6/16

D0447037

The King and Queen of Comezon

CHICANA & CHICANO VISIONS OF THE AMÉRICAS

CHICANA & CHICANO
VISIONS OF THE AMÉRICAS

Series Editor
Robert Con Davis-Undiano, *University of Oklahoma, Norman*

Editorial Board
Rudolfo Anaya, *Albuquerque, New Mexico*
Denise Chávez, *Las Cruces, New Mexico*
María Herrera-Sobek, *University of California, Los Angeles*
Rolando Hinojosa-Smith, *University of Texas, Austin*
Demetria Martínez, *Albuquerque, New Mexico*
Rafael Pérez-Torres, *University of California, Los Angeles*
José David Saldívar, *Stanford University, Stanford*
Ramón Saldívar, *Stanford University, Stanford*

The King and Queen of Comezón

Denise Chávez

UNIVERSITY OF OKLAHOMA PRESS : NORMAN

Also by Denise Chávez
The Last of the Menu Girls (Houston, 1986)
Face of an Angel (New York, 1994)
Loving Pedro Infante (New York, 2001)
A Taco Testimony: Meditations on Family, Food, and Culture
(Tucson, Ariz., 2006)

This book is a work of fiction. Names, characters, places, and incidents are either the product of the author's imagination or are used fictitiously, and any resemblance to actual events, locales, or persons, living or dead, is entirely coincidental.

Publication of this book is made possible through the generosity of Edith Kinney Gaylord.

Copyright notices for song lyrics used by permission in this book appear on pages 308–309.

Library of Congress Cataloging-in-Publication Data

Chávez, Denise.
    The king and queen of Comezón / Denise Chávez.
        pages cm — (Chicana & Chicano visions of the Américas series ; volume 13)
    ISBN 978-0-8061-4483-2 (paperback)
    1. Mexican American families—Fiction. 2. New Mexico—Social life and customs
    —Fiction. 3. Domestic fiction. gsafd   I. Title.
    PS3553.H346K56 2014
    813'.54—dc23
                                                                    2014010382

The King and Queen of Comezón is Volume 13 in the Chicana & Chicano Visions of the Américas series.

The paper in this book meets the guidelines for permanence and durability of the Committee on Production Guidelines for Book Longevity of the Council on Library Resources, Inc. ∞

Copyright © 2014 by Denise Chávez. Published by the University of Oklahoma Press, Norman, Publishing Division of the University. Manufactured in the U.S.A.

All rights reserved. No part of this publication may be reproduced, stored in a retrieval system, or transmitted, in any form or by any means, electronic, mechanical, photocopying, recording, or otherwise—except as permitted under Section 107 or 108 of the United States Copyright Act—without the prior written permission of the University of Oklahoma Press. To request permission to reproduce selections from this book, write to Permissions, University of Oklahoma Press, 2800 Venture Drive, Norman OK 73069, or email rights.oupress@ou.edu.

2 3 4 5 6 7 8 9 10

For my sister, Faride

Comezón:

1) An itch
2) The anxiety of mind produced by a long-standing desire
3) A misplaced longing that can never be satisfied
4) A small town on the U.S./México border

CHAPTER ONE

The Enchanter Struts a Hello

Arnulfo Olivárez stood in front of the Plaza kiosco, looking directly into the descending sun. He was bejeweled, a silver-threaded sombrero from Juárez on his head, his black charro suit nearly bursting at the seams, the buttons nestling like luminescent fish in the ever-changing light. His enormous belly quivered with the force of his hearty voice: "¡Buenas Tardes, Caballeros y Damas! ¡Damas y Caballeros! ¡Bienvenidos a la Fiesta!"

The still-strong sun caused Arnulfo to squint. He was caught off guard and shaded his eyes from the uncontrollable glare. Behind him the Lágrimas Mountains alternated colors—now crimson, now cerulean blue. His weak eyes adjusted to the enormous beauty that spread out before him. It was one of those sunsets that made his heart ache.

As he turned his face away, his lumpish profile was highlighted in what had now become the glimmering violet of the sky. Like the sunset of his desert land, he was moody, never to be taken for granted. Without warning, his phlegmy cough came up hard from the ancient depths as a great gurgling to remind him, despite his forced gaiety, how bad off he really was.

He extended his arms to address the growing crowd that was beginning to gather in front of the kiosco stage as his mirrored suit drew the light of the sun and flared out in front of him in random pockets on the heated pavement. It was good to know that he, the present King of Comezón, was the extension of that magical spirit light. For a brief moment, in its sudden and surprising beauty, Arnulfo Olivárez forgot his pain.

To strangers, Arnulfo Olivárez appeared to be a jovial old man.

To those who knew him, he was that viejito atrevido pendejo más que cabrón who thought he was better than anyone else. To himself, he was a man wasted with that comezón of longing and with the fragile, futile urge to live. What had happened to his bravado? What had become of his wayward and lusty joy? All he knew as he stood there in the hot sun for another pinche Cinco de Mayo Fiesta was that he was overheated and could barely stand.

Sadly, the King knew that the day was nearly done, his time was nearly spent, and soon the darkness would envelop him.

Arnulfo looked warily at several young men who wandered past, unsmiling, unsure, dumb with unknowing. No one knew he was dying of lung cancer. He asked himself how much longer he'd be able to stand in the middle of the Plaza and talk to these fools, babosos todos, the drooly-mouthed ones who never listened. The greatest mistake in his life was that he always ended up talking to people who never understood what he said. Sometimes they listened politely, sometimes not, and if they did pretend to hear him, they never really followed or finally grasped his intention. ¡Ay, que chingada es la vida, esta vida arrastrada!

A moment of wheezing uncertainty was followed by the same dark heaviness in his chest, a dread that spread out just underneath his throat and then traveled down the lower left side of his right lung, finally ending up on the numbed toes of his large right foot encased in the scrolled leather boot. Hell, his callo was killing him. The corn on the side of his big toe was as hard as the hoof of an old horse. With a wistful sense of impending finality, Arnulfo looked around to see his daughters, the half and the whole.

Juliana sat nearby in her wheelchair by the side of the Plaza closest to the church and tugged at her large drooping black bows. Velvet in May—what was anyone thinking? She leaned her twisted flesh into her metal throne, a blue scapular to the Immaculate Heart of Mary wound twice around her neck. She straightened the scapular while secretly running her forearm over her lush right breast. In the background, the bell of Santa Eulalia summoned errant worshippers to the 5:30 P.M. Saturday Mass. The church was named after a thirteen-year-old Spanish virgin and martyr who had been subjected to thirteen forms of torture, including being placed in a barrel with knives or glass—it was uncertain which—and with the barrel then rolled down a street. She was also subjected to the cutting off of her breasts, a crucifixion on an X-shaped cross, and finally a decapitation. Only the most heinous of tortures were remembered, but no doubt the rest were equally vile. They had to be. Sainthood came at a price. At the moment of her death, a white dove flew out from either her throat or her mouth. There was also some dispute among the citizens of Comezón, New Mexico, as to whether the Santa Eulalia they honored was the Spanish Santa Eulalia from the persecution during the reign of Emperor Diocletian or the Mexican Santa Eulalia from Mérida. Did it matter? Yes, it did. The overwhelming vote was for knives, her mouth, and México.

The Church of Santa Eulalia was a fitting place to meditate on the fragility of life. Throughout its dark history, the church had been host to a gaggle of Spanish priests who attended to their errant Mexican flock.

Few enough people would be found in the quiet interior of the ancient adobe that evening, and El Padre Manolito Rodríguez knew it as he peeked out the heavy wooden door to see what stragglers would be wandering in. Somehow his impatience at the lack of his parishioners' faith was heightened at times like this. Maldita fiesta. Malvada gente. Miserable celebración. Cinco de Mayo, bah! ¡Coño, me cago la leche! I shit sperm! Spain was the first to conquer this vile land and could vanquish it again if it chose. The French weren't the first to come to this godforsaken New World and see that it was inferior. El Padre had been exiled too long to this outback post and longed to return to his hometown of Madrid. At least there people knew how to speak. This desolate and heathen land may once have been México, but the language and the roots of this so-called culture were a porquería that wasn't this or that. Just to see Olivárez out there dressed up like a prancing monkey made his pure Spanish blood boil. Aunque la mona se vista de seda, mona se queda. ¡Coño! Even if the monkey is dressed in silk, it is still a monkey, he thought as he crossed himself in preparation for the Holy Mass.

And not only that, but Olivárez was the cause of his daughter Juliana's dangerous predilection to evil that was causing her to backslide in her Holy Faith. He'd observed her hesitation lately in confession to tell him everything she was experiencing. As her counselor and confessor, it was his sacred duty to know everything about her life—from those late-night religious inquietudes to the early morning moral lapses of the flesh—which in her case were mostly imagined. Were they? But invented or not, as he looked at her—a pretty, dark-haired young woman with a full, firm figure, a woman in her mid- to late twenties, albeit with crippled legs—well, her spiritual needs were paramount, and who, if not he, was her buttress in all things holy?

Lately, for some reason, he had felt a terrible foreboding sensation when he saw her. His throat tightened up and his hands became damp and hung thickly by his side, weighted down by a torpid uncertainty about something. Surely he was transmuting some kind of evil force that had surrounded her? Perhaps a demon had entered her body? No, he wouldn't think about that. It wasn't possible. She was as pure as a child. Wasn't she? He wasn't sure, but he knew how to keep an observant eye on this situation. Too many exceedingly attractive young women's souls had been lost through inattention. God grant him the grace, it was his sacred duty to guard this one errant lamb. ¡Dios en los Cielos! Juliana Olivárez would have been here at Mass if it weren't for her father, that madman Arnulfo Olivárez, standing out there in the middle of the Plaza dressed up like a weary clown in a much too small flea-bitten mariachi costume.

El Padre Manolito closed the heavy wooden church door and crossed himself three times in a very grandiose manner as he sighed out loud, hoping someone would hear his exasperation. Lorenza Tampiraños slid through the door just in time, with her long black rosary wound around her right hand, and chirped a hello. Ay, Lorenza! She was forever running late, forever smacking her pinched lips with who knows what swirling around those fractured, barely clinging yellowed dentures of hers. How dare she arrive at this hour for the Sacred Repast and with mortal food in her harlot red mouth! ¡Coño!

He had repeatedly scolded her about eating just before Mass. What would it take for her to remember? She was a cook and around fast food all day. Why hadn't she eaten earlier at that grease pit of a restaurant she worked at, La Reina Mexicana, the most popular drive-in restaurant in Comezón? He avoided it entirely. He might accept an invitation for lunch or dinner from his friend Don Clodimoro Balderas, or from the women from the Altar Society at another local place called La Única where he ordered the sirloin steak rare with as many Riojas as he could to ferment that slightly less inferior food in its juices. The food in Comezón gave him gas. It was a greasy fare that the natives enjoyed, lard being one of the main food groups. It was just another of the hardships he endured in this rural outpost. What could he do to teach these people how to cook?

He noted that Lorenza was sipping from a Sprite bottle. She always had it nearby and would slip it in and out of the old brown purse that she carried. What did she have in there? Maybe it was more than soda. He would make sure she wouldn't be allowed to take the Sacred Host this evening.

El Padre Manolito was known for locking the church doors minutes before the Mass began. If you weren't seated in your pew or kneeling in holy prayer in front of the tabernacle by the time he locked the door, you were jodido equally by the Father, the Son, and the Holy Ghost.

Lucinda, the festival queen, sat nervously on her throne on the raised stage in front of the kiosco. Without regard to who might be watching, she rearranged the inescapable metal wires that held up her strapless white satin queen's dress. The itchy tulle cut into her tender breasts, but that wasn't the worst of it. It was her time of the month, and she was afraid that her usually heavily clotted menstrual blood would seep through the layers of that rich, slick, very white cloth. But there was nothing she could do, at least not right now. She had layered one Kotex atop another like two conjoined tacos and pulled on an old, tired, and much-stained girdle that her mother, Mamá Emilia, had given her. She hoped it would pin down and hold the hated sanitary napkin in place, which wasn't so sanitary or so napkin-like. She didn't want the Kotex sliding halfway up her back like it usually did, like a misplaced shoulder pad.

And on top of it all, you had to use a girdle to keep the panty hose up, and even then they got all hüango and pooched unpleasantly at the knees. The girdle didn't help with the saggy knees, but it did cut the slack and irritating elongation of the hose that stretched with every movement. Lucinda used her girdle at just these times to hold her tamales in place, even though she was as thin as a matchstick and hated the feeling of being bound and trussed down there. But it was better to be safe, after all.

She remembered when her friend Elora's blood came on unannounced in the middle of her Quinceañera and how two of her madrinas had to dramatically escort her, one in front of her, the other behind, like female bodyguards except dressed in pink velvet, as they made their way to the women's restroom at the Salón Tres Reyes—make that the former B and B Body Shop on the east side of town—a lo todo made over to look like a fancy salon de baile, except it wasn't. The owner and former head mechanic, El Gancho Gutiérrez, was standing out there in what had once been the lube pit, looking all Moctezuma Reincarnated dressed in a 3-for-$10 black sleeveless muscle shirt from a Korean store on El Paso Street in El Chuco, with his huge hairy arms splayed out a good foot from the trunk of his body. He was that beefed and buffed, his rug-like sobacos in full glory as he waved to a Chrysler full of tittering viejitas, motioning to them where they should park. The gaggle of pouffed, trussed, overheated, and over-perfumed women made their way to the back of the salón. Outside, Elora's mother was sitting shotgun as one of the madrinas drove the poor unfortunate home to change, but not before El Gancho helped them back out and sent them on their way with a booming "Vuelven!" Like hell. The Party was over. Que Salón de Baile ni que Salón de Baile. Salón Tres Reyes smelled like old pee and wet dog fur.

Lucinda didn't want this to happen. Who would she find to shield her from prying eyes, she thought, looking around furtively. Who would wrap herself around her and her steaming telltale chorro of blood that couldn't be hidden on white satin? Chingao. Better to wear a damned old-woman's girdle in this heat with a hot, thick pañal between your legs like a grown-up baby than to live the endless shame of seeping blood in front of strangers.

Lucinda looked over to Juliana. Worse it was to be paralyzed from the waist down and have to have someone like Isá, face like a metate, the family's long-term servienta, to clean your woman's juices. No other way to say it. Isá was a servant, and at her advanced age she accepted the calling fully. She had no place to go, and why should she go anywhere? She'd never been outside of Comezón and didn't miss the travel. What was there to see that she hadn't seen in the Olivárez household? Uúuuuquela! And what was she lacking? She had a nice warm room with a nice warm little bed and a nice warm colchón she'd knitted herself with little almohaditas, her soft little pillows that she'd made from fabric scraps, and a nice warm little flannel nightgown and store-bought slippers from La J. C.—Penney's, that is—that La Patrona, Doña Emilia, had given her pa' Crismes. It was all very nice if it weren't for Juliana.

Ay, pero ni modo, everyone's hot meal comes at some price. And hers, may God remember this when she got to Heaven, or Hell, it could go either way at this point in her life, was the care of a crippled young woman who was coja from the waist down— make that the panochita up—because she had to clean that too. And she was heavy for someone with such little deformed bones and the legs of a newborn calf, aguados y sin fuerza.

Pobrecita, thought Isá automatically. And yet she felt little pity and certainly no mercy for Juliana. Better it was to be Lucinda, the adopted daughter, la Consentida, the chosen, spoiled one, the one Isá doted on and loved. Like her, Lucinda was an outcast, and because of this Isá became her protector and confidante. Ay, but everyone was smitten by the Julianas of the world, and though they seemed to revere and honor the Lucindas, it was truly the Julianas they adored. Juliana was the imperfect statement of her parents' life and so-called love, and everyone knew it. But it didn't matter. Only Isá knew that underneath Juliana's frail exterior lay a woman with an immovable heart and a will that would never be tamed.

Let's get this over with, over with, over with, more than one person thought as the sun finally began to set in the west.

Both sisters eagerly awaited the darkness, as did their father, Arnulfo Olivárez, who intoned his endless, tireless, monotonous litany of welcome thank you goodbye.

"Welcome to Comezón! That's right, Comezón. Itch, New Mexico. Homeplace of living history . . . birthplace of legends . . . this was México before the signing of the Gadsden Purchase, yes it is, or it was. You are standing on Tierra Sagrada, Sacred Earth. ¡Qué Viva México, nuestra patria pa' siempre! And don't let them tell you otherwise. This is México, and it will always be México! I'm a Mexican first and an American second. Except on the 4th of July, and then it's ¡Qué Viva Los Estados Unidos! A que la chingada, ¿qué pasó con el micrófono? El mic went off, el pinche micrófono se apagó! Can somebody help me? Luisito, ¿'onde 'stas cabrón?"

Juliana sat in her wheelchair atop the scrubby yellow grass just to the right of the kiosco with the smile of a contented cherubim. Arnulfo gesticulated wildly and yelled to his assistant, Luisito Covarrubias, a mirthless man of indeterminate age with a dark furrowed face who was already very inebriated. Luisito darted from behind the kiosco like a confused crab, tucking a small wadded-up paper bag that held a small bottle of Ripple wine under a battered poncho. He crept up behind one of the wooden posts, between the folds of green, white, and red streamers that cascaded down from the top of the wooden bandstand. Unsteadily, but with gathering courage, he weaved his way to center stage, nearly tripping over Juliana's wheelchair to get to Arnulfo's side. He checked the microphone as best he could without knowing anything at all about microphones. He lifted it up and down. Dead, it was dead, and good thing, too, as the echo of his formidable and resonating belch could be heard. Arnulfo pushed Luisito away with irritation and waved to the crowd as if to say, "Ignore this pendejo. We'll be right back."

Arnulfo was fiddling with the chingao micrófono de la puta madre when it suddenly came back to life. Several women yelped with surprise, whether at the sudden high-pitched noise or the cursing, no one was sure.

"I'm jest fine," Juliana cooed to a very proper white lady who had heard that reverberating curse and decided right there and then to move on, dad blast it, past Juliana Olivárez, who was in her God-blessed path. There was nothing Mercia Crawley could do; she just had to greet the poor girl, and that was fine, it wasn't her fault she had no functional legs to stand on, and her father was the town fool and a fat slabby drinking whoring wreck of a Mexican without tolerance or restraint. Mercia stopped to greet the pitiful twisted thing for the sake of her mother, Miss Emilia, a living saint who used to do her ironing.

"Yew been taking care of yewself, Julie-Anna? Yew been a good girl?" the leathery Gringa inquired as she patted Juliana's hair, messing it and displacing a bow.

"I'm jest fine. It's so good to see jew, Mrs. Crawley. How jew been?" Juliana knew the old woman and disliked her, but for her mother's sake she feigned friendship.

She remembered La Vieja Crawley coming to the house once with half a melón for her real good friend Miss Emilia. But Miss Emilia wasn't there. As Mrs. Crawley held the drippy specimen aloft, Juliana saw how selfish and self-serving she truly was when she said to both her and Isá, "Now, you make sure Miss Emilia gets all of this, yew'll hear?"

All Juliana could think about when she saw La Vieja was her thoughtless offering of an already pasado melón.

"How's yew mama? Give her a hello from her old friend, will yew? You 'member me, don't yew, Julie-Anna?" Mercia Crawley asked with vexation. Of course The Girl remembered her. And what was worse was that Mercia knew the Poor Sickly Thing didn't like her, never had, despite all her generosities to that Poor Mess of a Family.

Juliana remembered as well that La Vieja Crawley never paid on time, nor paid enough, always forgetting to bring her purse with her or forgetting her checkbook, but she was her mother's friend, if it could be said that her mother had any friends, especially women who were white and who owned land and had grown up in the desert heat like her mother and knew what it was to be tied to a man who rambled and roamed the way their two husbands did. It wasn't the ironing that brought them together. Ay, La Vieja Crawley, esa vieja repunosa had messed everything up! She had reminded Juliana once again of the disparity between her thought life and her outer public life filled with other people's pity and pain.

Why did la Gringa Seca always ask her the same questions? What did she really want to know? I'd like to say a few things to that metiche asquerosa, that fetid meddler, with her overpowering smell of Vicks and dust. Why was it that tall, rich Güera always looked down on her short Mexicana mother? Especially since the two of them were so alike, both saddled to men who weren't worth a startled giggle or a sigh of joy in the too-long darkness.

For the sake of her mother, Mamá Emilia, whom she loved and who was always told to stay home and who knew she was unwanted, unloved, and unappreciated by most everyone, Juliana would be nice and polite to La Vieja Crawley. She answered La Vieja in her quiet public voice, with a gentle and wounded smile, a smile both miraculous and terrible that spoke of something unreachable and inconsolable.

"Goodbye, Mrs. Crawley. I'll tell Mamá you said hello. She's fine. Jest fine. And I'm fine. I'm always at the house, Mrs. Crawley. Descansando. Jew know. Resting."

La Vieja Crawley moved away because she couldn't bear feeling anything anymore for either the daughter or the mother, much less the father.

"Well, goodbye now," La Vieja Crawley said with an unpleasant side glance at Arnulfo, who was waving his arms with jerky puppet-like movements behind them. He was unsuccessfully trying to make a point about something.

Juliana couldn't really see or hear her father anymore. She had tuned him out, just as she tried to ignore La Vieja Crawley. All she could think about was her hair. ¡Ay, La Vieja Crawley! La Gringa had messed up her hair, and it had taken so long for Lucinda to fix it that afternoon. It had been so hot out there in the patio of their house on Calle de La Acequia even in the shade of the mulberry tree. The large tree was full of ripened berries that that old drudge, her caretaker, Isá, would never let her eat.

"If you eat them," she had warned, "you'll get empache, the stomach gas and the burning stool."

Juliana knew that mulberries never gave anyone anything like that. She did remember once putting a handful of berries in the chest pocket of her white blouse when she was around ten years old. She was sitting in the little wheelchair on the playground of La Reina del Cielo Catholic School eating the rich, purple-red berries long after the school bell had rung. When she finished, she hurried back through the schoolyard, where the principal, a short, dark Mexican nun, La Hermana María de La Concepción del Sagrado Corazón de Jesús en Su Gloria y Majestad No Last Name, another mummy from Guanajuato, had scolded her for being late. When she finally got back to her classroom, her teacher, Sister Betita, chided her as well. Finally back at her desk, she fingered the few remaining mulberries in the pocket of her blouse. She could feel the roundness of her ripening breast and knew her nipple was wet with the dark juice. The berries had stained her white blouse, and she knew that Mamá Emilia would be angry. She hoped the blouse would wash clean. The truth of the matter was that the blouse would never be the same. And what did it matter to her mother, anyway? She never did the laundry. It was always Isá who washed the clothes. It was Isá who knew all their secrets. Who washed and who didn't. Who slept alone and who didn't. Who was loved and how often and who wasn't and why.

That was just before her father took her out of school, saying she didn't need to learn anything there that she couldn't learn at home. After that, she felt a stronger and sharper pain run between her feet and knees. Maybe having a burning stool would make her feel like a woman. In everyone's mind she was a little girl, a pitiful little girl without legs or a thought in her head. If only her father had let her finish her schooling!

What did she know about life? And with whom could she share her thoughts? She knew about glowing sunlight on the dark leaf of a plant, the instinctive terror of insects, who, just like humans, lived deeply and with fear of the Other. She knew about the rhythmic humming of a bee and its incessant need to dance. She knew the high-pitched chirrup of cicadas who for that one long night knew all there was to know about surrender. And she understood how hard it was for any living thing to let go of the incandescent miracle of life. She watched roaches in their agony, and always when she saw yet another poor creature dying, she lifted it and took it outdoors to lay on earth, where she hoped the grass and the sky and the cool or the heat of the day or night would give it peace. That's all each of us can give another.

Oh, she knew so much, felt so much, longed for so much! And yet—who knew what yearnings she had—what profound, implacable, unrevealed longings she had—oh, who knew of her comezón, that secret, long-held desire to be touched, to be loved?

Oh, if only others could share with her what she knew about life. If only she could get away from all the people who would never let her grow up or grow old. She hated her black bows and the way her mother dressed her, like a little girl, in taffeta and lace. She longed to be a woman among other women and a woman next to and under a man. Would she ever make love to anyone? She was ashamed to know so much and yet so little and to be unable to speak her truth to anyone. Not even her sister, Lucinda, understood her or wanted to know what secrets she had.

Not that long ago, Lucinda had tugged and pulled Juliana's long dark brown hair. She had hurt her, pulling her thick hair into compliance in a braid that dropped down her back. She complained that she didn't have time to fix her sister's hair; after all, Juliana wasn't the queen, so what did it matter what her hair looked like anyway?

And why was Juliana in such a hurry to get ready for the Fiesta and the dance? She couldn't dance, she would never dance, and she didn't have a boyfriend and would never have a boyfriend. And not only that, she would never have anyone to look at her naked except Isá, La Vejona, that old pockmarked mare of a helper she called La Caca behind her back.

It was true, and most likely no one would see her naked, not the way a man would see a woman naked. With that thought, she turned toward her father, then turned away. She didn't want to think about her parents making love . . .

Arnulfo stood on the stage, larger than life. He could be so polite and dignified in public. And yet Juliana could hear her father taunting her mother one more time . . . "otra vez el burro al maíz . . . "

"You and Juliana, all you do is rest. Gorda, have you ever wondered how hard I have to work to support two sick animals, one old, one young?"

Otra vez el burro al maíz . . . Here we go again . . . here we go again . . . the burro goes round and round in the chaff . . .

"No! You can't go to the Fiesta this year. Why do you ask me, Gorda? What would an old woman like you with an uneven step and a bad back be doing with normal people who are celebrating Cinco de Mayo when you can barely hobble from one piece of furniture to the next, standing there like a drunken Mexican sailor from Veracruz anchored to the trastero, that old ugly bookshelf of yours, for support? Stay home, mujer, do you want people to see you and feel even more sorry for you than they do now? And when they see you—in your state—and our daughter—in her state—they will look at me and think to themselves: He's a damaged man. His seed is Tainted. How could a man be so unfortunate as to have a manca for a wife and a tullida for a daughter? Double cursed is what I am! Double triple quadruple cursed to have four dead legs in my life, make that five since my last illness. ¡Ay! Might as well die and get it over with!"

Arnulfo had said this to his wife earlier in the day, his wife of too many years, the proverbial long-suffering Emilia Izquierdo. He looked disdainfully at her short right leg that hovered in space a good ten inches above the left. He had once had sex with a prostitute without a leg, but that was something else altogether.

With a sigh, Juliana touched her heart and felt the comforting roundness of her left breast. She could feel the ripe purple mulberries again. She loved to touch herself secretly, especially in a crowd of people. As she touched the round swell below her nipple through the armhole of her sweater or blouse, she would often think about her breasts. They were beautiful. They really were. If there was anything lovely about her—and there were a few things—the greatest of these was her supple breasts, breasts that Isá had once told her were wasted on a cripple.

Juliana had never told El Padre Manolito how she felt about her breasts. Prideful. Maybe even superior. First of all, it would be a shameless thing to mention her anatomy to a priest, one of God's elect, and then again, she didn't want to be a further cause of temptation—she'd already seen El Padre Manolito staring at her chest in an unpriestly way—the way a man would look at a woman—a real woman, until he realized that she had the legs of a five-year-old and the bound feet of an Oriental woman. It was true that the lower part of her body was useless for most things.

La Caca summed it up most crudely: "Not that it matters if you know a man's hot, smelly pinga or not. You should thank God you'll never know a man's dry plow on your unfurrowed flesh. Thank God you'll be spared that splitting of the earth. But then, of course, Nuestro Señor most likely cares about His fellow men's pingas and might even feel sorry for them—which is probably likely—because after all He is a He and not a She and has an It."

This was a sorry summing-up and horrible to hear. As if this weren't enough, La Caca went on as only she could, without mercy or decorum. She was a loud, rude, untamed nanny goat who brayed without decency or restraint.

"It's not your fault you're a renca, m'ija. I'm not telling you that you might not find someone someday who wouldn't mind having a coja in his bed, only God make him strong enough. Here they probably think you're a sack of potatoes when you're more like a goat with engorged teats. Someone has to take over soon. I'm getting tired of lifting and cleaning you. It's the age coming on and your being a dead weight. And how could you lie in some small man's arms and then have him turn you over to get what he wants? If you ever do find someone, I pray he's an ox, for that's what you'll need to lift you, someone fully in his flesh, and not afraid to touch the woman you are underneath all the bows and the lace."

Talking about sex made Isá reflect on her own sex life, be that what it was. What was it? A warm, soothing wet towel between her legs on Sunday afternoons during her weekly bath in the shed behind the main house. Yes, it was on a Sunday, but always after Mass. An alone time that was just for her. And for her little pan dulce wanting café con crema.

"Ay, m'ija, que Dios te ayude. You should find a man, some bull to tame you, and then you could love him back the way I know you could if you could. But you can't because you can't, and for that comezón I am truly sorry. You should find a man, but who, who? And when, when?"

Twisted Juliana with her full woman's breasts, and what did it matter if they were there at all? They were breasts only three people had seen, and one of them was Isá.

Saint Juliana sat on her metal throne, she lived on that veritable cross, offering her eyes, her heart, the firm flowerings of her unknown flesh, to the Great God who called her daughter.

Saint Juliana looked toward her father and blessed him with the sanctity of her bemused look, as he called out to the audience with his booming voice, the microphone, for the moment, dead again: "No te vayas mi gente! Don't go away, no, not yet, the Fiesta has just begun!"

Arnulfo Olivárez attempted some modicum of dignity despite the heat and the fact that Luisito was pulling on the microphone cord just under his large splayed right foot, almost knocking him over. Arnulfo's pumped-up walrus cheeks obscured his tiny blue eyes. They were the eyes of a once-shrewd boy, a dauntless lover, a self-important older man who wanted to be remembered in the still-undefined history of this small forsaken pinche town where no one cared about him or his true work, his mission for greatness or fame. But not only for him, no, not only for him. If truth be told, Comezón—this rolling, roiling piece of glorious untamed earth—was the only woman he would ever truly love.

People would say a hundred years hence, "Comezón. Ahhh, Comezón. Arnulfo Olivárez lived there. You've heard of Arnulfo Olivárez. He was Mr. Comezón. The Goodwill Ambassador. Mayor . . . no, he was never mayor, but he should have been. He was a businessman and a farmer. He was the one responsible for the annual Fiesta. He's the one who brought the town to life. Before that, Comezón was just dust on the banks of the Río Grande. Imagine Comezón nothing but mesquite and espinas! That's how it was, vast empty land full of thorns. That's the way I remember it. Fields full of rabbits. That's how it used to be when I was a boy."

Arnulfo's wild mustache was once black, once lush, once a point of pride, once a show of masculinity. Now his fleshy lips sputtered and sprayed over yellow-white hairs that looked like the dusty mange of an ancient wolf. No one had kissed him in a long, long time. He hardly remembered what the inside of another person's mouth tasted like. He only knew his own stale smell of Camel cigarettes and watery Coors Light and the sensation that haunted him like that one bad tooth in the back that seeped a nasty juice. The inside of the tooth was now impacted with the remnants of his luncheon tacos de buche, his beloved cow gullet. He would have to find a toothpick soon or he would go crazy.

Ay, he was tired, and yet he had to go on, get it over with. But it was Fiesta, how could he be weary? He would be exhausted when it was over. Then he would rest. The illness would wash over him and he would stop. He would sleep all day if he wanted to. And he'd tell Isá to fix his favorite tacos de tripitas the way only she could make them, crispy on the outside and tender on the inside. He'd tell her to clean the tripas good, as only she knew how, for after all, tripas were tripas and you couldn't be too careful, could you, they being the conduit for untold shit. If anyone knew what to do with shit, it was that old brick-faced woman, ugly as she was. Sadly, she was the best thing about his life now, she and her food. Really, that's about all he had left, the taste of food on his tongue. The last organ to go. But now, tonight, he had to endure, tenía que aguantar.

With an enormous puffy hand, he twisted and twined his impudent mustache hairs. A huge belly and truncated torso supported a turquoise-studded bolo tie and matching concha belt, a gift from his compadre at the pueblo, his other brother, the man he knew as spirit kin, Donacio Quiroz, the only man he had ever trusted or loved.

Thinking of Donacio Quiroz gave him hope. Hell, there was always hope. Pinche vida, there was always hope. When the sun went down, there was the dance. Animal-like, unrestrained, Arnulfo's strange hungry eyes peered out with joy. They were unquiet pilgrims, they wandered this way and that, and they saw all things, all people, as they glanced around the Plaza, seeking out impressions, faces, darkness, someone to love.

Arnulfo's eyes momentarily rested on his Tony Lama boots. His were the feet of a large, robust man, splayed outward, without consideration or restraint. They hurt, especially the right one with that corn, which probably needed medical attention, but there was nothing he could do, not now.

He looked into the shadows that loomed larger and larger as night was coming on. Maybe there was a face to be seen through the trees. He saw his old drinking buddy Joe Kiratz sitting on one of the Plaza benches. Joe was absorbed in something, someone. Who could it be? They were both older men, but Joe had the advantage. He was not yet sixty, and the man was still attractive to women. Ay, the same couldn't be said for Arnulfo, who at seventy-two was well past his prime. Although if truth be told, Arnulfo had more ánimo than his often self-effacing compadre, who was so damn reserved. It took a lot for the man to get worked up, but when he did, he was a man on fire. Whereas

Arnulfo, pinche cabrón that he himself knew he was, was always holding himself in check lest someone see how starved and desperate and truly jodido he really was for talk, for anything resembling human contact.

If he looked long enough, perhaps he would see the outline of a woman waiting, waiting out there for him, just for him. Yes, he had faith, the desperate darkness of a small belief that this year he would find love. Maybe he would take a woman in the shadows behind the Mil Recuerdos Lounge, his compa Rey Suárez's bar, like he had some years ago.

Dominga "La Minga" Maez Hornbarger was the woman who had cleaned up there at the Mil Recuerdos. She used to let Arnulfo visit her after the late-night shift sometimes, the two of them grunting like overheated pigs in the little rincóncito where Rey stacked up his used beer bottles. Dominga was the widow of Glenn Hornbarger, another of his old drinking buddies. Uúuuquela, en el año del caldo! She was one of those crazy Maezes everyone in Comezón talked about, but hell, old Glenn was long gone. What he didn't know wouldn't hurt him. It was dark back there, and while their encounters were good in one way, they were bad in another. There was always the unpleasant smell of stale beer and pungently acidic and acrid urine that permeated those furtive encounters. And the worst thing was that it wasn't his own urine that he was forced to smell.

One time he'd caught Luisito meando back there, his dirty chones down around his knees. The man swore he had to strip down to take a decent pee. If he took a crap, it required full nudity and the time to enjoy. No hurried pace or feverish urgency. A shit was to be enjoyed as one of God's greatest gifts, Luisito expounded in a moment of true lucidity, between drunks. Thank you, Lord Jesus, for this one true gift! Arnulfo chuckled to himself thinking what Padre Manolito would think about this theory. The man was so tapado he would probably never know the glory.

Ay, no, Arnulfo reasoned, probably nothing was going to happen this year. Dominga had moved to Deming to be with her daughter, Concha, and had become a Jehovah. And then again, there was the matter of his Cross. Best not to think about it. There were other things to think about than a quick mero mero en el mero mero. After all, he was the Master of Ceremonies of the Fiesta. The town elections weren't far off. Arnulfo was running again for mayor, like too many previous years. And this time, this blessed holy hotter-than-ever pinche year, he would win!

Arnulfo bellowed greetings to the crowd of local townsfolk and a few confused shell-shocked tourists. For someone from northern climes, it was hard to adjust to the heat, much more so to the way people lived, without hurry or expectation. That's what the cabrones think, Arnulfo had formulated, as if unraveling a great mystery.

¡Estúpidos! What did they know about heat, little rain? Hell, what did the strangers know about anything? Did they listen? Could they hear him? Who cared? Arnulfo was the voice of the protective brother, the devoted father, and the faithful lover. He spoke earnestly and with great enthusiasm, "We are proud of Comezón. We love our Comezón!"

His speech was a prayer, a long chant, a rant filled with wind, much wind: "We are her citizens, her men, and yes, her women." And with this phrase he looked sideways at Juliana, who blushed and turned away. The girl was always perverse, would never change.

She'd become even more so after consorting weekly, some-times daily, with S.S.—the Sanctimonious Sacerdote—as Rey Suárez, the owner of the Mil Recuerdos Lounge, liked to call El Padre Manolito in one of his many epistles about the current state of religion and how jodido it was. La Gorda, his wife, Emilia, had decided that Juliana needed Catechism classes, and so now S.S. came to the Olivárez home once a week on Tuesday after-noons, and whenever else he felt like it, which was often.

S.S. stood for the short, Napoleonic, albeit somewhat hand-some sawed-off version of what a Spaniard should be. A dandified runty Don Quixote with his airs, that's what he was. Dreaming up things to cloud Juliana's head, tales of a heaven that didn't exist, of saints who walked among men, of a way of life that could never be, the lion peacefully next to the lamb, the pinche unsuspecting lamb unafraid of the beast. All lies, all of it. The next thing that was going to happen was that he'd find out Juliana wanted to go to the university and get a degree! What was the world coming to? Lies, all of it lies!

"We've come to celebrate the annual Fiesta and to give thanks to God, who's given us this time together."

With hands upraised, Arnulfo urged the locals to pay heed and to rejoice. He scanned the audience for some sign of understanding or recognition. Good. No one could see that the God he spoke of so reverently he deemed an arrogant fool, or worse, a cruel deceiver, the arbiter of fates. And that the destiny of Arnulfo P. Olivárez had been sealed long ago in the annals of the Pinche Jodidos on the Wall of the Cabrones Perdidos in the Great Heavenly Hall of the Desamparados y Cagados.

And yet, did he see, could it be, out of the corner of his eye, Dominga Maez Hornbarger back there, behind Don Raúl Espuelas and his wife, Flujcinta? Yes? No? Was she alone? No? Yes? Dominga, or someone who looked like Dominga, waved to him, and with the greatest unwavering hope for some shard of compassion from a God who too often looked the other way, the hungry young boy in him waved back. It was Dominga, wasn't it? Oh oh oh, whoever you are, whoever you are, dream woman, don't taunt me . . .

And if it wasn't Dominga, hell, it didn't matter. He wasn't sure his palo seco could meet the occasion.

But damn it, this was May 5. Tenía que darle El Try.

In groups of two or three, the young girls sauntered past their mothers' booths, where gorditas, tacos, and hamburgers were sold, driving smells of green and red chile and hot lard into the air, permeating nasal passages with the lingering odor of aunts' houses, feast days, weddings, and days of mourning, when the family of the bereaved would not cook but accepted food, and were fed royally by relatives, friends, comadres and compadres, all of those who had known the deceased when there was food, song, breath, a chance.

The young girls walked by slowly, lingering a little too long by the young couples who floated past, lost in their miraculous union. They were plump, with bad skin and little panzas, puffy stomachs, that stuck out from underneath tight halter tops. They had high, hard little breasts that ached when they stopped to pull up an errant bra strap. They were lost girls in tight jeans that their mothers unhappily knew showed the clear outline of their sex, or in shorts that folded into the cracks of their butts. Their disdainful and all-knowing eyes encountered crazy boys with cowlicks, rumpled white t-shirts, and faded jeans that fit too big in the seat. They were farm boys who lived with their abuelitas. They huddled in groups snorting at jokes in Spanish and smoking unfiltered Camel cigarettes while holding crumpled brown plastic bags with a Pabst Blue Ribbon or Hamm's inside. They were the night's boys, the boys of growing older women. They were lusting boys, half-grown. They were boys. Just Boys.

And the girls, with their heavily painted black eyes, were made for them. They all circled round—they circled round—the girls—the boys—moths—not dancing, but wanting to. They clung to the light as they dreamed of future encounters, not here on the Plaza but somewhere dark, by the river, in a car near the middle of nowhere in the middle of the summer night. No mother worrying, no father caring, no one bothering them and their sweet flesh. They knew the hope, the imagined fever, the sweetness of flesh, and the dream of flowing nights of love.

Arnulfo introduced his daughter, Queen Lucinda, beloved of this night with its colored lights. Lucinda walked up the steps to the kiosco stage, her long white taffeta train carried daintily by little girls who followed in her footsteps. She was enshrined in turquoise, a crown befitting the Land of Enchantment, a sunburst of molten silver inlaid with vivid coral.

Arnulfo took his daughter's small white-gloved hand into his own large, rough, sunburned hands. Her fingers barely touched him, so light she was, a wisp of wind not wanting to touch land.

He held her, tiny leaf, to his mountainous chest. She fretted. And yet it felt so good to hold someone. Ay, if only he weren't her father, and she was older, much older. Lost in a daydream, he was unwilling to let her go, and yet he knew he must. He released her, and she thankfully returned to her handmaidens, children between the ages of five and seven. They were her pages, minions of some higher order with their innocent cherubic beauty and untainted bodies. They stared at her with luminescent eyes that been painted with dark eye makeup. They leaned into the light, were held in their brief glory, and then collapsed by their Queen, an omnipotent star that shone brightly as they basked in her majesty. She sat, to reign. The Plaza's boys were her other, dearer pages, the lonely, lovely girls with their still-unspoiled flesh her true servants.

Arnulfo called out for everyone to dance. It was time for la Marcha de La Reina. Lucinda rose, gathering her long train around her, and motioned for her princesses to assist her as she danced the Queen's Dance with her escort, who until now had been hidden among her pages. He was a tall, skinny, bumpy-skinned boy who had large hands and larger feet. Ruley Terrazas was his name, and he was the son of Comezón's chief of police, Cuco "Matamosca" Terrazas, who was known for his abiding hatred of all flying insects and always carried a multicolored plastic fly-swatter on the dashboard of his police car. He was a man who liked to kill anything that got in his way. Bugs. Frogs. Mice. Dogs. Cats. Birds. It was even reputed that he had once killed a belligerent mojado by the river one moonless night in a rage for calling him a joto. Damned wetback was trying to cross the Río Grande. The insult was intended to hurt, and it did; what did it matter if it was true? What the chief of police did in his off hours was his own business.

But for this one night, Cuco, or "Mata," as everyone called him behind his back, and his errant son Ruley, who had already shown signs of cruelty to small animals, were—despite their matching burgundy tuxedos with turquoise boutonnieres—insignificant specks on the murky canvas of life—make that microscopic mites—in the blinding radiance of Her Majesty, Lucinda I of the Royal House of Olivárez.

Arnulfo's voice rattled time. A side of beef was won, a guest was introduced. Dr. Balderrama González from the university. Mr. López from the governor's office. The governor couldn't make it tonight. I'll read the telegram.

Arnulfo was annoyed. Did Lucinda need a drink? Was Juliana sleepy? It was time for her to go home with Isá, the old housekeeper, face like ancient inscrutable stone. He looked in the direction of the Mil Recuerdos Lounge. He was very thirsty. He would catch up with his compadres, Rey Suárez and Joe Kiratz. He would forget all of this soon enough. It had been a very long day.

But before that, he had things to do.

Juliana was flushed. She had sat primly all night, knees bound by invisible ropes, hands folded over onto themselves. Surrounded by white, green, and red chrysanthemums, she smiled attentively to anyone who passed by, but her thoughts were far away. She sang quietly to herself—the quiet forgotten song of herself—the song even she didn't know she sang to herself, a haunting intake and then expulsion of air. It was a sigh that over the years had deepened and become song. Hm . . . hhmm . . . hhhmmm . . . hhhhmmmm . . . hhhhhmmmmm . . .

"It's your bedtime, querida," Arnulfo said gently. "Come on, Isá and I will take you home. Your mother is waiting."

After what seemed like an eternity, Arnulfo returned to the Plaza. He had left the women behind, to their holy cards, to their dark prayer books, to their evening chores: to the slow rinsing of old dishes, the washing up of aging faces, the care of those few loose ancient teeth, the creaming of dry heels, the rubbing of aching knees, the self-placating automatic gestures that brought rest as their softened hands searched for and finally found humid rosaries. Their barely audible voices intoned incessant supplications, first to a tired body and then to a silent

God. Somehow knowing this gave Arnulfo some peace. The peace of knowing that someone was praying for him. He looked in the direction of the Mil Recuerdos Lounge.

The women lay down, unwinding long thin sheets
they lay down in the darkness of their cool beds
they felt that blessed breeze
tears forgotten
sorrows forgotten
the flesh finally the flesh forgotten
sleep the long glorious sleep
summer just begun

CHAPTER TWO

Too Early Too Late

It was still early. Too early to go home. Too early to go to bed. Arnulfo Olivárez wandered back into the shadows that sustained him. He looked back toward his home with a certain longing. It was equidistant to the Mil Recuerdos Lounge. Either way was fraught with sorrow and self-loathing. He slowly made his way across the Plaza toward the bar, regretting his weakness with every step. He was exhausted and knew he'd have to stop and rest along the way. Was it worth it? If he headed in the other direction, he could rest. Maybe. Better to have a drink and think it over.

The Fiesta had wound down. No one was around to play any more silly games. The racing mice had finally been put in their cages to rest. The booths were gone, the water from the duck moat emptied. A careless child threw the dirty water from the trough onto the pavement in front of the church. A woman called out to him with irritation in the darkness, the street lamps suddenly coming on, illuminating the filthy water that flowed down the brick street. "Watch what you're doing. Give the water to the trees. They need it!"

The giant turkey legs, roasted corn, Navajo tacos, and gorditas were gone, and all that remained was the murky water the cleanup crew used to rinse the blackened burners. The trash bins were full of greasy paper plates and bent food-crusted forks, half-chewed corncobs, and turkey legs with their tough sinews and protruding bones. A few stragglers, mostly tourists, wandered through the Plaza, lost, waiting for something to happen and knowing that nothing would.

Bah, turistas! Arnulfo sat down on the bench nearest the church and looked out to the scurrying booth owners and their families, who were scrambling to clean up their little turf, the vans and trucks hauling off the canvas tents and metal poles that had held up the small businesses that not so long ago crowded the Plaza. There was a clanking and yelling going on that irritated him. The Plaza cleanup crew took down the red, white, and green streamers from the stage. One lone wistful handmade red paper flower hung from a viga.

Arnulfo wondered where Lucinda had gone. The girl had taken off with Ruley Terrazas without telling him anything. Ruley was still wearing that awful burgundy tuxedo, and Lucinda had on her white queen's dress, the one he had paid for dearly at the White House Department Store in El Paso. Where would they be going dressed up in those outfits? Either to Juárez to drink or to the river. At one point or another they'd take off all their clothes. There might be some way to salvage Lucinda's dress. The girl was always up to no good. She'd come home one day with news about a baby, and then what would he do?

Well, come to think of it, he'd be happy to hand her over to the Terrazases for safekeeping. She was as wild as they were, and as headstrong. Let Ruley tame her if he could, and if not Ruley, then old Mata, who would lay down the law once and for all. Lucinda had never been a sweet child like Juliana. Little did anyone know how much of a torment she would become to them all.

Juliana was probably asleep by now. Isá would have rubbed her shrunken legs and twisted feet with her special medicine and then wrapped them in her soft flannel leggings and little shoes. They were handmade by an old nun from Ciudad Juárez, La Hermana Clorona, who made all of her clothing, making sure it was comfortable and loose-fitting and wouldn't ever chafe. The soft socks were very yielding and allowed Isá to adjust Juliana's little toes through the fluffy cloth when they cramped or shifted to one side, for even though they were stunted, Juliana still had feeling in her extremities.

After praying the rosary like they did every night, Emilia would kiss Juliana goodnight, giving her the final nightly bendición, and shuffle back to her room. Before she lay down she would go into Arnulfo's room and pull back the covers, so that his bed would be ready for him when he got back.

They had slept apart for so long, he had forgotten what it was like to wake up next to her warm body. He couldn't remember the last time he had slept all night with a woman and awakened to her presence there in the bed next to him. A few random women had met his needs as best they could in the past—ay, who was counting—but now he never had the pleasure of luxuriating in a bed with anyone other than his dog, Chamorro. When he accidentally reached over and touched the animal, his hairless body almost felt like a woman, it was so soft, so yielding. He loved the incandescent essence of living flesh. When he touched or was touched, he felt himself disappear, a spirit without the confines of space, extending out to reach only more space.

Arnulfo's thick, numb hands would stroke the small Xoloitzcuintle, the completely bald Mexican dog given to him by Rey Suárez. A native of México, the Xolo was considered sacred by the Aztecs and was believed to have healing properties. Arnulfo could attest to Chamorro's strength, agility, strong guardian nature, and his sweetness. A friend of Rey's from Chihuahua, Don Clodimoro Balderas, had given Rey the little dog, but Rey had found him ugly. He was going to take him to the pound but instead offered him to anyone who'd take him. Arnulfo won the dog by default in a raffle that Rey had devised, and now Chamorro was his constant companion. As a matter of fact, the dog was probably waiting for him at this very moment by the front door, as he was wont to do.

Both Emilia and Chamorro would be waiting for him when he got home. The dog was smart, loyal, and best of all, he couldn't talk. On the other hand, Arnulfo would have to listen to Emilia's eternal infernal monologues about what had happened during the day. Nothing of consequence ever happened, but she would spin her tale one more time, otra vez el burro al maíz, going on about how she thought the well was clogging with dirt or leaves, or how she'd noticed that the wasps had returned to that one nest by the back door, or had he noticed how the ants had moved from their usual spot near Dulcita, the oldest of her bougainvilleas, to a spot near the statue of La Virgen de Guadalupe out by the lawn chairs where she liked to sit in the summertime and eat watermelon with Isá? No, no, and no. He didn't know, he hadn't noticed, and he didn't care. Why was it that she cared so deeply about the animals and the trees? They weren't people. And yet . . . Chamorro was the closest thing he had ever found to a person, with a strong, placid will and a loving heart contained in that short, soft little body. Joe Kiratz pointed out to him that Xolos were often pictured in the murals of Don Diego Rivera, the great Mexican muralist. Chamorro was worthy of a painting, Arnulfo agreed.

"Oye, you better watch out, Olivárez, or I gonna come after that pinche perro," Luisito taunted him once after Arnulfo had rebuffed his company yet another time. "Yeah, I eaten dog," he proclaimed proudly. "In Guatemala."

"That was most likely Tepezcuintle you ate, not Xoloitzcuintle," Joe Kiratz, Comezón's present mayor, said with authority. It wasn't a job he'd wanted; it had been thrust upon him recently, after the last mayor, Telesforo "Tele" Pinchada, was deposed for bad behavior.

"I don't care what type of cunt-le it was, it was pretty good," Luisito sneered in Arnulfo's direction. Serves him right, the old goat, he thought. He never treated Luisito very nicely except when he was really drunk. Then they were the best of friends.

"What the hell were you doing in Guatemala, anyway, Luisito? Was that when you snuck over here to the U.S. with all your pinche family?" Arnulfo shouted back.

"I got relatives over here, over there, what it to you?"

"Oh yeah? Well, no wonder you're so messed up. Growing up eating dog like that. Listen, cabrón, you leave my poochie alone. He's buena gente. If I ever catch you messing with Chamorro, I'll twist your huevos in a knot. You hear me?" Arnulfo felt that he had to speak to Luisito with authority. The authority of balls. The only thing the man understood was the power of a man's testicles.

Yeah, Chamorro would be waiting. He hadn't been fed yet, and Arnulfo was the only one who was allowed to feed him his twice-daily ration of hamburger meat, red chile powder, and a raw egg mixed in. That was the first guilt that hung on to him for a moment, quickly followed by the second.

Arnulfo knew that Emilia was still awake. This made him feel bad, and he didn't want to feel bad. Well, let her wait. He had things to do. People to talk to. Who? Luisito? Rey? Joe Kiratz? Joe was writing a book. Mr. Philosopher of the World. But hey, the guy was pretty good, he knew a lot about this and that. Yeah, he was also a rival, but yet one day he and Joe had started talking, and now they sometimes sat together over a beer and looked at the world from the heights. Joe could talk if he wanted to, and he had a lot to say if you cared to listen. Most of the time he was hunkered down in some corner working on his book. Maybe Joe would be there. There would be a little music, even if it was from the jukebox. He knew all the songs. C2. N6. His favorites.

From where Arnulfo sat on a Plaza bench in front of the Crystal & Bead Shop, he could see Rey Suárez. Rey was the owner of the Mil Recuerdos Lounge. He was a good man. And that was saying a lot. And this is what Joe was writing about—good men, or rather, what it meant to be a good man. A good man in an evil time. Or at least that's what he told Arnulfo he was writing about. It was hard to understand what Joe was talking about sometimes; he used strange words, and mostly he talked about ancient Rome. Arnulfo didn't have enough to think or worry about, but Joe started talking to him about some Roman emperor. And the problem was he liked to listen. He hadn't known that Rome was, well, so Roman. Full of bad people, weak people, bad things and good things. It reminded him of Comezón in some ways.

Hell, even one beer makes all men good, or at least a bit interesting.

He saw Joe Kiratz hurrying by, pretending not to see him. It didn't matter. Arnulfo yelled out to Joe in his loud, booming voice so that the cabrón had to turn around. He waved back. He had to. Just because he was the mayor and was writing a book didn't make him king of the world. Hell, he was just another drunk who hung out at El Mil Recuerdos Lounge.

Arnulfo got up, his Tony Lamas pinching that cursed callo, his knees stiff, especially the left one, which was nearly locked. He felt overheated, water streaming down his forehead. He thought about his father, Bascual, and how before he had died he sweat a chorro of water each and every day. The man was always drenched in his own juices, which once he began sweating began to embarrass him. Arnulfo felt the same way. He'd watched how dying people began to perspire like that and cling to tables and benches. It was hard to touch them, and after a while they carried handkerchiefs and towels to wipe their own ooze. Soon afterward he'd be using a cane. Then he would need a wheelchair, and before you knew it, Isá would be wiping his butt with a soapy rag.

In the darkness Arnulfo could hear all sorts of sounds. Someone was whistling. A cat let out a high-pitched shriek. Someone coughed. The air was full of humming. More than one something was answering another something. The insects were active, and he swatted another fly. Where was old Mata with his flyswatter when you needed him?

The wind was coming from the south. It had been so long since he'd sat outside, listening to the birds, the wind. He wanted to lie down on the earth and rest. If it weren't so hot even at this hour, he would do just that. But the bugs would get him; there were the mosquitoes that had followed the recent rain, there were ants, and of course there were cucas—hell, he'd never known a life without Comezón's variety of persistent devil-may-care in-your-face roaches. Damn, there was just life out there, overwhelming and insistent life out there, waiting to get to him.

He would have to lie down soon. But where?

Arnulfo stood up, railing against all manner of things and cursing the inevitable.

In the distance a train moved north, the shrill whistle breaking the silence. Arnulfo wanted to sleep for a thousand years and wake up whole. But he trudged forward, stopping at another bench briefly as he adjusted his hat and cleared his throat, hurling an unceremonious glob of mucus on the street. There was a little blood in the spittle. Someone drove by and honked. Pinche puto scared him. He straightened up and waved back.

CHAPTER THREE

The Ants

Rey Suárez was rinsing Coke bottles on the side of the building with a faded leathery hose that emitted a weak trail of water a good ways away from the original nozzle opening. Hell, he kept forgetting to replace the damn thing. It was only a matter of heading down the road to the Walmart, but somehow Rey couldn't bring himself to go inside. He hated shopping in there. The last time he'd been in there, he had found himself face to face with El Padre Manolito, who hissed to Rey from one side of his snively little Spanish mouth, "Al fin nos encontramos en el templo." No way he wanted to run into S.S., that Sanctimonious Sacerdote, again, even though the Padre had it right and they had both found themselves unhappily in the temple of consumerism.

You could tell the time of day by when Rey came outside to rinse the Coke bottles. The man was regular in his ways, he always was. And there was something comforting about that. But something was wrong. Rey should have been inside the lounge, and not outside rinsing his Coke bottles under the flickering streetlight. Something was bothering him. He didn't want to think about things right now. Later, when he got home, he would think. Now he had to work. He'd forgotten to come out earlier when the light was better, and so he was stuck in the darkness estimating which bottles were clean and which weren't.

Rey had once told Arnulfo that he rinsed out his Coke bottles "so the ants won't come. The big ones. The red ones. You know. They bite the tourists. And you know, we like the tourists."

After carefully rinsing out each bottle as best he could, Rey gingerly placed them in the slats of the stacked-up wooden cartons that stood to the side of the lounge next to the Crystal & Bead

Shop, owned by an aging extraterrestrial channeler who went by the galactic name T'ernaita Astrominsle. Human or alien, the woman was looped. But she paid her rent on time and was a good tenant, and that was all that mattered. After a while Rey got to like her and referred to her as Terna. And that was how she became known in Comezón. Recently she'd hired some girl named Vela, a fortune-teller who always had her sidekick boyfriend around. They'd started hanging around the Mil. What the hell, they were something new to stare at.

The fiesta was over, and soon the tourists would be wandering in for a beer. He knew he'd better get inside. La Pata was on duty, and so was Emy. They might be swamped momentarily. Let's hope so, Rey thought. It had been an off week in an off month in an off year. Business had been slow. He turned off the hose, picked up a black plastic bag of garbage he'd left near the door, and dragged it to the dumpster. As he did, he pushed the crumpled-up local newspaper, the *Daily Comezón*, deeper into the garbage bag. He'd read an article tucked in the back of the newspaper, and it had disturbed him.

BODY OF YOUNG WOMAN
FOUND IN DESERT NEAR DEMING.
The body of a twenty-four-year-old Mexican immigrant, María Lourdes del Carmen Auriola, was found yesterday by a rancher and his son.

The article went on to give skimpy details. The rancher had found a bloody Kotex near the body. No water was found nearby, and it appeared that the deceased had tried to suck the sanitary napkin dry for whatever moisture there was.

That woman's story. Was it true? Was it something someone had told him? One of the Border Patrol guys? Or had the story come from someone who knew someone who knew the story?

Hell, any one and all of the stories were true; just wait long enough and something bizarre and unbelievable would become true. Who could make up a story like that? Desperate people do strange things. He hadn't been around for so long not to know more than a few choice stories. Ah hell, that was in the early days when he was out there in the dirt, and not in the office doing what later became his specialty.

What was the location of that ranch? He'd have to ask Chapo. Chapo would know.

Now there were other things to worry about. Many other things.

Rey couldn't get the story out of his mind.

María Lourdes del Carmen Auriola. Her death reminded him of the other woman—in that faraway, long-ago life.

Did María Lourdes del Carmen just lie down like that in the heat and finally go to sleep? And exactly where was it that she died? Rey would have to ask Chapo to show him. Would there be some sign of her death in the dirt and scrub brush, a pile of stones, a rough-hewn cross, a letter to someone? Probably not. Most everyone who died out there died without fanfare and in the extreme summer heat that blistered and boiled a man's blood and brought pustules of blood to his face. What of a woman, delicate and alone? It was an excruciating death. Nothing left but rotting bones, brittle water bottles, a rosary, or a faded photograph of someone loved, and yes, another false ID.

Rey saw Arnulfo resting up against a bench and shook his head. The man had no sense. Few people did. Where was that ranch?

The wind was picking up—life is this busy circle of action—and there was no stopping the inevitable. There was always a story out there, a story to be listened to and a story to be told. A story that floated on the hot breeze and burned your soul.

The story went the usual way of all stories: I mouth words. You respond in gestures. I become irritated with you. You find me difficult to be around. I want more. You want less. Your mind is so slow, mine too fast. I want to be alone and sleep. You want exterior noise, music. There is a depth of otherness in me. I frighten you. You've always had close friends. I wonder if I've ever had a friend. For a while, but then we got irritated and grew weary of each other. There's always a selfish need. You want something from me, and when I get tired, you hurriedly leave.

We were friends once. Maybe lovers. Each with our own selfish needs. We tired each other out. We wore each other down. We outlived our usefulness to each other. We bored and infuriated each other. We forgave each other one time too many. We disappointed each other. We knew each other's actions/motives/needs. We loved the same man/woman. We both slept with that woman/man. We resented and had never forgiven the lies. We were unfaithful in any number of ways, all ways. We were sidekicks until we couldn't stand each other's side and kicked back hard. We strained and shit on each other's dreams until we couldn't dream anymore. We confused each other's dreams for our own until we were afraid to dream. We cursed each other with nightmares, walked through dread-filled rooms anxious with each other's grief. We cried out: I'm tired of your pain, your lack, and your sorrows. Your endless stories of loss. Your dramatic beliefs of who you are or could be. And friend, if I bore you, revile you, suffer torment for you, imagine how I feel about myself. I am tired of my very skin. It pulls and stretches me and lays me out flat.

Rey coiled up the hose and put it away. It was time to go back inside the lounge. Time to get back to work. To figure out what to do. Don Clo had called him to say he was coming to town. Rey would have to give him an answer. It hadn't been so long since he'd seen him with his wife, Lita, but this time it was a different type of visit. He wouldn't bring Lita and their two little daughters with their flouncy little dresses and white gloves. This time they wouldn't go to lunch after Mass with El Padre Manolito. Hard to believe Don Clo and S.S. were friends.

Don Clodimoro Balderas was coming all the way from Chihuahua. Alone. Just to see Rey. Maybe he wouldn't make it. He said he might not. He said he wasn't sure he'd make it this time. He would let Rey know for sure.

That was last week.

Rey had been an expert on false IDs. It wasn't a job he'd ever thought he'd be doing for so many years for the Immigration and Naturalization Service, but he was good at it. As a matter of fact, he was famous at it. He traveled all over the U.S. consulting. He had a keen eye and could spot a false ID faster than you can say undocumented alien. Although he always hated the word "alien." Alien never said it well. Nothing alien about anyone on this God-Blessed Earth, unless of course they were an alien from another planet. And he had an idea of some who might be. He'd always believed in life on other planets. Why not?

One night, out there in the field, he and his then partner, Bruce Winford—ole Bruce Winford, where was he now, ole snively snorty watery-eyed Bruce Winford, cough up a storm and let everyone know they were out there in the darkness and shadows, waiting, waiting—he and ole Bruce had seen a flying saucer. It came over them in the blink of an eye, and then it was gone. Bruce wanted to let it go, but Rey, he wanted to know more. Funny thing was, Bruce refused to talk about it. Never talked about it ever, never wanted to. He was that kind of guy, always shutting off. Maybe that's why they got along so well. Hell, yes, there was life in the universe, and it wasn't all human. Working for Immigration taught you that. Most especially some of the so-called rank-and-file. Damn if they weren't from other planets!

And there they were working the Marfa Sector. No wonder they'd seen a flying saucer. Anything and everything was possible out there. Rey had never see the Marfa Lights, those legendary balls of light that came at you and then sped away, but he'd seen other things, creatures, elementals, whatever you wanted to call them. Best-to-leave-it-alone kinds of things. Several times he'd even seen the Devil himself. The Devil lived in a cave near Redford, Texas. But he didn't want to think about it now.

Rey Suárez was a Migra All-Star. An expert on false IDs.

What was it about false IDs? It was in the tilt of the head, the angle of the pose, the way the subject looked at the camera. Rey was a natural at what he did. And that's what he did for years, too many years. After a while, he started a scrapbook to show the other officers what to look for. And that scrapbook grew to two and then three and so on. When he retired, he put the best IDs in a number of scrapbooks and took off with them. No one really cared, anyway. What did it matter if he kept one or two or three or even ten scrapbooks? To anyone else, all the photos looked the same. All the information was repetitive, boring, and tedious. María this. José that. Poor fools caught and sent back. He was the only one who was really interested in those photo IDs. He was the only one who remembered all those people. Never forgetting a single one. He was the one who saw them for what they were, he was the one who saw their hopes their dreams their lies their sorrows. Maybe he even saw their deaths. Hell, he saw something move around them, and it wasn't the wind. What he saw, he could never tell them or anyone else. Who would believe him? Yes, he saw the ones who would make it, the ones who wouldn't, the ones who would die trying, the ones who would get by, and those who'd thrive.

That was his job, to assess, to understand, to know more about people than they knew about themselves. And he did. It was both a curse and his livelihood. Never made the money he should. And he was the best. But he got by. At the end, he was doing pretty good. Pretty good. Pretty damn good. But it was never good enough. He wanted to get away. Have his own business. Be his own boss. Open up a lounge. Never got the recognition or the money he really should have after all was said and done. There were plaques and awards and bullshit dinners and at the end a semi-valuable watch if you like gold. He never wore anything that wasn't silver.

He could tell where a person came from by their accent. By the way they said certain words. By the way they moved. By their stance and the stillness of their fear. He knew too much, and in the end it was too little.

That was his talent. He didn't have a name for it, but there it was.

Naming. That was the thing. To have a name for a thing and call it out.

Now that he'd left that job behind, he was still using his talents; that would never go away. Who better than a lounge owner to need to know the ways of the world? His knowledge had served him in the past, and it still served him well. He immediately knew the con artists from the homeboys, the vato locos from the bull-shitters, what passed as the power in Comezón, the twitchy, the itchy, and the just plain jodidos.

In the boredom of Rey's work out there in a hot car waiting for something to happen and in the office waiting for nothing to happen, he had begun to realize a skill he didn't know he had: that of memorizing faces, information, postures, stances, and of knowing and separating what was true from what was a lie. He was good at interrogation and better yet at reading the quiet des-peration of any ID, false or otherwise, and at observing and then understanding the person who handed it to him and stood there in front of him waiting for the light to change from red to green.

He was good at judging people, and this was what he was paid for. But in his own life he was sometimes as muddle-headed as they come.

How often had he looked at a stranger's photo ID, analyzed their look, the slant of their body, observed the angle of their body to see if their ID was a forgery or not? Once determined, he would relegate their life to one pile or another: Resident Alien. Undocumented Alien. American Citizen.

Rey was an expert on false IDs. And his life was the falsest ID of all.

Ah hell, he couldn't leave town. Not now. If he left, Don Clo would be angry. Eventually he'd track him down. Might as well get it over with. Although it wasn't a bad idea to just up and leave. Just for a little while. It would give Rey some time to figure things out. And he needed that time.

No, he couldn't leave. Not yet. And yet it was almost time for him to make that trip he should have made long ago. To find those people. Names in a scrapbook. Faces that stood out in a book of too many faces. Most of them posing proudly with their false IDs. Many people had lied to him. But not those people.

Their names were real. How did he know their names were bona fide? How did he know their stories were authentic? How did he know they spoke truth when they said the names of their towns, the names of their mothers, their fathers, their brothers and sisters? Why truth from so few? Was it the way they breathed truth, with such longing?

"They're just lying wetbacks," Chapo said with disdain. Chapo would say something like that. He was the nastiest kind of Border Patrol agent you would ever want to meet. He looked pure Indian from some dark heartland of Hell, and he hated Mexicans because he was one. Rey had had the misfortune of knowing Chapo in that past life, back there in the history of his forgetting.

"You ever notice how much those people smell? I mean it, they smell. Don't you be trusting not a single one of them, Rey. Hell, man, you look at those IDs too much, they start coming alive for you. All's I can say is, they're all lying hijos y hijas de la puta madre from over there trying to get over here. And our job, don't you forget it, Mother Teresa, is to keep them over there and not be letting them slip over here. You just keep looking at those faces and those IDs and tell me which one is a good ID and which one is wrong, and I'll do the rest, Mr. Migra Man."

It was at that moment that he hated Chapo Martínez the most. The man had a bad mouth, a foul temper if you pissed him off, and damn if he didn't smell. He was one to talk about smells. It was because he smelled that he thought they smelled. He was always ducking into the bathroom, but it didn't hide that nasty butt smell of someone too far gone with bleeding. Hemorrhoids? No, something worse.

Someday. Sometime. Sometime someday Rey would find those people. He would call them out. Maybe some were dead. He had no way of knowing. He was good at what he did. He'd track them down and see what had happened to them. If they were where they said they came from, he would find them. Find them all. After all, he had their names, their information, the names of their towns, the names of their mothers and fathers.

It was as if all the IDs began to have a life of their own. It started when he took one of his albums home to check on a few facts. Chirrión. A small town in the state of Tamaulipas. México. Sierra de Chirrión. Latitude 23.5166667°. Longitude −99.7166667°.

Call them the names of ghosts if you want. But even ghosts have names: San Juana Fierro. Rosaura Muñoz. Plutarco Carmona. Adelma Sánchez. Evangelina Duarte. Jesús Senaiba, the old man with his huge battered hands and scarred arms from the barbed wire.

Someday Rey would find out what had happened to them all. But now he was in a fast car going down a deserted road. A faraway sign beckoned out there in the darkness. You see that light? That was the future.

Now he was the owner of the Mil Recuerdos Lounge. Life was pretty good. Except for that one thing and for that one person. Don Clodimoro Balderas. He knew what the man was capable of doing. He had known that someday Don Clo would come looking for him to settle things. Oh, but those things were things that could never be settled. Not in this lifetime or another. And that was his comezón.

CHAPTER FOUR

The Mil Recuerdos Lounge

Arnulfo Olivárez slowly made his way into El Mil Recuerdos still wearing his soggy, sweat-stained mariachi suit. He held his hat in his hand, and it kept bumping into people. Some stupid biker looked at him, pointed, and laughed.

Although it was nearly 7:00 P.M., it was still 90 degrees in the shade. He had wanted to go home and change, but then he would have had to talk to La Gorda, and as far as he was concerned, there was nothing more he had to say to her. Not today, anyway. They'd already spoken. Tomorrow would be another day.

He'd huffed and puffed as he made his way to the bar, crossing the Plaza on a diagonal to save time. Once he got near the door, he took off his sombrero to make sure his hair was not too flat. He would find a place to park the hat, probably Rey's old coat rack near the men's restroom. He'd have a beer or two or three and then head home. The women would all be asleep then, well, most of them, anyway. He'd see how he felt when he got back. If he was hungry, he'd have La Gorda make him some huevos rancheros or warm up some menudo that Isá had made for the day. She always made menudo for Sunday breakfast; it was an Olivárez family tradition.

That was one good thing he could say about his life—he was never hungry. Well, for food, anyway. And if he was, there was always someone around to cook him anything he wanted. He made sure they knew that he was to be attended to, day or night.

Por Dios, all you had to do was look around and see the sad faces of too many men who'd lost their ability to command their home the way they should. It was an epidemic, and he was one of the few healthy men who ran his household the way it should be run, with a firm hand and no arguments. He could tell Joe Kiratz a few things about life if he'd listen. His other compa, Rey, said he'd heard it all, being the owner of a lounge, but he, too, never listened to what needed to be heard. As a result, both of them were soft and spineless, lost within themselves. And the worst thing of all was that they didn't even know it. Ay, but he was tired out from worrying about other people. What he needed was a Coors Light with a shot of tequila on the side. He sat down away from the jukebox, as far away as he could get from Luisito and close to the restroom. He could feel something gurgling inside and felt a pull near his sphincter. Best to be on guard.

The Mil Recuerdos Lounge was aptly named because it called up a thousand memories of love and loss, the wistful, weighty sadness of its dark front room with its well-worn bar and the two even darker side rooms. Too many dreams nested in the languid air. It was a place where too many small-town drunks searched for Nirvana or at least a minutia of compassion from Rey Suárez and his crew: Patricia González-Curry, a flat-chested former brunette who had gone blond a few husbands back and liked to wear her clothing very tight—showing off not too much of this and a lot of that. "La Pata," as everyone called her, often wore low-cut blouses, sometimes even tank tops, although she should have had more sense. Once a patrón had mercilessly ragged her about her lack of charm(s). Rey then barred the poor unfortunate from ever entering the lounge again.

La Pata was the Mother Superior to her undisciplined brethren, and she liked it that way. Rey, of course, was the Father Confessor and the Bishop of the Town all rolled up in one, and he and everyone else liked it that way. Everyone but his nemesis, El Padre Manolito, who imagined himself Pope of the World and the Head Inquisitor all rolled up in one, and who went out of his way each Sunday to mention the lounge in some form or another in one of his blistering sermons about Sodom and Gomorrah and the end of the world border style. In his version, that disreputable place would slide into the lapping, burning waves of lava that would engulf what had once been desert, carrying it out to a sea of burning, smoldering rock, a newborn conflagration that would lap up against the shore of what once had been. Yes, all this land was once underwater, El Padre Manolito continued, but now it's a sea of filth and stench and pestilence that needs to be erased from all memory, etc., etc. On the days he had forgotten to take his Metamucil, the more he berated the Mil Recuerdos bar and its owner, Rey Suárez.

"Bar, hell, it's not a bar. A bar is a place full of drunks," Rey liked to brag. "Our clientele are some of the deepest, most intellectual thinkers in Comezón, well, other than Luisito Covarrubias. I don't think that walking excuse of a man has had a straight thought since day one. Heard he was dropped from a height headfirst as a child, but shoot, that doesn't even explain it. I'll have you know plans and plots have been made here, and once some big honcho from the Highway Department laid out the blueprints for some new cloverleaf up north and proceeded to make his corrections on the pool table while I handed him a cold Bud. Not to mention the fact that the City Council meets here after their meetings, and the Lions, Elks, and Women of the Moose have frequented our establishment. Yeah, Women of the Moose. Don't you ever be calling them Cows. Show some respect."

The other staff member of El Mil, as it was called by those who called it home, was back-up bartender Emmanuel "Emy" Ramos, a retired truck driver who'd gotten injured on the job and now worked whenever Rey needed him or felt like letting him work. It wasn't a good arrangement for Emy, but then again, he didn't want to work too much, and his so-called job was an excuse to get out of the house, which had been bought for him by his girlfriend, Minerva, who never let him forget who the real breadwinner was.

Emy's sometime part-time job got him away from "Nerva," who worked at the State University, and in none other than the president's office.

Minerva's former boss had just recently moved to a job in a state where roses grew lushly and the humidity was higher. As a result, Minerva was really busy, preparing the path for the new Grand Lizard. Emy knew who David Icke was and had read all his books.

Minerva, on the other hand, didn't believe in all that Lizard crap about the Queen Mother and the Royal Family drinking the blood of blond blue-eyed babies. Emy didn't want to think about all that Matrix shit, but someone had to before the Hopi prophecies came true. But try and find anyone to really talk to about underground human breeding colonies run by Greys and secret tunnels crisscrossing the U.S., or about the nearby cattle mutilations on Red Roybal's ranch or the latest sighting of the chupacabra at the dam where a USO (Unidentified Submerged Object) was reported in '89, and it was all over. Might as well have another Coors Light.

"Coming up, Nulfo!" Emy called out to Arnulfo Olivárez, who was waving to him to bring him a cold one. The viejito was looking bad as far as he was concerned. Emy would try to talk him into going home early. He had no business here, but as Rey used to say, "It's not our business what the business is. It's all just business." Not in this case, though. Old Nulfo, or Nuffie as some called him, looked worse off than usual with his left leg elevated on a chair, one giant leather boot blocking the door near the men's room.

The hot topic lately in El Mil was the three-day fire in the Lágrimas Mountains and speculations on when the winds were going to die down and when it would rain. Other topics included the hope that the pecan tassels would soon quit affecting the air quality, causing the usual seasonal allergies, and just why in hell the old Dairy Queen had been bulldozed for a Walmart gas station when there were already two other gas stations in the proximity of several blocks. In other words, it was a regular sort of night at the Mil, comme si, comme ça. The weather was always a topic. Bets were going as to when the temperature would reach 100.

If Emy had to work, it might as well be at El Mil, where he could count on an occasional beer on the house—that is, if Rey wasn't looking or if he was feeling pretty good, which was pretty much how Rey felt most of the time. Yeah, it was pretty good this, pretty good that. He was a good-natured guy as long as you didn't mention religion or Mexicanos getting food stamps. Emy also steered clear of giving the U.S. military any shit and talking about taxes, especially who paid and didn't pay and why. And yeah, the job was pretty good if you could take a bunch of bullshit stories from a bunch of shit-kicking rowdy bullshitty shit-kickers. Emy could, especially after experiencing Nerva and her family. What he couldn't take was his boss's very rare and overpowering occasional rage.

Emy had only seen Rey Suárez angry or sad a few times, and that was because some shit-kicking drunk was trying to kick shit or because someone had died, like the Pope or Mother Teresa, usually a famous Catholic who would someday be canonized.

Rey was a lapsed Catholic and never attended Mass unless someone he knew had died, but like many other dyed-in-the-wool-don't-mess-with-my-religion-I'll-be-a-Catholic-until-I-die-a-Catholic-and-am-buried-in-Santa-Eulalia-Cemetery-en-frente-de-la-mera-mera-larger-than-life-plaster-of-Paris-statue-of-Santa-Eugenia, he was faithful to his God, if only in spirit. He was a Catholic, and damn it, no Bible-quoting Jehovah gemelos dressed in twin monkey suits were going to change that. Let them try.

Rey had a pantheon of his preferred saints and heroes on the wall behind the bar in photo frames, along with his favorite political figures, all Democrats, as well as a smattering of popular icons: Old Blue Eyes—Frank Sinatra, Pedro Infante, and Al Martino, as well as a framed newspaper ad of a concert at the El Paso Coliseum with Willie Nelson sporting a crew cut. Yep. Rey also had all the usual Chicano heroes in attendance: John F. Kennedy, Bobby Kennedy, Pope John Paul II, Freddie Fender, and of course Tiny Morrie at the piano playing "Lonely Letters." El Mil's Hall of Fame also included Al Hurricane, Sr., Trini López, and Baby Gaby.

Oyeme, Rey was a child of that time, and for him, there was no time like that time. And if you didn't know who Baby Gaby was, you were probably a Gringo or a pendejo desgraciado who'd lost his way in the sixties and had never gotten home. Aw, give me a break; just don't get all agüitado over what I'm telling you, man. The simple cure for it all was a couple of cold Tecates with lime as he sat you down and gave you the history that both of you knew you were missing.

When it came down to it, the Mil Recuerdos had algo, call it an atmosphere. It wasn't a memorable place, and yet to those who frequented it, it was very special. No one planned to remember the women's restroom with its lack of stall doors or the pee-saturated hallway near the men's room. There were just some things about the place you could never forget, and that's maybe why the old regulars who'd moved away kept coming back. Call it nostalgia for the past. Call it anything but sophistication. What it lacked in style, it made up for in the nature of its clientele. And this clientele was what could be termed faithful.

El Mil had a smell. That smell. Its own smell. It was hard to get away from the smell and much harder to describe it. Many had tried. It was the smell of too many beers delivered, dropped, dripped, and downed. It was the smell of too many tears, too much anger, and too much lust that came bubbling up from untold human cavities. If the bodies were human, as Emy often wondered.

The smell was a cross between booze and perfume, cheap aftershave and alternating hot and cold piss, horny men and hornier women on and off the proverbial gara. It was the smell of semen, sand, old farts, moldy dust, and red enchiladas with an egg on top, over medium, New Mexico style. Add the seasoning of age to that, and you might could probably approximate something. Maybe. It was a dingy nest of a place, an incubation chamber of possible despair, and despite Rey's attempts to keep it fairly neat, the inside of the Mil Recuerdos was tawdry and rundown, but only if you looked at it closely and in full daylight, which was an impossibility. First of all, Rey would never have let you look at anything with the lights going full blast in daylight, and secondly, you never wanted to look at anything in there too long or up too close. Maybe that was the reason La Pata often wore thin plastic gloves while serving drinks.

To an outsider, it seemed cheerful enough with its long wooden bar, the colored Christmas lights over the Budweiser sign, and the

Chicano Hall of Fame that spread out lengthwise across the spidery and smoky mirror with the rust-colored swirls that added a certain touch of something from another era, what a swiggling late-night drunk might even call class.

Often Rey was to be found at the bar, reading the local newspaper, the *Daily Comezón*, or maybe the *El Paso Times* or *El Diario* from Juárez. In the background you could hear Elvis warbling "Blue Hawaii" or, there it went again, "Wasted Days and Wasted Nights," or the ever-popular "Volver, Volver," which everyone sang to themselves through their beers and watery rum and Cokes, and which stunted their pain as they honked out the chorus with a vengeance.

"Quiero volver, volver, volver . . . a tus brazos otra vez . . . I want to return, return, return, to your arms again . . . "

A large jar of dill pickles sat on the counter alongside a greasy plastic container of Slim Jims. There were always a few bowls of chile popcorn available if you didn't mind a stale taste and an occasional mustache hair. A drippy glass bowl of hard-boiled eggs stared out like ghost eyes as Pep Turgino, a regular, fished out two large orbs, popping them both in his mouth. Pep held the award for the most eggs contained in a human mouth at the same time: eight. Or was it seven? Rey couldn't remember. Hell, Pep couldn't remember. And why should he? Someone did remember, but it wasn't worth knowing who.

Occasionally there was live music, most of it not good, not bad. The bands had names like Johnny and the Texas Teasers or Velvet Urge or Hamburger Necktie, a too-loud punk rock band that was never invited back. The flip side of the rock bands were groups of sad-looking mariachis who never smiled, like Pancho Puentes y Los Pilotos or a Cumbia/Norteña fusion group like Mexican Diamond in the Rough or a popular group from the valley called Así Me Gusta that played everything from "La Puerta Negra" to "Layla."

At that moment Joe Kiratz, one of the regulars, peeked in the doorway of the bar, thinking of his mother, Sofía. Her memory frequently came up hard when he least expected it. She had often told him that his ancestors were Native American and that they considered alcohol a spirit. "And like all demons, before you know it, they can take possession of you."

Joe could hear "Wasted Days and Wasted Nights" being sung in the background by Freddie Fender. As usual, the bar had the animal smell of too many drunks.

Sofía was part Apache from way back, although in her lifetime she had always denied being anything but Spanish. That's how it was for people in her day and age. If someone was Native or part Native, no one spoke about it, although everyone was part Native when you came down to it. To be from México, too, was something of a burden as well. Sofía's family had once lived in the Mexican part of the county and became law-abiding citizens of the Territory of New Mexico under President Franklin Pierce. They were the part of the family who decided to stay on the U.S. side when all the land around them reverted to México after the Gadsden Purchase. The treaty had broken up so many families and damaged so many lives, but then again, nobody ever talked about that.

Joe, as a result of his mother's confusion, was one of the most confounded of all the denizens of the bar and of his town, a Mexi-Gringo, an Ang-lino, an Anglo-Latino man looking for his country and his roots who wanted to claim his lineage but was never allowed to be truly what he was: a mestizaje, a mezcla, a mixture, just himself, a man from many worlds. And that world was Comezón, his itchy little town.

Another thing that set Joe Kiratz apart, at least in his own mind, was the seriousness of his life's work. For the most part, he saw the others who frequented the bar as below him intellectually. It wasn't their fault, he thought, it was just a matter of heritage and breeding. He didn't want to feel this way, but Sofía had done a number on him. Joe was working on a biography of the Roman emperor Antoninus Pius, 138–161 A.D. He often worked on his opus at his special table at the back of the bar. At this time the book consisted of a number of manila folders containing sheets of onionskin paper with beer-splotched notes. It was all coming together.

Joe glanced at Luisito in full drunken thrush at the counter and then saw Arnulfo sitting by himself near the restroom and thought of Sofía's fire-and-brimstone admonitions and how she had tried to save his mortal soul one too many times. Who would save Luisito? What about Arnulfo? Sure enough, there were more than a few full-blown possessions in plain sight.

Wasted days and wasted nights,
I have left for you behind
for you don't belong to me,
your heart belongs to someone else.

Why should I keep loving you,
when I know that you're not true?
And why should I call your name,
when you're to blame
for making me blue?

Don't you remember the days
that you went away and left me,
I was so lonely
prayed for you only,
my love.

Why should I keep loving you,
when I know that you're not true?
And why should I call your name
when you're to blame
for makin' me blue

Don't you remember the days,
that you went away and left me
I was so lonely

prayed for you only
my love.

Why should I keep loving you,
when I know that you're not true
And why should I call your name
when you're to blame
for makin' me blue

It was around that time when the drinking became serious. La
Pata was bartending because Emy had had to leave early because
Minerva's coven, call that her family, was gathering and he couldn't
get out of it. He had offered to bartend the birthday party of
Minerva's stepfather's brother, Gallo, who was visiting from Syl-
mar, and already that visit had impacted Emy's life and run its
course with Minerva's overextended family, who wished he'd
leave, and as soon as possible. Only one more borrachera to go.

"Okay, I'm headed out, Rey," Emy said with resignation.

"We'll be here . . . ," Joe called out to Emy.

"Yeah, I know . . . "

"Until the pendejos go home . . . "

Always the same goodbye from Rey.

Emy nodded to Rey.

Rey nodded to Emy.

Emy nodded to Joe.

Joe nodded to Emy.

Rey nodded to Joe.

Joe nodded to Arnulfo.

Arnulfo nodded to his Coors Light.

If anyone had seen them, they might have thought they were
four crazy nodding men. Make that five. Luisito nodded to everyone.

"Nuffie's waiting for you in the corner. Has secrets to tell," Rey
said to Joe.

"Can't do it. I have to work on the book. I had a breakthrough
this week. Might have to leave early. "

Joe lived in the apartment above the lounge, which Rey had rented out to him about a year earlier when he separated from his wife, Laneen, who was dying of cancer.

"Oye, compa! Let's have a drink, just you and me, eh, Joe? I got a table in the corner. We can talk real good back there," Arnulfo snorted through his beer, his eyes watery, expectant. "So what's new, Jefe? I saw you out there on the Plaza in the shadows. Yeah, another Fiesta. No lo creo. Were you there when the wind came up? It blew through my soul, compa. I had to get a drink to settle the wind. Lots of people, yeah, lots of people. Turistas. Most of them didn't hear or understand a thing. Another year. Allí te espero, I'll be back there. Tú sabes, there in the shadows. We're just a couple of cucas rebeldes, two rebel cockroaches, we're going to outlive this bola de locura, all these fools . . . "

The atmosphere of the Mil Recuerdos had never varied much; it was a late-night place, the kind you might find in a border city, or in Juárez, México, after 1:00 A.M. Usually there was a sad and haunting version of "Camino de Guanajuato" on the jukebox, someone belting out its famous lines "No vale nada la vida, La vida no vale nada." Or maybe an older Chicano veterano who once lived in California was playing "Pipeline" by the Chantays on a cheap guitar on the upraised platform that was the so-called stage. El Mil was a local hangout with not much happening in the usual sense of happening on the Texas–New Mexico–México border. En otro sentido, in another sense, it was the only place in Comezón that was really happening.

But in the old sense of no sense, the usual regulars kept waiting for someone new to walk in. So far no one had walked in. Luisito stood in the middle of the lounge scratching his balls with one hand, the other holding a longneck Coors. He then unbuttoned his shirt and was up to his usual somewhat obnoxious yet tolerated habit of sticking his middle finger inside his ombligo—where he'd nest his finger and then pull it out to smell it. The action seemed to calm him down. Sometimes he sat with a beer, his finger resting comfortably in his large dark hairy belly button while he peacefully contemplated his world the way a baby might suck on a teething ring. After a while no one seemed too concerned about what might be considered aberrant behavior.

Moving back to a table, Luisito sideswiped Rey's old dog, Diablo, who was sleeping in a matted ball near the jukebox.

Diablo was arthritic and cranky, and he always left an oozy trail of strong brown pee behind him. Suddenly, as if emerging from a bad dream, he arose with a lurching movement that catapulted him close to Arnulfo, who was at the jukebox selecting a song. The mangy dog—ignored by all and relegated to the dark, nasty corners of the lounge or forced to sun in the doorway where no one had to breathe his acrid smell—suddenly found himself the center of attention. Something long deadened in the creature came alive, and like all maligned and scorned creatures who are ignored, he reacted as his nature allowed and peed right in front of Arnulfo. Then the old dog farted loudly, leaving a smelly oozage behind. There was a long and uncomfortable pause after this wild toot of wind that caused Luisito to break into uncontrollable laughter. He snickered his way to Arnulfo, who greeted him like a long-lost brother, forgetting in his loneliness that he'd earlier disdained his company.

The two hermanos sat down as Arnulfo took off his other boot and was beginning to unbutton the charro vest. Pata knew it was time for him to go home. She walked back to him and whispered in his ear. After all, he was married to her madrina, the good-hearted woman who had baptized her so long ago. Her mother and Doña Emilia had been good friends.

The Plaza finally began to wind down for the evening as El Mil heated up.

CHAPTER FIVE

Night

Juliana Olivárez twisted in her bed. She couldn't sleep and dragged her torso up from a sleeping position. She was restless, thinking of El Padre Manolito. He had such beautiful eyes.

El Padre Manolito was in his kitchen, drinking a glass of cold milk and thinking of the sermon he'd given that morning. It had not been a good one, and he was dissatisfied with himself. No one had come up to tell him how moving it was and that they were glad he was now the pastor of Santa Eulalia. They had at one time, but that was back when he first arrived. What had changed? Why didn't anyone appreciate all his hard work, his teachings, what he had to say? The only one who appreciated him was Juliana Olivárez. Maybe she even loved him. She did love him, didn't she?

Emilia Olivárez got out of bed, fully clothed, and made her way down the long hallway to the kitchen, moving from one piece of furniture to another. Her left leg was tight with pain, and her short right leg was numb. She angled down the zaguán, almost knocking over a floor lamp. When she got to the dining room, she turned on the lights. She suspected that Arnulfo would be hungry when he returned. She wanted to get her favorite sartén ready, just in case he would want some huevos con chorizo or his favorite güiso, pork with green chile.

Ay, Arnulfo, when will you grow up! Life was moving so fast, too fast. Juliana wasn't young anymore, and she'd started having problems with her right foot. No amount of massage helped ease the pain anymore. Something had to be done. It was nearly time for her annual checkup. What would Dr. Diosdado say this time? Would he try and amputate, like he had wanted to do last time? Juliana had cried so much they had abandoned that possibility right away, although it was true that something had to be done. But when?

Emilia doubted that she could make the long trip this year to see the specialist in San Antonio. She wasn't feeling so good herself, and there was no way Arnulfo could drive them. Ay por Dios. There was no one to talk to. As always, she had so many things to say and no one to talk to. She was most active at night, just when everyone else shut down. Isá was in bed and had been asleep for a while. Emilia could hear snores coming from her little room behind the kitchen.

Where was Lucinda? Lucinda would be gone all night again with that boy, the sheriff's son, Ruley. That nasty boy left her mangled, a bruised flower. She could smell him on Lucinda's skin, and it was ugly to think about. Soon Lucinda would leave home, hopefully not pregnant before her marriage. Emilia was afraid.

Lucinda was Arnulfo's child by that other woman. Adopting her had never worked out. Lucinda had been cold and uncaring even as a baby. She cried when you picked her up and never wanted to be touched. Now that she was grown, she was worse. Now all she wanted was to be touched and loved, but by all the wrong people.

Lucinda was always demanding, always unpleasant, never loving. The only person Emilia had hope for was Juliana. All brightness and life surrounded her daughter. What could she do to help Juliana?

Emilia crossed herself, "Ay, qué familia, Diosito." They were all lost souls, and worse yet, incapable of ever changing. There was a curse on the family as surely as the night was long, so very long. Long with only the noise of her unstoppable thoughts, fervent prayers, feverish wishes, and dreams of peace.

She took out her favorite sartén, the cast iron skillet that had never seen water, and oiled it. There were beans to heat up in hot grease, a tasty güiso Arnulfo loved. She'd call over to El Mil, and

La Pata or Rey would give her a report. Her ahijada La Pata would have someone walk Arnulfo home. She was good about that.

The night was unquiet, charged.

Wake up, cabrones! Arnulfo stood up at his table, pounding his fist on it and upsetting his and Luisito's beers. He passionately expounded on the lack of moral fiber in most men, especially the heads of families. It was a favorite rant of his, and no one bothered to listen. He spoke to everyone and to no one. If anyone did hear him, they ignored him. He thought he was speaking clearly, eloquently, saying important things. From his vantage point at the counter, Rey looked at him and shook his head. Somehow in the din Pata heard the phone ring and answered it. It was Doña Emilia calling.

"Sí, Madrina, he's here," Pata reported.

"How is he?"

"He's taken off his boots."

"Make him put them back on and send him home."

"What if he refuses?"

"Have someone walk him back."

"There's no one here who can do that . . . lo siento."

"You know what to do, Patricia."

"Ay, Doña Emilia, I'm sorry . . . I tried to send him home earlier, but he refused. Ay, all right, I'll see what I can do."

"Tell him I made him some red enchiladas and warmed-up fideos. He's not well."

"No, he's not. He just took off his waist cincher."

"What about the hat?"

"We put it away."

"Tell Luisito to bring him home. I have some food ready."

"Sí, Doña Emilia."

"Luisito will take care of him like he does."

"Así es."

"Gracias, Patricia. I was thinking about your mamá. I miss her. She was a good woman. Muy buena gente."

"Buenas noches, Madrina. Don't you worry, we'll get him home."

"Buenas noches, Patricia. Te agradezco el favor. I'll say a prayer for your mamá. How many years has it been?"

Emilia was the only one who called La Pata by her real name. She had known Patricia's mother, Clarita—they were good friends. Clarita had become her friend when she first moved to Comezón. She knew when Patricia was a little girl, she was always taking off her clothes outdoors. She liked to be naked.

Emilia was thankful. Arnulfo would be back soon enough. He would be hungry. Luisito would help him get back. She would feed them both, and then Luisito would take off to his mother's. She would then put Arnulfo to bed, leaving him at last to sleep off his long sustained drunkenness.

It had been a very long day.

Emilia had wanted to go the fiesta, but Arnulfo had refused to let her leave the house. It was just as well. She'd taken a chair out to the front yard and sat there, listening to the mariachi music and singing along to the songs. One of her favorites was "Paloma Querida" by José Alfredo Jiménez.

Por el día en que llegaste a mi vida
Paloma querida me puse a brindar
y al sentirme un poquito tomado
pensando en tus labios me dio por cantar
Me sentí superior a cualquiera
y un puño de estrellas te quise bajar
y al mirar que ninguna alcanzaba
me dio tanta rabia que quise llorar

Yo no sé lo que valga mi vida
pero yo te la quiero entregar
yo no sé si tu amor la reciba
pero yo te la vengo a dejar

Me encontraste en un negro camino
como un peregrino sin rumbo ni fé
y la luz de tus ojos divinos

cambiaron mis penas por dicha y placer
Desde entonces yo siento quererte
con todas las fuerzas que el alma me da
desde entonces paloma querida
mi pecho he cambiado por un palomar

Yo no sé lo que valga mi vida
pero yo te la quiero entregar
yo no sé si tu amor la reciba
pero yo te la vengo a dejar

It wasn't so bad. The time had passed. Later she and Isá had cleaned some dried red chile outdoors in the backyard, twisting the stem tops and shaking out the seeds. They then soaked the chile in boiling water in the little storage house out back that Arnulfo called La Tumbita, and when it was softened they put it through the colander to make the red chile paste for Isá's menudo. They cleaned the tripe and cooked the hominy and put the menudo to simmer on the stove.

Arnulfo would be home soon. He would put his arm around her waist, teasing her, talking, talking, while she pulled off his boots. She would take off his socks and rub his feet with Bengay. He might try to coax her into getting into bed with him. They'd tussle, and he would sigh and roll over like a child, asleep long before he had a chance to finish telling her whatever he was trying to say in that voice she knew so well, low words, intimate and thick, words garbled but full of meaning, words full of something she couldn't explain. He would speak to her from his dark place, and she would hear his black words and let them slide off of her into the light of her prayerful intent.

Emilia fingered the rosary inside the pocket of her nightgown as she prayed for Arnulfo and for all men like him and for all women—women like her who were waiting for men—men like him. Qué Dios los cuide.

She could hear Juliana stirring in her bedroom and moaning in pain. Her feet were bothering her again. They would have to do something to help her soon. Dr. Diosdado in San Antonio had suggested surgery. Maybe it was time.

Emilia could hear the cicadas outside the kitchen window. It was their time again. Pobrecitos. Nomás tenían esta noche. They had only this one solitary night to feel the cooling-down after all those years underground. How would it go for them? Was it enough to have this little moment of joy? They would mate, bury their eggs, and then what? Fall down and rest in the earth again? If they could tell their story, what would it be? Dreamers dreaming a dream of coming up from the dark earth of their living tomb to breathe the shallow air of this one May night?

The night was full of stories. Who listened? Who cared?

Emilia would wait a little and then put on the sartén to güiso the beans. The hot grease would caramelize the beans, giving them that added flavor, el toquecito, the touch that meant home.

CHAPTER SIX

The Assumption

"I assume you know about the Assumption?" Padre Manolito asked Juliana as they sat on the patio of the Olivárez home near the bougainvillea, sipping cold mint tea from Doña Emilia's garden. It was time for their Catechism class, that special event they both looked forward to in the late afternoons.

"No, Padre, I don't, but I am waiting for you to indoctrinate me." Juliana spoke in Spanish and used the verb "indoctrinar," to indoctrinate, but what she really meant was that she was ready, willing, and enthusiastic to learn whatever he had to teach her, even if it was boring Catholic doctrine. She always feigned ignorance when she was with people, but most especially when she was with El Padre. If people thought she was simpleminded, let them think so. She knew she was bright, and not only that, but she always learned the truth about so many things when people thought she wasn't thinking. Everyone was delighted to learn that she was so innocent, so pliable, so unknowing. It was to her advantage to act dumb, ever the sweet fool. With El Padre Manolito, it gave him such pleasure to know that he was the one to teach her the ways of men, and most especially the doctrine of his bright and glorious and heavenly God.

For all his sternness, unrest, and slight stature, he was a handsome man. There was no denying that. She turned to look at the window. She didn't want him to think she was staring at him. Did he see her looking at him with interest? Oh, he was short, and maybe in some women's eyes that was a failing, a point of weakness, but in her eyes it was comforting. She was short, too. And perhaps because he was so short and so good-looking and so saintly, that would help him understand her, and if he understood her he would give her room to breathe. That's what she most desired, a space to breathe with someone she loved. She lived in a hothouse, and she was the rarest plant. She was always on display, ever guarded, and yes, overwatered. She looked back to El Padre, who looked at her with a strange expression. He had such beautiful eyes, with full, thick lashes. They were slightly sunken and very mysterious. What was he thinking?

"The Feast of the Assumption, which falls on August 15, Pausatio, Nativitas, Mors, Depositio, Dormitio S. Mariae, is the principal feast of the Blessed Mother. It is the day we as Catholics celebrate the Assumption of Mary into Heaven. Let's pause to reflect on that, mi niña preciosa. What does this mean to us? Mary, may her name be forever praised, the Mother of Our Lord Jesus Christ, was assumed bodily into heaven. She did not die, niña, she was assumed or lifted into the Heavenly Realm, into the Reign of God, into Spirit, without passing through mortal Death. Do you understand the significance of this, mi reina? No, you don't. God, as a gift to his beloved Mother, spared her from Death. From Death! Now do you see what I mean?"

She did not. She was still admiring his lashes and those finely shaped eyebrows. He was a pretty man, very pretty. And the Mother of God, well, it's too bad she didn't go through physical death, she thought. Everyone comes into this life to live and to die. Really, it was a waste of the Blessed Mother's time when you thought about it. How could one come into this world and then miss the meaning of life? For life was a duality. What was life without the fearsome, glorious, and transformative expectancy and charge and greatness of the Other? Dare she express her thoughts to El Padre? She didn't want to upset him. Especially not today. He looked rumpled, as if he hadn't slept. His clerical collar was on crooked and was slightly dirty.

"Padrecito," she began . . . but he interrupted her.

"Niña linda, I want you to call me Manolito, for we are friends. We are friends, Julianita, aren't we? We have known each other over a year, and you have been under my private instruction for over three months. It is time for our working association to change. What do you say?"

"Oh, sí, mi Padrecito, I mean Manolito, you are my friend and I am yours."

"That's how I want it, mi cielo. That's how it should be. I am your earthly Father and you are my child. By Father I mean Confessor, not true flesh-and-blood father. Each of us can only have one father and mother. Although it is to be said some of us are born of aberrant parents, wayward kin, and strange relatives. Such is the fate of many. Do we choose these irregularities, this punishment? No. Does God choose this for us? No. It is the result of Original Sin, that blight of Adam and Eve's that sends us shivering and lost from the Garden of Eden into places of famine and thirst, into the desert of emptiness and far away from our true home."

"Would you like some more tea, Padre?"

"Gracias. Where were we?"

"Mary had just been assumed and you looked very thirsty."

"Ah, sí. The Second Vatican Council taught in the Dogmatic Constitution Lumen Gentium that the Immaculate Virgin preserved free from all stain of original sin, was taken up body and soul into heavenly glory when her earthly life was over, and exalted by the Lord as Queen over all things. Do you understand this doctrina, mi niña?"

"Pan dulce, Padre? Fresh today from La Reynita, the panadería, our local bakery. Isá just brought them. Would you like a concha?"

"One must concentrate and reflect on the power of this gift."

"Yes, Padrecito Manolito. I love pan dulce, too."

"La Santíssima Virgen, the One and Only, and not what our local riffraff call La Virgen de Guadalupe with her dark skin and rough hemp dress and her peasant and revolutionary ways, did not decay. She was too pure, too dignified, too, too . . . do you see, do you see what I mean? She was above mortal man. And most definitely above all women. She was the greatest of all women. As we know, women are weak. Despite the inherent impairment of all women, the Blessed Mother had the ability to rise above, yes, rise above her sex, and for that reason alone, it might it be said, El Señor chose to bestow upon her the greatest gift. The Gift of Bypassing Death. 'Sidestepping' perhaps is a better word. Or just moving around or through. And for that reason and others, we will continue to explore this unfathomable mystery in a later class. You do understand?"

"No, Padrecito, I don't. Can you explain it further?"

Juliana leaned toward El Padrecito. As she did, she accidentally brushed his hand as he reached for a puro, a little flute of pastry shaped like a sugary cigar. She felt a bolt of pure electricity and dropped her elote, a corn-shaped delicacy with cherry jam inside, onto the floor.

"Ay! Oh, excuse me, Padrecito. I'm so clumsy. You were saying . . . ?"

"There are some who mistakenly believe that the Blessed Mother, may she be praised, ascended into the Heavenly Realm, which is an error of Holy Faith. It was Our Sacred Lord who ascended into his glorious Kingdom by his own power. It was La Santíssima Madre de Dios, Mary, who was assumed or taken up bodily into heaven by God without passing through Death. Note the verbs I am using: 'ascended' and 'assumed.' You don't need to be a linguist to know the difference."

"Padre, what is a linguist?"

"Reflect on this mystery, my child, while I drink my tea. May I pass you another pastry, niña? You need your strength to bear witness to this Sacred Mystery."

"I'll have a beso, Padrecito. I mean Manolito. That one there—it's called a kiss. Excuse me, just give me that piedra instead."

"Which one was the beso? And which one the rock?"

"I'll take the piedra or an oreja. The one shaped like an ear. It seems to be listening, no?" She laughed weakly and then turned away.

"Which? It's a confusion of bread, my child! Who came up with these names?"

"Oh, that's not all. There's the cuernos, the horn-shaped ones, and the maranitos, the little pigs. Or the trenzas. And the bigotes."

"Mustaches. Braids. It's all vanity. Pass me another beso. Now, just rest your spirit and reflect. That's it. Breathe. Breathe deeply as you meditate on the Holy Mystery of Our Mother's Gift from Her Son."

El Padre Manolito watched Juliana's chest rise and fall. Rise and fall. Rise and fall . . . rise . . . rise . . . and then fall . . . It was a lovely chest, he thought, and then took a large bite of his beso. If only . . . but no. No. His mind was wandering. He hadn't slept much the previous night. Oh, maybe for an hour or so, but it was a tormented sleep, a sleep of anxious dreams and worms. Yes, worms! But he could not show this holy child his doubt and his delirium.

"Are you reflecting, reina?"

"I am, Padre. I am meditating on the Holy Mystery."

"I am as well, my child. Now breathe again, deeply . . . as you ponder the Impossible, the Unfathomable, the Sensual, I mean the Essential."

Juliana wanted to reach out and touch him again. She had felt the heat of his skin, and it burned through her. She felt a twinge in her thighs, or was it near her knees? It was hard to tell where she felt the movement. Something had come alive down there. Tonight she would dream about him, and in her dreams he would be holding her and rocking her back and forth as you would a child.

El Padre started in again. She wished he would be quiet and just sit there. But he was a talker. An incessant talker. He seemed nervous, overwrought, and yes, very hungry. He'd eaten all the maranitos, most of the besos, and all but one of the elotes. Now he was starting in on the orejas. He would take a gulp of tea and then several large bites of pastry. The crumbs nested in his dark shirt and on his rumpled collar. He made wild gestures, and the crumbs followed the arc of his hand and landed in his thick, dark hair. Hair that needed to be stroked and loved and kissed again and again. Hair that needed to be pulled and crushed with a rough hand while having sex. And still he went on and on!

"We celebrate the Feast of the Assumption on August 15 of each year although we are not certain of the day, year, or manner of Our Lady's death. It's best we not know. How could we, being mortal sinful men? It is not for us to know the Divine. After our class is over today, I would like you to reflect on the brevity of life and the transitory nature of all flesh. We are here but a glorious moment, only to know the sweetness and its other side, decay. And yet: Our Father so loved his Mother that he did not allow her woman's flesh to undergo corruption. She could have been your age, my child. How old are you? It doesn't matter. She, like you, was vibrant, young. She was still a woman, although few saw her as such. Much like you. You are a woman despite your crippled body. Few see you as a woman. But you are. You are. You are a woman. Do you understand? And that is how we must see the Assumption. From the point of view of a woman. The eye of the needle, yes, let us meditate on the eye of the needle, my child. The Assumption is God's act of mercy to womankind. Oh, the dark agony of a woman's life! The Feast of the Assumption es el Colmo, the be-all and end-all of grace bestowed on the lesser being, which in this case was the Mother of God. This Divine Gift should succor us as we sit, much like in this garden, in our private Gethsemanes waiting for our blood to be shed. Now do you see? August 15. This year it falls on a Friday. Remember that date, niña; for that is the day we will celebrate with a High Mass at Santa Eulalia. I would ask you to engrave that date in your memory, for that is when I would like you to crown the Blessed Mother's statue with a diadem of roses. Don't worry; we will bring the statue down from its high nicho. What do you think? It is a great honor bestowed on a young virgin in the parish. I will expect you at the church around 5:00 P.M. for the Feast Day Mass."

"I thank you, Padre, for the honor, but I can't accept."

"What?"

"I won't be here."

"Why?"

"I won't be here."

"You won't be here? But you're always here. Juliana, you are always here. You're always here!"

"I won't be here."

"Why?"

"I can't tell you now, Padre Manolito. I am sorry. Perhaps later."

Juliana felt a certain shame rise up. She didn't want to tell El Padrecito that she might have to have her foot amputated. Dr. Diosdado had recommended it. She didn't want the congregation of Santa Eulalia to see her with a cast, or worse yet for El Padre Manolito to pity her, she who never had pity for herself.

"Juliana . . . " El Padre Manolo exhaled in exasperation and disbelief.

He felt jangled, disordered, and suddenly very sick. What was going on? He reached out to implore her just as Isá came out onto the patio to check on them. It was her habit to do so every fifteen minutes or so. The old woman was bothersome to him, and he noted that she often smelled. She wasn't particularly clean, and despite everyone's praise of her cooking, he couldn't bring himself to touch anything that came from her kitchen. She was as bad as Lorenza Tampiraños, the cook at La Reina Mexicana. He was haunted by ugly old women in this vile town. Even the young ones were cross-eyed and cow-faced with buggy hungry eyes or had the bodies of long-married women with saggy breasts and the nipples of a wet nurse. And he hated every one of them. He hated all women. Except two. The exceptions being the Mother of God and this innocent child of beauty who sat in her wheelchair looking at him with a funny expression. He could almost swear she was taunting him. She was a virgin, wasn't she? Had he been mistaken to ask her to crown the Holy Mother on her feast day?

The old worn-out cow filled their glasses with tea, bowed with exaggeration, nearly toppling over, and then took away the plate of pastries, but not before he grabbed one last one. It was a beso.

"I must leave now. I have an appointment, Juliana."

"But Padrecito, we still have some time."

"Not today. And besides, you aren't well, are you? Another time. You are too busy and too distracted. Perhaps you will get back to me when your spirit is less defiant. I will leave you to reflect on the Mysteries," he said with some malice, watching her squirm in her chair as she adjusted her malformed torso and weakly cleared her throat.

"Padre," she started to explain. But whatever excuses she had, she knew he wouldn't accept.

"You seem weary. Shall I call your nurse? You mustn't get over-tired, must you? Your body can't take it. Until next time, Señorita Olivárez. Me despido. I must say goodbye."

He put out his hand, but she did not take it. Instead, he made the sign of the cross in the air with a dismissive wave.

"In the name of the Father, the Son, and the Holy Spirit. Amen."

He turned his back to her and left her there, a crushed flower in a very hot garden.

CHAPTER SEVEN

San Manolo

Juliana worked with her hands. She had little formal schooling—only what her mother, Doña Emilia, had taught her—various prayers and some basics and what she had learned up to age ten, when Arnulfo took her out of school.

Her fellow classmates at La Reina del Cielo Catholic Elementary School were merciless and unnecessarily cruel to her and saw her only as a crippled girl. Arnulfo didn't want her suffering any more than she had to. To her, it was a heartbreaking jolt to be taken out of school and uprooted so violently by her father, but there was no recourse; he stood firm and refused to let her be victimized. It never occurred to him to home-school her; that wasn't something he would have thought about, nor was it part of that vision of his for her life. And so instead of learning what she could from a full-time or part-time teacher at home, Juliana absorbed what she could from everyone, anyone, at any time.

But Juliana was never one to be pitied. She was very bright and very able, and her abilities were many. Limited in certain physical actions, she became dependent on the strength and talent of her hands.

She could do anything with her hands. She was a seamstress, she crocheted, she was a cook, her biscochos and pumpkin and apple empanadas were renowned, her capirotada was a rich miracle of bread and fruit. She made piñatas, paper flowers, and masks, and yes, she painted little miniatures that were spectacular in detail.

Best of all her work were the holy cards she hand-painted and edged with crocheted lace. She was working on one now for El Padre Manolito. Somehow she had found out that his birthday was August 24, the week after the Feast of the Assumption. He had wanted her to be in that ceremony at the church, but she'd told him no. She might be having her operation before then or around then, and she didn't want people to see her in bandages, especially up on the altar. They would pity her more than they had before, and she couldn't endure that. She didn't want the operation, but it seemed necessary.

Juliana wanted to surprise El Padre with her gift, a handmade holy card depicting San Manolo, his patron saint. The only problem was that she couldn't find any sign of a saint named Manolo. There was nothing even close! The name Manolo was a derivative of the name Manuel, but when she thought of El Padre Manolito, he was no Manuel. His name, Manolo, should have been in between Saint Manirus and Saint Mansuetus. It was nowhere to be found. But she knew that somewhere, dear God, there was a Saint Manolo. What he was the patron saint of, she would never know. If that was the case, she would invent a Saint Manolo, no kin to Manuel.

The holy card showed San Manolo holding a book and a feather. The feather was a pen with which he would inscribe the names of the holy into his book of judgment. Well, it wasn't his book but God's. Saint Manolo was wearing the usual white shift with a green sash; no, make that leather leggings and a short tunic; no, better yet a dark suit with a white sash and a hat; no, no hat. The holy cards went through many transmutations as Saint Manolo aged from thirty to thirteen, fifty-five to seventy-something, and then back again to maybe twenty-eight. Juliana was twenty-eight, and it was a good age if you were a saint. Not that she was or ever would be. She wondered how old Padre Manolito was. She would have to find out. Then she could paint her Saint Manolo at the age of the other Manolo. The real Manolo. Creating the gift would take her months. It was very taxing, as she wanted it to be perfect. No one knew she was painting San Manolo. Mamá Emilia thought it was San José, ay que pretty, and Isá didn't care who it was, although one day she did notice that it looked startlingly like El Padre Manolo Rodríguez, the pastor of Santa Eulalia Church. Yes? No? Of course not, Isá, Juliana told her. Besides, there isn't a San Manolo. There's never been a San Manolo. You're probably thinking of San Manuel. Her father never did see the painting, and so who was there to care what saint it was?

Juliana began to pray to San Manolo, holding the holy card in her hands, placing it on her breast, next to her heart, right up against her nipple, and staring at it intently as she thought of healing. Her healing. May God concede to her this blessing.

Maybe the operation would allow her to sit up at a table without the brace she wore under her clothing to keep her spine straight. It might give her more mobility, allow her to do more things. It would, wouldn't it?

Querido San Manolo.

Please help me to get well. I may never be fully well, not in the way the world would see well. But make me well enough to be a bride. Make me well enough to love and be loved. This I ask in prayer and devotion to you, San Manolo. And if there truly isn't a San Manolo, then I send this prayer to you, San Manuel. And if there is no San Manolo, only a San Manuel, I ask for your forgiveness in calling out to San Manolo instead of you, San Manuel. Amen.

Maybe if she kept praying, they wouldn't take away her right foot. If Dr. Diosdado took away anything from her, she would never recover. Nothing could be taken. She would live in the body that was given her. She had come to accept it and felt comfortable in her skin. That was what people didn't understand. She was not suffering the way they wanted her to suffer. She knew who she was and how she felt, and to her that was not suffering. Her hands fanned the air. The heat in Comezón was unbearable and never-ending.

If it weren't for her art and her books, Juliana didn't know what she would do. She had been good in her studies and of course had learned to read. She could read quite well, thank you, but she hid her talents from her father. He didn't need to know everything about her. He wanted to, oh, he wanted to, but he would never know she had read *El Castillo Interior* by Santa Teresa de Ávila. The going had been rough, but over time she had come to understand more of the seven crystal mansions that would lead her to God. Mamá Emilia had the book on her bedroom bookshelf, and from time to time Juliana would borrow it.

Mamá Emilia's room was always in disorder, with an unmade bed and books and papers scattered pa' qui pa' ya. Such a strange contrast to the way she kept her husband's room. It was always organized and very clean. She might not have kept Arnulfo's room so clean if he hadn't demanded it. Oh, yes, she would have! Juliana always suspected her mother of keeping tabs on her father, and one way she did it was by going through his things on a continual basis, looking for any evidence of other women in his life. Over the years, this desperate kind of action had lessened.

Emilia might have welcomed another woman into their lives, especially now as they'd gotten older, someone who would cook and clean and keep up with his moods. As far as sexuality went, not to mention it. She was a one-man woman and always had been. She didn't want to think about Arnulfo's sex life with anyone else. It pained her to think of Lucinda's mother, Senaida, and how she and Arnulfo had come together. She wasn't a fool or blind. After all was said and done, she had to pity the poor girl. It was a story to be told in the shadows late at night. No words would pass her lips in daylight or to strangers. If you want to know about it, she thought, you'll just have to wait, for what she wasn't sure. All she had to do was look at Lucinda and see what that wayward life of his had produced. She and Arnulfo had stopped having regular sexual relations over twenty-two years ago, just after Lucinda's birth. Shortly afterward, Senaida had left town, and she hadn't been seen since.

Of course Emilia had taken Lucinda in. She had to. Era propio. It was proper. Well, maybe not proper, but expected. Maybe not expected, but Christian. It was the only thing to do.

What had happened over the years? Every once in a dark moon on a night with many stars, and after a long, sustained borrachera the likes of which would render him nearly senseless except for certain body parts, they would have occasional couplings, and truth be told, she wished they were more frequent. It was on those magical nights he would coax her into his bed, throwing himself upon her like a young man of forty, yes, forty, for that was when he had been in his prime. Most often he couldn't perform, but by then he was so sleepy and tired he didn't care. And if he did care, it was only briefly, and by the time morning came and he hadn't performed, he would have forgotten being overcome with desire for anyone, most especially his wife.

There was the one time she'd forgotten her handmade flannel calzones in his room. Later she found her underwear on top of her bed in a paper bag fastened with a clothespin. There was no note. She'd noticed that her chones were torn, oh yes, it had been quite a night! She retrieved them, and no words were ever spoken between them about this episode, but for months afterward Arnulfo looked at her shyly. She would smile at him broadly and he would turn away. That time había cumplido, he had completed what he set about to do. Arnulfo hadn't been as drunk as Emilia thought, and she hadn't fought him back like she usually did. All in all, it was a memorable and amazing night, and it passed too quickly. At daybreak Emilia crawled out of Arnulfo's bed back into her own. For he was a man of dignity.

After that, Emilia hoped things would commence with them again and that he would ask her to visit him more often, but it didn't happen. After putting him to bed on those various intermittent and drunken nights or on those other strange, sullen nights when he locked himself in his room with his long-playing records, she stood outside his door listening and humming along to "Begin the Beguine" by Ella Fitzgerald or "O Sole Mio" by Mario Lanza. She knew he could hear her. Unlike him, she had perfect pitch and a beautiful voice.

After a while she'd move away, down the zaguán to her bedroom to read. She read as long as she could. She read until her eyes couldn't stay open and the book became heavy and dropped out of her hands onto the bed. She would then wake up and begin to read again. She never had a bookmark, was always losing her place and rereading the same passages and even chapters over and over again. It didn't matter; this was how she had worked her way through the Bible and all the works of Santa Teresa and Saint Augustine, and most recently the biography of Padre Pío, the Italian priest who had the wounds of Christ on the palms of both hands, what were called the stigmata. His hands were always bandaged and his side was pierced, as was the Lord's.

She read until the sun came up, and then she slept an hour or so before getting out of bed to oversee the making of Arnulfo's breakfast by Isá. She rarely made up her bed, and she left her books lying about for Juliana to find. Now and again, most especially in the summertime, she would lie down for an hour or two in the afternoon as everyone else in the house did. In 100-degree weather, a siesta was mandatory.

Emilia knew that Juliana was a secret reader and let her wander in and out of her room at will. She left Juicy Fruit or Licorice Beechnut gum around on the tables, both their favorites, and if Juliana wished for a moment of sweetness, there was always a plastic container of Orange Slices or Circus Peanuts on top of her bureau next to the statue of Our Lady of Guadalupe.

Sometimes she would find Juliana in her room perusing a book, but she never said anything. Her philosophy of life was akin to Padre Pío's motto: Pray, Hope, and Don't Worry. Emilia always did worry, but she kept trying to work on that part of her life. She let Juliana read and learn as much as she could; it was good for her to know the world, at least in small increments. Of course, as a mother Emilia wanted her to be happy. That joy would probably never be with a husband or family, but then again: Pray, Hope, and Don't Worry.

Isá would find Juliana awake each morning when she went into her room. She never once had to wake her up. The girl was always one step ahead of her. And it was an unpleasant task most of the time to work for someone so kind and affable and irritatingly perfect. And for this reason she didn't really love Juliana. She never could. Although to anyone who saw Isá attending to Juliana with such apparent care and devotion, it would seem she was the best of attendants.

Juliana knew otherwise. Isá was careless, and yes, sometimes cruel. She would accidentally prick Juliana with a safety pin or catch her skin when she was clipping her toenails. She left hair on the floor and never liked taking care of Juliana's toilet. She would say things to her about her bodily functions that weren't nice and made her feel dirty. And she complained so much about having to lift her. She grumbled about this the most, but only when Mamá Emilia wasn't in the room. Isá was fast, furious y fastidiada. She was always bothered by the seemingly insignificant. A moan and she would go off, a sigh and she would pout, an expression of confusion and she would sulk. The woman was getting old and unhinging rapidly. Juliana would have to talk to Mamá Emilia about her soon. She didn't want the old woman to take care of her anymore. Ay, what was to be done?

Juliana sat in her room near the window. She was propped up, with a wooden board on her lap. This was the easel on which she placed her miniature paintings. Over the years she had refined her technique and was now a fine artist. Her specialty was paintings of the saints on cloth. These she would sew onto another piece of cloth that was backed by cardboard. She would then crochet the cloth pieces together to form a band around the image.

Last night Juliana had been reading *El Castillo Interior* and wanted to ask Padre Manolito a question about *The Mansion of Exemplary Life*, but then again, she didn't want him to know that the weekly Catechism lessons he gave her were elementary and ultimately unsatisfying. She hungered for a true discussion every time they were in each other's presence, but El Padrecito treated her like an unthinking child who didn't know much. If he realized how bright she was, maybe he'd stop coming to teach her things she already knew through reading her mother's religious books. Once again she had to feign ignorance and act demure. How tiresome the charade was!

Juliana didn't dare tell El Padre Manolito about her encounter with Santa Teresa. If he knew, he would surely grill her and go on and on as he did about everything. He was a slick broken record when it came to anything Spanish. Los Ethpañoles ruled the Old World and Forever the New. And nothing got him going like the memory of his beloved country's food. ¡Ay, el bacalao!!

El Padre Manolito breathed bacalao. Several weeks ago he'd interrupted the Catechism lesson on the Mystery of the Transubstantiation, the change of the bread and wine into the Body and Blood of Christ, as he suddenly remembered his mother's recipe for bacalao, prepared with tomatoes and fresh roasted red bell peppers.

BACALAO Á LA ESPAÑOLA

A Recipe from María del Carmen Rodríguez de García Given to Juliana Olivárez by her son, Padre Manolo Rodríguez.

- 2 lbs. dried salted boneless COD (No replacing the Cod with Tilapia or other white fish, unless you are mexican)
- 1 large white onion (yellow if there is no other choice and if you are mexican or they are on sale as they are often during the summer since this is one of your people's crops)
- 3 chopped garlic cloves, more if you are SPANISH
- 3/4 cup SPANISH olive oil (none of the other types, oh you can try them but they won't be the same thing!)
- 28 ounces of crushed fresh tomato (canned only if necessary and if you are mexican)
- A small amount of unbleached white flour to roll the fish in (GOOD FLOUR—none of that cheap flour mexicans buy in dollar stores)
- 1 hoja de laurél (Try and show a mexican herbs other than comino y oregano. Do you know what a bay leaf is, Juliana?)
- Fresh roasted and sliced red pepper, none of this bottled or canned red pepper. If you absolutely have to get other red pepper, get it in a jar that comes from SPAIN.
- This recipe should serve a table full of people. I never have more than 4–6 people at one sitting. How can you ever really talk about anything? And if you do have more than 6 people, it usually doesn't go well, I can promise you.

- You need to soak the bacalao overnight, or maybe two days. The fish is very salty, and you need to change the water various times or else you won't be able to eat it. LISTEN TO ME, JULIANA. You need to desalinate the bacalao pero con su tiempecito and with love.

Dry the bacalao. Set it aside while you get your pan with olive oil ready. Fry the bacalao. Set it aside. Add the onion and garlic to the bacalao and sauté. Add your fresh tomato sauce and bay leaf and simmer otro tiempecito. How long? Not long. Incorporate, yes, incorporate the fresh roasted red bell peppers with love and gratitude that you are Spanish and not Mexican. ¡Qué Viva España! ¡Bacalao! Now, this is God's food! ¡Coño!

The light was dimming, and it was time to put aside San Manolo for another day. She didn't want to overwork the painting now that she was getting close to finishing it. El Padrecito would be coming in a few days, and she wanted to check his eyebrows. Perhaps she'd made San Manolo's eyebrows too dark and strong. The eyes seemed fine, deep-set, large. The hands were strong, a little hairy with short, thick fingers. With some wistfulness she thought of them. She looked at her hands.

"Isá!" she called out in a voice she hardly recognized. "Isá!"

"Sí, Señorita Juliana. A sus órdenes." Isá was scowling, and Juliana could tell she had interrupted her as she huffed and puffed with irritation in front of her. She was getting the dinner together and didn't like to be bothered when she was cooking.

"I'm done for the day."

"Oh, you're done for the day, eh? Well, I'm not, my Little Queen. I'll be back in a little while to put up your toys."

With that, Isá turned around and left Juliana in her chair. As best she could, Juliana put up the contrived easel and the box of paint and sat there in the darkening room to await her caregiver's return.

El Padre Manolito was still in a state of shock. How dare Juliana refuse his offer to have her place the wreath on the Blessed Mother for the Feast of the Assumption! Little did the child know what an honor he was bestowing on her! Ungrateful little girl! He would take her aside at the Sunday morning Mass. It was unlikely he would have much time to speak to her in the presence of her bodyguards, but he would try. He needed her for his ceremony. Let these heathens see what could be done when someone with talent addressed a need. Juliana would look beautiful with a diadem of flowers in her long, dark hair, her hands placing a crown of roses on the Blessed Mother's head. The thought of that scene made his eyes tear up.

Beautiful hands they were, with long fingers and finely curved nails. They were always warm, expressive, and sensual. To take her hand and hold it was a pleasure. She would take his hand with tenderness and place her other hand like a soothing blanket of flesh over his. He lost himself in her soft, gentle touch. When she took his hand in greeting, it was hard to say goodbye. And saying goodbye, he only wanted to say hello again.

He wanted to hold her hand and hold it for a long while. He wanted her to touch him in places no one had touched him in a long time, her palm bandaging his weary brow, the flesh inside his wrist, the tender skin inside his elbow. He wanted her to touch him in places no one had ever touched him, places too dark to say.

And he, in turn, would take a firm grasp of her neck from the back—she would know that he was behind her, steering her forward onto that fast-speeding train of desire into the darkness of another country, that country being the flesh, that faraway land where they would lose language and the ability to speak, as they wandered blindly—still sensate beings but without a will of their own—so enamored they were with that touch that touch that touch that bound them to each other. He would grasp her by the nape of the neck and propel her forward into the burning room of passion.

Juliana sat in the darkness in her room. The sun had gone down, and still Isá had not returned. It was all right. Soon Doña Emilia would come in to take her to dinner. She would sit here and think of her painting. Of Padre Manolito Rodríguez.

Several Tuesdays ago at the Catechism class, El Padre Manolito had brought her a gift. It was a pendant of La Virgen del Carmen. He explained to her that Our Lady had appeared to four young girls, Conchita, Jacinta, Mari Loli, and Mari Cruz, in the village of San Sebastián de Garabandal in Spain beginning in 1961 and ending in 1966 with the usual warning to the world: to repent, pray the rosary, or else. The Or Else was the usual End of Time. And the warning was urgent. Padre Manolito had been to the small village of several hundred people and seen the church and believed the miracle to be real.

Thankfully, Isá was out of the room when Padre Manolito came up behind Juliana and lifted up her hair, which was in a large chongo, a thick braid that went all the way down to her knees, or approximately there, before he put on the silver chain with a pendant of Our Lady of Carmel. As he fastened it, he held her neck the way you would hold a small live bird, with caution and extreme care. The touch was light, feathery, and then suddenly he squeezed her neck tightly and held it a moment in his warm hand. Before he moved away, he ran one errant and naughty finger down her neck from the bottom of her hairline to just below her shoulders. The abruptness and the intent were unmistakable even to Juliana, who had never been touched like that before. The sudden touch sent an escalofrío down her body. She could feel that shiver all the way to her feet. She was not totally dead down there, she knew it now.

Juliana's hands fluttered and danced, pulling wispy ends of dark brown hair from her lovely face, away from those large, serious, immensely deep eyes.

El Padre Manolito moved away, walked in front of her, and inspected the pendant, which now lay heavily on her chest. He pronounced all things good. No, not all things were good. Juliana was chilled by the touch of El Padre's hand on her neck. She would never forget it.

"Juliana, now you are protected by una Española. La Virgen del Carmen, La Estrella de Los Mares. ¡Qué Viva La Virgen del Carmen!" he exclaimed with a little too much energy. Isá came in, concerned about the noise, but he dismissed her.

"She's much better and more beautiful than Our Lady of Guadalupe, that simple peasant girl. I'll bring you a holy card, my child, so you can see how glorious she is. In a way she reminds me of you with your thick hair."

Without pausing, he went on to describe to her his day in San Sebastián de Garabandal, a small village of hamlets in the Cantabrian Mountains in northwest Spain. Then he started in on the annual feast of La Virgen del Carmen, which was held throughout Spain, and then he talked about bacalao some more, and then their time was up.

"Do you have any questions for me, child, before I leave?" he asked.

"Padre, what is a hamlet?"

"A hamlet, well, a hamlet is a small, simple hut. But why do you worry yourself about insignificant details. Child, I am speaking of Nuestra Señora del Carmen. For God's sakes, listen up. Coño!"

This lecture on all things holy, and therefore Spanish and not mexican, with a small m, did not deter her fervor to create something of beauty for El Padre's birthday.

She wondered how she could get hold of some bacalao. She'd never heard of it. Bacalao in Comezón? Ay, Reina de Los Cielos, beloved Virgen de Guadalupe. And you too, La Virgen del Carmen! Help me! Where in the world would she find bacalao?

CHAPTER EIGHT

The Last Shooting Star

Lucinda laid the dress down in the sand atop a dune. Good to be done with it. Finally. She didn't have to be queen anymore, and she was glad. She had never wanted to be queen anyway, but Arnulfo had insisted. She couldn't call him father, dad, daddy, not even papá; nothing like that came to mind. He was an old man, and he wasn't her real father. Just look at him and Emilia. They weren't her real parents, you could tell that right away. All you had to do was look. And not even look hard. They were strangers, practically. She lived with them but she wasn't like them. They were all old and old-thinking, and she was young. She had to get away from them, and as soon as possible. The only person who really liked her and took care of her was Isá. She was old too, and more than ugly, but she was the only one who was nice to Lucinda. Some people might say that Juliana was good to her, but it wasn't true. Juliana tried to be nice, but she was too sweet. Lucinda couldn't breathe when Juliana was around. Everything had to focus on Juliana and her needs. Juliana always came first, and what she wanted and needed was always first on everyone's mind.

And she was always asking Lucinda questions. Questions that she had about life. The life she herself would never have. Her questions were stupid. How does it feel to kiss someone? What is it like to have someone hold you? Have you ever, and what was it like? They were questions no one should ever ask. It was only because Juliana was crippled that she asked those questions. She didn't have a life. Well, neither did Lucinda, but her life was better than Juliana's. At least she had kissed someone and knew what it was like to be held and loved. Ruley loved her. He did. And she loved him back.

So what did it matter that she'd gone away after the Fiesta and not let anyone know? What did it matter that she and Ruley just took off, she in her queen's dress and he in that ugly tuxedo? They wanted to go to the river to drink, but then they decided to go to White Sands. White Sands, are you crazy? It was a full moon, and the park was open until midnight. It seemed like a good idea. They stopped at the Walmart to buy some clothes to change into and got some food for a picnic. Everything was going good until Ruley swerved to kill a dog on the side of the road. She begged him not to—it was an old dog and it looked sad. But Ruley wouldn't listen to her. He never did. Sometimes he did crazy things for no reason at all. She didn't like that. He was just like his daddy, he said, so get over it.

After they got to White Sands, they stowed Lucinda's queen's dress and Ruley's tuxedo in the trunk of the car. He had to return the tux on Monday to the Elegant Penguin so they had to keep it clean. He wanted his deposit back. Lucinda didn't care about her dress. Oh, it was pretty enough, but she was tired of it. And it belonged to her; she could take it off and then take it home, and no one would care.

After a while Lucinda decided that she wanted to leave her dress there on a big dune. Hey, it looked spooky and nice as the moon came up, and she was lying next to her dress in her purple capris and spaghetti-strap tank top thinking about her period. She had bought some more Kotex, but she wasn't sure it was going to be enough, especially if they were gone a while. Did they have Kotex in Mexico?

When she had to go to the bathroom, she went out a long ways by herself and decided to urinate on the dunes, making a little hole in the sand. She squatted there and it wasn't dark yet, and she could see the blood come out in a clot like it does sometimes, and when it came out she covered the hole, and you know, it felt so good and so natural to have a period like that outdoors, nobody watching you and away from people and noise, just you under the stars and with your body doing what it does and that being normal and natural and the way it should be. She felt like she wasn't herself, but another woman from another time just squatting there in the white sand.

It felt so good, she let Ruley make love to her later on one of the dunes under a blanket. He didn't care if she was on her period. Things like that never bothered him. You could even say he liked it. He liked her however she was. He liked her the way she was, the way she tasted, the way she smelled, everything about her, even her blood. And when she found out that this was so, well, it made her free to be herself. He would never be afraid of her like some men might be of a woman or a woman of a man. She could be herself with him because he liked her in all ways and in any way and at any time. Blood to him was nothing. And yet, why was he always killing dogs? She made him promise her he would never hurt her the way he hurt animals, and he did.

They lay under the blanket until it got too hot, and then they sat up and watched the sky, the way it went on forever, and saw lots of shooting stars and made all kinds of wishes. And that's when they decided that this time for real they would get married. No one could stop them. She was the Queen of Comezón and he was the King. Her King. They would drive to Juárez and get married. She was old enough and he was old enough. And they loved each other, and why should anyone care? He had a job. She didn't have a job, but she would get one. She wanted to go to beauty school, and he said he would help her make her dreams come true, and she believed him. The last shooting star he'd proposed, and the next one she'd accepted, and that's all there was to it. They made up their minds right then and there. It was getting late and they didn't feel like driving to Juárez, so they went to Alamogordo instead to spend the night in a Motel 6. They would drive to Juárez the next day after returning the tux, and they would spend their honeymoon there. He had just gotten paid and everything was set. They wouldn't call anyone or tell anyone anything yet, not quite yet. Mamá Emilia would just look at her, and Arnulfo would start yelling, and Isá would be sad and start crying, and Juliana would ask her too many questions. Ruley's family didn't need to know right yet either, even though his dad was the sheriff. He'd call him first once they got married so he wouldn't send a squad car looking for them, thinking they were lost or on the lam. Were they on the lam? Hell, yes! They would stay there in Juárez a few days to celebrate, and then they'd come back to Comezón and rent an apartment, or maybe stay with Ruley's family until he got his next paycheck, as they'd probably spend most of the last paycheck in Juárez at the clubs. His mom, Terri Ann, would like it if they stayed with them, and his dad, well, he didn't care as long as he knew what was happening. That way they could declare their independence from the world and all those people, particularly the Olivárezes, who would try to hold them down and make them over and want them to eternally feel sorry for themselves because that was what it was like living in that house of ghosts.

The ghosts had always been there, even when she was a little girl. When she was little, she saw and felt them maybe more than when she got older. They were always there, but they, too, changed when she changed. She could hear them in the night, rustling around and coming down from the top room of the house where Arnulfo kept his old trunks and his dusty things, guns, pictures of his family, her old toys, and Juliana's first wheelchair. He had all sorts of things in there, and he kept the door locked. Sometimes he forgot to lock it, and she went in to rummage around. Not that she liked being in there, but she had to see what he kept locked up. Junk. Old magazines, old newspapers, old bills. Everything was old, like him.

The ghosts that lived in the room would come down and spy on her when she was in bed. They would just stand there and stare at her. She would fall asleep and they would wake her up. One time a little old man sat in the corner in a wooden chair most of the night. Once he came over to look at her sleeping in the bed, and she shooed him away, get away, get away, but he wouldn't. She tried to get up but she was in that sleep lock, she couldn't move.

He knew she couldn't move, but he finally did move away, to his little corner. He came to visit every now and then and just stayed in that corner of her room. The last time he had sat in a chair next to Arnulfo. The two of them just sat there. She told Isá about it, and that was when Isá gave her a limpia and prayed over her and told her not to think about it anymore. The old man is Bascual Olivárez, Arnulfo's father, she said; he worked on this adobe house and comes back now and again to see how things are going. He wouldn't hurt you, but he is bothersome. As far as Arnulfo being there, well, mija, that's another matter. He's very sick, and Bascual wants him to go with him to the Other Side. But he's not quite ready yet. I don't blame him. Just forget about it; I'll give you something for you to get better.

Isá did give her something that tasted bitter and that had little twigs that she had to spit out.

But she didn't feel any better. She couldn't. Not in that house.

It was good she was leaving. It was time to leave. She wished she could have said goodbye to Isá, but she would see her later.

She had memories of the house. So many memories. When she and Ruley first got together, they used to meet in the little casita, La Tumbita, the house behind the house where Arnulfo took his baths and Isá cleaned the chile. She knew where Isá kept her key, and she knew when Arnulfo was there and when Isá was there and when the house was empty. Ruley met her there when everyone had gone to sleep and it was dark. He wanted to make love in that old tinita of Arnulfo's, but there was no way she would tolerate that. She would forever feel Arnulfo's skin on her, and she didn't want that. He was a nasty, smelly old man. And he wasn't her father. Her father was someone young, handsome. And her mother was beautiful. That's what someone had told her once. You're not the daughter of Emilia Olivárez. Your mother, Senaida Ojeda, used to work for the Olivárez family, and she was from México. She got pregnant and she had to leave. But then the Olivárezes adopted you and tried to raise you like their child. And this is where the story she invented and imagined came to life. But you were never their child. Your mother was very young, and your father was a soldier from Fort Bliss. They met in town and fell in love. It was a love story, except the sad part was that you never knew them or saw them.

No one had loved her until Ruley loved her. But sometimes he wanted too much. Ruley wanted her to stand in that tinita and take off her clothes. He said he would wash her, but she said no. Let's move to the back, there in the shadows, someone might see us.

And someone did. She could feel someone's eyes on her, except she couldn't see who it was, man or woman. It was someone old. It could have been Arnulfo or Emilia or Isá watching her make love to Ruley in that little house. Afterward she stood in that tub of Isá's while Ruley washed and then dried her off, and then they made love again on an old serape of Isá's, and when the morning light came up they were exhausted and Ruley left, and she wandered back inside the house, and that's when she saw the shadow of the old person looking at her. She said to herself: Go ahead, it doesn't matter. Go ahead and see what it's like to be a woman in this house. For I am a woman, the only woman. Go ahead, imagine yourself young again. And with a man. Or like a man. Because that's what you dream about: being with a man and being like a man. And she remembered the way the old woman Isá touched her when she was a baby and then as a little girl, the way she cleaned her and put cream on her body, and she wondered why she did it so carefully and so slowly. And sometimes when Lucinda couldn't sleep, the old woman rubbed something on her body to make her relax, and it felt good, and that's what she said to her, it'll make you go to sleep. Children need to sleep, and they need to know they are being taken care of and loved. It's very natural. Now close your eyes and sleep. When you love someone the way I love you, you can touch them and help them relax, and then they can go to sleep and sleep without fear. I don't want you to be afraid, Lucinda. When you're with me, you'll never be afraid.

But she wasn't quite sure which old woman it was who stood there in the shadows looking in on them. One or the other of the women had stood out there in the darkness watching her and Ruley make love in the little house. And for different reasons.

If it was Emilia, she would want to know what it was like to be loved again. She would probably wonder if Lucinda's body was like her mother's. Was it like that body that gave pleasure to her father and brought her, cursed child, into this world? Why was it that Senaida went away and never came back? What happened? Wasn't her loving enough for her father, whoever he was?

If it was Isá, then the old woman watched her little girl with that man. He was ugly and he was hurting her. She wanted to yell out, to say something, but her voice was gone. Her hands twitched, and if she could have, she would have strangled him. He was hurting her. She was a little girl with bad dreams, and only Isá could calm her down and help her sleep. It was what she wanted. To help her to help her to help her. She wanted to kill him because he was hurting her. She would have to clean out the tub and burn the serape. She stared through the window. She knew Isá was the only one who really loved her. The only one.

Lucinda knew that one of the old women was out there in the darkness.

She saw someone retreat and fall back into the shadows that enveloped her. Which old woman was it? Or was it the old man?

Lying there on the dunes at White Sands, between shooting stars, white sand sifting through her fingers, she thought of that shadow person in the darkness. Who was it? Who?

No matter. It was her dress, and she could do to it anything she pleased. After all, she was the Queen of Comezón.

CHAPTER NINE

Niños de la Tierra

Ay, what a night it had been! The Mil Recuerdos Lounge was dark and nearly empty. Dark was how Rey wanted it—so dark you couldn't see the shabby pockmarked adobe walls where centipedes and niños de la tierra lived. The walls were full of children of the earth, also called Jerusalem crickets or early babies or potato bugs or old bald-headed men, what Donacio Quiroz, Arnulfo's best friend, that wise old Navajo, once called wó see ts'inii, a skull insect.

Let them live out their brief lives in the dark, Rey figured. Who was he to meddle anymore with creatures' lives, even the smallest? The old walls were dusty and encrusted with layers of fine silty loamy earth, the lodo of his hometown, Comezón. The dirt trailed on the floor where the white and pink stucco ended. The sand pocketed on the cement floor, later to be swept away by a sharp-tipped broom, leaving another determined gouging on what had once been a solid adobe wall. If the niños de la tierra wanted to live in his walls, he didn't have a problem with it. Live and let live.

Sometimes when he was alone at night, he could hear them making a rasping noise as they rubbed their hind legs on their stomachs. Leave it to Luisito to get bitten. Hell, it might have stung, but it didn't kill him, and he got a free beer out of the episode. What Rey didn't tolerate was cruelty from humans to any living creature. He had stopped Luisito from setting fire to a niño de la tierra—Luisito had wanted to hear what he said was their legendary high-pitched cry, the cry of a child. Damn, the man was a cabrón!

Little by little Rey was sweeping away the past, hiding in the darkness of his personal sanctuary where the bottles of liquor lined up neatly and were an orderly display of human frailty contained. He liked being the owner of his little place, the Mil Recuerdos Lounge. A thousand memories, hell, more!

He liked being the bartender, the gatekeeper, the bouncer, and the confessor as well. He was there all the time, except on Sundays, which was the day he spent with his elderly mother, Florigunda, who prepared lunch for him, as she had for over fifty years—that is, whenever he was in town. Now that Rey didn't travel anymore, he could be found every Sunday afternoon at his mother's house.

Florigunda prepared a meal that far exceeded what even the legendary film star and beloved singer Pedro Infante, a known gourmand, was said to enjoy at his mother, Doña Luisa's, table.

Doña Flori, as Florigunda was known to her family, had seen Pedro Infante in person, on the stage of El Colón Theater in El Paso, Texas, with an all-woman mariachi review in the 1940s. She was a young girl then, and very pretty. Pedro had handpicked her out of an auditorium full of people and sat her on his lap, bouncing her back and forth with a peculiar rhythm she later came to know. She would never tell anyone that he had excited her, and she him. She was a mature twelve-year-old, and she remembered how he called her niña preciosa and invited her and her mother to join him after the show for a late dinner in his hotel room.

"He kissed me here," Florigunda said with wonder and slightly misty eyes, pointing to her lips. She saw the face of her only living son contort in pain in front of her. If her other son, Armandito, had lived, he probably would have disapproved as well. ¡Hombres! They could brag at length about old girlfriends, past love affairs, property they could have bought cheaply a long time ago, as well as their stamina in and out of the bedroom, but when a woman had something to say about love or romance, they couldn't tolerate a single moment of sacred recollection.

"It was a good kiss, too, with a slightly open mouth. Pedro smelled fresh, not at all like old milk or decaying eggs or stale beer, which is what I find most men smell like these days. You know

I have a good sense of smell, Hijo. He was a short man but very handsome, and he had a nice cuerpo. But of course I was too young then to know things a woman would know about men and their bodies. It's a shame that in this life we are either too young or too old."

Rey didn't like to hear his mother go on and on about the event that had colored her youth and made her who she was—someone who wanted more and only got less. Also, he didn't like to think of his mother as a compliant virgin, which was how she came across when she talked about Pedro Infante. Lately Rey had noticed that his mother's mind was wandering more and more. She was leaving—se estaba yendo—and there was nothing either of them could do about it.

¡Hijo mendigo! What did he know of her dreams? All he knew was that she was his mother and had been married to his father for over sixty years, all of them a living crucifix of disquiet and misunderstanding, one day after another strung out like dark beads on a sticky rosary. It was a life she endured like a long, monotonous prayer.

And yes, it was she who intoned religiously to Rey every Sunday at 1:00 P.M., "Oye, Hijo, why aren't you eating? Don't you like the food I've spent all day cooking? Eat! How are you ever going to be strong enough to do the work you do serving borrachos and destroying marriages unless you have something to back you up? I never wanted you to go into that business of yours. And when it goes under—which it has to—I'll be the first to say I was glad I didn't lend you the money to buy it. Who you got to lend you the money I don't know and I don't want to know, ever. I never liked the way the money just appeared like that, all of a sudden, and you never even going to the bank. It can't come to any good, Hijo, and you know it. And you wouldn't have bought that place if my mother had listened to Pedro Infante that night after the concert and sent me to school en La Capital, El D.F. Pedro was interested in my welfare, and it could have worked out for all of us. I wouldn't be here and you wouldn't be there. And your father, well, let's just say it could have worked out."

It didn't matter that his father was his father and that Pedro wasn't his father—or was he? In her dotage Florigunda had started believing that Rey was Pedro Infante's son. Pedro was reputed to be a ladies' man, and he was known to have many children. Rey could be his son, ¿Por qué no? Except his mother was only twelve or thirteen when she met and kissed Pedro Infante, or rather he kissed her and bounced her on his lap. It was possible some sperm had seeped out or in or out and then in. It was very possible. Pedro was sweaty, overheated, and had just given a tremendous concert. She did touch him with her legs spread out and wearing just a thin skirt and a pair of old chones that had a large hole right in the place where her little empanadita was. Someone forgot to sew those little panties, and as a result Florigunda believed that Pedro Infante had impregnated her. Anything is possible on this miraculous earth, and yes, they did have dinner with him after the concert, and there was a short while when her mother had to go to the bathroom after she'd gotten sick on some greasy chicharrones and later came back and found things were disordered. It was possible! Sure to the day or almost, give or take a little time, she had met Rey's father, Armando, in the pisca and they had gotten married. Flori had tried to cover all the possible consequences of that night she sat on Pedro's lap when something she wasn't sure happened might have happened. She had had a little wine even though Pedro was a diabetic and a teetotaler, and yes, she was confused. She remembered the sound of a zipper, but who was sure? Time was shifty, and there was much confusion for Flori at that time. Best to marry Armando, who wasn't bad-looking and was very sincere. And yet—there was always that comezón.

"You, Hijo, whether you want to believe it or not, are the true child of Pedro Infante," Florigunda Suárez said with authority, passing the red chile con carne to her son.

"Sí, Mamá." Rey agreed but one more time, sopping up the red chile with a fluted flour tortilla. He didn't believe her for one second, but who was to refute Florigunda Suárez when she got into her Sunday rant? Surely not her son! It was better just to eat and remain silent. He'd learned over the years to let her carry on, wind down, and then take a breather. It was time for her daily siesta. Her helper, Claudia, would clean up, then go home to her family. Flori would wake up in time for her novela, eat a little cottage cheese and peaches or some Sugar Pops con leche, pray her novena, and then go back to bed.

Florigunda was a very Catholic, very devout woman who prayed her novena every night.

"Oraciones Dudas Al Sexto Sello. Templo de Mediodía."

"Prayers and Concerns to the Sixth Seal. Temple of Midday."

During the lunch she had referred to the section that said people shouldn't work on Sunday, and if they did, they should give back something in remuneration for working on the Lord's Day.

Los Preceptos de Moises de Jesús y los de Elias El Hijo del Hombre.
The Precepts of Moses of Jesús and Those of Elias the Son of Man.

Precepto #6: No harás trabajo lucrativo el día de Domingo, y si lo hacéis, por tu pobreza o compromiso verdadero, impondrás un penitencia conforme a tus circumstancias por pertenecer este día de Dios.
Precept #6: You should not do lucrative work on Sunday, and if you do, because of your poverty or true compromise, you should impose a penance according to your circumstance on this day of the Lord.

It was true that Rey closed the lounge on Sundays; however, according to precept #6, he should have done some sort of penance to make up for the other times it was open.

Flori also knew her son, Qué Dios Lo Cuide, was breaking precept #9, drinking alcohol, as she knew he did, and worse yet, giving others that known poison. It was the same veneno that killed her brother, Ricardo, and the same drink that killed and will continue to kill countless others. Que Dios Los Proteje.

Precepto #9: No tomarás bebida embriagadora.
Precept #9: You should not drink liquor.

Rey was teetering dangerously on the edge of precept #9, and although he was a good son in many ways, he was a stubborn one. He needed to be prayed for constantly. Since Armandito had died, it was always Rey she was fearful for. That business of his would ultimately come to no good. She had always been afraid he would die suddenly and violently. Sometimes she woke up nights with a premonition of evil. Someone wanted to hurt her son. Que Dios Lo Defende. Call it a mother's intuition. He was too precious and too special for this ugly world.

Flori hummed her favorite Pedro Infante song, "Amorcito Corazón," as her maid Claudia cleaned up the kitchen.

Amorcito corazón
Yo tengo tentación
De un beso
Que se prende en el calor
De nuestro gran amor,
Mi amor.

Yo quiero ser
Un solo ser
Un ser contigo.
Te quiero ver
En el querer
Para soñar.

En la dulce sensación
De un beso mordelón quisiera,
Amorcito corazón,
Decirte mi pasión por tí.

Compañeros en el bien y el mal.
Ni los años nos podrán pesar.
Amorcito corazón serás mi amor.

On Sundays Rey was first a son, the most chiple consentido son of Florigunda and Armando Suárez, and secondly he was father to his two daughters, the big one and the little one. Their mother, Dulce, had divorced Rey and moved to Utah. Her new husband was from New Jersey and went by the name El Huevo. What she saw in that no-account son of a bitch, he would never understand. Yeah, he was a huevón, all right. Lazy as hell and expecting Dulce to support him. And she did on her teacher's salary! He didn't expect the marriage to last. If she came crawling back, which he knew she would, would he take her back? Probably. Oh yeah. He still missed her. They had had some good years. He figured Dulce just got tired of being alone most of the time. He was always traveling to one place or another, and after one trip she announced she'd met Rogelio "El Huevo" Licón and that she was moving out of the house.

They'd shared a lot, too much maybe, too many scares and dark nights of people coming to the door looking for him when she was in bed. He was always on alert status as far as she was concerned, and she didn't like the fact that he was on duty twenty-four hours or more. She had never liked his work. When El Huevo deigned to work, he was a jardinero; he liked plants and was good at gardening. From what Rey had heard, the man was trying to start a nursery. Good luck in Utah, cabrón!

Dulce and Rey had two girls. The older one was named Raquel and at nineteen was already living on her own in student housing. She was a lot like her mother. She and Rey weren't that close. It was her mother's fault; she'd been coddled and made to think she was more than she was. As a result, Raquel wanted to get on the fast track to making money. Good luck as an English literature major with a minor in creative writing!

Rey's second daughter was called Ruby, and he loved her more than his mother, his ex-wife, the big girl, and now his son, a forgotten assignation who showed up at El Mil one hot summer day two years ago. His name was Rico, and he was big-eared and needy, telling tales of I am and she was. No one knew about him but his mother, the young woman from México who had been his mother, and of course now Rey, his startled but not totally unsuspecting father. The kid came and left without an address or any real information. He had grown up with his grandmother and didn't know too much. He was medio pendejito, and it was probably a good thing.

Rey couldn't remember Rico's mother's name at first, although he remembered her body—young, taut, smelling of onion. They'd met at the pisca. As a teenager Rey had worked alongside his father during the onion harvest.

Rico's mother was from somewhere deep in the interior of México, some long unpronounceable name, Tlatle-Tlotle, something that as soon as he'd heard it and tried to say it out loud, he'd forgotten it. He didn't want to remember the name of the town. But in her honor and in memory of those times they were together, he'd promised them both that he'd make something of his life—away from his parents' limitations, far removed from the smell and heat of this scorched, too familiar earth.

Her name was Rosa María, and she was from Parral. A dark rose. Yeah, yeah. She was from a small town and smelled of both woman and little girl, searing heat and earth, the dampness of sex and the sweat of small hands.

Her name was Lourdes, and she was from Durango. She was a miracle, the first in his life or maybe the last.

Her name was Felicidad, but she was never happy. Theirs was a furtive and hard copulation that left his gusano, his little worm, crying for mercy. She disappeared one hot day in an Immigration roundup, and he never saw her again.

Her name was Estrella, or was it Estela, and she was a dreamy and distracted girl. She only let him make love to her late at night, and when she did, she hummed an unfamiliar song that still haunted him—it was a tune he would always remember. And in all his years of listening to music of all types, he never once ran across a melody like hers.

Her name was Erlinda. Sanjuanita. Cherissa. Clarita.

Her name was Lodo. Mud. Tierra. Earth. Cielo. Sky. And she was from Guanajuato. The place of mummies.

What was her name? He had wanted to name his youngest daughter, his precious Ruby, for her, but in daylight he couldn't remember her name. Or maybe he didn't want to remember. El dolor de los recuerdos. It was too hard to go over things anymore. And if he did, what could he do to change the immutable past?

And yet, in the middle of the night, between the hours of three and five, her name came to him. Around 4:48 A.M. he remembered everything: the way the soft, damp grass tufted underneath her firm hips, the way the crescent moon sliced the sky under the planet Venus. In the middle of the night when he was asleep on a high and faraway mountain facing the destruction of the earth by water, he was suddenly saved. As he climbed a high promontory and saw the devastation below him, and as he thanked God for sparing his life, he remembered her name. In the darkness of his lounge around 1:30 or 2:00 A.M., with the jukebox playing "Volver, Volver" and that same old medio sordo viejito Don Tomás Revueltas singing loudly "Quiero volver a tus brazos otra vez," he remembered her name. It was a name he never spoke out loud. He was a haunted and hunted man.

All those women. They came back to trouble him. The thousand memories. Los Mil Recuerdos. El Mil Recuerdos Lounge. Owner Rey Suárez, Esquire. Mr. Reymundo "Rey" Suárez, Proprietor. The Mil Recuerdos Lounge. Comezón, New Mexico.

Rey had wanted to own a drinking establishment during all those years of government work. The kind of work that can drag your unsheathed balls across a hot summer gravel-covered road far from water, an espina goat-head-filled badlands of a place called Devil's Lick or Valle Escondido or Camino del Diablo or a town named Perdido or Crump, a place reminding you that you didn't know anyone there, and that if you disappeared and were never again to be seen, no one would know or care. His father was born in a little town called Tierra Seca, and thankfully his parents, in their sage wisdom and abhorrence of the obvious, left that sad dark place to move to Comezón after their eldest son, Armando Junior, died without medical aid and as a result of a terrible fever.

Why Comezón? Comezón was the place where his father, Armando Sr., had once worked the pisca. It was a place Armando Sr. liked to say he remembered more for the good than the bad. Although in later years he would say it was the place he'd had his huevos removed and hung out on burning alambre to dry. No good came from bad, although he didn't know that what he thought was good was really really bad. Who would have thought that La Flori would divorce him after sixty years of marriage? For no reason. People of their age didn't divorce. Leave it to La Vieja to mangle him at the end and spit him out like a worked-over sunflower seed now that he needed family and a place to rest.

Coming from such unhappiness, what could a son expect?

From dirt to drag, Rey used to say, from nothingness to poverty to work for the Man. That Man being El Mero Mero. The U.S. government. But he was retired now. Let's not go back.

Government work will do that to you. It had almost made him forget who he was. Reymundo Suárez. El Rey. The King. Some king! He didn't want to remember those years on the payroll, of running on a time card, sweating over a ticking clock, someone else's schedule, or wearing a stiff and starched uniform, and always fearing for his life.

Well, it wasn't so bad. The paycheck was all right, and with his savings and a little help from a special friend, he had bought the building and the two apartments, at last converting the lower floor into El Mil. That was five years ago. Now he was settled into his new life as el dueño of a negocio. Yes, he was now the owner of a business. But there were problems. He thought things were going well, and suddenly there was a downturn. He wasn't able to make his mortgage payments every month, and now he was behind. What was he going to do? He still owed the friend who had loaned him money, and now he owed more. Would he declare bankruptcy? Hell, no! That was the coward's way out. And Rey Suárez was not a coward.

Would he go into Foreclosure? Hell, no! He never used that F word.

Getting up from his mother's table, he said what he said every Sunday around 3:00 P.M.: "El que tiene tienda, que lo tienda, o si no lo tienda, que lo venda." He who has a business had better take care of it, and if he doesn't, he should sell it. It was time to get back to work.

Maybe it wasn't much of a negocio to the outside world, but to him it was a dream. Forget the come true part. It was a dream that would never totally come true. Hell, he didn't really believe in dreams, but if he did believe in them, El Mil would be part of that almost-impossible-not-really-feasible-why-even-harbor-dreams dream. His sueño was a small hope that called itself life, his life.

Would he ever remember the song he had forgotten and once again sing its words? Would he ever again feel that heat and taste the damp earth and bury himself in that flesh and remember that name, the one true name? All the others imposters.

No.

His past life was just that, past. Whatever he was or whatever he did before was past, never to be resurrected. Why even talk about it?

He remembered Dulce. She had allowed him to forget that name. And he was grateful.

Rey kissed his mother goodbye. He returned to El Mil to prep for Monday. It was reassuring to return to the lounge. His mother's house had been stifling and he'd eaten too much.

The walls of the lounge were dingy and damp. But in daylight they appeared to have a pleasant rose-hued glow. At night they came to ethnic life and became that beloved illusion: a Mexican joint full of ambiente, with the glow and penumbra of well-being, with its hot pink rosa mexicana walls and a plethora of beer signs that made those irrefutable and indelible statements: Fun Place. Good Times. Relax. Let Go. You're at Home. Drink Up. Enjoy. Now Forget.

He took a cold Coors from the cooler and sat down at the bar.

Rey had never understood the Coors boycott. He was born in the 1940s, and yes, he knew what the sixties were about, but somehow he had missed something. One of his favorite songs was Frank Sinatra's "My Way."

Rey never smoked mota, never did drugs. Nor did he ever force anyone to have sex with him in the back seat of a steamy Camaro. From age thirteen he'd had all the women he wanted, it didn't matter what age they were or if they wore a wedding ring or not or maybe had it tucked in a secret compartment in their purse or they twisted it around to look like a friendship ring. He didn't care. He was very circumspect.

Yeah, he knew what his way was, except on Sundays.

He took out a small toallita and turned on the tap, soaking the rag in the not too hot, not too cold water. He had his methods, and it was best to clean the counter with warm water. It was a luxury for him to have time to straighten things with care, and this is what he did late Sunday afternoons after having lunch at his mother's house. He would head back to El Mil, park around back, making sure the front and back doors were locked, and he would clean. And he would open the door to no one. Those were the unbroken rules. He lifted and then swabbed the container of bright-colored red and blue swizzle sticks, the olive and maraschino cherry compartments, the lemon and lime holders. He would fill them tomorrow after everything was perfect and the napkins were laid out like a fan.

It was good to have a business and work. He was sixty-two; he'd taken early retirement. What he did he did because that was what he wanted to do. El Mil was his life now. And the people who came into the lounge were his family. Of late his tenant, Joe, had become a good friend. Joe used to come in for an occasional beer. More often than not, he just sat in a side room or by the far back table near the men's restroom—and did whatever he did with that little notebook of his and all those manila folders.

Recently, Joe had begun to sit at the bar and talk to Rey. He wanted something from him. Information about people, a history of Comezón. The man had a lot of questions. Too many questions.

Joe said he was writing a book. What the hell! Who would ever read it? All of it was probably lies. Who was he writing the book for? Joe said he was writing the book for himself. That it mattered to him. If he wrote the book, he said, he would understand something about himself. If that was the case, then maybe Rey should write a book.

But it was Rey's life now not to ask questions or to answer any of them too fully.

Leave the questions to someone with nothing else to do than wonder about what Arnulfo Olivárez would call pinche unfathomable sometimes insufferable but so very precious life.

CHAPTER TEN

El Chingón

Arnulfo woke up chueco. It must have been the way he slept. Chueco. Crooked. He was never that, not really. Not crooked the way other people in Comezón were crooked, property owners and businesspeople, fleecing poor people in small and grand ways, robbing land from hardworking farmers, hard-of-hearing old women, unsuspecting out-of-town relatives, taking a bit of this and that and not offering much in return. Don't get him started about El Padre Manolito, offering hope to the hopeless, a God to the Godless, and Eternity for a Tithe. What did it matter that Arnulfo had rigged a few Queen of Comezón contests? There was no way Emilda Urquide would ever have gotten to become Queen if he hadn't intervened. It meant so much to her, poor fish-eyed enanita, ugly little dwarf that she was with those watery orbs staring back at you with glassy wonder. It also meant so much to her parents, Consuelo and Wilfredo. Who would have guessed that the little gnome had a rare form of leukemia and would be dead the year following her brief reign? It made her so happy to wear that little crown with glass insets on her oversized bald head wherever she went.

It was only God who knew how two normal-looking people like "La Connie" and "El Wiffie" Urquide could produce a child with a Taint. Blood was sometimes more than blood, and some-times the blood was bad. He, of all people, knew this all too well. Look at him and La Gorda. They had also spawned a damaged child. Ay, his Julianita, she had been such a beautiful baby. And for the longest time they had covered her small malformed feet, more like fish fins, and her twisted legs with embroidered pink dresses and soft woolen blankets. They told people she got cold easily and then moved on to the story of her brittle bones, and finally one day her legs just stopped growing, and there was nothing they could do or say. While the rest of her matured, her legs and feet stayed the size of a five-year-old's. It was a curse that surely came from La Gorda's side of the family.

Los Izquierdo were known for their Strangeness and their Ways. The name came from some ancestor who wrote with their left hand. Eep, they had their Ways, all right! They were country people from the darkest recesses of New Mexico, those little landlocked northern villages in the mountains where people clumped together to keep warm on those cold winter nights and then begat offspring with little tails or webbed toes and extra ribs. They were people who mumbled incessantly to themselves. All the sisters and brothers and primos and tíos and tías lived next to each other on their family plots without straying far. They were fearful of so many things and disdained company. They were often funny-looking, with large heads and elongated ears and wrinkled, hard-thinking brows, and they had THAT LOOK, which isolated them even further, as they didn't know or care much about the real world. They were, in short, artists.

Bah, if you call that art! They carved tortured wooden Christs with dripping bloody crowns of thorns and anguished saints who didn't have the sense to find another way to live. La Gorda's father, Persignato Izquierdo, was a Penitente who flagellated himself and once played the Christ in their ceremony where they lifted an hermano up and suspended him on a cross. Oh, he had a lot to beat himself up for, that was for certain. Persi, as he was known to those who knew him too well, was a drunk. He was a womanizer as well when he got the chance on an out-of-town jale, any work that allowed him a brief escape into anonymity and a blessed respite from his overbearing wife, Anunciata, who was also an artist. Anunciata did repujado, the punched tinwork that had made the name Izquierdo known and respected in many circles and was so valued by wide-hipped, hairy-lipped white women who lived summers in Santa Fe and tall, freckled, overheated businessmen from Florida or New Jersey who found the Izquierdo art, especially Anunciata's, quaint and authentic. Persi worked part-time for the Highway Department cleaning up the roads, and when he wasn't kicking up holy dirt and heaping it on his family of twelve, eight daughters and two sons, he was carving those nasty bloody Cristos in his backyard by the cottonwoods near the river and then crying himself to sleep after finishing up yet another Sebastiana, the skeletal figure of Death in another blasted cart with her arrow facing outward, ready to pierce the hearts of mortal men.

Persi would etch his name on another Sacred Heart or San Isidro and then fall into a slumber that lasted for days, he was so depleted. If that was art, then spare me, Arnulfo thought to himself more than once. As he saw it, it was useless to suffer so long for something so ephemeral. Just like his compadre Joe Kiratz at El Mil. Working on those damn notebooks or that book or whatever the hell all those papers were. Useless suffering, y 'pa qué? Who would even care about their creation once he was gone?

No wonder they were so unhappy. Persi. Joe. What about him? Why was he so unhappy? Oh, there were the obvious reasons: old age, bad teeth, legs that ached and wouldn't let him sleep at night, no sex, and now lungs full of dust and death. And now what could he do about it? Things had once been different, hadn't they?

Emilia hadn't been La Gorda then. There was no sign that her two best features would droop and sag and head south and then girth out. The woman did have nice breasts in those early days, but more than that, and that was what drew him to her, she had a sweet nature. She was pliable and gave him hope. She succored him and nurtured him, and yes, that was what he hated most about her now. Her passivity and her damn goodwill. The woman was incapable of arguing with any sort of gusto, and when he reached a feverish state of caring about anything, she would smile and say, "Ay, Arnulfo." Sometimes she even had the audacity to pat his hand or kiss him. She treated him like a child. He hated her equanimity and even temper. What it engendered in him was not love anymore but a vile sense of pity, and yes, jealousy and envy, because secretly he knew she was a better person than he could ever be.

He should have looked at his mother-in-law more closely; they say you can see where a daughter is headed by taking a good look at the mother. Well, he really should have seen that Anunciata was a tangle-headed soft-bodied mollusk with down-sloping nipples that she didn't have the decency to sheath in a brassiere but paraded around without respect for anyone who had to face those teats at eye level. She was a tall woman. The vision of those breasts still haunted him.

Little did he know that later in his life his Emilia, the tender-hearted little princess, would have to have surgery on her legs, leaving one of them shorter than the other, causing her to hobble around the house, dragging herself from one piece of furniture to the next, while snuffling from a chronic nasal problem that caused her to sleep with her mouth open, which led to drooling, which in turn caused her dental problems, which over time caused her heart problems, which eventually affected their sex life. They slept in different bedrooms and had for over twenty years. And it was a good thing, too; La Gorda snored very loudly, especially with that nasal situation. The lovemaking had never been that good to begin with, he had to admit, although at first it was promising. Well, it was good for about a year before Juliana's birth, but then it was all downhill, just like her breasts.

Arnulfo stirred in bed. He had to get up sometime.

He had to try and see a man about a dog. That was what his father had always said about having to take a shit. For some unexplained reason, Bascual always had to announce his needs to his family.

"I have to see a man about a dog," he would call out loudly to anyone who was within range as he headed to the outhouse and then later the indoor bathroom, where he locked himself in for an hour or so reading the newspaper and contemplating whatever it was he contemplated.

Fucking. Shitting. It was all necessary. Primal. And when Arnulfo couldn't shit, he was chueco. Which is what he was today. Crooked. Torcido. Twisted. Body bent. Out of sorts. Constipated and stuck. How did he know? He just knew. He hadn't gotten out of bed yet, and he could already discern what kind of day he was going to have by the sound of his tripas. He knew whether he would be able to shit or not. Fucking, well, that was out of the question. On the Fuck-o-meter, the big hand was broken and spinning. But he knew that. Nothing new.

He could read his body and knew all the signs just lying in bed with the sheet over his head. More than anything else, he wanted to stay in bed. But that wasn't possible. It was possible, but it wasn't probable. He had to move around or he wouldn't shit tomorrow, and then things would go from bad to worse. Once he had asked his father, who lived to be ninety-three, his secret for a long life. Muévete, keep moving, was Bascual's terse reply. Just keep moving.

But not now, Arnulfo thought as he peered at his watch in the growing light. It was a little after 6:00 A.M. He slept with his watch on his right wrist, the timepiece facing inward. He'd thought it was a distinctive professional thing until he saw a joto bartender in Juárez wearing his watch that way. Oh, who the hell was going to be visiting the Club Carnaval and noticing the bartender Rogelito's watch facing inward?

The wind on the Plaza had blown right through him yesterday. Sunstroke he knew. Heatstroke he knew. But windstroke? Now he knew that as well. He didn't remember a year that had been so windy as this one. Why? Why was the wind so nasty and ill-behaved? It was May, and the winds were more persistent than ever and never abated as they often did, one windy day followed by a good day, one dusty cloudy wind-blown day followed by two or three days of heat, followed by a day of rain and a beautiful sunset, followed by an ugly tumbleweedy day that set off a string of accidents in Deming and a pileup near Akela Flats that led to a highway closure, followed by a glorious day like no other without a cloud in an immense blue sky. That was Nuevo México for you. Irascible and unpredictable as a woman.

Let's talk about the wind.

No, seriously, he thought as he lay in bed talking to himself, let's talk about the wind.

After the Fiesta he'd gone over to the Mil Recuerdos for a short one, which turned into a long night of too many memories. Earlier he'd seen Joe Kiratz out there on the Plaza in the darkness and nodded to him. Joe pointed a finger in his direction, which said gotcha and catcha later, which meant only one thing: the same old but not so same old at the Mil Recuerdos. Another nightcap that didn't cap off the night but left it dangling in a dream. He'd walked over there with his Tony Lama boots pinching him badly. That one damn callo cried out for release. He'd taken the boots off at El Mil trying to free up that crusty corn. It had helped for a while, until he had to put them back on and walk back home. He barely made it, leaning on Luisito all the way. La Gorda had fed them both and then shooed off El Compadre. Together the two of them struggled to get to his bedroom. He felt his stomach with probing, prodding fingers, but it didn't appear he needed to mear. Better to say mear than pee. "Pee" was a joto word, whereas "mear" was a word with strength. Later it turned out he'd already done wee-wee in his chones. That would probably wreck the mariachi costume.

He'd called out to La Gorda to have her help him take off his boots. He hated that she waited up for him, but at the same time he was grateful. This infuriated him further. Damn it, why did the woman always wait up for him? And yet, she was the only one who could help him take off his boots. She knew how to do it without any muss or fuss. Like taking off a pair of soft gloves.

He'd thanked her and kissed her on the cheek, but not before asking for a glass of her special milk drink, her ponche with cinnamon that included the white of an egg. Few women could make a ponche the way she did. He needed that milk to settle his stomach. He depended on that milk. It brought him calm as he lay down to sleep, praying to his version of God for a night of no dreams. He'd waited until Luisito left to ask for the ponche. The next thing you knew, he'd be coming over and expecting that sacred ponche, he who didn't deserve anything but maybe a raw egg thrown in his face. The man was an alcoholic and a fool. Not a good combination. How his soft-spoken saintly mother tolerated him was not to be believed. The two men had nothing in common, nothing!

The wind. Yes, he remembered the wind. it was already late, and the Mil Recuerdos had been crowded with turistas and a few regulars like Pep Turgino and Don Tomás Revueltas, who sang softly in the corner next to Luisito, who had followed him over like the puppy he was. Arnulfo talked to Joe about the wind.

"Bring me another round, will you, Rey?" Arnulfo called out in a barely recognizable voice. Had that sound come from him?

Out of the blue or the dark or the horrible emptiness, Joe had said, "Why is it that we don't have a name for the wind around here?"

"What do you mean, why don't we have a name for the wind? First of all, who is 'we'? And second, what the hell do you mean? What are you talking about? Oye, Rey, bring me a pickle while you're at it, and wrestle me a couple of eggs before Turgino gets them all, with some salsa and chips."

"I mean to say that we don't have a name for the wind. 'We' meaning anybody. Why is that? Nobody has a name for the wind around here."

"¿Cómo qué around here? Around here where? What wind are you talking about?"

"Wind. Wind. Any wind. Wind from here. North. South. East or west. Although I have to say each wind is different. Don't you think?"

"Okay, you want a name for the wind? I have a name for the wind. You want to hear my name for the wind?"

"Oh, so you have a name for the wind, Olivárez? And what would that name be? You making this up? Hell, you have to be making this up. I don't know why I'm listening to you. You make things up. I swear, you're always making things up. I mean, there's the Mistral in France, the Sirocco in the Mediterranean, the Harmantan in Africa. Then there's the Chubasco in Central America and the Ostria in Bulgaria. Haboob. Leste. Shamal. It goes on and on. What do we have here in New Mexico, tell me?"

"Never heard of any of those winds."

"So, what's your name? And your answer can't be Mariah."

"I have a name all right. Who's María?"

"It's pronounced Ma-rye-uh. Not María. So, what's your name? Go ahead. Might as well cough it up. I can take it."

"El Chingón."

That was what Arnulfo named his wind. El Chingón. It had moved through his entire body yesterday and today as he stood on the Plaza during the Fiesta, two long days of noon to midnight. The wind had pierced and skewered him and left him exhausted and panting as if from an arrow of one of Persi's Sebastianas. Old bony skeletal Death moved through him and left her unmistakable calling card of despair and dread. He felt the cadaver's caress and wondered, how much longer? Dear Unknown Unseen God, how much longer?

He had stood on the Plaza, the crowd going home as the vendors pulled up and folded their tents and another Cinco de Mayo drew to a close. A remolino, a fast-swirling dust devil, came up, a blast of cold evil air with its spiraling pressure filling his already compromised lungs with a heavy, uneasy grit. That was the wind that moved through him and left him staggering and out of sorts—the curse of this land and its heat and dryness and eternal infernal lack that caused him to lie in bed with a sheet over his head wondering if he could drag himself out of bed and why; why should he get up and go on, knowing that lack, always that lack?

He knew El Chingón. He knew him too well.

So why get up?

He had to. Muévete. Keep moving. He had to finish that one piece of business he had started. It couldn't wait. He rose from his bed, raw, feverish, with all the pinche hope he could muster. He called out to La Gorda.

"¡Oye, Vieja! ¡Gorda! ¡Traígame mis botas! Where are my boots?"

Another day.

But first he had to try and see a man about a dog.

CHAPTER ELEVEN

La Tumbita

Arnulfo peered through the dusty windows of the shed behind the main house. He called the little casita La Tumbita. It was dark in there and always a little cool. It was a good place to get away from the rest of the world. The casita was still one of his favorite parts of the property he called Rancho Comezón. It had served his parents first as a shed to dry herbs and later as a place to stretch skunk and fox pelts, and then it stored canned food. Finally it had evolved into Arnulfo's bathhouse.

The glass was dusty and the vines were beginning to cover part of La Tumbita's adobe walls. He would have to get Luisito out here soon to clean things up. He had let things go, and now the little building was covered in dusty spider webs and was dotted with little tufts of yellowed grass that grew randomly and miraculously in the most inconceivable places. He'd seen a small frog inside the last time. It had hopped away and hid behind a table, and he hadn't seen it since. Several weeks ago he'd seen a small lizard on one of the walls. Pendejito just sat there a lo todo contento. ¡Cabroncitos! Just as long as the lizard and frog remembered who was in charge.

On one side of the room was a large freestanding vintage copper tub that had belonged to his grandfather and had been carried all the way from México. This area was sectioned off and had some lovely old Mexican tile on the walls. A nearby table held a ceramic basin, and a folding screen with scenes from the Battle of Puebla reminded him to always stand firm. Arnulfo had also saved all his previous Fiesta programs and pasted them on the screen and added some Mexican flags on the corners. A comfortable old chair with a footrest was nearby, and this is where he sat after his bath. Sometimes he would fall asleep, and Emilia would have to reheat his dinner.

On the other side, near the back of the building, was a very large basin, this one ceramic, that had been and still was used to clean anything else that wasn't human and named Arnulfo Olivárez. Isá used this sink to clean her red chile and to bathe Chamorro, Arnulfo's dog.

Once—the story went—one of the farm helpers, Lázaro Fonseca, had been caught in a snowstorm. He was nearly frozen, and they brought him to the shed and put him into the metal tina, which they filled with hot water. This brought his temperature up. Lázaro came sputtering back to life, and it was all due to the healing immersion in that tinita, everyone said. Let it be said that the nearly dead man, a true Lazarus, was the only one besides Arnulfo who had ever used his tina.

Let it also be said that the little house was segregated. The front part was Arnulfo's domain, and the back part was Isá's territory. She had all kinds of jars back there, with canned fruit, herbs, and what she called her chucherías—her whatnots, gewgaws, and scraps of cloth, which she stored in boxes. Isá made blankets, tablecloths, and aprons. Her domain was half infirmary and botánica, and she always had some project on a worktable near the back door. A clothesline separated the two sections and created a pronounced swath across the space. During the rainy season and in the winter, the casita was full of women's clothing, mostly undergarments, hanging disrespectfully from the tendedero, which greatly displeased Arnulfo. He hated seeing his wife's drawers hanging overhead side by side with Isá's cotton leggings, which were next to Juliana's brassieres or soft little footies or Lucinda's skimpy Day of the Week underpants.

The front part, which was Arnulfo's, was comfortable and always clean, and the back part, which was Isá's, was always in creative disorder. This also irritated him. At one point in the past he had tried to evict Isá from his turf, but she refused to leave. She would leave, she said, only if he began to cook the meals. Well. That was that.

Each side had its own entryway, and the two parties never visited each other's sector. Isá had been preparing for her summer fruit canning, to be followed immediately by the harvesting and roasting of green chile. Soon afterward would come the making of red chile ristras and the final canning of the late summer fruit. There were jars on the table next to plastic freezer bags. Predictions were that this year's chile harvest would be the best in years.

As he peered in the darkened window, Arnulfo could see Emilia getting his bathwater ready. Good. She was heating the water in the large metal bowl that Isá made her menudo in. It was important to get the temperature just right. Arnulfo liked his water hot. He also liked the idea that his bathwater was heated in the menudo olla. Some red chile energy would undoubtedly seep into him during his bath. He was a believer in hot red chile tea for colds and chile poultices for sluggish body parts.

Today was Arnulfo's designated day for bathing. His scheduled bath was a ritual he'd never ignored, not once in the last fifty years. If he was out of town, he took a bath wherever he was on that day. He tried to time it in the late afternoon, but sometimes he had to wait until it got dark.

On his bath day he would clean up his room, attend to what needed to be done in the house, and then head for the little casita where the metal tub that had once belonged to his mother awaited him. It was a comforting reminder of who he was in the scheme of things. It was his rejuvenation and his respite. And no one and nothing ever bothered him when he got into that tub.

Sometimes before he stepped in the tinita, he would have Emilia brush his skin with a long-handled brush made out of vegetable fibers that he had bought in the mercado in Juárez from a Rarámuri woman who had come up from the Copper Canyon in northern México. It was helpful to get rid of dry and excess skin. While he enjoyed La Gorda's brisk brushing and the glow that followed her ministrations, that was the extent of their companionship in the shed. He called it La Tumbita with great tenderness.

Not because he was morbid and felt a death wish, but because when he emerged from a bath he felt like Lazarus. The real Lazarus. Reinvented. Renewed. Reborn.

At various times in his life he'd had oil, mud, clay, and all types of herbal baths in that tina, depending on his ailments. Isá knew all the tratamientos for whatever ailed you and passed along her suggestions to Emilia. The back wall was filled with little jars of things called Uña de Gato, Estafiate, and of course her Gobernadora, the chaparral she used for many things, including arthritis, cancer, cramps, and your everyday aches and pains. She was the one person in Comezón consulted in cases of aires, empachos, sustos, mal ojo, coraje, and bílis. There were few hostile vapors, impacted stomachs, fears, evil eyes, angers, or biles that Isá hadn't met or couldn't deal with. Arnulfo had always known that the woman was part bruja, but she could cook, ugly as she was, and she knew more than a thing or two about healing. She'd kept Juliana going at times they didn't think she could go on.

What about the time Juliana had that terrible pneumonia when she was ten years old? That was after she'd left school and Arnulfo decided she should stay home. Whatever she needed to learn, she could learn just as well at home, away from the Sister Servants of the Blessed Sacrament. They were nuns who'd come up from México during the revolution and were still teaching children in California after all these years. One of them, Sister Betita, had retired from a school in Calexico to move to Comezón, and it was she who taught Juliana. Better his daughter got an education from a woman who hadn't known the violence of that past. He wanted Juliana to be a tranquil woman, not a fighter, not a rabble-rouser. If she was home, he could watch her closely, she would be under his scrutiny.

The sad thing, he pondered when he had time to reflect, which was usually in his tinita, was that Juliana hadn't grown up demure or calm or mild. Underneath her quiet exterior burned a wild heart, ay! And yet secretly he cheered her on, yes he did.

He knew what it was to rail against the pendejadas of the world. And she, Juliana Olivárez, in her own muted way, was a rebel, just like those fearless Mexican nuns who'd survived Villa's raids, having to leave their convent at a moment's notice, those women who hid their prayer books in haystacks and had a secret set of tunnels that they used as escape routes when the soldiers came. By the time Arnulfo realized what education would do to Juliana, it was too late. She had become a quiet anarchist. There was something good about it and something bad. The good he'd seen, and the bad he didn't want to know about.

Arnulfo entered La Tumbita. He would forgo the scrub-down with the brush and the loofah on his feet tonight. Nor was it the time of the month to have his toenails cut by Emilia. His hair was fine, not to worry about a trim, and his mustache was long and hearty, the way he liked it. He would clean his ears after he emerged from the bath, when the wax was soft, and brush his teeth with a soft toothbrush and sea salt. He would also gargle with the same salt. He still had some of his teeth and was proud of that. Look at Luisito; the man was ten years younger and had few teeth to call his own. Of course he couldn't compete with Joe, who had really nice teeth, or Rey, who had pretty good teeth and a way with women. If he had wanted a way. Since his wife Dulce had left him, Rey had been celibate. He was waiting for her to return. Ay, let him wait!

The man didn't know how lucky he was, Arnulfo thought as he stiffly got out of his clothes, locking the door behind him. He was still exhausted from the Fiesta. He wondered how much longer he could be the Master of Ceremonies. The job was finally wearing him down. People didn't seem to care about the Fiestas the way they had in the past. It was a disrespectful, cynical world. It was time to let go. Well, maybe after next year.

Arnulfo carefully put a few toes in the tinita, gauging the heat. Very hot. Good. He eased his other toes in, then his right foot and then the left. With one long surge he swooshed into the water. Ayyyyy!!

He always locked the door now because he didn't want Emilia hovering with a wet washrag to scrub his back or Isá to come barreling in with a pot of beans to soak. Once the old servant woman had caught him with his chones down. Of course she looked straight at his pito and smiled at him. It was an approving smile, no? For an old man, he still had a pronounced member. Sadly, it was good out of the chute but unable to win the race. Best not to think about it. But he had to. No, he didn't. Por Dios, it was just a bath! His puro wasn't being graded and wasn't under attack, and he didn't have to report it to anyone. Gracias a Dios. Women don't know how tiresome it is for men to constantly account for their penises, which sadly, over time, become nuisances.

The water in the tinita was perfect. It would start off very hot, and then it would become warm and then cool. He had a resistance to the heat and could tolerate high temperatures. Must come from living in Comezón! As he soaked in his tinita, he began to relax as the many thoughts came to him:

What had happened to Dominga "La Minga" Maez Hornbarger?

How many years was it since ole Glenn Hornbarger had died?

When was the last time he and Minga . . . ?

Was the mariachi suit going to be all right?

Just where the hell had Lucinda gone with Ruley? She wasn't back yet, and Isá was beside herself. If she didn't come back by tomorrow, he'd have to report her missing.

He had a meeting with his lawyer on Wednesday at 10:00 A.M. Cabrón, he'd try and take all his money. How expensive could it be to make a will, anyway?

He had to see the doctor sometime soon. He was beginning to have trouble breathing. When he was on the Fiesta stage his voice would suddenly stop, just like that. He had trouble catching his breath after a long-drawn-out grito. This never used to happen. He had always had a voice like a flamenco singer; it could go on and on for a long time without a breath. Just recently he'd had trouble projecting mid-sentence. What was happening?

Ay, bendito sea el agua del baño. He knew it would break up the empache that had come on after eating all that Fiesta food for two days. Too many gorditas red chile enchiladas funnel cakes curly fries horchatas not to mention the giant turkey legs the roasted corn and the caramel candy.

Yes, he could feel something loosening up in his stomach. He hoped he would be able to make it out of the tinita in time to run back to the house. Someday soon he would have to put a toilet in La Tumbita. That's all it lacked. More than once he'd watered or fertilized the herbs that Isá grew behind the shed. And then there was his little bush near the back door, his shit bush, a sad-looking white oleander that he also often fertilized.

Lying back in the tub, he rested a moment with the warm toalla on his chest. Caress me. Bandage me. He wanted to stop feeling bad. He drank to assuage his pain, but do you think he'd ever tell anyone that? No one wanted to be around a sad Arnulfo Olivárez. If he stopped drinking, he'd have to face his long-standing grief about so many things. He leaned his head back and lay there immobile. His head hurt. Ay!

It was that time again. Juliana had her doctor's visit coming up. He didn't have the energy this year to drive her to San Antonio, Texas, to see her specialist, Dr. Diosdado. Someone else would have to take her this time. Who? Maybe he could find someone to drive her and Emilia. Who?

His thoughts always came back to Juliana. The one easiest to be around and to love. And still even she was a thorn in his side.

Would Juliana ever leave Rancho Comezón? And if so, how?

Ay, Julianita! His precious girl. She was only lovelier every day. And sweeter. She had a good personality and was always cheerful. But she wasn't too cheerful, not like her mother. She was always upbeat, but not artificial. His poor Gorda, she did suffer, didn't she?

He should visit Gorda sometime soon. That last time had been good. She hadn't resisted like she usually did. And she was soft. He would try not to drink so much. But of course he had to pretend he was drunk. Otherwise. Otherwise. She might think he was coming back to her the way a husband comes back and stays with a wife, and a wife with her husband. They were married, but she'd never forgiven him for so many things. Lucinda. Don't think about it. It was a mistake. They'd never spoken of it. Emilia had gone out to Erenacio and Chanita Lucero's place and brought the child home. Their niece Senaida was living with them. She had been working at Rancho Comezón as a maid for a while. It was she who was Lucinda's mother. It happened. It just happened. And for that happening he was truly sorry. She was a young woman of twenty. Oh, he was sorry!

He had loved Emilia then. Oh, he loved her. But she was so so so so, ay! And he was very restless. He was still restless.

Arnulfo stretched his legs out as far as they would extend and flexed his toes. They were always numb now, especially the last three on his left foot and the farthest two on the right. Probably diabetes. He didn't want to know.

The water felt good. He put the warm washcloth on his face and sighed.

The will. Now, that was something to think about.

Who? Who? What? What? And why? Oh, he knew the why. The why was the hardest part.

The most important thing was just to rest right now. Rest.

The many thoughts twirled round and round his head and then just lay there in the warm water like his wet cosita, floating, floating in his soothing bath. Hopefully the water would bring him back to life. In the water he was a baby boy, soon to be born.

CHAPTER TWELVE

Las Comadres

Isá Lugo was a woman of the earth. All day she lifted, carried, moved, removed, put back, and made whole. She wasn't afraid of work. She'd started working at age four, and she was still attuned to every day's cycle of movement and challenge. Nothing changed her center. That center being the reality of the job at hand. There were things to be done, jobs to be accomplished. And it was her lot in life to take hold, to be in charge, and to clean up other people's messes.

How had Isá come to live with Doña Emilia and Don Arnulfo, then later Juliana and Lucinda Olivárez?

She had grown up in Aguacero, just down the road from Rancho Comezón, and when Arnulfo took a wife, she came looking for a job as a housekeeper. She and Emilia took to each other right away—it was as if they were childhood friends, but they weren't. Doña Emilia was always a lady, kindness itself, and this suited Isá, who in her own rough way, and with her crude voice and unpleasant demeanor—not to mention that ugly face—was a woman of prescribed behavior and formality.

From the very start, Doña Emilia treated Isá as an equal. Despite Arnulfo's protestations, she eventually came to live with the Olivárez family. At first she would come over on Fridays to clean the house, each morning to cook the day's meals, and on Saturdays to water the trees and plants. This schedule varied depending on the season. In the summertime she became a regular fixture, until one day Emilia approached her with a proposal. Would she consider living in? Juliana was about to be born, and Emilia needed the help.

Isá was the partera, the midwife who brought Juliana into the world. The girl was born without a sound; it was only when Isá cleaned her face and little body that she noticed the child was deformed. She didn't have the heart to tell Emilia that first night, nor the second. The labor had gone on for so long. She just swaddled Juliana in cotton and gave her to her mother to nurse. Emilia's joy was profound. It was only several days later, after she was stronger and Isá had fed her healing broth and yerba buena, that Isá found Emilia with her child at her breast, all the bandages removed. Emilia was oiling the small inverted feet and the crooked toes and singing to her. Nothing was said. Doña Emilia was a very strong woman, and this is why Isá was still here, nearly twenty-nine years later.

She wasn't still here because of Arnulfo, who paid her well enough. She had few needs and had saved most of her salary. She kept it in a box near the back of her closet.

She'd had no use for Don Arnulfo at first. He was a useless baby, always would be. But he was Doña Emilia's baby, her niño querido, and that counted for something. Doña Emilia loved him and Isá loved Doña Emilia, so he was to be tolerated, and yes, respected.

Over time she became accustomed to him, as one would to a temperamental ten-year-old, make that a five-year-old. She knew how to control him. Through food and structure. She had discovered that besides being a pompous, self-absorbed, self-serving sin vergüenza, shameless with women, most especially his wife, as well as a braggart with delusions of grandeur, the man needed parameters. She kept him on a short leash, and as the saying goes, she had him by the pelitos, the very short not-so-fine hairs. She had his meals fixed on time, kept his house neat and clean, didn't bother him with a lot of talk, and never discussed religion. All of this suited them both. They had little eye contact, and that also was good.

Isá went to Mass each Sunday at 6:30 A.M. and was back home to have his breakfast ready by 8:00 A.M. He might decide to sleep in, but he knew it was ready to be served on time. Mealtimes were punctual. Arnulfo was an aficionado of her tortillas, her pipían, and never failed to compliment her on her Pescado al Mojo de Ajo, which he ordered up for company. Theirs was a match made through necessity and inventiveness and acceptance. Arnulfo acknowledged her fierce, sometimes brusque and unpleasant ways, her scowling pockmarked face, her shadowed stealthiness, the sudden surprise of her appearance in a room without warning, except of course his bedroom, which was always off limits to everyone, and the occasional interruption without warning—for the steady, organized care of the house and all things pertaining to his comfort, most especially his dietary needs.

Isá, for her part, accepted that he was Doña Emilia's husband, and this sole fact eclipsed all she felt about his drinking, whoring, and lack of faith. She would never truly accept him as a man of principle, virtue, or spirit, but he was, in his own way, singular, someone she'd become accustomed to. She knew by looking at him when he needed a bowl of red chile for an oncoming cold, when to cut back on his bean intake, and if he needed more fluids. Likewise she knew if he needed soft food, roughage, or something to jumpstart his kidneys. And if he needed to adjust his salt. Like an old dog, she could assess him by his gait, the whites of his eyes, and the watery or dry tone of his voice. She knew more about him than Doña Emilia did, because she also washed his laundry.

Few words were ever spoken between them. They never discussed anything at length. It was usually a "Buenos diás" or a "Buenas noches," with a few questions about food thrown in for good measure. The rest she came to know about him when she and Doña Emilia, the two comadres, sat in the little grape arbor near the well, in their usual chairs, on the hot nights, the air finally cooling down and transforming into one of those miraculous and perfect evenings, a cool breeze coming down from the north, from Doña Emilia's little village, Aguacero, that she was always talking about. The two friends sat together enjoying cold sandía, the best watermelon of the season so far, or a slice of homemade cheese with membrillo and a fresh limeade.

Doña Emilia talked in a hushed and reverent tone about her family, Los Izquierdo, and how much she still missed her parents, Anunciata and Persignato, as well as her favorite sibling, her sister Dorotea, whom she called Doro. Isá talked mostly about her mother, Gertrudis Azucena, as well as her father, Crodifacto, who had died when she was five. They often said a rosary or two together, one for each set of relatives, and then continued eating whatever little snack Isá would have prepared for them alone.

When Crodi, Isá's father, died, their world was upended, and everything went wrong for her brothers and another sister. But that was the past. The present was the cold watermelon and the great calm of two large and always hungry women alone with each other. Who knew where Arnulfo was? It was too early for Emilia to start worrying.

—Come and sit, Doña Emilia. Aquí le tengo su plato de sandía. It's your special plate, the little one with the flowers you like. I brought you your fork and knife. I've cut the watermelon slices the way you like them. Here's your salt. I also brought us some chilito to spice things up, that's if we want them spiced up. Come and sit down, you've been on your feet too long today. It's time to rest.—

—You're the one who should be resting, Isá. Are you tired? It's been a busy day.—

—Busy? Today? No, today wasn't too busy. Busy is coming up. Will you remind Don Arnulfo that this year I'll need more green chile? We almost ran out last year. He was one costal short.—

—He forgets things, Isá. I'll remind him when he goes out to Don Fidencio's farm to get the extra sack of chile this year. We still have some time before the harvest, but yes, do remind me.—

—It's never too early to start reminding Don Arnulfo.—

—You're right. He seems so distracted lately. What do you think is wrong?—

—Now sit down, Doña Emilia. No more talk of what to do and for whom. Although I'm the one that brought up the "To Dos."—

—That's all right. You're good to remember so much. What would I do without you? I'd be lost.—

—Ay, you lost without me? I'm a little speck of nothing on the face of this earth, no more than a gnat or a bee, así es.—

—Always working, always moving. I envy your freedom to move. I never thought I'd end up this way. How I wish I had your strength. I've always been delicada.—

—You? Delicate? No, Doña Emilia. You are not weak. Look at what you've endured. I don't have to tell you.—

—It hasn't been so hard. You've been here to help, and for that I am grateful.—

—Me, a help? It's you who's helped me. More salt? You saved me from that horrible man who wanted to marry me. I meant nothing to him, I was a work animal.—

—Pass me the chile powder. And the lime. I feel dangerous.—

—More limeade?—

—Let's have a little tequila with our limeade. Let's. You know how I like things.—

—The bottle is right here. I brought it out, just in case.—

—Juliana? Does she want to join us?—

—I asked, Señora. But she said no. She's in her room.—

—What is she working on?—

—A new holy card.—

—I thought so.—

—It looks like him.—

—Who?—

—El Padre Rodríguez.—

—Oh. I see.—

—Yes.—

—I'll have a little more tequilita.—

—She's absorbed.—

—I'm glad to hear the doctrina classes have helped her focus on God's graces. Yes, it's good. Isn't it?—

—It's what it is.—

—Do you think? . . . if you thought . . .—

—Absolutely not. And yet . . .—

—Then? She's a child.—

—Yes, of course, she's like a child. But him? He's not without his problems. He's a man. That says it all.—

—Does it?—

—Yes, he's a man. But he's a priest. And the priest part is so ingrained, he'll never be anything else, except . . . He's not a holy man like El Padre Zamora, our last priest. Now, he was a living saint.—

—No, he's not. El Padre Manolito is always very irritable. Have you noticed?—

—Very impatient.—

—But he's good at his work. He's a teacher. Juliana is learning the sacred doctrines."

—No one likes him. Quizás es lo Español. But we've had priests from Spain before. This one is different. He's young.—

—And handsome. Do you think he's good-looking?—

—He's a Spaniard first. Before being a priest and a man.—

—Should that worry us?—

—Yes and no. Perhaps. Do you want me to check on Juliana now?—

—Let her be. It's her time to create.—

—She spends too much time alone.—

—She's an artist. She needs that time.—

—She's spent too much time alone, I'm telling you. When young women are alone so much, many thoughts come into their minds.—

—Yes, he's very Spanish.—

—Puro Español.—

—Shall we go in? The mosquitoes are coming out.—

—What about dinner?—

—We'll eat the leftover meat with papas and red chile. I'm not sure when Arnulfo will be coming back.—

—Señora Emilia . . .—

—¿Mande?—

—I was just thinking. No, never mind. It's nothing.—
—You worry too much.—
—You are the one who worries too much.—
—Someone has to worry around here.—
—All right, then, let's both worry.—
—Es puro Español.—
—Puro Español.—

CHAPTER THIRTEEN

Las Lágrimas

Arnulfo had nearly died from pneumonia some years back. What he saw in his worst moment was an expanse of shocking blue sky opening up to clouds, those clouds becoming families, and those families turning into whole towns and continents. He saw and understood everything with a startling simplicity—the clouds were kin, the trees were brothers, sisters, and sometimes they rested alone, but they were never that—alone. Each was connected to the other, as day is connected to night and night to infinity. Infinity was connected to each álamo seedling, for that is where all potential, all life, rested—in the core and pulp and root. In that way, life, and yes, even infinity, continued to be what it was: potential.

Arnulfo loved his daughter Juliana, but too often he was afraid to tell her so. When she was little, he'd sworn to God if only if only, and nothing came of that. He'd held her little twisted body and whispered in her tiny ear: "I love you. Te amo querida, and please don't die on us. Emilia's heart can't be broken. Dear God, break mine instead. Punish me, do what you will to me, but spare this angel." Little did he realize then that God would do just that.

It was true Juliana was an angel—if ever there was a perfect child, she was it—so lovely, so very lovely and so broken. She hid her deformity from him, and he was thankful. To see her with her feet and legs so stunted and so thin was his greatest sorrow— she who was so perfect otherwise. And he knew that she knew he suffered, and this brought him greater pain. Why had she been born so twisted? What in him or in Emilia had caused the Taint— for that was what it was—a dark, evil flow of blood and semen mixing murkily over the pure water of his daughter's pulsing life? What would become of her once Emilia was gone, and yes, what would happen to her once he'd moved to Infinity, if that was what awaited him? Who would take care of her? Not Isá, not that old piece of leather. She was paid help, and it was obvious she didn't love Juliana, not the way a mother would. Who would wake her up, clean her, dress her, bring her her sewing, and help her cook and do her painting? Who would wrap her legs in flannel every night after rubbing them with alcohol and herbs, the liniment of the old, beloved, never-forgotten country? The little bags of marijuana coming to him from Mata himself. Everyone in Comezón knew he was the one to find when you needed what you needed. And what Juliana needed was that magic oil, El Aceite de Marihuana, that Isá rubbed on her legs each night just before she went to bed.

Who would love Juliana the way he and Emilia loved her? No one. And until Arnulfo found someone who could love her, really love her—with even the smallest approximation of her parents' love—he would hold on to her tightly. She was a precious child, too precious for this ugly world.

Arnulfo saw the way Padre Manolito looked at her. No good could ever come from that. And yet her mother insisted she needed the doctrine. What doctrine? What laws or rules were there to learn the basics of living?

His Credo was reality.

Arnulfo believed in the power of Power. Power of the land, the rise and solidity of mountains. Especially the Lágrimas Mountains. Mountains named after the tears of God, legend said, tears that God shed after he formed the world. According to the legend, God did not rest on that fateful day, as Padre Manolito would have extolled to his parishioners from the pulpit; no, instead of resting on that seventh day, God wept. But first he meditated on the lives of men, the lives of women, and their descendants, all to emerge in the coming forth of race, the propagation of the human family.

God meditated on the fragile brevity of Creation and on the impermanence of Beauty. These ruminations did not bring tears because to live is a miracle, and in that miracle we awaken to the splendor of the Divine. If there is impermanence, then by deduction there exists through the veiled shadowing of the unknown sacred knowledge of the permanent. And this is what Padre Manolito would never understand and could never teach Juliana in those Catechism lessons Emilia insisted on.

What was permanent? He didn't know. But he knew it was permanent. Who was God? He didn't know and he didn't care, but he did know there was a Power greater than himself and all life. Call it the sky or the clouds. Too many people had called it God. And their God was a sniveling bag of lies, a sham protector and a conceited and vain specter who ruled the hearts of men through fear of the unknown.

Arnulfo's God was not a man in his thirties who walked the Americas leaving signs of his passage, staurolite crystals in the shape of red, white, black, brown, and yellow crosses. His God wasn't the broken, nearly nude body on that cross of sorrows; God wasn't even a man, although this wasn't a conversation he wanted to have with anyone, or at least not sober, and most especially not with El Padre Manolito.

The only person Arnulfo could talk to about God was his compadre from the pueblo, Donacio Quiroz, and that conversation would be through looks and the long silence of nods and on the rim of the Lágrimas Mountains, where they'd once stood as boys and then later as men, contemplating the beauty of a sunset, the sky turning orange-red and then purple-blue, the horizon lit with immense majesty, as below the lights of Comezón came twinkling alive to remind them who they were: nothing and everything.

The concept of a Mother God came from Donacio, who knew his grandmother María was the incarnation of the Divine, the feminine and all that was right with the world, the loving Mother of Life, who guarded her children as clouds guarded the mountains, and then wept, bringing rain, sometimes soft, sometimes hard.

Arnulfo was a hungry child at her breast; that was Arnulfo, tasting beauty. He liked the idea of La Abuelita María being Donacio's and his God; he knew the old woman, respected her, trusted her, knew her teachings well, acknowledged them because they were just, equitable, and without pity. She could kill a lame horse, putting it out of its misery, the horse not knowing anything but love and surrender as she stroked its neck, talking to it, looking into its weary glassy eyes, telling it to sleep. She brought grace to illness, peace to the dying, bravery to the fearful. She talked to the wind when it raged, telling it to sleep, and it did, it rested and was not resentful. She talked to the sun and it abated its fury, and with water all she had to do was lay her hand in it and it cooled down and satiated any traveler.

María had once been a soldadera in Villa's army, traveled with the troops, and met La Destroyer, the other María, María Zavala, who helped the soldiers die without remorse and with dignity. That was the irony of La Destroyer's life: she was the one who dynamited the tracks at the end of the revolution. How could she be called merciful when she brought death? Ay, that was the great mystery of La Destroyer's life.

When the fracasos ended or transformed or absolved themselves into another time and stage, another platform, and Villa was shot, dead, and buried, Donacio's grandmother, María, traveled north through Chihuahua and Ciudad Juárez, and it was she whom Donacio's grandfather, Lobardo Quiroz, took as his wife. She was an indígena as well, but it wasn't until she met Lobardo that she claimed her healing. It was María's mother-in-law, Morning Light, who taught her to follow in the footsteps of her ancestors.

Few Apache women were honored with names, but Morning Light was a rare woman who brought healing to her people in the early morning hours, invoking the power of the rising sun as she prayed atop the small cerrito near her home, the place Donacio came to call El Resplendor.

When Arnulfo passed from this earth, he would call out to Doña María, who would call out to Morning Light to assist him. They would both come to him, because that was what Doña María had promised. She had told him that once, and he believed her. She was a woman of her word. She was incapable of lies, just like her son Donacio. And that was why his God was named Doña María Quiroz. She was a small woman with thin gray braids, little trenzitas, and the amused smile of someone so old they are young and so young they would never grow old. At that end time, or it could have been the beginning time, he wasn't sure, Arnulfo would call out to Doña María and she would come. She would stroke his forehead like the time she cured him of the curse of Ramírez, but that was another story, another time, another darkness. She would place a towel on the back of his neck, the sacred place where heat rose and fell; she would quell and stanch the sorrow and would talk to him and then sing the song of life:

Cloud Brothers
Cloud Sisters
Gather 'round
Sit in stillness and attention
As I tell you the story of how we came to be

You are a form of the formless
Ya-hay
You are a child of the Divine
Ya-hay

Out of the formless comes the form
Out of the darkness comes the light
Out of spirit comes the child
Out of the child comes the man
Ya-hay . . .

CHAPTER FOURTEEN

Don Clo

Don Clodimoro Balderas was coming to visit Rey. And to Rey Suárez this was bad news indeed.

Don Clo, as he was known, had no hometown. If he did, only those people who had seen him being born knew who he was and who his parents were. He was entitled, that you could see right off. And it was an entitlement that came from generations of breeding, like the lineage of an old but glorious fighting rooster whose progeny still fought and killed.

But Don Clo was too refined to be thought of in such coarse terms. He was a gentleman who stood by his manners and his soft-spoken but unbending word.

A dapper man, tall at six feet, two inches, and athletic still for a man in his early fifties, he was respected and feared. But the fear only came to those who displeased him, and those people were few.

Lita, Don Clo's wife, had once been a beauty, still was, except for the little roll of flesh around her middle. Never call that fat by its vulgar Spanish name, panza. Her little belly was something Don Clo loved to touch on those many excursions of her still-desirable flesh. Lita had been a finalist for Miss México in the Miss Universe Contest. That was where she met Don Clo, her husband-to-be, in a red bathing suit on a beach in Acapulco. It was love at first sight. Don Clo was a judge, and while Lita Ornelas from Torreón didn't win the contest, she did win Don Clo's vote. Theirs was a happy marriage, with two young daughters to prove the validity of the saying "Two beautiful flowers, one without thorns, the other still bleeding." No one was sure where this dicho came from, or what it meant; many say Don Clo penned it himself, but no one was sure. The man was a mystery. And yet he had published a chapbook of poems, *Desde La Noche Sin Luz: From the Night without Light*. It could also be said that Clodimoro Balderas was the most successful of businessmen. He was reputed to own a large, luxurious home in El Districto Federal and to have houses in Miami, Rome, and Martha's Vineyard, but who knew, who knew? Only his birth mother and those who were present for the birth knew who he was and where he came from. But those people were long gone, and their stories had been erased. Don Clo was an enigma to the world, and he liked it that way.

While he was an engaging and erudite person, he was alternately cold and unforgiving, but this side of him few enough knew. And yet he was well mannered, impeccably so, and charming. This is what won everyone over. He was kind. And he was generous. And above all else, he was a devout man. A believer. In what, no one was really sure, but he was passionate about certain things, and from all outward appearances he seemed to be a good man. Buena gente.

This is what impressed Padre Manolito when they first met at Santa Eulalia after a particularly frustrating Mass in which all manner of things had gone wrong for the poor Padre, recently arrived from Madrid, torn, you might say, from his home and heartland. It was a brutal awakening to the reality of life in Comezón. Who could work under such conditions? Listening to confessions from those who would only return the following week with the same sad tale of sins mortal and venial, sins sometimes so silly and aberrant in their stupidity that it was hard to believe this was the so called New World and that this ragtag gaggle of brethren was even considered the faithful. They were faithful to nothing except their own skin and its needs. He would never find his place in this humid pit of lackluster humanity. No one here had read a complete book; they were ignorant of the finer things in life: opera, good poetry, or an excellent meal with a bottle of fine Spanish wine. The denizens of this backwater hellhole were the lame, the blind, and the jodidos. The women were inferior specimens of womankind, and the men were worse, boorish mules who thought themselves superior to anyone, and who, in their primordial state of evolution, loudly declared their masculinity to all within earshot. Oh, how they shouted out that they had penises. How tiresome it all was! That was, until El Padre met Don Clodimoro Balderas, poet and author of *Desde La Noche Sin Luz*.

They met at the early morning Mass at Santa Eulalia. Don Clo came up to El Padre, who stood just outside the door of the church greeting people. You couldn't escape him if you tried. He stood there, a pillar of salt, with a firm but cold handshake, an unforgiving look, the many unsaid words on his tongue that somehow were revealed in his demeanor toward his poor brethren. Few people he deemed worthy of his time, and they knew it as they sideswiped the Padre, the most despised man in town, known for his haughty, condescending ways, his heavy, oppressive air of sanctity, and his great sorrowful eyes like the eyes of a screeching raptor, eyes that followed you and haunted you, eyes that you remembered long afterward. There was a pitiful quality that he exuded, and yes, he was handsome, and yes, he was short, and yes, he was Spanish. He had a beautiful deep, sonorous voice, but he made it ugly with his rants and his vile curses and railings against all human beings, so enamored was he of his one true unforgiving Father God, a God who only tolerated those few chosen ones. "Pobrecito," said Don Tomás Revueltas long after El Padre was gone from Comezón. "No," others said, like Lorenza Tampiraños, "he always made me feel dirty and ugly, when it was he who was the ugly dirty one." "Pobrecito," said Don Tomás again and again, shaking his head and remembering so much about the little priest, things no one would ever believe, they were so unheard of, so ridiculous. "He's to be pitied." Oh yes, others said, he who showed no pity for any living soul. He is to be pitied.

Don Clo liked Padre Manolito from the start. He was a formal, respectful man, and so was Don Clo. El Padre was orderly and tasteful and, it was apparent, of better mettle than most in this stinking little town that Don Clo had come to like, maybe even to love. He was drawn back to Comezón, almost against his will, and came often. His wife liked coming here; she found it restful and quiet, and his little girls liked it as well. While Don Clo for the most part lived in México, he was a true citizen of La Frontera, traveling back and forth between the two countries, those miles easily traversed.

Few here understood the man that he was, not that Don Clo wanted anyone to understand or appreciate him, and yet this little Spanish priest did understand him and did appreciate him. It was rare to find an intelligent man anywhere, much less in such an out-of-the-way place and under such circumstances. They became best friends. Now, this was odd because neither had friends. It wasn't that they were truly friends; it was just that they knew enough about loneliness to understand each other's need for solitude.

"Someday you'll come to see me in my place in México, no, Padrecito? I will show you around, and you will come to know what there is to see and learn about the world that is out there, waiting for you. But maybe you'd like my place in France better. Tell me where you want to go, and we'll go there. Your talents are wasted here. Have you thought of leaving the priesthood? You should. You would do well in business. Let me show you what life is really about. I will show you myself what it is to be a man in this world. You have potential for the life. What are you waiting for? There isn't anything here for you. Oh, maybe there is, but is that dream worth it? Someday, I tell you, you will leave the confines of this little town. You'll come with me. And never look back to this this . . ." Here Don Clo gestured widely, taking in the Plaza. They sat on a bench in the late afternoon, and as the sun went down, each fell into reverie.

"What life would that be, Don Clo?" El Padre asked, but he knew the answer to that question. How easy it would be to go off with Don Clo to any one of his houses in any number of places and see any number of countries in a way that few would ever see the world. It was tempting. El Padre was reminded of how the Devil tempted Christ by showing him the world in all its glory, letting him know that all this could be his, if only . . . It was tempting. Yes, it was. Don Clo was the Devil Incarnate, and yet Manolo couldn't hate him. He was too perfect, too full of ideas and words—words understood, loved. He could never hate Don Clo. Both of them were special human beings. And it was to each other that they spoke their secret and most beautiful sentiments. For they alone understood.

Manolo was there when Don Clo first read his favorite poem to him.

Desde la noche sin luz
noche impenetrable
noche sin estrellas

Amarrado de sueños
Te he buscado
Te he buscado

¿Dónde estás, amor?
¿Por qué te fuiste?

Since the night without light
Impenetrable night
Night without stars

Bound by sleep
I have looked for you
I have looked for you

Where are you, love?
Why did you leave?

The poem was dedicated to someone named Vicenzia Glakowki. Who she was, Manolo would never find out. He didn't care to know, either. It was enough that those words to her came crawling and slithering to him out of an immense darkness, the two men hissing their truth to each other.

Someday Manolo would leave this town. Where would he go? And with whom?

CHAPTER FIFTEEN

Los Cuatro Milpas

Stanley Wabatt's office was on the third floor of the Archuleta Building. His father, Zomley Wabatt, had bought the building from Eliseo Archuleta. As Comezón's only dentist from the 1920s to the 1960s, Eliseo had done pretty good. Yeah, pretty good, Arnulfo thought as he climbed yet another high, slippery step, pausing to rest after each one, but not great. The cabrón hadn't put in an elevator. It was unlikely that Stan would, either. Ay, qué El Stan Wabatt! Chinchy as they come.

Arnulfo was basing his opinion of Stan on facts: the two had been in the same class at Comezón High together, and they were both members of Los Caballeros Reales del Valle, a social and service club that took baby blankets and library books to México. Stan was the treasurer of the senior class, and Arnulfo had been on the Entertainment Committee and had run for president, losing to Guillermo "Memo" Urquide, Wiffie's older brother. He and El Stan were also longtime Grand Men at Arms, reaching the highest rank in the Caballeros' hierarchy—and both were known for their zealousness to do good and their put-everyone-else-under-the-table drinking skill. They were compadres 'pa siempre except in daylight and on U.S. territory. Once they had taken two putas to bed in the same room with two loud waffley and lumpy double beds that creaked with every thrust. Come to find out they were twins. Stan and Arnie, they had shared many secrets, which they both tried to forget, and had more than once cried on each other's shoulder as they bemoaned the pinche fate of all mankind. To live. To live too fast. To die. To die hard.

Somehow in México and under the influence of a round of Dos Equis, or better yet an Indio beer, this irreversible fact brought out the poet in each of them, and Stan, who barely spoke a phrase of Spanish other than "Otra cerveza, pour favour," could be found humming along to "Los Cuatro Milpas," that haunting song of longing for the past, that little white house of one's memory long gone, ay, ay, ay!, embracing Arnulfo with the hearty joy of a long-lost brother. Arnulfo, on the other hand, would often declaim an improvised poem that spoke of the deepest bond—that being between men—or reveal some profound insight into the great mystery of being born in this world in his particular and unusual and very loud voice. These he would dedicate to his hermano, El Stanley Wabatt.

The Caballeros liked to get away from their wives and drink and party hard. Every once in a while the wives went along to socialize, but those outings were rare. Emilia Olivárez was never invited on one of these trips. The club members wanted to get as far away from home as they could, to lose themselves in the atmosphere of foreignness that allowed them license to do as they pleased without anyone censuring them. For people like Stanley Wabatt and Arnulfo Olivárez, nothing was better. Each of them had their prescribed roles, their heavy duties, their burdens and sorrows at home, but when they crossed the border they shed the known: family, all worries, becoming two long-lost amigos they never had been or ever would be in the harsh glaring reality of their lives in Comezón.

Some years ago they'd gone to Chihuahua, Chihuahua, with a delegation from Comezón. Oh, there were speeches made, all right, most of them late at night and in the many cantinas he and the other members frequented. During the day they delivered books to the local library, blankets to day-care centers, and at night they drank themselves into a stupor as they munched on tacos de rez or sopes de pollo con guacamole, downing one Carta Blanca after another in some out-of-the-way taquería with their fellow hard-drinking Mexican counterparts.

Somehow one day a mistake was made, and a Mexican official introduced Arnulfo Olivárez as the Mayor of Comezón. No one in the delegation corrected him, not that they might have if they'd known, for no one other than Arnulfo spoke very good Spanish. So it remained on the rosters that Licenciado Arnulfo P. Olivárez was Alcade, el Mayor de Comezón, Nuevo México. It suited everyone to let things stand, especially Arnulfo, who finally got the respect he deserved when he was called up to the bandstand to give a greeting to the populace on the occasion of the delegation's yearly visit. Fitting it was that mariachis should greet him with the Mexican and American national anthems and that a late-night conjunto should dedicate one or two or three songs to him while he sobbed through another Indio beer and repeatedly blessed his ancestral homeland and then sang along with them in a blubbery falsetto.

The funny thing about all of this was that Stan was his best buddy out of the country, and yet when they got back home, he never saw him. The guy wasn't cultured and never came to the Fiestas on the Plaza. He never saw ole Stan anywhere, as a matter of fact. Too busy with church, maybe? He was a deacon at the First Baptist Church of Comezón.

How would Stan find him today? Overheated, out of breath, and anxious. Arnulfo was worried he couldn't muster the energy to gather Stan in as an hermano and lay out to him what he wanted him to do. The task was too hard to ponder. They were not remotely connected to each other's universes except on foreign soil and under a dark moon. How would Stan find him in daylight? An old man with a dry, explosive cough that made the hair on his back stand up while sending a chill to his heart. So this is what it was to age. No wonder his father used to complain and rail against growing old. Now he knew, oh yes, now he knew!

When Stan went to the State University and then on to law school, Arnulfo stayed at home taking care of his father's property. He never liked farming or taking care of cattle, but that was his lot. He tried to break away and moved up north to work one summer on a ranch, and that's when he met Emilia Izquierdo. The rest, as the saying goes, became his life. They moved back to Comezón after that winter, when Arnulfo felt the cold of the northern climes and realized he couldn't live anywhere near his in-laws, Persignato and Anunciata, or as he called them, El Chivo y La Rana, the old goat and the ugly frog.

Arnulfo had changed from his Tony Lamas earlier that morning and was now wearing—against his better judgment—a pair of camel-colored Hush Puppies that Emilia had given him last Christmas. Joto shoes. His callo had hurt so bad that Emilia had to lance it and then put some moleskin on it. It hurt him to be seen in such mariquita mano doblado shoes on the streets of Comezón. Not that anyone was out there in this heat checking out an old man's loafers. What did they care? Hell, if they didn't care, at least he cared, someone had to care.

He was proud of the way he looked and would often go home during the intermission of an event he was emceeing to take a quick shower and put on a new shirt or pair of pants. Sometimes he would come back with a completely different outfit. No one ever acted surprised, either. Lucinda called him a metrosexual, but he took offense. He was a man who loved women. Not men. As far as being a dandy, if he was, so what? It was known that Arnulfo Olivárez was a man of fashion. Call him a dandy, he didn't mind. And he was always a gentleman. Sometimes the event would start late on account of his attention to his grooming and constant clothing changes, but it didn't matter. And if it did, ¡Qué comen mierda hijos de la chingada!

The show would begin adrede when Arnulfo Olivárez stepped onstage with his mic. Not that he needed a mic. Mics were for jotos. He had a big, booming voice and had never needed a mic. Well, until recently. As surely as he was getting older, his legendary voice was dying. Withering like his palo seco. Now he sounded like an old woman, all breath and phlegm. Might as well throw in the old toalla mojada.

And that was why he lumbered up the stairs to Stan Wabatt's office. He was ready to start letting go—well, in a way. Not totally, but then again. Then again. It was time to start looking around the chingao bend of life to see where the hell he was headed, yes, maybe even there. Most of all he wanted to secure a future for Juliana. He didn't want her to worry after he left this earth and his pinche vida for what he hoped would be a beautiful little jacalito atop a cerrito below an immense sky of blue standing next to Doña María and Donacio Quiroz and all the echelons of the Olivárezes who knew him and accepted him the way he was porque así era. You have a problem with that? Mámame la verga.

Finally reaching the third floor, Arnulfo paused and leaned up against the wall. He saw the sign on the door:

Stanley Wabatt
Attorney at Law
Hometown service for over 50 years.

Leaning into the door, he stumbled into the office. At one end of the waiting room was a receptionist who sat behind a small enclosed counter. Her window was closed and she was looking down. The room was empty except for an old woman who sat at one end. ¡Ay! It was Mercia Crawley, old Curtis Crawley's wife. As he made his way into the room, the old woman looked up. She was displeased as well to see him.

"Miss Crawley."

"Mr. Olivárez."

"Good afternoon." At this, Arnulfo took off his hat and bowed. She didn't deserve it, but she was a woman, after all, and he was a gentleman.

"Yes, it is afternoon. Well, I suppose you have an appointment. Because I have an appointment and Mr. Wabatt is late. Someone is going to have to wait."

"Sí, Señora. I understand." After the vieja's mini-rant, he sat down to wait. For how long, he wasn't sure. No, he didn't have an appointment. But his compa would let him in sin nada. They were compadres, and the annual trip to México was coming up in the fall.

Arnulfo pretended to read the *Christian Science Monitor* while Mercia Crawley worked over a *Good Housekeeping* magazine from 1992. There was not much news in either. The last thing either wanted was to have a conversation. There was a certain amount of harrumphing and hacking and one unexpected fart that just as well could have been the squeaky movement of an old leather chair like the ones they sat in primly with their assholes contracted tightly on the sticky seats. Crawley winced, and Olivárez looked out the window. Finally, Stanley Wabatt came out of his office. The secretary looked up from her crossword puzzle and called out Mercia Crawley's name. She got up, looked at Arnulfo with disdain, and shot into Wabatt's office. They had been in there about fifteen minutes when she emerged, sidestepping Arnulfo and making a hasty retreat for the door. He stood up to say good-bye, but she was gone. It was then he released a good thick pedo with her name on it and sent the fart running after her. The secretary called his name, and Stan came out and shook his hand. Pumped it, you might say. He also sniffed the air suspiciously. They did the customary Caballero handshake, which was a combination of hand movements that had to be learned over time and when seen from a distance looked very similar to the Chicano Brown Beret militant sixties handshake, but with a limper wrist and a sudden jiggle thrown in at the end.

"Brother Olivárez."

"Hermano Wabatt. Buenas tardes."

"Sorry to keep you waiting, Arnie. Next time you might want to make an appointment."

"I didn't know I was coming in, Stan," Arnulfo said, but it wasn't true. He'd been planning this trip to see Stanley for a long time. He knew he had to get it over with once and for all.

"You know Mercia Crawley, Curtis's wife?"

"My wife knows her."

"Have a seat. She was in here to complain about the Cinco de Mayo Fiesta. Says it has to go. That it's a mess and that it's too loud and that it has nothing to do with America. Said it just like that. That it's not an American holiday and it's a waste of time.

I tried to calm her down. She's an old boot, but she does have some power. 'Mercia,' I told her, 'do you know where you're living, woman?' 'In the United States of America,' she says. And I said to her, 'Miss Crawley, look around. You're in Mexico but for the Gadsden Purchase,' and then she got all in a dither hissy fit, and then she got up and said, 'We'll just see about that.' I know her point of view and what she is capable of, and I have to tell you, Arnie, we haven't seen the last, oh no, we haven't seen the last of Mercia Crawley. As a Brother, I wanted to give you a heads-up. You packed?"

"Not yet, Stan. You have a roommate yet?"

"I told Brother Candy Lystrum we could room. Of course, you being down the hall. We have to have that. I have to tell you we have quite a few books this time around. Brother Ron Quantley has been collecting books all year long from garage sales, estate sales, even publishers. He has three sets of encyclopedias. We're really going to make an impact this year. Yes, siree!"

"Stanley, I need to talk to you."

"Sit down, Brother Olivárez. You're looking a little shaky."

Arnulfo was hot and sick, and more than that, afraid. He explained to Stanley, after a glass of water and then a bracer of whiskey that Stan brought out from a locked drawer when he saw how feeble Olivárez was looking, that he was there to make a will.

"Good idea. You mean to tell me you, a man of, well, a man of you know what, doesn't have a will? Everyone needs one. You never want to go into probate, let me tell you, never."

After discussing executors, living wills, living trusts, powers of attorney, and what they were going to present to their fellow Mexican Caballero counterparts as a gift from Comezón this year, that taking the greater part of the hour, Stanley decided on a set of roadrunner trivets with a set of red chile ristra–decorated hand towels, which he would buy and wrap up in preparation for their trip.

Arnulfo shook hands Caballero style with Stanley. Stan grabbed him and hugged him hard, causing him to get a crick in his neck. Might as well have lifted him up and shook him up and down.

The man didn't know his own strength. It had come in handy once when they were up against some mocoso punks who threatened them on the streets of Reynosa after an all-nighter. They thought they saw an easy target in Stanley Wabatt, but they were mistaken! Hell, yes! And they *were* from Hell, that's what Stanley said after he beat up the gang leader and then prayed over him with more Jehovahs and Holy Be's in one breath than Arnulfo had ever heard.

As Stanley went on about the upcoming trip to Ciudad Apodaca in Nuevo León, Arnulfo pondered the inevitable. He had a list of things he needed to do before formalizing the will. He had to look at various papers and make sure that he understood what was Emilia's and what was his. She was the one with the money. Rather, she was the one who had started out with the money. What was hers was now his. He needed to go over a few things with her, and this left him with a sense of unease. He knew she would agree to anything he proposed, but somehow the idea of confronting her with the sad spiraling end of his life's assets was numbing. Although he knew that at heart they wanted the same thing: for Juliana to be taken care of. Forget about Lucinda. No love lost there for her or from her to them. She would soon be pregnant and married and a Terrazas living on the outskirts of town in a big two-story house, which would someday become hers and her brats'. The writing was on the adobe wall.

An appointment was made for the following week. By then Arnulfo would have spoken to Emilia, Emilia to Juliana, and all the papers would be signed. Everything going to Juliana, and of course her guardian. That guardian being Emilia until Emilia's death, and then . . . that was the part that needed to be worked on. The and then . . .

Juliana was twenty-eight years old. Who would take care of her? How long would she live? With whom would she live? Would she ever marry? What of the house? Juliana's as well. Everything to Juliana. Everything.

With feet numbed from diabetes, too-tight shoes, and a callo that had bled through his socks, Arnulfo took one step at a time back down the stairway, cursing all the way. Cheap was Stanley Wabatt's middle name. What the hell was a trivet? And who in their right mind wanted bath towels with a red chile ristra on them? Couldn't Stanley have thought of a manlier gift? Probably his wife suggested the gifts; she did own a junky little gift shop off the highway called Candice's Closet, and hell if Stan wasn't making money on the sale. Leave it to old Wabatt. Forget the roommate thing as well. The man snored and was known to walk in his sleep. If Arnulfo went on the Caballero trip, he would get a room by himself. Just in case. You never knew. There was an American woman in the delegation that one of the Mexicanos had started calling "La Milk Shake." Marsha Milfort was hefty-chested, and she liked to shake her breasts when she danced, which was as often as she could, in loose low-cut tops, her passport and cell phone tucked between her enormous chichis for safety. This year maybe he would end up dialing a couple of her numbers. Marsha was a pharmacist, and like old Stanley she let her hair down when she was in México. She was the one who took condoms and birth control pills to her Mexican Caballero brothers and sisters, passing some out to the delegation with a wink. She never knew that the men in the group talked about her breasts all the time. She wasn't a Caballero, but she tagged along with Munchie Morales, a former president of the Caballeros. When Munchie moved away, Marsha become their mascot. If Arnulfo had a room to himself, maybe Marcia would come visit him, and if not Marcia, perhaps one of the more attractive Hermanas Mexicanas? Single or married, it didn't matter. Well, maybe married was better. Life was full of possibility. Or was it? Ayy, this damn stairway. One step. Another step. Right leg first. Then the left. Leading with the right leg, his stronger side. Coming up with the left. Right leg. Now the left. Gripping the rail. Damn Stanley! And damn that old Crawley woman! Damn them all! It was an ugly world if you thought about it long enough, and yet . . . and there he went again with that and yet . . . he loved life, and yes, he wanted to live and as long as he could.

All he wanted, all he ever wanted, was that one thing . . . that lost sad never forgotten thing . . . ese comezón . . .

Arnulfo hummed the tune to "Los Cuatro Milpas" to himself. When he got home, he would put on the music of his tocayo, Arnulfo Flores, singing "Los Cuatro Milpas." He would lock the door, cry a little in his room, and then go to bed until dinnertime. He would eat a good hearty meal and then lie down again, maybe to dream.

LOS CUATRO MILPAS
by Francisco González

Cuatro milpas tan sólo han quedado
Del ranchito que era mío ¡ay, ay, ay, ay!
De aquella casita tan blanca y bonita
Lo triste que está.

Si me prestas tus ojos, morena,
Los llevo en el alma, que miren allá
Los despojos de aquella casita
Tan blanca y bonita lo triste que está.

Los potreros están sin ganado,
la laguna se secó
la cerca de alambre que estaba en el patio
tambien se cayó

Si me prestas tus ojos, morena,
Los llevo en el alma, que miren allá
Los despojos de aquella casita
Tan blanca y bonita lo triste que está.

Las cosechas quedaron perditas
Toditito se acabó, ¡ay, ay, ay, ay!
Ya no hay palomas, ni flores ni aromas,
Todo se acabó.

Cuatro milpas que tanto quería,
Pues mi madre las cuidaba . . . ¡ay!
Si vieras qué solas, ya no hay amapolas
Ni yerbas de olor.

Si me prestas tus ojos, morena,
Los llevo en el alma, que miren allá
Los despojos de aquella casita
Tan blanca y bonita lo triste que está.

Las palmeras lloraban tu ausencia
la laguna se secó ¡ay, ay, ay, ay!
los piones y arrieros
todititos se fueron y nadie quedó

Por eso estoy triste morena
por eso me pongo muy triste a llorar
recordando las tardes felices
que los dos pasamos en aquel lugar . . .

"Esa casa tan blanca y bonita . . . el ranchito que era mía . . . ya
todo se acabó . . . y nadie quedó . . . Todito se acabó . . . ¡ay,
ay, ay!"

Everything . . . everything would soon be gone . . . no one
left . . .

¡Ay, ay, ay!

CHAPTER SIXTEEN

The Confession

Juliana couldn't sleep. She looked over to the alarm clock by the side of the bed. 10:19 P.M. She had lain in bed for over two hours, and sleep had not come. She didn't like going to bed so early, but Isá always put her down around 8:00 because that's when *she* liked to go to bed. Mamá was always up late, often till two or three in the morning, but she had weak arms. She would never have been able to lift Juliana because she was almost dead weight. Arnulfo might have helped, but he was usually gone from the house, especially at night, depending on the day of the week, or locked away in his room listening to Augustín Lara or José Alfredo Jiménez, and he considered any household chore to be women's work. Attending to his daughter Juliana fell to Isá, the caretaker. That's the way it was.

Juliana called out to her mother and then Isá. Emilia finally heard her and woke up Isá, who got Juliana up from bed. Isá grumbled loudly but managed to get Juliana into some clothing. Juliana told them she couldn't sleep and wanted to spend some time painting. It was Padre Manolito's holy card she was working on. Little did she know they knew whose sacred face adorned the painting! Against her will, Isá wheeled her into the dining room.

Juliana made sure that Isá placed her in the wheelchair by the side of the dining table that had the phone next to it on a small stand. She would paint awhile, and then when it was quiet, she would call El Padre Manolito. He had given her his private home phone number. She had to talk to him.

"How will you manage, Hija?" Mamá Emilia said to her with concern.

"Mamá, you know that sometimes I paint for hours late at night. I'll sleep tomorrow. When Isá wakes up at five in the morning, I'll have her put me to bed. I'll be all right. I have a pañal and I haven't had liquids all night. I won't need to go to the bathroom, I'll have my pads. I'll be quiet, Mamá. I know your head hurts. Take one of those pills Dr. Marías gave you for those headaches you've been having!"

"They put me to sleep, Hija. When I take them I can't wake up."

"You need to sleep, Mamá. What I need to do is paint. I have an order from La Pata, your comadre's daughter. She needs her holy cards for her grandson's Holy Communion in a few weeks. Don't worry. I can wheel myself into the bedroom if I get tired. I'll just recline the wheelchair and go to sleep; you know how I do it."

"Ay, Hija. I understand. Doña Emilia, now you go to bed. You've done all you can, and you have to get your sleep. Go on!"

Isá complained loudly to Juliana, "You have no business up at this late hour, Juliana, and you know it. No good can come of your working at this time of the night. It's not good to tempt the Devil in the midnight hours. That's when the Duendes, the little spirits, come out and give you dreams. Don't forget to pray over your work. Now, don't you be soiling yourself. I don't want to wake up to any messes, you hear me? ¡Buenas noches!"

Juliana sat in her wheelchair in the dining room in a long bata that covered her legs and kept them warm. The ample dress gave her room to move her arms and allowed her movement when her legs or feet jerked in a reflexive action, as they sometimes were wont to do. She never knew when those involuntary movements would come on, and sometimes they embarrassed her.

Harrumphing and complaining, Isá set up Juliana's tools and her paints. Mamá Emilia kissed her goodnight with a look of pain. Her headaches were getting worse, and the only thing that brought relief was a pill that made her sleepy and gave her gas. Her life was disrupted by the headaches. And there seemed to be no relief. Reluctantly she made her way to her bedroom, looking wistfully toward Arnulfo's locked room. He was out again. She didn't know when he would come back. And when he did, she doubted if she would hear him. The headaches were beginning to affect him as well, as no one was around to warm up his calditos and güisos and make him red or green enchiladas at any time of the day or night. For sure, after 8:00 P.M. Isá was off the payroll. Ay, life in the Olivárez household was turvy-topsy!

After several hours of working, maybe longer, Juliana listened to make sure that everyone was asleep. She could hear her mother's distinctive snore, as well as Isá's roncas. Two completely different modalities and melodies, both hard to describe. She was an artist, she should be able to describe them.

First of all, her mother had permanently plugged-up sinuses caused by the nasal drip that had led to her dental problems. The sleeping pills added a little music to the already high-pitched snorkeling followed by that unusual little wheeze. She sounded like a trapped baby pig.

Isá, on the other hand, sounded like a man who had eaten and drunk too much and was fighting with an unknown assailant. There was a deep urgency in her snores; they came irregularly and were frightening to the uninitiated. And yet everyone in the house had gotten used to them. They didn't seem to bother anyone anymore except Isá, who was woken up often by her own deep bass sputterings followed by an occasional hiccup attack. She kept sugar water by her bed for just such moments.

After making sure that the snores were regular and confined to their quarters, Juliana put away her paints and moved to the phone. It was well past 2:00 A.M. She dialed Padre Manolito's private number, which she had memorized. No answer. The phone rang and rang. Again she tried calling. There was a long series of rings. Finally, a heavy, gravelly voice answered. It was El Padre!

"¡Coño! ¿Quién es, por Dios? ¿Bueno?"

"Padre Manolito," she whispered, making sure that her voice was quiet so no one could hear her. "Padre, it's me. Juliana Olivárez."

"Juliana! What are you doing calling me in the middle of the night? I'd just gotten to sleep. Do you know what time it is, princesa? ¡Coño! It's either very early or very late. What are you doing up at this hour? Are you all right?"

"Padre Manolito, can you hear my confession?'

"¿A estas horas? Confession, now? ¡Coño! Child, have you gone mad?"

"Padre, I need to confess. Please. Can you hear my confession?"

"But Juliana, I just confessed you on Tuesday. What have you done that needs confessing at este puta madre tiempo de la mañana?"

"Padre, please. Just listen to me."

"¡Qué putada! Excuse me, but Juliana, it's very late."

"You're my confessor . . . "

"Yes, I am."

"And my counselor . . . "

"I am that as well."

"Now hear my confession."

"Let me get my stole. It's in the other room."

"It's important. I have to talk to you. Now. I can't wait. If I wait, I won't be able to make my confession."

"Empieza, go on, start, I'll keep looking for my stole. I put it somewhere. I'm not sure where. Hijo de la . . . where's my stole? Can't we do this tomorrow? I could come over tomorrow, or you can come to the church . . . Coño, I can't find my stole, and I never listen to a confession without it!"

"Father forgive me, for I have sinned . . . it's been some days . . . "

"Three days . . . "

"It's been three days since my last confession . . . "

"Go on . . . "

"Padre Manolo, I've sinned in thought, word, and deed."

"Let's start with the deed first . . . or is it deeds?"

"Deeds first?"

"What have you done, Juliana?"

"Padre, I touched myself."

"You touched yourself?"

"I touched myself."

"Oh, I see. Where?"

"There and there. Up high and then down low."

"How high and how low?"

"Ay, Padre, this is hard for me. Don't ask me to explain."

"No sin is too great for God to absolve, child, no matter how evil or what time of the day or night. What did you touch first?"

"I touched my breasts."

"Both?"

"First one and then the other. And then both at the same time. And then I licked my finger and brought it to one nipple and made circles."

"Did you do it on both? I mean, that motion."

"Yes, Padre."

"¿Y qué más?"

"I put my hand between my legs and I felt my wetness inside. And then I tasted myself. It tasted salty but sweet. A little like fish juice but tastier. Is that what bacalao tastes like, Padre?"

"Hija, por Dios! I understand. You tasted yourself. And then . . . ?"

"And then, Padre, I felt a sudden shivering sensation you know where, and I kept touching myself until it went away, and then a heat came over me and I moaned and kept touching myself down there, and then I'd touch one breast and then another, and then I called out a man's name but not too loud because I was afraid Isá would hear me . . . "

"You called out a man's name?"

"Yes."

"How many times?"

"How many times did I call out?"

"No, how many times did you touch yourself up and down and inside, and then how many times did you have that fever that came and then went away . . . "

"Ay, Padre, many times. I lost count."

"You lost count!"

"I couldn't help myself. I was on fire."

"What name did you call out?"

"Padre, I can't say."

"You must tell me. I am your spiritual advisor, and your eternal soul is my charge. The sanctity of the sacrament must be honored even if it is early in the morning and we both have our pajamas on and the confession is taking place over the phone. You do have pajamas on, don't you? What are you wearing?"

"I have clothes on, Padre."

"You do?"

"I'm wearing my nightgown but no underwear."

"No underwear?"

(She didn't want to tell him she had a thick rubber pad underneath her and that Isá had put a thick night diaper on her. God help her, she was lying in the confessional! But that was the way it was; sometimes you had to make the best of the worst. And besides, he didn't need to know everything. He was a man, he didn't need to know. Well, he was a priest first and then a man, but anyway, it was none of his business, really!)

She could hear him straining on the other side of the line. What was he doing? By that time she had pulled her bata up and was moving her fingers inside the diaper. Forget that. Too much trouble. She wet her finger and circled a nipple. Ay!

"Child . . . child . . ."

She could hear his strangled, faraway voice.

"I just found my stole. Where were we? Ay, Dios en los cielos, where were we? You were telling me that you weren't wearing underwear . . ."

Juliana could hear him panting. Clearly, he was panting.

"I made love to the man in my dreams. It was so beautiful. I could have died without regretting anything."

"In your dreams. In your dreams! Well, that's one thing. Do you have these dreams often? And if you have these dreams, who is the man? You need to tell him. Who is this man, Juliana? Who is he?"

"I think about him all the time. I want to be with him and tell him I love him. But he's unreachable. Our love can never be."

"Is he married?"

"Yes. In a way. And no, in a way."

"A married man? Who is he? Hijo de la puta . . . "

"He's not married married, but yes, he's, he's . . . taken."

"Who is he? What is his name? I demand that you tell me his name, as your mentor, as someone who loves you, I mean your priest. Your priest, I am your priest. Who is he? ¿Quién es este capullo soplapollas mamonazo cabrón? Who is he? ¡Hijo de la puta madre! Coño!"

"I can't tell you, Padre. Not right now. But you know him. Very well. He's handsome and he's young. Too young and too handsome to be what he is. God forgive me for confessing it."

"You have sinned in word and thought, child. You have sinned against the Tabernacle of the Almighty."

"Yes, Padrecito. I have sinned."

"Who is he?"

"I am burning with love. I am consumed and on fire. Please, Padre, please help me!"

"Are you touching yourself?"

"Yes, Padre, I am. My breasts are his. One and then the other. They are his. My lips and my eyes are his. My hair is his. And my neck. My hands are his. My nails are his. My wrists and the inside of my arm are his. My armpits and my shoulders. My back and my backside. My sex is his. My body is completely his, as are my mind and my soul. They're his."

"Ay, Dios mío. Juliana. What are you saying? What are you doing? Are you alone? Can anyone hear you? Santa María Virgen del Carmen, what are you saying?"

"Only you can hear me, Padre. And God. God hears me."

"Yes, He does. God hears you. He loves you. God loves you. He loves you, Juliana. I love you. I love you, Juliana, I love you."

"And I love you. I love you, Padre. And I love God, Padre."

"I know you love God. And that is why I need to come and give you the Absolution."

"Yes, Padre, give me Absolution."

"Manolo, call me Manolo."

"I want the Absolution. I need the Absolution. Give me Absolution!"

"Absolution. Yes, the Absolution. I pronounce you free of guilt or shame. I relieve you of your obligations and your burdens. I pardon you, Juliana. I reconcile you to the Lord. I set you free. I unloosen your clothes, I mean your bonds."

"When, Padre, when? Come soon!"

"I will come. I will come . . . I'm coming . . . I'm coming . . . "

"Ay, Padre, I mean Manolo . . . "

"Princesa, I think I just came . . . The Absolution . . . yes, the Absolution. When will I find you there? When will you be alone?"

"The day after tomorrow at ten in the morning. Mamá Emilia and Isá are going on mandados, they have many errands, the grocery store, J. C. Penney's. Papá is leaving them at the mall. Mamá's borrowing my extra wheelchair. She can't walk too well, and she gets dizzy. Padre, my Absolution! What is my Absolution? You almost forgot."

"Me forget, never! I was just cleaning up here. Five Our Fathers and Five Hail Marys. In the name of the Father, the Son, and the Holy Ghost."

"I'll be waiting for you. Come through the back door."

"Are you sure you'll be alone?"

"Yes, Padre, yes."

"Now go to sleep, my child."

"I can't sleep Padre. Can we talk some more?"

"I have heard your confession, mi reina, but I suppose we could talk a little while. Since we're up."

"Sometimes I stay up late and work. I'll sleep tomorrow."

"I can't talk too long, I have Mass at six. What time is it?"

"We could stay up and pray awhile."

"Try to get to sleep, you need your strength. ¡Coño, I know I need mine."

"Padre, do you understand? These days I'm awake . . . dreaming."

"I do."

"Ten o'clock."

"Ten o'clock. Padre, forgive me. Forgive me my sins."

"You are forgiven, child. Now go to sleep."

"Padre . . . "

"Si, mi Amor…"

"Padre, I'm afraid."

"You're strong, niña."

"No, Padre, but I want to be."

"Pray. Pray for forgiveness."

"And for love."

"For love."

"Amen."

"Amen. Buenas noches, Juliana."

"Buenas noches, Padre."

"Manolo. Call me Manolo. No, better yet, Manolito."

"Buenas noches, Manolito."

It was here they both paused and reflected on the enormity of their sins, and on all that had happened, could happen, or might never happen, and if it did happen . . . ¡Ay, Santa María, Madre de Dios!

There was a silence that can only come from the depths of inscrutable night. Those hours when the shadows are fullest and animal life is most fecund. The time when leaves move inward to protect themselves from the cold, and the stars are at their brightest and clearest in the heavens. The time when the ancestors come back to earth to stand in front of you and say things to you but without using words. It was dawn. That special time. That time wherein all hope resides. The world is new. It is the time when all sins—past, present, and to come—are forgiven as surely as the sun rises on a new day.

CHAPTER SEVENTEEN

Absolution

Manolo would confess his sins, and they were legion, in a few days. But not today. Just as Juliana had made her confession last Tuesday and then again last night—or was it this morning?—Manolo Rodríguez would initiate the action of Divine Reconciliation knowing full well that his act of contrition would be heartfelt, dramatic, and completely bogus. He had sinned deeply and with abandon, and today he didn't care. A la Puta Madre. Add that full-bodied curse to his list of sins.

From all outward appearances, nothing had really happened. At least in the outward physical manifestation of the laws of cause and effect. On the other, deeper plane of intent and will, everything had happened and would continue happening. The only problem was that he didn't know what had really happened, and most of all how it happened. The real question was: What hadn't happened? The dilemma was also in the not happening and in the happening. One way or another, something had to happen to let the happening unfold. But how and when? Also, he didn't have an inkling of what would happen next, if anything would happen. And if it didn't or wouldn't happen, well, what would he do? He had no idea. All he knew was that he needed to make his way to Juliana Olivárez's home to give her Absolution. His Absolution. Not God's. God's would come later. For both him and her.

Now, there's a word for you. To absolve, untether, release, and forgive. First and foremost in the case of Juliana, there was nothing ever to forgive. Not in his book, and most likely not in the Holy Text of the one and only God's Manifesto of Truth. She was an unspoiled child, a handmaiden of the Divine. All one had to do was look at her. And he had looked long and hard.

She always sat in her wheelchair on the left-hand side of the church, in the first row, the row without a kneeler. Her mother was behind her in the second row. Doña Emilia couldn't kneel well because of her one short leg, so she sat during the entire Mass.

Manolo would approach that side of the church first during the communion offering, giving the host first to the mother and then to the daughter. He would lean into the mother, causing him to tilt slightly into the side of the wheelchair. From that very fleeting vantage point he could smell Juliana's full-bodied fragrance, and then as he arched in to give her the Divine Paraclete, he would sometimes touch her warm hands as she extended her open palms to him in complete submission and humility. There was something beautiful and sacred about the way her delicate fingers cupped upward, willing flowers of flesh.

Once he leaned too far in and had to grab her arm to right himself. It was a supple and strong arm that helped him straighten out. She was not a weak woman, by any means, and that he knew from that quick furtive touch that saved him from pitching forward and embarrassing himself in front of the congregation. Not that they were looking at him or cared what he said, or that he had spent long hours in the hellhole of his little house, that either too cold or too hot ugly hut that passed as his living quarters, writing another sermon that would go unloved and unheard. ¡Coño!

As he looked out—not to a sea of animated and interested faces, but to a miasmic wall of confused stares—a few of the elect nodded in agreement at some irrefutable truth, but many more stared back vacantly or dipped their chins with fatigue, their eyes closed in half-sleep. Worse were the ones who looked somewhat alert but couldn't give a damn about either him or God. Yes, the yawling yawning were the worst, those who planned their day's activities while in a wooden pew in Mass leaning on the seat and never kneeling as they should as they kept looking at their watches and then in loud stentorian voices intoned an amen as they rose stiffly and most piously. Let them all burn in Hell.

They were far removed from God. Tan lejos como un culo de gato. It was a phrase his father used for something very far away. The asshole of a cat.

It wasn't surprising that he couldn't help but stare at Juliana during the Credo and then the Gospel, but most especially the sermon, which found him broadcasting his homilies to the left side of Santa Eulalia Church. Mercifully, Lorenza Tampiraños sat on the right side. He avoided her gumming and snickling with her barely clinging false teeth. He skimmed over the tops of the heads of a few other regulars who weren't worth looking at for their open-mouthed expressions of complete incomprehension or vapid indifference. They were spiritual swine and not worth a glance.

Only Juliana Olivárez, the town's most beautiful woman despite her short legs and small feet, was worth a second and third and fourth look. The lower part of her anatomy was always covered. Often after seeing a crippled person, Manolo paused for a moment of prayer as he imagined them whole, as God had originally intended, but for the need of their mortal soul to come into this world jodidos por una razón u otra with some spiritual need to absolve or absorb.

Yes, for some reason, and this was rooted in the concept of original sin and the need to expiate something or other in this life or another, the very lovely Juliana Olivárez had come into this valley of tears and sorrows the happiest of cojas. Her illness, if you could call it that, never seemed to bother her, and for all intents and purposes she was the most complete and well-adjusted person, male or female, he had ever met in her condition, or in any condition when you came down to it, on this continent or any other.

Despite being a Catholic priest, Manolo believed in reincarnation and past lives. He also believed that each of us chooses our birth parents long before we come into physical being, a manifestation of the ultimate divine. In spite of his belief in what his mother called Oriental babosadas, he still pondered his unavoidable bafflement and dismay at finding out that Arnulfo Olivárez was Juliana's flesh-and-blood father. No, it wasn't true. It couldn't be true.

Surely Emilia Olivárez had once had a youthful discretion and gave birth to Juliana before she met Arnulfo. Such a perfect soul couldn't have emerged from such a polluted vessel as Arnulfo Olivárez! Padre Manolo continued to probe his hypothesis during Doña Emilia's weekly confessions, but so far nothing had come to light to shed any insight on his theory. He knew in his heart that she had commingled with someone before Arnulfo, he just couldn't prove it. The name José Victor kept popping into his mind. José Victor. That was the name he started calling Juliana's imagined true-blood father to himself.

Juliana Olivárez was a precious being he had come to love. And he knew that she was the living embodiment of her mother's carnal and doomed love for an unnamed lover. José Victor? It was an intriguing theory, one he hoped to someday prove. But for now he had to content himself with looking at la Señorita Juliana Olivárez, the spirit child of a forbidden, passionate, and reprobate love.

Looking out at that dead sea of errant souls, Manolo felt a bitter salty bile in his mouth. What was he doing here? Why wasn't he in Madrid?

Manolo's flock was a ragtag group of half-believers, infidels misinformed and despairing. Why was he so cynical and bereft of joy? What was the story he told people? Where did he come from, and what was his comezón, besides longing for love, the flesh aside, and that too, the flesh of that sweet girl. The one. The only. The holy. The one true Queen of Comezón.

Manolo had been the sacrificial lamb in his family; he was the one elected to be the priest. His mother, María del Carmen, had chosen him from birth to serve the family in this life and in the other. His path was chosen and set for him, and he knew it. He decided to excel at his carrera, but it was a heartless task and career that he nevertheless embraced as one would the caress of an aging aunt, his best years spent in Madrid, his exile and cross his immigration to the United States. He was a Jesuit, and as a bright young priest he should have been sent to Rome to study.

He was misled by his great-uncle Padre Sebastian Rodríguez, who had come to the U.S. as a priest and had promised his parishioners he would send someone back to the world that had embraced and loved him, and where he had died penniless, defrocked, living under the care of a woman who was paid by the estate of a wealthy older benefactress who had once been his lover. All of this Manolo did not learn until he had moved to Comezón and realized it was too late to return to Madrid. Grudgingly he took up the mantle of poor Padre Sebastian and decided to stay on.

Against his will, Manolo had come to the U.S., and to Comezón, this backwater community without culture, language, or even good sausage, its traditions an amalgamation of folk religion and quackery. He, who came from the perceived darkness of the old country, with its burden of centuries, encountered a truly loose way of living, at once formal, traditional, and skewed. He would never understand this border between the two worlds—each dependent on the other—each with its dreams. Who were these people?

And who was Juliana Olivárez?

Manolo tried to understand this frantic fanatic need of humans to save one another, their seemingly useless attempts to resurrect hope within themselves by giving selflessly to those less fortunate, most especially to those who were both attractive and crippled. Was he, too, guilty of this sin? Why was he attracted to this girl? Would he have loved her less if she had legs or was complete? No, he loved her more because she was needy and couldn't walk. And because she had a mind that was stronger and more noble than his, and yes, because her breasts were beautiful. He wanted to make love to her, not violently but tenderly, and without a clock ticking in the background. He wanted to know her flesh, he who had made a vow of celibacy on God's holy altar in La Catedral de la Almudena, named for Nuestra Señora de la Almudena, the female patron saint of Madrid.

As a young seminarian, he thought he'd fallen in love with his cousin Merecedes's best friend. Inez was her name, and she was attracted to him as well. They did, in fact, consummate their affair, but the ending was unsatisfactory. Inez disappeared one day without a word, never to be found. He had decided to leave the priesthood to pursue the romance and marry Inez but then found it was unnecessary. Since then he had buried himself in his work and knew that someday he would minister in a foreign country. Perhaps in the Congo or the rain forest. But little did he know how truly foreign his post would be. His cross and martyrdom was named Comezón, Nuevo México. The flaming, itching culo of the universe.

Looking out to the unfaithful, he realized the difficulty of the sermon he was about to deliver. He had labored over it since Juliana had called him on the phone. When was that? A day ago, two days ago? Since then he had felt feverish with strange aches and pains. Did he have the swine flu? He'd refused the shot and now was sorry. And then again he wasn't, as he knew someone older who had died of the shot, and someone young as well. The U.S. government was attempting to rid itself of the unwanted— the old and the young—the lame and the diseased—and those who survived now had microchips in their bodies that could be traced even to the shithouse. Oh yes, it was true. He'd read about it back in Spain and was sure that nefarious world powers were plotting the downfall of the crippled, the senile, and the syphilitic. And who knows, it might not be such a bad idea. He trusted no governments, no mass programs of health, and much less the local doctor, who also worked part-time as a realtor and had amassed a fortune selling fake adobe houses to elderly white people who moved into the valley for their health. A few of them were starting to come to the Saturday night Mass, and they were a welcome addition to the church's revenue. Most of them were stiffbodied, hard of hearing, and totally devoid of culture, even more so than the natives, and he held a healthy disdain for their meddling, pandering ways, but what could he do? They were the moneyed elite and the new parishioners of Santa Eulalia, they with their honey-colored eyes and bobbling arthritic walks, their short white hair sticking out this way and that, their skin pasty and flabby, with the texture of wrinkled chicken meat. They smelled of swimming pool chlorine and insect repellent and were always on time to Mass and late to leave, calling out with accents that bleated and brayed, "Evening, Father Man-oh-low." One had even called him Father Manilow, like the limp-wristed singer with the greyhound-colored eyes and the big nose. But there was nothing to do but take their money and look the other way.

Manolo looked out to the audience of faces, most of them long-time Comezónites. The sermon had begun roughly the day before. He had labored over it all day and long into the night.

ABSOLUTION
By Padre Manolo Rodríguez
One day, dear brethren (they weren't so dear, but after all, this was a sermon on forgiveness)
 One day (when?)
 One day, dear brethren. Dear Ones? My children?
 Dear brethren, one day I pray you will forgive me of my sins, the way I have already forgiven you.

Was that last sentence too arrogant? Hell, yes! He'd forgiven them for keeping him out too late and waking him up too early, for feeding him bad food or nothing at all. He'd forgiven them for assuming, supposing, intercepting, interloping, and intruding. Also for their thousand and more petty sins: forgotten Masses, for not praying, for praying too much, for not loving enough or too much, for touching themselves too much or other people that they shouldn't be touching, for missed opportunities of grace, for this, for that, all egotistic self-absorbed and indulgent behavior. Hell was paved with little sins, the venial sins building up over time to nothing more than one really big sin, the sin of overindulgence. Even the mortal sins were tame and easily repairable with a 5-and-5. Five Hail Marys. Five Our Fathers. Oh, the same tedious and boring 5-and-5! The worst sins of all were usually covered by a rosary or two. ¡Ay, humanidad! Blazing, blind humanity!

He loved them so. No, gente, it was true. Despite the fact that he was the chosen sacrificial lamb of his family—he truly loved the idea of healing the world, one living soul at a time. And God Bless Her, he had chosen Juliana Olivárez as the one soul who was worthy of salvation and his special ministrations. Her potential for sainthood was enormous. And the surprising thing was that she had no inkling of her majesty.

Manolo Rodríguez had come to Comezón with such hope, such promise. He had come here to save his immortal soul. How little he knew then—that in fact he would lose both heart and soul here. And more . . . honor and pride. He was startled when his plane flew over the great vast sea of blue-gray earth. He had never noticed before how mysterious and ethereal the land looked from a plane. How did the earth become so blue?

Was it the memory of water this parched land remembered? Was it a teeming of underground life lifting itself up to the sun, the mountains reaching to a ceiling of stark blue sky? Was it the blue of the ocean calling him home?

Oh, this blue earth, this desolate sorrowful llano of longing, was this blueness to be his? Would it envelop him in its magical unknown vastness and bring him peace? It was that idea and ideal that had sent him forth—from the sureness of his dark known land—to the surprising shock of blue, blue sky, blue land, blue mountains.

The mountains were called Las Lágrimas for the tears of God. In his previous world, his God had often cried. He was a bloody, battered Christ who had been scorned and spat upon. In Comezón, his concept of God began to change. Imperceptibly at first, and then with a growing intensity, Manolo's God became a nicer man.

And sometimes, to his great amazement, as he was praying alone in Santa Eulalia Church in front of the side altar where he liked to meditate in front of the statue of Saint Francis, or in his private prayer spot at home, in front of a picture of La Virgen del Carmen on his leather-covered kneeler that was cracked and sometimes pinched his skin and which he accepted as just another cross, he began to see the face of God shifting in front of him.

Sometimes God now appeared to him with the face of an old woman with kind, loving dark brown eyes and weathered skin, burned from hours of labor in the sun. She was an Obrera God, a worker en los files, as people called the fields here. He called her La Viejita Milagrosa. She knew the hardness of dry earth and the miracle of growth: plots of chile, onion, iceberg lettuce, cotton, corn, and alfalfa, dry weather crops, and the harvest of a lonesome, nearly forgotten land that had burnished and bronzed the luminescent skin of this woman who came to him from out of the darkness of his dreams. He was startled to see her at first, and then he came to look for her. She brought him a quiet peace, a respite from the tumultuous thoughts that moved within him, a churning wave of uncertainty and dread. For the first time in his life, Manolo was afraid. Of what or of whom, he wasn't quite sure. And this not knowing, this not understanding, was what caused him more pain and confusion.

Only La Viejita Milagrosa brought him peace. Last night, or was it days ago, Juliana had called him in the middle of the night, or was it morning, he couldn't remember. He'd fallen into a hard sleep. Always La Viejita came to him as a colorful and lively presence, and now she stood before him, energetic, fun-loving, and wanting to dance. She extended a sunburned arm to him— her hands graciously coaxing him to join her. A music he'd never heard played in the background, and he, Manolo Rodríguez, a non-dancer, danced with La Viejita, bodies not touching but somehow melding, as a warmth of love enveloped him. He stood on blue land, and suddenly a winding metal stairway stood in front of him that moved to blue sky. Something beckoned him, and he began to climb. Oh, dream stairway, stairway of old in dream! Stairway with the missing rungs, with uneven steps, no steps, stairway to who knows where, dangerous, perilous stairway, I know you I know you. He climbed that ethereal, frightful, and yes, desired stairway, and still it led him on.

La Viejita sang to him. First in that droning ecstasy like the chorus of women's voices at Santa Eulalia, that off-key whine, that utterly pitchless and indescribable chant epitomized by the terrible voice of Lorenza Tampiraños, the toothless devout whose low gurgling passed as song. He turned his head away to see Juliana sun-framed in front of him. He heard her clear, strong soprano singing that song, that old song, the song of all the ancestors come and gone. "Bendito, bendito, bendito sea Dios. Los Angeles les cantan . . . y alaban a Dios."

Juliana was the missing rung, the step, the leap. And he would crawl to her even if she led him to Hell and back.

He began his sermon, his voice small and at the back of his throat. He sounded like a drowning man: "My children, one day I pray you will forgive me of my sins, the way I have already forgiven you . . ."

Juliana was waiting for him to give her Absolution, and as he turned to face her on the left side of the church, the living, pulsing side of hope, he felt her dark, burning eyes on him, breaking into him like the mighty current of his damnation or his salvation, he wasn't sure which.

CHAPTER EIGHTEEN

¡Salud, Amor y Pesetas!

There was a constant, steady noise. Someone was knocking on the door! ¡Coño! Who was it at this hour? Manolo stirred fitfully. Unwillingly, he finally dragged himself out of bed and peered through the too-bright yellow curtain of his bedroom. It was Don Tomás Revueltas, who relentlessly rapped on the door and called out in a shrill voice, "Padre, Padre!" His voice was high-pitched and sounded like a wild squawk. All the world—meaning most of Comezón—could probably hear him and his squealy parrot dirge. The man was nearly deaf and didn't realize how loud he was yelling.

"¡Coño!" Manolo answered back, his voice submerged, far away. He filled the air with puta madres and caraja viejas and other harsh and vile expletives like arrima tu prima cabrón y déspues tu madre porque me cago en la virgen santa quien te parió that were all lost on Don Tomás.

After what seemed an eternity, Manolo lumbered like a drunken man to the front door and opened it. Suddenly he realized he was naked. He usually slept in silk pajamas that his mother, Doña María del Carmen, sent him from a specialty shop on la calle Jorge Juan near the Museo Arqueológico Nacional in Madrid. His mother's friend, the Spanish designer Meye Maier, had just died. What had happened and what would happen to his preferred underwear? Ay, he sighed as he leaned up against the wall. He was a lost man!

He rushed a flustered, red-faced, confused, and sputtering Don Tomás into the small dark house as he grabbed a stole that was draped on the couch and put it on, but not before blessing and kissing it. Realizing it covered little, he pulled a chasuble on top, but quickly removed it. "Pica," he explained to Don Tomás, meaning the wool itched. He grabbed a small nearby tablecloth and sat down on the lumpy ancient coyote-colored sofa, shielding his unstable privates from Don Tomás, who was clearly impressed by El Padre's large member and his prodigious balls that rested like two large flesh-colored cupcakes on the tablecloth, just waiting to be served.

"Padre, Padre! What happened? Everyone was in the church waiting for the Mass, and you weren't there! You also missed the Altar Society meeting and then the Third Order of St. Francis lunch. I was sent to find you. Are you all right?"

"Can't you see I'm sick, man?"

"Yes, I mean, no," Don Tomás sputtered. It was true. Don Tomás could see that El Padre was not himself as he sat on the couch giggling like a schoolboy wrapped in a lacy tablecloth, a hand-knit mantel made by La Hermana Dometilia Domínguez, his very discernible male organ tenting through one of the scalloped edges that showed an airborne Holy Spirit, its wings white against a blue sky. Don Tomás smiled to himself as he imagined La Hermana seeing her handiwork put to such elegant use.

"I've been very, very sick, but not in the way you think, Don Tomás," Manolito said, out of breath. "Coño, hombre, sit down. Sit down, por favor, you're making me dizzy!"

Oh, vile is the lie! Dark and evil is the lie! But darker and more evil is the truth! What was the truth? Manolo wasn't sure at this time of the morning, was it morning?

As it turned out, it was 2:00 in the afternoon, and El Padre Manolo had left the 7:30 Mass group waiting, as well as skipped the Altar Society at their 10:00 meeting and the Third Order of St. Francis devotees plantadas, flat-out forgotten, at their monthly luncheon meeting at the parish hall with a kitchen full of paella that someone had made in honor of him and his culinary heritage.

The last straw was the luncheon, and nobody could understand how El Padrecito could be absent from a meal that represented what to him meant everything: Ethpaña! Ethpaña! Ethpaña! Paella!

Ceviche! Gazpacho! La Conquistadora! Not to mention Real Madrid! Don Tomás had even snuck in a bottle of Rosa Tinta, as he knew El Padrecito liked his wine. This latter event, the missed Franciscan order meeting, had been el Colmo—the zenith, the final turning point of what came to be known as the Downward Spiral of a Once Holy Man. This overlooked function was the one that everyone in each organization, they being one and the same people, figured had to be the reason that something sinister had happened to El Santo Padre.

Little did they realize that at the time of the Mass and the meeting and the luncheon, their living saint was half-asleep and half-awake twangling on his guitarrito, playing it with a mighty and creative hand as he alternately saw the face of his lost love Inez La Española, his tiny-bodied little harpy with her thin dark lips and her panochita like a well-turned Tortilla Española, in competition with the great breasts of his other love, the crippled girl Juliana, who haunted him now with her dark and fierce energy that had sapped him so recently and caused him to lose all sense of time and space. He alternated between their two faces, one hard, one soft, one dark, one light, both hated, both loved. At one point La Viejita Milagrosa's face passed in front of him and he cried out, but maybe it was only Don Tomás's tremulous and fearful voice that caused him to awaken with a jolt. And yet, and yet, just thinking about Inez/Juliana made him salivate and yank his arma even more. He felt his nabo, and it was sore. He'd been asleep too long with too many dreams.

Don Tomás was the Distress Emissary, and to him fell the unpleasant task of finding El Padre in a state of total disarray and desorden and then asking him what the hell was wrong. Just in case there was some untoward feeling or something that needed to be resolved through a Higher Power with or without prayer, Don Tomás had brought the aforementioned bottle of Rosa Tinta with him as a backup. One could never be too sure when and if a bracer would be needed to steel one's nerves. He also had his rosary in his back pocket and a novena to Saint Jude, the patron saint of Impossible Cases, in his wallet, along with his good-luck horsehair key chain that his mother had given him when he left home back in Durango, Durango en el año del caldo.

An hour later, both men sat on that same lumpy sable-colored couch in the living room. They had finished the inferior Rosa Tinta and moved on to a bottle of Riojas that Manolo had in reserve for such an occasion. What was the occasion? Half wake, part wedding, a little of the Last Absolution, more than a little Confirmation, and most definitely a necessary Confession. Whatever was said between those two men stayed with them.

After all was said and done and then said and said again amidst all the gossip and the shame and the sheer out-and-out audacity of it all, and when the repercussions came around and back again and backfired and bit the town of Comezón on its nalgas, Don Tomás was never to breathe a word of what transpired during that hour or two or three between him and El Padre Manolito.

What was said and to whom? Don Tomás actually didn't remember too much. He remembered sobbing, but he wasn't sure if it had been him or El Padre crying his heart out. He did remember lying down at one point and falling asleep, and when he woke up, El Padre was gone. They'd prayed the rosary, or had he prayed it alone? Both had confessed, but to what he wasn't sure. One of them had made sandwiches, he thought that was El Padre. He remembered eating a very delicious ham sandwich. And he remembered they drank and drank and drank. At one point El Padre was naked, and then when Don Tomás woke up from a tormented sleep in which he roamed around that underground tunnel he was wont to visit nights, that familiar hellhole of his nighttime yearnings, he realized he was naked as well.

Don Tomás didn't remember taking off his clothes, but he must have because they were neatly folded next to him on the floor. He was the only one who folded things that way, with the shirt side in and the chones tucked in the legs and the pants sideways, the cuff folded in like a little shelf. He must have taken off his clothing at some point in solidarity with El Padrecito, but he couldn't remember exactly when he disrobed, whether it was before or after the ham sandwich. It must have been before because he found quite a few crumbs in his thinning pubic hair. Garlic bread.

It all came so easily, and it was without embarrassment or shame. Why should two friends be cowardly in their true feelings, having divested in that short time whatever lay between them as men, men who were sensitive to the world, conscious men who didn't have the time or the need to hide their true selves from each other, one a misunderstood and lonely old man, the other a lost saver of souls who wasn't sure he would ever save his own.

They were in the same boat, this being the long old-fashioned yellow sow belly–colored couch rolling and rocking to their private sorrows and laughing with joy at their impending dissolution, call it by its true name, freedom, at least that is what they said then to each other in the strictest confidence, without a backward glance to the open portals of a blazing Hell.

At one point one of them took a knife and drew blood to seal their pact, and the other did the same. Whose knife was it? And what was it they professed to uphold or sanctify with this gesture of brotherhood? Maybe this was when Don Tomás got naked; it was hard to remember. What mattered was that now they were brothers in blood.

Don Tomás knew that he would always believe in the young priest, no matter what anyone said to the contrary about him. Manolo knew that he would never meet a kinder man. Both fell in love with each other as men can fall in love with the missing in themselves, the brave and good in another man, and the blessed memory of how they once had been, could be, once were, were likely to be, aspired to be, and dreamed themselves to be. Each saw in the other good and bad, and that was both bad and good. With each sip of wine came greater clarity. Don Tomás was impressed. The young priest, who wasn't really that young, could hold his own in the drinking realm. And yes, his pinga was impressive and a waste for a young priest. And the old man, who wasn't so old, matched him one on one at the place where faith and hope meet. All said, it was an afternoon to remember, and they did, each feeling tenderness for the other, the listener and the listened. The priest became a man, and a man became a priest. ¡Salud, amor, pesetas y tiempo para gastarlas!

Who knew how soon the world as they knew it would come crashing down, a pinche derrumbamiento, a terrible landslide eclipsing all that was known, all that was good. This, too, they would both remember and regret.

CHAPTER NINETEEN

Sounds of the World

Arnulfo Olivárez sat on a Plaza bench listening to the sounds of the world. His throat was dry and full of dust. He'd been caught in a sudden remolino, a freakish dust storm, and had to sit down to brace himself against the attack. The predicted gusts had reached forty miles an hour, leaving him wind-beaten and sandblasted. Most of his life he had felt that same way—sunburned, a little raw on the outside, with a deep, dry interior that needed water and a long rest. Dr. Marías had prescribed six months by a quiet lake some years back, but he had not been able to comply. Six months by a quiet lake! Ha! Him? How? What would he do so far away from Comezón? And where would he go to find that remote lake?

What had brought on the cancer? Was it the dust, the interminable wind, or the unsatisfied, always persistent, always unattainable longing to rest?

We come into this world esquintles crying out and leave it the same way, clutching for a teta, some teat to calm us down. What was it that would bring him peace? Loving and being loved could be that balm; maybe it could still be his healing.

He remembered the sounds he most loved: the roar of the Fiesta crowd, someone calling out loudly "¡Qué Viva la Fiesta! Bravo!" Someone behind him gave a grito and someone else a long chiflada, whistling in that way that made him want to get up and throw his mariachi hat in the air.

A young woman, well, she was actually a not-so-young woman with dry, thin painted hair and tense red lips, sang the National Anthem, and most everyone stood and put their right hand over their heart. Some even sang along to that mierda. Ooohh say can you sí . . . He hummed a bit of the song, but the words escaped him. His hand stayed in his pocket adrede, and there it would stay. He was a rebellious Napoleon. Hypocrites!

He still remembered how in the late 1930s and early 1940s many undocumented men, farm workers and their families, had been rounded up, manacled, and forced to walk the dusty streets of his town, yes, his town, Comezón. He felt a terrible shame on seeing Don Elberto Enríquez in that group, his father's best friend, and Elberto's son Librado, who had grown up with Arnulfo and helped on the farm. Both of them had their hands bound, and they shuffled along sadly. There was nothing he could do but watch the chota, the damned police, take them away. No one ever heard from them again, that is, until Librado sent word through his sister, Chela, who was married to a black soldier at Fort Bliss, that their father had died of a broken heart in Chihuahua. Arnulfo asked himself, how could he salute a country that would do this to its people?

And now things were worse. There was so much racism, exclusion, and downright fear that sent hardworking people back to México. Once they got home, men were being decapitated, young women raped and murdered and thrown out on street corners, children buried in suitcases, and all for what? Money, money, money, power, power, power. Mierda, mierda, mierda. He could not honor a country that would punish kind and decent men like Don Elberto and Librado. He'd just heard that someone in Morelia, Michoacán, that beautiful place full of art and culture, had been hacked into four parts and that the pieces had been scattered in different sections of town. What kind of monster would do that? Oh, it was a hard world to understand. He never would. He was a man who lived fully and wanted the same for others. There was no need to abuse, to maim, and to kill. And yet, had he been responsible for sorrow? Well, yes, he had to admit it, he had.

First there was his mother, Doña Lolita, and then his wife, Emilia. He didn't like thinking about his mother. Poor thing. She was a simple girl from a small village in México, and she was unschooled, as many women were in those days. His father had been taken with her as men are taken with the innocent and the pure. But their temperaments were unsuited, and as sure as the sun rose and the moon beguiled and bewitched, Bascual had found another woman who bore him children. Two families came from that proud, haughty root of a man he never truly loved. The children, all of them, and there were many, battled all their lives to find themselves in the giant shade of that great álamo, the father who loved each child less and less the more his seed was spread around that burnt land. Arnulfo was the second-to-the-last child, and every one of them was now dead. Nothing was left. The old dreams left behind in that little poverty-stricken and haunted village called Refugio de Los Santos. The trouble was that the village was no refuge, and as far as he knew, no one there was a saint.

México had been his beginning, and if he could, he would make it his ending place. Oh, he wanted to die in Comezón, but he wouldn't mind if a few of his ashes were scattered there in Refugio, as the people called that little way station off the carretera going to México City, the only signpost a large, looming ancient nopal that the locals called Papá Grande. A path was cut through the cactus and led back a ways to a small outcropping of houses. That was where Refugio was, and that was where Arnulfo's people came from, that labyrinth of pads and thistles. What he wouldn't give for one of his mother's tacos de nopal!

What was happening to his beloved México? The Evil began this side of the border and spread south, touching goodness and infecting it without regard to age or background. That was what it was, Evil, pure and simple. He had heard too many stories, known too much, and each retelling of the same old Evil story chilled his heart. What was he to do? It was time for revolution! It was time for the people to stand up. Oh, if only he were younger. And if only he had been less fearful when he was younger! What would he have done? What more can be done to a people than what the United States has done to the people of the world, even its so-called own? He was an American, but he would never be an American, not fully. He didn't want to believe that his country would kill immigrants and the women and children in other countries not their own. Not like this, not this way. Never. And all because of power and money and oil and drugs. U.S. weapons moving through the many labyrinthine Juárez tunnels, and drugs from México going back the same way. He had heard things, too many things, and too many people had come seeking a safe house with him or those he knew and trusted. There were too many rumors, too much darkness, and what could he do about it sitting on the Plaza, winded and out of breath?

He could hear his heart beating rapidly and felt the wind searing his very being. And why should he curse the wind, that impetuous, childlike, never-to-be reckoned-with-or-explained wind, that never-to-be-taken-for-granted wind that came up one minute soft and caressing like the gentle hand of an experienced and kind woman and then turned the corner, slapping you like a surly puta with a sudden blast that nearly knocked you down and then kicked you in the heart. El Chingón was puro chingón. He was wind-tired and had been so a very long time. His throat was dry and sore and clogged; he spat out an ugly brown clump of mucus that was flecked with blood. He wanted to die, and yes, too soon, his wish would be granted.

But for now there were the sounds of the world. The Fiesta swirled around him in memory. Never mind that a surly dog was barking somewhere nearby, and he could hear the long wail of a child being abused by a screaming parent in the apartments behind the Plaza. He immediately transposed these sounds to others, instead hearing things inside his head that he never wanted to go away. He heard the clamoring crowd, the hushed expectation of their hunger, and behind it all he heard the soft voice of a woman calling his name: "Arnulfo, Arnulfo, mi amor. ¿Dónde estas? Are you there?" And finally, finally he heard her quick exhalation of breath and a long contented sigh.

For a moment time stood still. And then the wind snapped at him and made him cough.

Last year's Fiesta was over, but there was always another one coming up. His year was framed by two important dates: Cinco de Mayo and Diez y Seis de Septiembre. These two dates were the two channels of his creativity, the only two times when the artist in him shone bright and glorious. If he had his choice, he wanted to die on Diez y Seis de Septiembre, the preferred festival, on top of his bed after returning from the dance on Saturday night, the tumultuous echo of the crowd a swirling vortex around his bed, as he announced the beginning of the Fiesta. He would have danced all night in the Plaza with the ghost woman who called to him, in between his responsibilities as Master of Ceremonies. And when he finished the dance, he would see Doña María in the shadows and behind her Morning Light. But before, he would call out to María Zavala, nicknamed La Destroyer, to ease his misery, she who mercifully killed the lame and the diseased. She was the one to rectify things justly. She would be fast and kind. She was said to have helped those who fell in battle during the Mexican Revolution to die a faster and less painful death. Certainly she would help him as well.

It was at that moment he felt a great hope rising up in him, causing him to catch his breath. At that moment he was a young man, and the world awaited his magnificence. He wanted to die like that, wearing his mariachi suit, the still-resounding echo of the crowd's excitement coming around again as he felt that catch in his throat and the pulse of his living blood. ¡Ajjjjuuaaaa!

But instead his throat burned as if he had ingested the long, sharp showman's sword, opening up to receive what to many appeared to be a mortal wound, the back of his throat pepper raw, the esophagus blocked and inflamed with some unknown dousing. It was the old hard spot on this throat where the cancer had begun that would eventually kill him. He was the fire eater, and the fire was consuming him each day as he swallowed back the unthinkable outrages and lies of a world he both loved and hated. Why couldn't he be happy? What held him back, and what would he have to do to find peace? Was there no one out there to help him? He had forgotten how to love. Or rather, he had never learned how to love. And the scraping of that vile sword, the long-standing metal choking, was what caused him to look out to the wind and ask it to sleep, just sleep, my furious and beloved little wind, just sleep. You who are so defiant and rebellious and without reason. Sleep!

There was no sleep for him, not yet. And this reality lay heavy on him as he sat on the Plaza bench, once again deciding which way to go, home or down the street the other way, into forgetfulness. El Mil was open and beckoning.

If only things hadn't changed so much. Things used to be better, life was more pleasant. And yes, he had been younger.

He was old, but he was not a viejito; there was a difference.

Cinco de Mayo had become a gabacho holiday, an American party party, college frat boys getting drunk and carrying on with a license to hunt and roam. There was something ugly about it now. No one remembered what Cinco de Mayo meant, the Battle of Puebla and freedom from France. Diez y Seis de Septiembre was more of a Mexicano holiday, for real Mexicanos, but then again, things had been blurred, and all the holiday meant again was getting drunk and making pedo with your fellow fart-balls. What about the glorious grito of Padre Hidalgo and the lucha of all luchas? Where had all the fight gone from his people? Why were they buried up to their necks in Miller and Bud and Coors Light?

It was early afternoon and he was bone tired and sleepy, yes, very sleepy. His nights had been restless since he'd been to see his Brother Conquistador, el pinche Stanley Wabatt. He would never again sleep well until that final long and desired sleep of all sleeps. He was worried about Juliana. Who would take care of her after he died? Emilia couldn't lift her, and Isá was getting old. And besides, he didn't trust his beloved hijita to that tired-out old woman who cooked his food. She was a good cook, he couldn't deny that, but she was unkind and unloving to his daughter; he saw that every day. How was it Emilia never noticed? They were best friends, but she should have observed how Isá treated Juliana, with carelessness and disrespect.

Isá would stay with Emilia until Emilia died, of that he was sure, but how long would that be? How many Fiestas did he have left? One, two, three? However many, they were too few. Ay, que pinche vida—to give you false hope for joy and then hit you hard with the blasted wind of misery!

What could he do to rest his mind, which had him twirling this way and that like fluff from an álamo tree, sticking to you against your will. He would have to go home and talk to Emilia, tell her he'd made plans for Juliana, that she shouldn't worry, it would all work out. Would it? Lucinda would be mad, for nothing would go to her. And she had hinted to him time and again that she was glad to be part of the family, a member of the Olivárez clan. He knew she was lying, that her words were a sham, and that she only wanted what she felt was her part of her inheritance. She, the adopted one, was the luckiest. She could go on without feeling the curse. Yes, that's what it was, a family curse. Only Lucinda would be spared. Wouldn't she? No, for she was part of the curse as well. She was the fruit of that buried nopal needle in his heart, and no one could ever take out that spiny reminder of his lust.

Too many questions posed. Too many questions unanswered. Too many too many too many. All of it mierda. All he wanted to do was lie down and rest, but even that wasn't good enough. The rest was never rest, and the lying down was always full of dread. He wanted to be left alone, and then again he didn't. He wanted to be taken care of, and then again he didn't. He wanted to love, and then again he didn't. Jesucristo, it was a dark and pinche world! And only Jesús if he was the real God knew the sorrows of the world. He had something to say to that God. But first he would go to El Mil and have a shot of tequila to talk to *his* God so that the other God would have some time to get ready for him. He had a lot to say to *that* God. The God in God Bless America the Land of the Not So Free and the Home of the Not So Brave, the killer vengeful God who lurked behind the thin veneer of this land and all lands of the corrupt and the home of the depraved. What, dear God, had Don Elberto and Librado done to deserve their shame? Arnulfo wished he could cry. He couldn't and he wouldn't. Too many memories of injustice stung him. He longed for release in tears for those two, for those many. What had they done that merited death and destruction, a sad ending in the desert slumped up against a nopal in a no-man's-land, far away from all water, their bodies dried out, leached of life?

CHAPTER TWENTY

¡Mi Vientre, Jesús!

Juliana Olivárez had fallen asleep in her wheelchair in the living room. The phone was off the hook when Isá came in to fix breakfast. She hung it up and wheeled the still-sleeping Juliana back to her room, where she put her to bed. The girl was stiff with cold, and her feet were twisted inward more than usual. Yesterday she had looked more supple. It was as if she had crawled, no, clawed, inside herself during the night. What had happened? Isá would have to work her feet and legs hard later today. As ever, Juliana was an irritation. Isá had known when she took her into the living room last night that she was up to no good. The creature was perverse for all her saintly demeanor and sweetness. She was not to be trusted. But then again, who was to be trusted in this house of vipers? Certainly not Don Arnulfo. Maybe only Doña Emilia now that Lucinda had taken off with her cuschispete, that no-good long and rangy boy, the son of the meanest sonna beech este lado o el otro.

Who had Juliana been calling?

It was six in the morning, and no one else was up. Emilia was sleeping late these days because of her headaches and wouldn't wake up for a while. Don Arnulfo was locked in his room most likely, although she didn't know for sure because sometimes he slept elsewhere. Where, she wasn't certain. Several times she'd found him asleep in La Tumbita.

She had left him alone, not wanting to cause him embarrassment, although he knew that she'd seen him, and once she'd even covered him up with a serape she had in the back near her things. Why, she wasn't sure. She had no regard for him. He was simply an animal she fed. But she was respectful toward that large and reckless animal. She stayed out of his way, and the old buffalo stayed respectfully out of her way.

She would make his favorite food today, tripitas. That would settle him down. She just knew this day was going to be hell. She just knew. She could feel it in her vagina, yes, that's where she felt disruption, upheaval, and decay. She knew by twinges in there between the folds whether the day was going to go badly or well. And last night she hadn't slept through the night as she usually did. She lay in bed tossing and turning, her internal organs on fire. There was no stopping what was going to happen, whatever it was.

Juliana was overheated, overexcited, and very brittle. In addition, Doña Emilia wasn't feeling well, ay, she hadn't been well for some time now, and soon she wouldn't be able to walk. And her headaches, they were getting worse. She would often have to go to her room and lie down in darkness. Sometimes Isá could hear her crying in there. Isá would check in on her every once in a while and bring her agua de melón or her preferred agüita de sandía, which Emilia sweetened up even more with a teaspoon of honey.

Something was happening to Doña Emilia, but only Isá could see the decline. To Arnulfo his wife was a constant presence, always there, always in the way, like a familiar pet. ¡Je! The pet was more loved than the wife, and the wife was treated like an animal. Only the daughter, that little princess on her powerful throne, was adored. Santa Juliana, La Princesa, wasn't so high-and-mighty today. She had been a burden to carry to her bed, as she winched up and refused to lie flat, her body twisted in a strange S-shape. She moaned as if with a fever. She had soiled herself, and she had a mess of a time with that. It had taken Isá over an hour to get the girl cleaned up and in bed, where she should have stayed all night. Ay, to think now that she was sick! When Juliana got sick, it was a true sickness, and there was no telling how things would go. Isá would have to attend to her all day long, swabbing her with cool water and then oiling her feet and hands with her special aceite de marihuana.

Don Arnulfo, uúuuqueee, now there was illness personified. The only one who had been normal was Lucinda, and now she was gone, oh, she was gone, yes, she was gone. And if and when she came back, it would only be temporary. She was surely gone. Poor girl had never really lived here, just as Isá was a necessary guest. The two of them had found a strange friendship, a friendship founded on acknowledged misery, but a friendship nonetheless, and now it was over.

Lucinda had sealed her fate by taking off with Ruley Terrazas, Mata's son. Isá would have never picked that skinny long-legged boy with his already overbearing scent of sweat, a large man smell that followed him like a shadow. She could see the outline of his coiled penis raised taut in his jeans, declaring himself to all he came in contact with. He was a boy-man, but he had an organ the size of his father's, people said. And that tranca was rumored to be, well, it was rumored. Isá had never had much to do with men; what did she care about them, really? Women had always interested her more. Everything that a woman was or could do was of so much more interest than a man's action and being.

But no one messed with the Terrazas men; whatever they wanted, they got. She could see that now. Lucinda, just like all the women in the Olivárez house, was lost. She had picked up the curse when she was adopted into this festering familia. Rancho Olivárez! ¡Qué rancho ni que rancho! It was a sad plot of earth, un terrenito maldito.

Who had Juliana been speaking to?

She thought about this as she brought out the tripitas that were to be their dinner. Isá always bought her cow intestines from Lalo Móntez, a neighbor. She took them outside La Tumbita to clean them because they smelled bad.

She would boil them in a large pot with salt on the outdoor stove she had rigged up, out there behind La Tumbita. While the tripas were boiling, she chopped cilantro and onion and set that aside. When the tripas were soft, she rinsed and drained them.

She would then take some Morrell lard and put them in a hot disco, her special round frying pan that she had bought from a traveling salesman from México. She mixed the tripitas with her special secret recipe of red chile and seasonings. Once they were crispy, she placed the drained tripas in a casserole dish. She would chop them when they cooled down, and she would serve them in bite-size pieces with homemade tortillas de maíz and top the tacos with cilantro, cebollita, and limón.

Oh, she didn't care for them herself, but everyone who had ever eaten her tripitas had come back for more. Maybe that was why she was such a good cook; she loved cooking but not eating her own food. She was both involved and detached. She ate simply, no grease or sweets. That was why, even though she was in her mid-sixties, she had the figure of a much younger woman. It was startling to see a woman of her age, an ugly woman, let's admit it, with high and proud breasts and the strong, muscular legs of a woman in her twenties.

But today it wasn't Arnulfo or his beloved tripitas that concerned her. It was Doña Emilia, who was still sleeping, who was causing her untold worry. She was also preoccupied with Juliana, whom she now heard moaning in her room. No doubt her feet hurt her. Yes, she was unable to walk for her weakness, but there was some vestige of feeling in those misshapen, infantile limbs. Emilia would have to go see what she wanted and what she needed. She felt a sudden burning itch in her vagina. What good could come of this holy and terrible day?

Isá decided to wait on frying the tripitas. She would keep them in the refrigerator until the evening. No telling who would be eating and at what time and how things would turn out. She put the already cleaned tripas in a bowl, covered them with a cloth, and headed toward Doña Emilia's room. La Reina could wait.

Doña Emilia's room was locked, which was surprising. She, of all people, never locked her room. Nor did she believe that anyone should lock their door. Now, this was ironic, because everyone in this hot house locked their bedroom door, well, minus the

Little Queen. Her door was usually open. The other doors, Don Arnulfo's, Lucinda's, and Isá's, were now always locked. They had to be, for each of these people demanded and got their privacy.

Isá used to go into Lucinda's room sometimes when she was gone, as she had an extra key, and she would sit on her bed as she looked around the room: a white bedspread with a canopy top, a wooden chest of drawers painted white, a little desk where she kept her few books and what the teenagers called a boom box, a large beanbag chair where she sat watching her little television set in front of her bed, large pink throw pillows strewn throughout, several chairs, and a small fan. Everyone had a fan in their room; it was the only cooling to be had in their rooms at night, other than an open window that brought in whatever freshness there was outside.

Things in Lucinda's room were ordered: her posters of teenage singers, none of which Isá knew. A poster with the words If It Feels Good, Do It. Another poster with a small cat next to a girl holding a bouquet of daisies. Lucinda's room was always neat and smelled of a young girl's perfume. It had been pleasant in there until she started locking her door. Isá discovered the smell of cigarette smoke and then later marijuana, and she was sure that several times Lucinda had sneaked Ruley into her bedroom late at night. After a while the room began to smell different. There were other smells: moist, dark smells, the smell of people who were making love, that strange fish juice and powdery acrid smell of crotch and heated flesh, the smell of strong unfiltered cigarettes and old beer, and most recently the smell of vomit. Was Lucinda pregnant or was Ruley drinking too much? Either way, people were getting out of control and sick in the room. It pained Isá to know that her little girlfriend was gone forever. Lucinda had started leaving her clothes on top of her chairs, and now she never made her bed. Her sticky balled-up panties were scattered here and there, and she went days without showering and washing her hair, she who used to take such pride in her cleanliness and in how she looked. Now she wore ragged jeans with loose threads on the hems that trailed behind her, and her t-shirts were full of stains. Or else she wore low-cut tank tops, her firm young breasts peeking out of the stretchy cloth, announcing themselves to anyone who looked—and one had to look. She and Ruley had begun to look alike, brother and sister messes, steaming and distant, lost to themselves, with little regard for anyone else. It was a sad transformation, and one that happened so quickly. What had happened to the young girl Isá once knew, the one with dreams and hopes, the one who only wanted to leave Comezón and make something of her life?

Lucinda always locked her room now, and no one had a key. She herself had bought and changed the lock. The girl was handy at things like that and could match any man when it came to doing typical male things: she could fix machines and appliances and cars. She loved being outdoors, and it wasn't surprising that her room was off limits. No use trying to get inside to smell the sweet perfume anymore. She was a woman with her dark secrets, and her sex gave off the offal smell of men, one in particular, the long-limbed tempter Ruley Terrazas.

Where was Lucinda, anyway? She'd taken off with Ruley after the fiesta, and it took her days to come back. There had been an argument when she finally returned, and Arnulfo had thrown her out of the house, against Doña Emilia's wishes. Now she hardly slept here anymore. She was staying with Ruley at his family's house, and she told everyone they were getting married before the next fiesta in September.

Now it was July, that month of heat and sudden rain, that month of thunderstorms and double rainbows, that month of uncertainty and dread, too much or too little, that month of celebration and depression, that summer month when one wanted to sleep, sleep, sleep and not wake up. Here it was July 8, and all one could hope for was an unexpected rain. Ay, few enough people knew what it was to wait for rain!

Thank God the 4th of July was over, with its horrible rattling and ongoing fireworks, the intermittent blasts that had kept Isá and Chamorro awake, the smell of sulfur and smoke, the overheated streets with their shadowy mirage of rising heat. Following what seemed to be the hottest month in Comezón, July was lazy, sleepy, full of furious imaginings, restless sleep, and torpor. How could anyone do anything great when all you wanted to do was sleep or disappear from everyone who wanted something from you and from the endless chores that made up what was called a responsible life?

July was an ugly month in this regard. Its few joys included sandía and melón, any kind of melón, and a wet washrag behind the neck and on the arms, a reminder that the body could be soothed, at least temporarily. The other few consolations of this struggling time were the beautiful occasional nights of cooling woman wind blowing through the bedroom curtains, a gift unexpected and greatly loved. Sometimes Isá lay in bed listening to the sounds of birds trilling to each other in their five-note patterns. She became fond of one little bird in particular, whose time was between three and four, the sacred Mother Time, when life was forming in the darkness. The little bird was insistent but never hurried, beautiful to hear in her syncopated rhythm. What news did she convey? What stories did she tell? Who heard and answered back? When Isá did not sleep, as she hadn't lately, which was burdensome and unsettling, she listened in the early mornings for her bird, her little woman bird, a spirit strong and certain, and she felt some peace. If only the little bird could stop her dread and calm her fear.

Approaching Doña Emilia's room, she again felt the locked door. She called out: "Doña Emilia! Hermana! Are you all right?"

Emilia had had an episode two nights ago, and it was terrible to behold. Arnulfo wasn't home, and Lucinda was at Ruley's. Isá had come into the living room to see Doña Emilia sitting in the growing darkness. It was around 8:00 P.M. There was still sunlight, but soon the night would come on. The Lágrimas Mountains were dark blue in silhouette, their dark fingers probing the sky. The horizontal lenticular clouds fanned across the horizon, umbrellas of navy blue. Suddenly a wind came up from the southeast. It was more an eastern wind, but it wanted to head south. The wind was cooling down after the day's long heat and stirred the trees gently at first, and then more insistently. A dog barked across the empty lot to the left of the house and then howled. Another dog answered. A truck kicked up dust down the road. What was going on? More barking, now awful and unpleasant. They were taunting Isá, who only wanted to get a little coolness on her skin. A woman with a dog on a leash walked by on one of those awful cell phones that Isá detested. The only person who had one in this family was Lucinda, and now she was gone. That was the only thing about Lucinda she missed. That unpleasant appendage of hers. The little pink phone was always ringing, and most of the time it was Ruley or one of her ugly little friends, young women without decency who dressed even worse than Lucinda and had tattoos and silver cow nose rings, and wore ugly little thin tops with their loosey low-slung chichis hanging out todos in your face from greasy, dirty bra straps. What was this insane world coming to? Lucinda had given her a cell number. Just in case, you never know. Just because, and why not? Isá would never call her if she could help it. She hated the little thing.

The trees stood out against the sky and were solid, deeply rooted. She had cut a new sandía and took a slice of it to Doña Emilia. They sat on the patio in the cooling darkness and ate their watermelon without speaking much. It had been too hot during the day, and what was there to say? Emilia was grateful and handed her plate back to Isá, only well-chewed rinds left. When Isá returned from the kitchen, she saw Emilia with her eyes glazed, her right hand reaching out to Chamorro, who lay next to her on the tiled patio floor. He was having a seizure of some type, and Emilia was trying to reach out to him. He buckled back and forth and gave out a terrible whine, and then she heard an ugly gurgling noise. Emilia tried to reach him, but her arm hung there loosely as she tried to say something. Nothing but garbled words came out of her mouth. It was a pitiful sight: a sick dog in undulating spasms, an old woman trying to reach out to him, both of them floundering, incoherent, jumbled, muddled, confused, and mangled. The scene chilled Isá's heart and made her vagina wince and then explode inside with heat. It was the beginning, clearly, and she wasn't prepared, no, not yet. Doña Emilia had most likely had a little stroke, and el perro pelón, well, who cared about him? She would tell Don Arnulfo, and he would take care of the dog. It was bad enough she had to take care of Juliana; there was no way she would be nursemaid to a drooling, dying dog. He had to be put down, and soon. What of Doña Emilia? When Isá went to take her hand, Emilia had a terrified look. She knew somehow what had happened, and her abject fear was something terrible to see. Isá led her to her bedroom and laid her down to rest. She took off her shoes and covered her with a loose sheet. The bed was unmade, as it usually was, and the room was disordered. Emilia refused to let Isá clean her room. The end table was full of books. Of what use were they now? It was probably the books and their overheated lies that had brought this on. Isá closed one book, leaving a bookmark between the pages, just in case. After all, she was a decent woman. She then opened the windows to that strange woman wind. She would call Lucinda on that ugly little pink phone and ask her to find Don Arnulfo and bring him home. His Gorda was dying. And so was his dog. Lucinda would bring Ruley and Mata, and from here on out, all hell would descend on them. Mother of God, the night was now here, the trees giant shadows in the sky, pulsating and reaching out to the heavens. The Lágrimas were washed over now, mere outlines, intimations of what they had been, the clouds moving over them. A loud treno broke the silence. Damn the fireworks! Now another one . . . when would it be over? Wasn't there enough ugly noise in the world? The darkness enveloped her now. Something dry skittered across the road. The wind now came from the east. El este. It swirled around her. Woman wind birthing. She knew then that Emilia would not die, not now. Not yet. Crossing herself, because she wanted to believe, she went inside and dialed Lucinda's number.

CHAPTER TWENTY-ONE

Otro Jueves/Another Thursday

It was a Thursday, and this was good, Joe thought, as he wiped down the bar near the cash register. Thursdays were good because Friday followed, then Saturday and then Sunday. The longer he was away from anyone calling him about money, the better. No one called him on Thursdays or Fridays. But Mondays and Tuesdays, those were the days he dreaded. Those were the days he either paid bills or avoided creditors. Someone might come in then looking for him and money that they were owed or imagined they were owed. He hated Mondays. Tuesdays were the same, and Wednesdays as well. But on Thursdays—now, on Thursdays things began to ease up, and the week seemed to go better.

If Don Clo came in, it was usually on a weekend, so that upset that plan. He was sometimes around on Sundays, visiting S.S., the Sanctimonious Sacerdote, parading his family around at the 9:30 A.M. Mass in Spanish, all of them convening at La Única for lunch.

Don Clo and El Padre were friends. Hard to figure that one out. A drug lord and a priest. A killer and a self-professed saint. One hypocrite befriending another hypocrite. One married, with two small girl children and a beautiful but nasty wife; the other celibate, and all the worse for it. What they had in common was the Spanish language and poetry. And the fact that they were selfish, haughty sons of bitches whom the world rewarded for their supposed good deeds and their invented veneer of goodwill and the way they apparently helped others in need. Nothing could be further from the truth.

"The problem with you, m'ijo," said Doña Florigunda to her son, Rey, "you too eh-nice. You seem not so eh-nice, but you eh-nice. All those white people sipping on white wine, they not so eh-nice, but they the ones get ahead when you working hard all the time to make the ends meet. And the ends will never meet with you because you too eh-nice. But don't worry, it all come out in the laundry. Yes, it all come out. I love you, m'ijo, because you eh-nice. You a good m'ijo, eres un buen hijo, que Dios te bendiga."

Well, she had it right there. What got him in trouble was being too nice. Don Clo would never forgive or forget what Rey owed him. Her name was Rosaura Muñoz. That was his debt. Where was she now? he wondered. He hoped she was married, with children and a husband who loved her. She deserved all good, all good, because she was good. Too good. And he, he was too nice.

The others were obligations as well, each of them with their price and their toll on his well-being. San Juana Fierro. Rosaura Muñoz. Plutarco Carmona. Adelma Sánchez. Evangelina Duarte. Jesús Senaiba. Sometimes they came to him at night to say hello; sometimes they just stood in the shadows, and oftentimes he felt their presence in the room, a fleeting energy seen from the corner of his eye. The thing they had in common was that they were still attached to him, as he was to them. Let a man have his suffering. And let him know who it was who caused him to suffer. It was better this way. At least he knew what held him down and what would eventually set him free. And yet, would Rey ever be free of Rosaura Muñoz, with all that bleeding that was part of her, and now a part of him?

And to whom was he indebted? A madman, someone insane who cared little for love and nothing for life. Oh, Don Clo was clinically insane, he had to be, but no one saw it. His kind lasted long and brought the world crashing down around him. His kind was the kind most everyone admired for their good looks, their wealth, their business acumen, their sexuality, and yes, sometimes their talent. Oh, whatever it was that these kinds of men brought into the world always got turned inward and served only them. They needed to be annihilated. Erased. Extinguished. Removed.

What pity had Don Clo felt for the young woman who'd bled all over herself and been transported from the Migra van to the office where Rey worked? She hadn't fully cleaned herself up by then, and when he interrogated her she was exhausted, nearly spent. She'd spent several days in the desert, and when she came into the office where he worked, she was covered in dirt and then blood. It was cruel to ask her questions at that time, but he had to. Agent Chaparro had brought her in, and as far as he could see, she had shown her no mercy, either. Ugly short woman without pity even for her own kind. She who enjoyed going out with her night goggles to hunt people. The question was, was he any better for sitting in front of all those people, and for asking questions for which he knew they were inventing answers? Well, except those few. Yes, there were those few. Remember them now. Remember them now.

What is your name?

Where do you come from?

Where were you going?

What is it that you were planning?

Why have you come here?

What is it you want?

It was then she told him her story.

And he, Rey Suárez, dutifully wrote it down. For that was his job. That was what he was paid for—to record and to witness.

ROSAURA MUÑOZ: I.D. #595
AGE TWENTY-SEVEN. SINGLE.
BORN CINCO PINOS, TAMAULIPAS, MÉXICO.
APPREHENDED NEAR EL PASO, TEXAS.

There I was in the back seat of the van crowded between two men, one older, one younger, an old woman by the window, and it was hot, over 115 degrees. There were too many people in the van, but there wasn't anything anyone could do. La Migra, they caught us and made us get in the van. We were sitting out there in the sun with no shade, and that's when I felt the familiar pulsing rush of blood, not a river, but the small familiar trickle, how can I explain it to you if you aren't a woman, that fish swimming into a net and that net unloosening and the dark water flowing downward? There I was in the back of that van pressed between strangers, some pinche Gringo yelling to someone while his poor dog salivated in the heat. I could smell myself: that wet sticky fish juice, and me without even a rag to wipe myself clean. When I stepped out of the car after what seemed like an eternity una eternidad de desgracia, I was wet down there and I was soaked, drenched, my thighs rubbed dark con el chorro de sangre. I tried to stay behind after the men, the younger one and the older one, got out of the car and the old woman slid out the door, but not before turning her head to me and looking down at me and then the van seat, and she shook her head and said nothing, what could she say, and I made a plea to her but her face said no I can't help you, and she moved away, and I felt myself sinking down with embarrassment and shame. I was soaked in blood. Someone asked if I'd been hurt. "You herida? Are you hurt?" this young Chicano asked me in very bad Spanish. He reminded me of someone back in Cinco Pinos, in the state of Tamaluipas, and I said, "No, I'm not hurt." "Oh," he said. "Oh." And I think he knew. He moved away quickly, and this woman came up. Una chaparrita. Looking like everyone back there in Cinco Pinos, except this was in los Estados Unidos and I moved away, leaned into the seat of the van, and it was wet with blood. I tried to wipe it clean. The lady Migra yelled to me, "Ándele, ándele, hurry," and before I moved away I wiped what blood I could from the seat. I felt a rush of new blood pull down from inside of me, and I shut my legs tight. La Señora Migra looked at me. I looked at her and at the dog. The dog tried to get to me like dogs do, smelling me the way dogs do. And the Gringo Migra pulled him back. I couldn't go on, and that's when I said to her:

"Ay, Señorita, por favor. Ayúdame. Me da vergüenza decirlo, Señorita. Traigo la bandera roja . . . Señorita, por favor . . . Como dicen allá en mi pueblito, 'Anda el burro con su caballo' or mejor, 'traigo el chango descalabrado' . . . Por favor, no me puede dar una garrita, algo . . . un taco o un tamal como dicen. Ya no aguanto Señorita. No me puede dar una toalla sanitaria. Por favor . . . Señorita, tú, que sabes como es . . . you who know how it is to be a woman and to bleed . . . help me!"

This is where Rosaura Muñoz broke down, and Rey called out to Officer Chaparro, who took her to the restroom to be sent from there to the detention facility. And from there . . . well, she would be sent back home. If Don Clo had not gotten in the way, she would have been sent home fairly soon. But the woman was young, and yes, lovely. It was all a great misfortune of a misunderstanding. Why had Don Clo been there to witness this story of all stories? And why had he decided to intervene? It was all a pitiful mess. Don Clo had said he would help her but he hadn't.

Yes, it was true. Don Clo had written a book of poetry, *Desde La Noche Sin Luz*.

Joe Kiratz had read some of Don Clo's poetry and said it was good. How the hell would he know? He'd been working on his opus for years, and still no one had seen anything in print. Writers! Artists! And yet they deserved respect. They knew about life, real life and the struggle to stay alive within systems that always rewarded liars and thieves. They told the truth—each in their own way—jodidos as they were by those who didn't respect them. They lived in a hopeful world doing their work painting writing dancing singing when no one listened looked or read. Their work seemed so useless, unnecessary. And yet it was the only real work, Joe said.

Rey's mother, Doña Florigunda, wanted him to be a musician, to play an instrument or sing like his supposed father, Pedro Infante. Except Rey couldn't carry a tune, never could.

It was around that time he joined the army and left for Vietnam, that time that became a burning hole in his life. He came back without tears to shed, ever again, got married and joined the

Border Patrol and found his calling. Some calling! But oh hell, he was good at it. He was so good at seeing the actor behind the act, the liar behind the lie, the man or woman behind the dream. And even now, he was able to discern a man's inner workings, to see his heart beating softly inside the stretched fearful flesh. He knew men like few others, and as a result he was always on edge. He was always waiting for something to happen, and it would soon. Don Clo would come in on a Friday or a Saturday and demand his money, and try to take away El Mil. He would come and try to take it all away. He or someone like him would want something from him that he couldn't and didn't want to deliver. And then what would he do?

He was thinking about this when suddenly S.S. stood directly in front of him. He came up without warning, stealthily and without noise.

"Vino tinto," he said in a husky voice. The man's eyes were bloodshot. Rey glanced at the clock. It was 7:24 P.M. Rey had a habit of looking at the clock when someone came in. He would look at the clock and imagine how much time they would spend in the lounge. It was a secret hobby of his, to gauge time. How much time was their delusion worth?

"Una botella de vino tinto," Padre Manolo said with a sad and dusty voice, ravaged by some untold sorrow.

Vino tinto! This was Comezón, not Madrid. This wasn't a bodega with Rioja wine and tapas. This was El Mil, and the hard-boiled eggs were $1 and the popcorn was free. Where did the man think he was? And who did he think he was? Jesus H. Savior of the World?

"This is Comezón, Padre, we don't have the Spanish wine you're used to," Rey said, not as an apology but with irritation.

He didn't like the way the man had suddenly appeared in front of him, wearing a wrinkled pair of black priest pants and a spotted white Lacoste shirt with a fucking alligator, demanding to be served. He didn't really know the man personally, but he knew what he stood for, and that was what he hated about him and his supposed mission on this earth. His sanctimonious spirituality. He was a slimy shabby shady subterranean shitball who reeked of self-preservation, self-aggrandizement, and an overpowering ego.

"Una botella de vino tinto. ¡Coño!"

"Don't you be cursing me, Padre. I'll kick you back to where you came from."

A veteran at identifying and controlling drunks, Rey could now see that while the Padre was holding it well, he was soused. No use in getting him more riled up. No telling what he would do, maybe start a prayer meeting. Yeah, and who would be in attendance? Rey looked around the lounge. It was a Thursday night, and the usuals were there: Luisito, Joe Kiratz, Pep Turgino, a table of Brothers from the Rebeldes Motorcycle Club. Nuffie would soon be limping in. The Knights of the Fucking Round Table, aka the Last Supper Gang, would soon sit down to call out to the Holy Ghost.

"Go sit down, Padre, and I'll have La Pata bring you a glass of red. Pata! Where are you?"

La Pata was in the back getting some ice, but sure enough she heard Rey call out to her. It was still early in the evening, and he'd been on edge all day.

La Pata came out in her low-cut top, but when she saw Father Rodríguez, she covered her missing bosoms with a napkin that she folded into the top of the peasant blouse. She pulled down her black miniskirt as well and coughed nervously.

"Father Rodríguez! My goodness! What a surprise. What can I get you?"

"Glass of red, Pata. I already took his order," Rey said in a sharp voice.

"Red, like really red?"

"Give him a glass from that special bottle."

The bottle had been given to Rey by Don Clo. Why, he didn't know. It was sure enough a red wine from Spain, and he might as well get rid of it now. Damn the Spanish!

It was a hell of a surprise for both Rey and La Pata to see S.S. in El Mil. He had never deigned to enter before. As a matter of fact, he chose to speak of it in excoriating terms every moment he could, whether at the pulpit or not. At the moment he seemed distracted, wanting to be alone. Good. Let him be alone. Manolito moved to the back of the bar where Kiratz sat, going over his bloody notes. Good. Let them talk if they chose. If not, they were both out of the way. Rey didn't need anyone making pedo or pleito, not today, not on a Thursday!

La Pata rushed to take El Padrecito his red wine, truly flustered. She nearly dropped her tray and came back to Rey with a look of wonder.

"Hell if I know," Rey grunted.

"Do you think . . . ," she stammered.

"Hell, I don't know."

"Do you think we should . . . "

"What, what? The man's drinking a blasted glass of wine. Leave him alone. With all his bullshit, he probably needs it."

"I didn't think he . . . "

"Well, he does . . . "

At this moment Arnulfo wandered in from the Plaza, panting like any overheated perro, uno de esos vagabundos de la calle. He was a worn-out street dog much the worse for wear. He had the look of a man defeated still trying to stay upright. He straightened up. Sorrows? None. Worries? Few. Joys? None of your business. No one would know anything at all. He wouldn't give in or let on. His name was Arnulfo P. Olivárez. Looking back at himself in the mirror that ran behind the bar, he saw a large invisible P on his forehead. Or maybe there were two. Puro Pendejo. He hoped no one else would notice. Seeing El Padre, he made the sign of the cross. En el nombre del chingado, del encabronado y el espíritu jodido . . .

CHAPTER TWENTY-TWO

Yohualli Ehécatl

The wind was a woman. Swirling, twirling, dancing. She forced her way into Arnulfo's bedroom and then left him without joy, a brazen hussy. Arnulfo got up with an effort and turned off the large fan that faced his bed. He wanted to feel the wind full force in its natural state. He waddled back to his bed and pulled Chamorro to him. The dog was soft and compliant and lay there quietly, shuddering every once in a while. He had developed some sort of involuntary jerking movement. He was getting old. If he were an old man, he would have some sort of palsy or Parkinson's disease. Eventually he would start jerking more frequently, and Arnulfo would have to put him down.

But the dog would never let that happen. He had his plans. When he got worse, he would simply leave Rancho Olivárez and disappear. He knew how. He knew the way out. He didn't want to do that to Arnulfo, who had been kind to him, but the man was brutal and would not find a soft way to end anything. He would shoot Chamorro without thinking. He was a man who did things without considering other sides. Chamorro knew that animals, like humans, needed to die in their own way and at their own time. Forget putting them out of misery. Didn't all life suffer in the dying? That was the reason to live, and that was the grace of dying. Transition. Transformation. Transcendence. How small and simple were men's minds.

When Arnulfo was home, which was seldom these days, Chamorro was always at his side because he was known as Arnulfo's dog. That was his mission in life, to accompany this old man through his life. But when Arnulfo was gone, he clung to Doña Emilia, who was good to him in her distracted way. She gave him special tidbits of food and sang a lot, sad songs mostly in Spanish as she sat doing chores. He felt sorry for her and loved her quiet ways and her warm brown eyes and the way she called him to her side when she knew Arnulfo would be gone for a long time: "Chammmuuuurrrito! ¡Venga! Come here, niño. I have something for you."

For Isá, the old servant, Chamorro had no regard. She was unpleasant, calling him Perro Pelón, or just Pelón, and when she said it, she sounded ugly. And not only that, she had a funny smell. But in his way, Chamorro felt an affinity to her, poor thing that she was, a slave, really, to the old man and to the old woman and to the house that encased and buried all of their dreams and hopes. She was to be pitied, a bit but not too much, for she was cold and uncaring despite her outward appearance to the world. So much feeling, so many little twinges and aches and pains, so many itches, small and large, so many known and unknown terrors and sorrows, so many hidden stories, so much loss for each and every one of them.

Chamorro couldn't understand how humans could hurt each other so much, why, and for what? And he didn't understand how humans could kill their animal friends so easily, shedding big snuffly tears because they couldn't see them hurt or hurting, when it was their own hurt and their own death that they were shielding themselves from, not their animal friends, who always died with dignity and bravery. Yes, humans often deprived their animal friends of their natural passage to the stars. Arnulfo wasn't a bad man, not really; he was merely so self-absorbed and so selfish that all he could see in front of him was his own sacred need.

The rain hit the tin roof, and it was a familiar and loved sound to both man and dog. Each loved the wind, the rain, the lightning that came from the west. Chamorro lay there and let the old man love him as best he could, talking softly to him as he would to a lover, stroking his soft hairless skin. Arnulfo moaned every once in a while, his lungs filling up more and more with fluid as the cancer ate its way into the fibers of his being and lay there, nested, like a viper. Holy Mother Rain, come and wash my desert clean.

The wind churned and spiraled outside. The raindrops came hard and fast, and suddenly there was silence followed by a cold, luxurious breeze that delighted and relieved them both. It was already so hot. There was no way to stay cool in a house that had only one functional swamp cooler. It was a big house, too big for Emilia and Arnulfo. And it was too big a house to be without air conditioning except in the main part. Juliana took up little space, as did Isá. When Lucinda was home, which was not much anymore, the house filled up and it got hotter, and sometimes it was difficult to breathe at night with only a small room fan spinning round and round, slicing through the torpid air, bringing little relief to anyone who lived and slept in that house full of fevers.

Arnulfo slept in the nude in the summertime; who was there to see him anyway, with the door locked? Sometimes he pointed the fan directly toward the bed; sometimes he moved its direction away from him so that he wouldn't be cold in the morning. He pulled the thin sheet toward him and Chamorro and reverently covered them both. The dog was grateful for all the small kindnesses, but the man was still a mystery to him. All men were, lying in their beds expecting something to happen, not knowing that life was already there, present in every movement and with each soft stirring breeze. Oh, life! And when the wind was done and then the rain and then the lightning, what would there be but sleep? Soft, delicious, eternal sleep, or else flight, high above the heavens, one star greeting another in the endless night. Chamorro would leave Arnulfo and not look back, because it was in the looking back that one got lost. It had been a good life, but something else was out there. He knew it, because he was, after all, a sacred animal, a Xoloitzcuintle who knew the story of the world. The Aztec god Xotol made the Xoloitzcuintle from a sliver of the Bone of Life so men could love and protect their little friends, and they, in turn, were deigned to lead them through Mictlán,

Death, toward Life in the Stars. It was Chamorro's destiny, and yet it was a hard blessing.

Chamorro closed his slanted almond eyes, his batlike ears at rest. He raised his long, sleek neck one last time and heard the wind, the Mother Wind. She told him that she would bring them both sleep this one time again without worry. Tomorrow, they both knew, was another day. Arnulfo coughed up some bitter bloody phlegm into an old handkerchief that lay on his nightstand and drank a small amount of water from a glass he always kept nearby, and then he lay back down on his humid bed. He was restless and knew he wouldn't sleep well. His gun lay nearby inside a drawer, always fully loaded. Chamorro beseeched the wind that moved around them: rest, rest, now just rest. Let us see you as the woman you are, sensual, cool, unafraid. Please allow Arnulfo at least a few hours of respite without suffering too much.

Chamorro thought again of leaving Rancho Olivárez, but he knew he never could, not really. Leaving was not his manda on this earth.

Yohualli Ehécatl. God of Wind. You whose breath moves the sun, who brings us rain who moves the universe and all physical forms you who has no form you who causes movement you who shakes and uproots trees mover of matter and all life in the universe father of the breeze the wind the tempest storm bringer of tornadoes and hurricanes father of the soft breeze lover of the cold woman wind bring us rest from this terrible and searing heat let us sleep this night this night this one night and allow us to awaken one more tomorrow refreshed children unafraid.

Yohualli Ehécatl
Yohualli Ehécatl
Yohualli Ehécatl
Yohualli Ehécatl
Yohualli Ehécatl
Yohualli Ehécatl
Yohualli Ehécatl

You are the answer to the One, the Many Questions.

CHAPTER TWENTY-THREE

The Real Question

"That is the question after all, Padre," Joe Kiratz said emphatically. "Do you see what I mean?" He waved his hands around with emphasis. His papers, what was understood to be his great masterpiece, the grand opus he'd been working on for years, flew all over the place. The onionskin sheets blew this way and that, landing on the dirty floor and underneath his table at El Mil.

El Padre Manolo picked up a wrinkled sheet and started to read it, much to Joe's dismay . . .

"From the Journal of Josefia 'Joe' Kiratz.

June the 9th. Lost.

If one were asked to describe himself to the others, those anxieties out there in the miasmic future, what recourse would he have but to split himself open, fruit-like, and feast on the acidic juice of his own pumping liquid fire, this thing called his life?"

Before Manolo had gotten very far, Joe grabbed the page from him and tore it up. It was unfortunate, as many of the pages hadn't been numbered. But at the moment, Kiratz was unconcerned about pagination. The matter at hand was the matter at hand.

"Mr. Mayor," proceeded El Padre Manolito, for Joe Kiratz was the official mayor, or rather interim mayor, of Comezón. Joe had been on the Board of Trustees, it was true, but no one had any idea that the previous mayor, Telesforo "Tele" Pinchada, would be indicted and taken away to jail. His wife, Agapita "Pita," claimed that he had embezzled money from the Comezón coffers and was out to get her. There was evidence; unfortunately, what it was hadn't yet been revealed, but that and a battery charge against his long-suffering wife apparently was enough to put Tele behind bars.

Alas, there were too many witnesses as he hit Pita in front of La Única after an evening meal rounded off by too many pitchers of Micheladas.

By default, Joe Kiratz was now the acting mayor of Comezón. The timing was unfortunate, but there you had it; such is the nature of politics in the world. "Unfortunate" is not really the word, for Kiratz turned out to be a much better mayor than anyone ever would have suspected, but this honor for His Honor, if you would call it that, was unfortunate, for poor old Joe got sidetracked from finishing his novel. The mayorship also occurred during his illness of his wife, or rather his ex-wife, Laneen, which was really the worst part.

"Your Mayor, Señor Alcalde," Manolito proceeded with a flourish . . . he was drunk, very drunk, and getting more so as time went along. He'd been in El Mil two hours, and already he'd engaged in a heated conversation with Luisito about his laziness in coming to church on Sundays, and now he accosted Joe Kiratz about his novel and its theme. He had also had a minor tiff with Rey Suárez, who insisted he go home or to church or wherever the hell he wanted to, just get the hell out of my lounge, Padre. The altercation with Rey began over the quality of the second bottle of wine he had ordered, the vino tinto having run out after a half-hour. Realizing that no quality wine was any longer to be found in this inferior establishment, El Padre had moved on to Irish whiskey.

"Yes, why not, what do you have against Irish whiskey? All Spaniards are Irish, and the Irish are real men," or so went part of the exchange. Rey was trying to get him to leave, but the Padre was going at it a lo todo dar. From time to time El Padrecito would stop, become silent, and wave his hands around as he absolved everyone in the room. Vestiges of sainthood. Traits of the old life. Just a bit too pinche holy. This, too, was getting on Rey's nerves. He was about to escort S.S. out when Joe said he'd take charge of him.

'What is the real question, then, Mayor?"

"You should know, Padre. You, of all people, should know."

"I should?"

"Yes, you should."

"Well, then tell me so I'll know for sure."

"The real question, the deep and abiding and true question for us now, for those of us living at this particular time in history, is this: What does it mean to be a good man in an evil time?"

"That is the question? Yes, I see, I understand. A good man. An evil time. You are describing life now, here. Here in Comezón. Yes, not only here, but everywhere. Yes, I see. I do see."

The Padre couldn't see anything at that moment, but it didn't matter. This was the liveliest conversation he'd had all year with anyone besides Don Clo. Oh, there was the session with Don Tomás at his house, followed by that blood-brothering, but that was another thing altogether. Manolito was hungry for dialogue and only now realized how starved he was for discourse, any intelligent and mature conversation. Who was this man, and what was his theory of goodness?

It was sad, Manolito thought; he knew few good men, if any at all. Himself he did not count as one of them. He was a depraved and soulless vagabond, a useless and now degenerate cipher. Add lustful sinner to that list, and you might get started on his litany of sins. He felt his manguera, his nervous hose, jump up at the thought of Juliana and what had transpired between them over the phone. There is nothing more lustful than the sin of the mind. His penis ached from hours of self-induced and self-inflicted watering. And now he was hiding out here in the darkness of this hellhole because he couldn't stand to face himself, nor her. He was a coward. He wanted to love her but he couldn't. It was as simple as that. He would run away, leave town. Tomorrow, after the 7:30 A.M. Mass, or better yet this coming Sunday, after the 11:30 Mass and his lunch with Don Clo. They had made arrangements to get together, and he would ask Don Clo to take him with him, to his home, wherever he lived. Where did he live? As far as he knew, Clodimoro Balderas had many homes. Which one would they go to? And once there, wherever that was going to be, he would send news that he had left Comezón.

What of Juliana? What to do about Juliana? They would leave together. He saw Arnulfo sitting in a dark corner of the cantina near the men's restroom. He was en sus copas, fully drunk with his head hanging down. From time to time he would have a tremendous coughing fit. The man was not long for this world. Yes, he would call Don Clo and ask him to make arrangements for them both. For him and Juliana. They would leave together. No, he couldn't do that. She would never leave Comezón, not with him, not that way. And yet . . . he knew she would if he asked. But he couldn't ask, he didn't have the will to ask. He loved her, but then again, maybe he didn't. Even if he left with her and they lived together, he knew that someday he would leave her. He, after all, wasn't a good man.

"Coño! Bring me another whiskey," El Padre yelled to La Pata, who stood at the bar staring at him.

The man had unraveled, and it was sad to see. She wasn't surprised at his deep-seated sorrow so much as his nastiness. He was an ugly, nasty drunk, and there was no reason for that. She had thought he was a gentleman. Another dashed veneer. Another sick son of a you-know-what. Another man another drunk another story of loss and dread, ugly, ugly, ugly. You saw it daily here at El Mil. She always felt a sadness for these poor louts. Padre Manolito was an alcoholic like most of the patrons here, only he hid it well. ¡Qué lastima! What a waste. And yet, who was she to judge? Not she, Pata González-Curry, a recovered alcoholic, a barfly who lived off the fumes and the energy of the other drunks. She couldn't give up the life, the hard, demanding life and its pace, no matter whether she drank or not, she was still that drunk inside. She wasn't a drunk when she was a González; it was the Curry part that got her.

One Melvin "Bud" Curry, her ex, the man she had sworn she would forget but never could, was her undoing. Now, there was a drunk. She had met Bud here at El Mil about five years ago. He was already far gone and would only live three more years. He was a charming drunk, a happy drunk, a funny and loving drunk.

It was only when he was sober that he turned on you. She rarely saw him sober, and it was good because it was the drunk she truly loved, the kind, thoughtful, generous, give-the-shirt-off-his-back man whom she loved with all her heart. One night after work they hooked up, and after that they never left each other's side. Bud was her best friend and her lover. The week before he died, they got married in Juárez on a weeknight when she was off. Bud must have known the end was coming. And then a week later she found him in their bed, dead drunk, dead, dead, dead. He was a man without pretensions and knew he would die this way. His liver was shot, and he was starting to forget things. The toxins were building up without any release, and he was soon unable to drive or to think straight. But even then he was a sweet and caring man. That is, if he was drunk. The rest of the time she had to watch him. That was when she started working at El Mil. Bud was a regular, and at least she'd know where he was. Pata lived a few blocks off the Plaza in her mother's old house. Her daughter, Ramie, was gone, and she was alone until Bud came into her life. And then, suddenly, he was gone. She didn't want to bore anyone with the story of their love. When you love an alcoholic, most of the stories are the same. She was grateful Ramie's father, Eddie, was gone. Pata had never married him, and it was a good thing. When he found out that she was pregnant, well, that was it. Another boring story. What she was interested in was the here and now.

Pata had never missed having breasts. They seemed to be a bother to most women. She never had that worry. The only time she'd felt bad about her sunken chest was that first night with Eddie. He'd seemed so disappointed when she took off her clothes and they lay in bed. He told her that she was small, hell, there was nothing there, so get it straight, Eddie. He was a liar even then. And what did it matter to him, anyway? He was without teeth and all banged up from the car accident, and she didn't say anything to him about that as they lay in bed making out. She didn't say, oye, tú, cabrón, tú y tus encías, no, she never made fun of him like his so-called compas did, calling him Gummy and Gumbo and the other nasty, ugly things that men say to each other freely. She loved Eddie, teeth or no teeth. Banged up or not. He was alive and she loved him. She would help him heal. Oh yeah, he was a drunk, but she would help him give up the booze. Once he understood that she loved him and would never leave, he would get better. All he needed was the willpower of her love. "M'ijo, just let me love you," she said to him. He'd just gotten out of the hospital and was on the mend. Or so he said. They went to a party at Mando Molina's because he was finally out of the hospital, "so let's get all pedo," he said to her, and she said, "No, Eddie. No. You're getting well. You're getting better. Can't you let the drink go? I love you, m'ijo, I want to be your wife. Let me take care of you, Eddie. I want to. Please let me." He said, "I love you too, Pata. Girl, I'll always love you." She knew he meant it, but somehow she also knew her loving would never be enough. "Baby, can't you let it go? I can't stop, woman. Don't ask me to stop. I want to drink. And that's all there is to it. You might as well kill me right now and right here. I can't stop. I love you but I can't stop. I don't want to stop."

There it was. That was it.

That was the night Ramie was conceived. And that was the night she realized that things would never work out with her and Eddie. How could they? He loved the drink. And she, ay, she loved him. Never the twain shall meet. Just what the hell a twain was, she didn't know. Well, whatever it was, it was on that side and she was on this side. Eddie over there with his booze, and she on the other side with her love for him.

Ramie was barely a year old when she left Eddie. She didn't want to think about it now.

There were so many things she put back on the twain side— Eddie, her life as a single mother, her life taking care of her mother, her mother dying, and then Ramie moving across the country to go to school. That's when she took the job at El Mil. And now there was Rey.

Pata looked over at Rey. He was a good-looking man and he was kind to her. He never made fun of her chest, and he was a good boss. She could love a man like Rey. She would take care of him the way she took care of Bud. But Rey wasn't interested in her; he was still sad about his divorce from Dulce. She'd heard through the comadre grapevine that Dulce was tired of Utah and wanted to come back to Comezón, but those rumors weren't confirmed. Whether Rey wanted to take her back was another matter. Rey was better off without that woman, and maybe, just maybe, Pata would have a chancita. You never know.

Lately he had seemed so preoccupied, distant. He was worried about the business. Ay, she sighed, looking around. What a business! A dying old man hunched over his cervezita near the restrooms, that would be Nuffie. He looked bad. Then back there in the rinconcito was El Padre Manolito going at it with Joe Kiratz. They were in a heated discussion about something. She'd never seen El Padrecito in here before, but he looked right at home. She hoped he wouldn't become a regular. Don Tomás should be coming in any moment. She needed to bring out the pickled hard-boiled eggs and make some more popcorn for Pep Turgino, who would soon be eating his main meal for the day. Luisito was in the front by himself, laughing at some solitary joke. And Diablo, well, the perrito was up there as well, near the door, waiting for someone new to come in, someone who would take pity on him and pet him. What a business, and yet it was a business, and yes, a family. ¡Ay, qué familia!

CHAPTER TWENTY-FOUR

Luisito

Luisito Covarrubias lived with his mother, Panchita, in a casita several blocks from the Plaza. She was a hoarder, and their little crumbling adobe was a disgrace, but they were too busy living inside the beehive to see how the outside world viewed them. They wouldn't have cared either if they knew. Mother and son lived in the eternal moment without shame or any sense of guilt. There were innocents in the deepest sense of the word. Pure they were not, but naïve, the world's feral children.

Francisca Manteca Covarrubias was in her mid-eighties and looked every day's worth of living hard. "Pancha" was a woman who believed that more was better, so move over, would you, so I can eat my tostadas and then yours. Not a devout woman by any means—religion, societal pressures, any conviction or leaning, any nationalistic pride, had slid over her and been relegated to its place of the non-essential. She was immune to the propaganda of the world. She was a freethinker only because nothing affected her, not the trashed-out porch with two old rusty washers, not the box springs covered with spider webs or the old lawn mower that housed a nest of bees, not any one of the ancient blue tarps with who knows what underneath. From the street you could peer into the house, where if you looked with attention you could see old rakes and a stacked-up pile of chairs and several old couches where any number of cats lounged day or night without concern, urinating with abandon and self-propagating a legion of gooey-eyed and infected offspring. The curtains were nailed into the wall and couldn't be opened. Panchita had a system where she pulled one ragged curtain edge and tacked it back when she wanted sunlight, which was not often. The pooched-out roof leaked chorros on those few occasions when it rained, usually during the summer monsoon season, which caused a bubbling effect on the walls, like old soft skin sloughed off. The hallway was crowded with floor-to-ceiling newspapers from some bygone era, and her bedroom was the only habitable place in what had once been a large and spacious house.

Luisito's room was at the back with its own private entrance. This was good because he came and went at all hours of the day and night. The room was little more than an alcove with a folding cot, but to him it didn't matter, as he was rarely home, preferring to wander the streets of Comezón during the daylight hours, looking on curiously at the world's actions, antics, and foibles. In the evening he was usually to be found at El Mil, snuggling with a beer from the tap.

The kitchen was a ghastly sight, as Panchita and Luisito lived off plastic plates and cups, all the usable, once-clean dishes stacked up with crusted remnants of previous meals. Most of the crustation was brown or red, bespeaking their diet of beans and red chile, with an occasional flecking of green. Did they care how the house, inside or out, looked? No. Did they care what their neighbors thought about their house? Hell, no.

Panchita spent most of the day in her room sleeping. She spent the nights playing solitaire and smoking endless Virginia Super Slims Menthol, several packs a day, the supply of which she always entrusted to her son, who was the one who navigated the world, bringing food and supplies in whenever needed.

Luisito was a handyman, but how handy was doubtful. He didn't know much about electricity or plumbing and couldn't tile, paint, or clean up worth shit. He was very good at sweeping. Sweeping was his forte, and that was mostly how he made his way in the world, sweeping the Plaza and the businesses that abutted it. For this he was paid by the hour. He always lost track of hours worked and never knew what the minimum wage was, what is it, anyway, so he pretty much worked for whatever people wanted to pay him. This wasn't a bad way to do it, as people felt sorry for him and would pay him twice the amount they would have paid him if he'd had a regular salary. He didn't pay taxes, had no medical bills, didn't pay rent, had no wife or children, and had no debts, so all was well in his world. And this meant his money could be spent at El Mil Recuerdos Lounge or on his daily candy bars, usually Baby Ruths or Milky Ways, at the Pick-It & Pack-It down the highway on the back road to El Paso. His needs were few and his life was simple.

Luisito's father, Amoldo, Spanish for "The Eagle Rules," never ruled at all. At this point in the story of Luisito's life, what did it matter what it was; Amoldo Covarrubias was long gone. He'd been killed in a farm accident, and his mother got his insurance. She lived on Amoldo's Social Security as well. All his property was now Panchita's, and maybe someday Luisito's, if he lived long enough to inherit anything. It was unlikely, for although Luisito was in his mid-fifties, he looked much older, and while he wasn't ever ill, he wasn't ever well.

Many people thought he was retarded, an unpopular phrase these days, an unacceptable term. No, he wasn't. He wasn't dumb, either, and he wasn't stupid. He was just tapado, a little plugged up. He infuriated and irritated people, but he never knew it, nor would he have cared. He was so much himself that you just had to accept him the way he was or you didn't. Oh, he had many good qualities—he was loyal and he was always on time. It didn't matter as much that you couldn't get rid of him once he was there, and he had no concept of early or late. This sense of timeless time could be either a good or a bad thing, as he was unattached to all things and all people. He was a regular in the small world of Comezón, but would he ever be missed when he was gone? Unlikely. His own mother sometimes forgot about him as she lounged around the house attending to cooking her perennial olla de frijoles and her chilito. That was about the only food she prepared, and if you were invited to eat with the Covarrubiases, you would have found beans and chile ready to eat at any hour of the day or night. No vegetables of any type passed through the house, and fruit was also not to be found. In the summertime you might find watermelon seeds scattered here and there on the floor and old rinds in the kitchen sink. The refrigerator would be crowded with Panchita's olla, her much-used clay pot, a large ancient chipped Tupperware container of red or green chile, and half a watermelon, left uncovered, the heart core scooped out and the edges plasticine-looking and slightly curled up.

No liquor ever entered the house; this rule was sacrosanct. Luisito had to do his drinking elsewhere, and he did. His mother was unaware he was an alcoholic. No one had ever told her, so what was there to worry about? In many ways her life was calm, unchanging, safe. Mother and son did their business, and that business was staying out of each other's way and keeping to themselves. After a while they forgot about each other, and all was fine until the day Luisito forgot to bring Panchita her Virginia Super Slims Menthol. That was the night Doña Emilia Olivárez had her stroke and the sheriff, "Mata" Terrazas, had to break into her bedroom to rescue her and take her to the hospital. It was a terrible scene—oh, not at the house, but at El Mil. Lucinda got a desperate phone call from Isá on her cell phone. Isá was worried about Doña Emilia, her adopted mother—let's not call Emilia her mother, she never had been her real mother.

"Emilia's locked herself in her room, Luci," Isá said with unmistakable worry. She was the only one who called Lucinda Luci.

"So?" Lucinda said with irritation. Isá had woken her up. She was still getting used to sleeping at her soon-to-be in-laws' and had gone to bed early to get away from them. Her soon-to-be mother-in-law, Terri Ann, was driving her nuts. Lucinda wasn't feeling well and wondered if she had gotten food poisoning in Juárez, or perhaps, she thought with dread, maybe she was pregnant. Can you get pregnant when you make love during your menstrual cycle? If so, then she was touched. Yes, dammit, she was touched! Caray, the damn finger of fucking fate had touched her and made her pregnant. Either that or it had been Terri Ann Terrazas's pollo enpanado that had gotten to her. The chicken had tasted funny, and all that greasy batter hadn't helped. Terri Ann wasn't a good cook at all. Maybe she was wrong to have left home early. She missed Isá's cooking, but that was about it. She didn't miss Arnulfo or Emilia, and when you came down to it, and Isá knew this, much to her chagrin, she didn't miss her, either. What she did miss more than anything was her big bed and her room. The Terrazas home was large but musky-smelling. It smelled of boy. Terri Ann had a house full of men of all ages, from four to however old Mata was, and her home smelled of boy pee, boy dirt, and boy sweat. If Lucinda did have children, she hoped they would all be girls.

"Your mother locked her room," Isá said emphatically.

"So?"

"Do you hear me, Luci? She locked the door."

"So she locked her room. Big deal."

"Your mother never locks her room."

"Everyone locks their room. Arnulfo locks his room. You lock your room. I used to lock my room. By the way, I'm never coming back. Well, except maybe to get my things. Can you get them ready for me, Mima?"

"Your mother, I mean, Emilia, has never, ever locked her room. I'm worried. I haven't heard anything coming from inside for a long time. We need to call someone."

"What do you want me to do, Mima?"

Mima was what Luci used to call Isá when she was feeling loving. She didn't use the name often because it showed her dependency and need and love for the old woman, and she didn't want to feel anything for anyone—well, except maybe Ruley when he was being nice, and for their baby if there was a baby. She wasn't sure. So can you get pregnant when you're having your period?

"Mata's there. Let Mata know. He needs to come over and open the door. Although I don't know if he can open it, maybe he can, either that or he's going to have to force it open. Emilia's been sick, m'ija. She had un episodio several nights ago like I told you. She was out of her mind. I've seen it before. Era un choque. Un derrame cerebral. M'ija, I think she had a stroke. I put her to bed like I told you, and the next day she was all right, but tonight, tonight she got sick again. I'm afraid. This time I'm really scared."

"Why didn't you tell me, Mima?"

"I told you, Luci, but you didn't listen, you didn't hear me."

"Oh, Mima! What can we do?"

"Let Mata know. Make him come here and check on Emilia."

"I don't know where he is."

"Find him."

"I'll have to ask Ruley. He's not here now, he went drinking with some of his friends."

"Call him."

"I hate to bother him. He tells me that he can do what he wants and to leave him alone when he's not with me. He might get mad. And I don't want him to get mad. He'd just as soon run over a dog as see it sit on the side of the road. As a matter of fact, he did that the other day. He hit a little puppy. On purpose. It made me sick. But that's Ruley for you."

"Luci, this is your mother!"

"She's not my mother, Mima. You are. Or you are like a mother. Emilia never liked me. And she never loved me."

"I love you, Luci, and I love Doña Emilia. Please. For me. Do this for me and for Emilia because she tried to love you."

"She didn't try very hard. Oh, all right, but Ruley's going to get mad. He hates being bothered."

"Tell Mata to come over. I'll go find Padre Manolito. He should be at his house near the church."

"Híjole, why didn't you tell me it was bad? So why are you calling a priest? Eeeh, so it's bad?"

Lucinda tracked Ruley down, and then he tracked Mata down, and then Ruley picked up Lucinda and they drove over to Arnulfo's, except he wasn't there because he was at El Mil. Isá ran to the Padre's house, but he wasn't there, so she ran to El Mil where everyone was, drinking and carrying on sin nada while her only friend was maybe dying or already dead. Mata was there bragging about nabbing some indocumentados in the desert and making them eat dirt, when one of the mojados then shit in his pants out of sheer nervousness, and Mata made him run around with his pants around his knees and made him clean himself up, and then he let them go, but not before getting a mordida, hey, he had to have a cut too. And then he called Billy Bonner at the Migra station to tell him their whereabouts, and then he just had to come into El Mil and brag about the whole damn funny thing.

"You should have seen the way I had that mojado dancing, his chones full of caca . . . "

Arnulfo was sitting with that snively Don Nadie, that little pipsqueak Luisito Covarrubias, at their usual table at the back of the lounge, and ay, as God is my witness, El Padre Manolito was sitting with the mayor, Joe Kiratz, and they were both drinking what looked like whiskey and talking about the Holy Roman Empire in hushed and very drunken tones.

It was a scene from some living hell, and Isá wanted no part of it all.

Don Tomás Revueltas was wearing Padre Manolo's priestly collar and singing a sad love song, which sounded like "Cucucuru Paloma," but not really. He was snuffly and out of tune, and El Padre was wearing what looked like Arnulfo's mariachi sombrero. ¡Caray! What was the world coming to? Meanwhile, Doña Emilia was in terrible need. She was locked in her room, she was locked in her room!

The scene that followed was remembered long after.

Isá went over to Mata and yelled in his face that Doña Emilia Olivárez was locked in her room and that he had to get over there immediately with an ax and tear down the door.

"I'm telling you that Doña Emilia had a stroke and she's locked herself in her room!"

The sheriff laughed at her hysteria, and then she punched him in the face. It still wasn't clear if she broke his nose or not; he was prone to nosebleeds, and it could have been one of his familiar bloodlettings that came on without warning.

Stunned, he stepped back and fell over Diablo, Rey's dog, who just at that moment was headed toward the front door to attempt a much-longed-for pee. Diablo didn't make it and urinated a long dark dank stream on the floor, causing Mata to slip over him, landing on top of Luisito Covarrubias's feet. Surprised, but not overtly so, Luisito kicked the dog to get away from the stream, knocking over his and Arnulfo's table, sending a domino effect of dysfunction further down the road as Arnulfo fell forward and chipped a front tooth. The sudden fall caused him to urinate unexpectedly in his chones, dammit, sending a blast of hot urine down his leg to his feet, which then commingled with Diablo's hot seepage. It was a bad combination, that mixture of human and animal piss, and created a veritable stench that rose up and caused Pep Turgino to upchuck his meal of five hard-boiled eggs and about four Budweisers. The vomit had its own foulness, causing Padre Manolito to get up and displace Joe Kiratz's pile of paper, his so-called masterpiece tentatively called *The Good, the Evil and the Rest of Us,* shooting it into the watery and cloggy clump of egg, beer, and urine.

Don Tomás began to cry, as he was wont to do about this time of night, followed by his sudden nightly prostration on bended knees with a quick rosary thrown in. He was a damaged World War II veteran and from time to time would go into a trance as if he were on a field in Normandy or some other godforsaken place across the sea facing his destruction in some ditch or trench as he fell to his knees in desperate prayer. The spell didn't last too long, and after it was over he would then get up and act like nothing had happened. Meanwhile Luisito stood in the middle of the room watching the scene with his middle finger in his belly button like nothing had happened.

La Pata had her hands full cleaning up one mess or another and went to the back to get a mop and a bucket, and Rey, well, he just looked at it all and took it in with disgust. He yelled for everyone to shut up and get over it and get on with it. No one was listening except Padre Manolito, who moved to Isá's side. With disgust she noticed that he, too, was drunk. The Sanctimonious Sacerdote tried to bless her, but she just shooed him away. This egotistical weakling was the man Juliana was in love with? Oh, if only that little cripple could see him now. She smiled with the knowledge that someday she would tell her how he'd looked and acted. Suddenly he, too, started crying out about his lost life and God knows what untold tonterías, and that's when Emy came in, Rey's sometimes assistant manager. He was speechless. Just then someone turned off the lights, and when they came back on, Isá was gone, Mata was gone, El Padre was gone, Arnulfo Olivárez and Luisito were gone, just like that, and La Pata and Emy stood near the bar in wonder. They then attempted to clean up the mess. Diablo lay quietly on the floor, exhausted from the effort, and that's when Don Clodimoro Balderas walked in and ordered a Rob Roy, his favorite drink, with Scottish whiskey, sweet vermouth, and bitters, three cherries, one for each of his daughters and the last in honor of his wife. He was, as ever, dressed impeccably and smelled wonderfully of Capri Orange by Acqua de Parma, that unmistakable scent of Sicilian oranges tempered by mandarin and Sorrento lemon with a touch of caramel and musk at only $104 a bottle.

It was then Pata noticed that Rey wasn't in the lounge. Ay, Bendito Sea Dios! She wondered if it wasn't Rey who had turned off the lights. Ah que . . . ah que. It was late, but the night was still young and things were just starting to heat up.

Pobrecita Madrina, Pata thought about Doña Emilia. Later she would have to go over and see how she was, but for now she had her hands full with all these squealing children in front of her.

CHAPTER TWENTY-FIVE

¡Duende!

Juliana woke up as if someone had put a hot towel on her face. And maybe Isá had; she was prone to do ugly things to her, thinking they were funny. When Isá did something strange, she always had an odd snort that accompanied her action. She was without a sense of humor and only found herself amused by her own aberrant actions. Juliana had no way of explaining this mean streak of Isá's to her mother, much less to her father. Lucinda had been brought up more or less by Emilia, and so she too displayed this same kind of unconscious sense of wicked play. There was no way to describe it.

Juliana felt leaden, as if a great stone were pressing her down to the earth. She was twisted to the left side, her left leg immobilized and rigid. Her right leg seemed more pliable and was folded inward. Her entire left side felt cold, and her left shoulder hurt—it was as if a giant malaise, a shadow of some type, had moved through her during the night and left her bruised.

She recalled the story Padre Manolito had told her about Moses's flight from Egypt and the curse God had placed on the Egyptians. An unworldly vapor filled the air and choked out the lives of the eldest from each family, royal or not. Each of the first children to be born was killed. A great wailing then reached to the heavens. But God did not listen to the cries, and no firstborn offspring was spared. The Pharaoh lost his only son. But the Israelites were saved, their houses marked on the outside by the blood of sacrificial lambs. The Lord God had redeemed his faithful children, and he would also save Juliana if only she would obey.

"Obey what?" she had asked El Padre innocently.

He snarled back, "The Laws of Life."

"What laws, Padre Manolo?"

"God's Laws. The Laws of Life," he hissed.

What these sacred laws were, she never found out, because Isá had brought out some freshly made capirotada with cold agua de limón, which the Padre proceeded to inhale with gusto.

She knew that some people were the chosen ones and some were not. How this applied to her, she wasn't totally sure. One might say that God had passed her house by and left her a sorry wretch without mobility and the possibility of a normal life, but she chose not to see things that way.

"Death had passed them by," Manolito said with a mouthful of the wonderful bread pudding that was one of Isá's specialties. "Just as Death passed you by, giving you more than a nod in greeting."

Juliana didn't recall that when she was born she was sick. Oh no, she was quite healthy, still was, despite her malformed legs and feet. That was, until recently. Since she'd met El Padrecito, she hadn't been the same. Something in her had winched up and tightened, and she was often in a fever or full of anxious nerves. Once she might have believed that God had called out to her to become one of his own, a nun who took Holy Orders, but now all she could do was think about other things, things too shocking to mention in the Sacrament of Absolution, much less in daylight to anyone who knew her well.

"The Egyptians were Pagans, Juliana, Evil Men and Women Who Thought Nothing of Betrayal. Child, that will never be said of you. You may have been cursed, but only slightly, as the Dark Shadow has passed your door and left you a pure Child, a Chosen One, without blemish. Well, except of course . . . " and here he coughed and then took a sip of the cool agua de limón.

El Padre's story was full of mystery and magic. She loved listening to his voice rise and fall with the excitement of his tales, heaving up and summoning that certain pitch of reverence and power, his eyebrows twittering with energy and his eyes growing large and filming over. He loved the sound of his own words and the strength and glory behind those words. He was a true orator, and even there, on the patio of her father's house, near her mother's large fig trees and the flaming red bougainvillea, he was the personification of all that was theatrical. She could have watched him for a long time, an eternity, never tiring of seeing his manly, hairy chest puff out, with its impudent hairs that peeped out from his black priest's shirt. She wanted to kiss his chest, perhaps even lick it. Would he permit it?

His explosive exhalations extolled and intoned the mysteries of God's love for us—his calling out of the chosen people, of which, he never failed to remind Juliana, she was one. OH BLESSED BE THE GREAT CREATOR WHO CHOOSES HIS SACRED LAMBS!

Sweet Manolito and his breathy, salivating, histrionic voice— the tratratratra of the castanet—always behind him. ¡Vale! He had that kind of voice, she heard someone say, that was suited to flamenco—that voice without visible breath—vale—as he did his verbal tapeadas and sliced through the air with his passionate and desperate words. She could hear the echoes of his native land, far away, longed for, desired, ay, ese comezón, the cool wind that whipped around him and stung him with the frothy foaming discontent of his nomadic exile, another Israelite in the land of Goshen, wandering this desert for who knows how many years. What would his manna be as he circumambulated the labyrinthine routes of his predestined banishment?

¡Duende!

It was then she wanted to take his hand and kiss it—it was then she wanted to lay his hand on her breast and whisper to him that it was all right—that soon their earthly passage would be done. He would see his beloved Madrid again, she knew it, but she, she never would, and this brought on a great sadness to her that was at once terrible and sweet. She was a tragic figure, and she knew it. And in that knowledge there was some joy, for she knew she would live fully, always, and he, she knew, never would. Together they were a broken and dark story of longing, best left to someone's plaintive corrido.

Soon she was crying, but still El Padrecito meandered in his chosen desert, his landscape of choice, barren, full of wild beasts, inclement weather, heathens, pagans, old women with sagging ponderous breasts, men with jiggly false teeth and foul breath, the rest fools, ingrates, the prisoners and parishioners of Santa Eulalia, God save her from the Pharisees who clamored round, circling like hyenas, zopilotes, brazen buzzards who waited a little ways off to pick his bones clean.

Juliana felt sorry for El Padrecito, a great yawning pity and a love that included mercy, the greatest of human gifts, this selfless tenderness and compassion. Why did he suffer so? She, who had many problems, did not suffer as he did. She could enumerate her aches and sorrows, but why? What good would it do? And would her list of problems advance anything? Doña Emilia's always defining question was, "Do I oppress others with my gloom?" And as far as she knew, her mother had never, ever been the cause of another's anguish. Her father's misery, like the Padre's, was self-induced. In many ways they were similar in temperament. Both driven, self-absorbed men. Difficult to love to those around them, but cherished nonetheless to those who cared deeply for them. She knew that Mamá Emilia loved Arnulfo with all her being. Pobrecita! And he loved her so little! It was hard to see his descuido, his lack of concern and care for her. Why was he like that? How little he valued his wife's goodness and loyalty. How tiresome it all was, truly! Why couldn't people just love? And with that love, accept what was. Her father and mother had chosen each other—once he had loved her. What had happened to make him lose that bright hope? She couldn't understand it.

It was Arnulfo's selfish fear of losing himself that caused him to meander that valley of imagined loss and dread—circling, always circling, never finding rest in the calm oasis of Emilia's love. And yet, who was she to try and make the story so easily understood? She who knew so little about the complexities of human love, the flesh coming together and then growing apart?

Like her mother and all the Izquierdo women before her, she was ever-hopeful. It was a sacred hope, a prayer-filled hope, a hope held against her soft breast, where her heartbeat held it and made it a living, pulsating part of her being.

Did she think she and El Padrecito would ever—no, she couldn't say it. Would they, could they? Hope against all hope!

In her hope there was no pity for her situation, for her small body, for her twisted feet. Her essence was intact, always had been, and always would be.

And this she attributed to her mother, Doña Emilia.

¡Bendito sea su Madre! Blessed be all Mothers!

CHAPTER TWENTY-SIX

The First and Forever House

Emilia had locked the door to her room and made the bed. She straightened out the books on her nightstand.

She then put on her best dress. It was gray with tiny purple flowers. It was an old dress, but she had taken very good care of it, washing it gently with Wooleet by hand and drying it outside on a soft towel near La Tumbita. She kept the dress in the back right-hand side of her closet, only wearing it on special occasions. The last time she'd worn it had been Arnulfo's surprise birthday party, which was such a surprise that Arnulfo missed most of it. When he did come home later, he was angry to see family and friends there at the house. He smelled of liquor and urine. Most likely he'd urinated in his clothes again. He had a cough now, a deep gurgling cough that caused him to hackle up and release a hot stream of urine down his leg. He actually had two coughs, a top dry barking cough that hid underneath it a sustained heavy wet cough. It was the second cough, that underneath cough, that worried Emilia.

Arnulfo was ill, but he refused to see Dr. Marías, who was ready, willing, and able to see him if only he'd drive to El Paso. That drive had once been a joyous thing, an adventure of setting out for them both. The drive had been nothing when they were younger. Before Juliana was born—that too-brief time of happiness—they'd driven to El Paso often to eat at the Oasis Restaurant or any number of places on El Paso Street. Arnulfo would order his chicken-fried steak or his flautas, and Emilia would order a grilled cheese sandwich with extra pickles and a cherry Coke. They'd take in a movie or two at the Plaza Theatre or El Colón down the street, stopping off for chicharrones and a beer. Some-times they walked across the old bridge to eat lunch or dinner at Martino's and would walk back arm in arm. Arnulfo hadn't needed the drink then.

"I need it to settle me, Gorda," he had told her only last week. "I drink because of my life—it's hard. There's you and Juliana, I don't know who's worse. No parent should have to go through such sorrow with a child. She'll never marry, and where will you and I be in all that mess when she gets older? Bone weary, used up, barely able to lift or bend our daughter, that perpetual child who never left home. I drink because of her. She needs her opera-tion; she's never used that foot anyway. What does it matter if she has it or not? Her feet will never touch the earth to dance; what does it matter if she has an appendage that goes missing? We all lose ourselves, a bit here, a bit there, in the passage of life. Look at you, a baldheaded old woman, yes, I have to say this, Gorda, you've lost a lot of hair, and your skin isn't what it used to be. You can't walk and you can't breathe, you have that sniveling wheeze, and you're a walking disaster, your one leg short, the other long.

"We're getting old, Vieja, and what do we have to tell and show for it: a daughter who is useless, the other one not ours in her independence, laziness, and selfish ways. She wouldn't have been Fiesta Queen if it were not for me. All of us know it. She doesn't respect me, nor does anyone in this house. Especially Isá. Ay, Gorda! I would let her go if I could, but we need her to cook. She's never cleaned well. I've seen her throw out the mop like she was casting a net, and then slowly drag it back across the floor without energy. You call that cleaning? The only place the woman has any passion is in the kitchen; otherwise her days would be numbered. If I could hire someone else, I would. I see you've grown attached to the witch, and what can I do? I am a man whose hands are bound by women. Amarrado y atado. Arnulfo P. Olivárez. Come to the end of his life led by women and their needs. Release me from this womb of despair!"

Emilia knew intimately the womb of despair. It was her own that never conceived another child after Juliana. And yet, who could ever despair with such a beautiful child, her face always full of flowers, open, curious, full of blessing? She was always cheerful and loving, always in fine spirits, tan cariñosa y tan preciosa. She was conceived in the deepest love, and if she had a deformity, it was, ay, Madre de Dios, it was that her father hadn't loved them enough. Mother and daughter, oh they were briefly loved and then forgotten. And yet, ay, in the ays and yets of this world she knew that Arnulfo loved their child, broken as she was. Who couldn't love a child without complaint, without rancor toward those bruised vessels who had formed her? If there was anyone Juliana should hate, it was her mother, Emilia Izquierdo Olivárez. Arnulfo said the Taint came on because Emilia was always hot and sickly and had too many fevers. Maybe it was true. Her body temperature was normally all right on the outside, but inside she was always burning. Waves of heat undulated in the dark rivers of her body; her blood boiled and seethed, and she was always a little sweaty, little beads forming near her hairline. The left side of her body was worse, especially near the back of her head, by the base of the skull, the place where intellect and good fortune reside, the place where mothers are rooted and bound to their husbands forever, the neck the pillar of well-being, the spine the backbone of order and joy, the bones receiving the shock of life and bouncing back, time and time again. The pain began there, in the dark base, when hope began to leave her, one minute, one hour, one day at a time. With her health problems came the need. That dark comezón. Why didn't Arnulfo love her?

She was a good wife. She was a good mother to Juliana, and also to Lucinda, whom she had tried to love as if she were her own. And in a way she was their own, their own mistake. Senaida had been her ayudante, her helper. Oh, that name! It was so hard to think it or say it out loud! Emilia didn't believe in having servants or maids, not in the way you think of it, "siervientas." Senaida had been another muchacha, but not as sweet and innocent as the rest. She had a willful, restless heart, and that was what had called out to Arnulfo. She wasn't ugly, either, and it pained Emilia to think of it now as she sat on her bed in the darkness, her door locked against all intrusion.

Senaida's skin was light, and she could have passed for a white woman. She didn't speak English, and everyone assumed she was an Americana, but she wasn't. The girl was from Aguas Calientes, and she needed to go back there.

Juliana was twelve years old at the time. In a way, Emilia couldn't blame Arnulfo for his indiscretion. She only wished it hadn't happened under her roof. She had first learned of it from Isá, who'd already asked the woman to move out. She hadn't and had instead locked herself in La Tumbita. It only ended when Emilia called her to come out, telling her she wouldn't be harmed. It was an awful time, and the memories still rankled every time Emilia witnessed a haughty scene with Lucinda, who had never known who her true mother was. Maybe she learned later, but this not-knowing caused her to become hard and unbending. She was a spoiled child, not out of love but out of shame. Both Emilia and Arnulfo catered to her whims, and when Isá in her loneliness saw that she could befriend her, she did. The woman took Lucinda under her wing, and Emilia was grateful, really. Now she didn't have to attend to the sullen little girl. As a baby, Lucinda slept in Isá's room, in a large crib until the age of four. She then moved to Isá's bed until she was six. She was then led screaming into her own room, which after some years truly became hers. Often Emilia would find her in Isá's bed, the two of them huddled against the coldness of an unjust world. It had all been simpler then, or had it? No, Emilia reflected in the darkness, it had never been easy.

Emilia gave up going north to visit her family because Arnulfo didn't like them. The most heartbreaking thing he'd done to her was cause a fissure in her relationship with her younger sister, Dorotea. She had rarely seen Doro after she married Arnulfo, and later, when Doro got cancer and moved to Arizona, they rarely talked to each other. She knew Doro lived in Phoenix with her son, Tony, and his family. Emilia wanted to go see them, but Arnulfo refused.

"Phoenix! Por Dios, mujer, who do we know there? Oh, your sister lives there? Well, you tell her to come and see us, if she dares. Her husband, Sixto, borrowed money from us and never paid it back. Oh, so he's dead now. Well, good. And on top of that . . . "

Otra vez el burro al maíz . . .

The Bible says a woman should leave her family and cleave to her husband when she marries. Emilia had once believed this, and yes, she'd cleaved. Or cloven. She had believed that once.

Emilia could take a bus and go see Doro. Tony could pick her up at the bus depot. She had saved some money. She had it hidden in her room at the back of her closet behind her good dress. It was a room Arnulfo never visited. She would buy three tickets, one for herself, one for Juliana, and one for Isá. They would go to Phoenix to see Doro. The two sisters reunited at last. Their time was running out, and it grieved her. So many years wasted.

She took out her old brown leather purse with her money inside. Her head was throbbing back there on the left side. It was like a large vein was trying to jump out of her head. Nearly two thousand dollars she'd saved over time. It was her money, and Arnulfo knew nothing about it. Not even Isá knew about it, and Isá knew many secrets. She would send her ahijada, Patricia, La Pata, from El Mil Recuerdos to buy the tickets and ask her to drive them to the bus depot. But first she needed to rest. Her headache was worse than the other day when she got dizzy and felt herself falling into the darkness. She remembered Chamorro barking, an imploring, plaintive, and sad bark, and then the next thing she knew he was writhing on the floor. She thought he was doing to die but then he didn't, and suddenly everything got dark. After that, she woke up on the bed. Isá told her what had happened. The dog recovered, sleeping all that day and the next. As for herself, she wasn't so sure she was all right. When she came back into her body, she decided to go see Doro. She needed privacy to prepare for the trip. She walked to the door and locked it.

The headache was bad. She wondered how she could endure it. If she didn't and couldn't endure, she was wearing her good dress already, and no one would have to bother. She lay down on the bed, her hands folded, waiting for the outcome, one way or the other. It was time to choose. Or else things were chosen for you.

"Arnulfo," she whispered softly. No one could hear her. She was behind the door she had promised herself she would never lock.

Arnulfo . . .

Remember when we used to put a blanket on the grass in the backyard and look at the clouds? We were young and nothing shamed you—not lying on a blanket with your woman and staring at the clouds. You weren't afraid of yourself or what others said.

There's a cloud woman, you said that time. She has big chichis. And her nalgas, look, see them? They're big, too . . .

Where?

Can't you see her?

No. I see a father cloud and a mother cloud. And look, there's the cloud baby.

Where? What are you talking about, Gorda? I can't see a thing!

Arnulfo's warm fingers were laced in hers. Time didn't stand still, ay, time never stands still, but it didn't matter. They were happy. Emilia breathed a deep and eternal sigh.

Arnulfo would understand why she had locked the door.

She wasn't going away.

She was only going into herself.

The Lágrimas Mountains were ever-changing. Now fierce blood red, now soft lavender, now a dark blue. The mountains were laughing. Now they were crying. The growing darkness enveloped them. The sky was full of animals, people, spirits.

Arnulfo pulled her to him.

They were complete.

It was over there, by the old álamo tree, that they had lain, in the yard of their first and forever house.

Arnulfo P. Olivárez y su Señora, Emilia Izquierdo Olivárez.

CHAPTER TWENTY-SEVEN

The Cloud World

Mata had to break down the door. He kicked it in and left it splintered, all the time swatting at imaginary flies with his hands. The man was neurotic about insects. What lay behind this extreme phobia, no one knew. But this neurosis of his dictated much of how he behaved in the world. He was like a fly himself, big-eyed, with long, dangling arms and a halting gait, half moving forward, half moving backward like a praying mantis, a close relative. Like the order Diptera, his body was divided into three distinct parts: head, upper torso, and below the waist. The nether region was dominated by a large appendage that he was proud to accent by his choice of clothing, skintight jeans with a sharp-ironed seam. His bulging member always seemed to enter the room first.

The next thing you observed when looking at him was a disconcerting sense that he had three, maybe four eyes. These almost visible feelers shifted around the room, taking everything in with oversensitive antennae. His red and fleshy lips were the major focus of his head region, his mouth his true sense organ. He used it to suck up the changing mood of a room. When he entered a room he breathed in the atmosphere, digested it, and then snorted it back inside to some dark understanding that he alone knew about. He could read any emotion, especially fear and dread, with that quick intake of air from his open, always-dry mouth. This snorting, sucking action of his always preceded any interaction and was a shadow movement not lost on anyone. Children and drunks made fun of him only once. If he caught you sucking in your breath and making fun of him, that was the last time you'd do it. He had ways to make people pay for ridiculing him. He could have been an Inquisitor in Spain in a past life, and he certainly knew enough in this lifetime to be capable of torture if he saw fit. He had done that work in South America and México, as well as some in the U.S., what work only he knew about and for whom.

At that time he had been a courier, then a government agent. He met Don Clo, El Jefe, during that time. He had the greatest admiration for him. Now, there was a man! El Jefe never had a name then, no, he was just the Boss. Later Mata knew him as Don Clo. Clodimoro Balderas, the most impeccable hijo de la puta madre he'd ever known.

It was in that country at that time with that work that he'd learned what life was really about. That was where he learned how to measure things and how to let them go, how to assess what mattered and how to get what you wanted before others got what they thought they wanted. It was there, under the direction of El Jefe, that he learned to maneuver in the world and outside it. It was the happiest time of his life.

He returned to Comezón after a drug raid during which a giant massacre had gone down to impregnate his wife, Terri Ann, still charged with bloodlust. Ruley never had a chance. Mata was a man totally given to the senses; the pulse of life and death was what he fed on. Sometimes he hardly seemed human. And maybe he wasn't. To see him eat was distressing, his slurping, churpling, chuggling an experience to be remembered.

That was the man who stood behind the door and was bothered by the inconvenience of this unpleasant task in front of him. He was made for greater, higher, deeper, more important things than witnessing the death of an old woman in a dark, stale house.

Behind Mata stood his son, Ruley, the proud offspring of this aberrant family. Like his father, Ruley seemed to have come into this world fully born, ready to conquer. Behind Ruley was Lucinda, who seemed listless, sleepy. She had been taking a nap and wasn't fully awake. She was also unhappy to be called back to a place she abhorred. Since she'd left Rancho Olivárez, her life seemed to have receded, and she was always far away, living in a dream. The only thing that seemed real to her was her times with Ruley, the two of them in their bedroom, hot animals without restraint. She lived to be with Ruley, and nothing satisfied her more than when she had him to herself in her bed. She had dropped out of the Community College, never wanted to go back. She would have Ruley's children and stay at home. Also her dream of beauty school had faded. She would never have to worry about working, he had told her. All she had to do was be there for him. And he would be there for her. I'll always be there for you, yes, I will, baby.

Raising a hand to rub her eyes, Lucinda had a moment to reflect on her old life. This house had always seemed so large, but now that she was living at Ruley's house, it seemed so small, so shabby. How could she have lived in such a dark, ugly place? She stood in the hallway wondering how she could have loved any of these people here. They were all strangers. All that mattered was Ruley. She and Ruley. And maybe someday their children. Yes, their children. She would have Ruley's children, and someday Mata and Terri Ann's house would be hers.

Isá rushed past all of them, pushing Lucinda, Ruley, and then even Old Mata aside. He lurched back and hissed at her, his long tongue foaming spittle as his huge arms swung back and forth, wanting to hit her, barely holding himself back. He tasted his last meal coming up and then backing down. He had been called out from El Mil and was mad about that. What did a man have to do to be left alone in peace during his off time? What he did and with whom was no one's business.

Tasting the air with that upturned tongue of his, he felt that the old woman was near death. He knew death. He'd seen it up close and was familiar with its scent, the acid bile of vomit coming up his gullet to burn his trachea. Doña Emilia was nearly gone and probably wouldn't make it. No matter. She was old, had lived her life, nothing to reflect about too long. She was done for. Another carcass to be thrown out. He would call the Comezón Mortuary to pick up the body sas no más. Done deal.

Isá went into the room first. She stood over Doña Emilia, who was unconscious. Her eyes were turned back in her head, and her body was cold. They didn't know she was watching cloud families come together and go apart. Now she was a single cloud moving quickly through the sky, leaving a shadow on the ground. Now she was wind without moorings, and she was finally free.

If it hadn't been for the other old woman rushing in and insisting that they place the dying woman in warm water in the bathtub in the shed at the back of the house, what she called La Tumbita, a request Mata would normally have ignored but for the fierceness of the woman's urgency and the powerful display of her lifting the other woman bodily and dragging her from the bedroom to the back door and then across the patio to a vine-covered shed at the back of the yard to the old claw-footed tub and propping her head up as she doused her with tepid water, he would never have believed that La Vieja Suárez would come back from the otherworld in one piece.

Mata was amazed at the old Indian woman's strength, not only with her arms like a man's, but with her will, which propelled them all forward, with her pointed desire and her ruthless demand that was not to be ignored. He found this at once heroic and startling. It reminded him of another old woman in that other place in that other country in that other time who had dragged the dead body of her bullet-riddled son out of the path of a tank and then held his broken body in her arms, his blood covering her like a mantle. She was a dark Pietà as she sat gently rocking him and singing to him in words he couldn't understand from some long-forgotten indigenous past, words he knew in his heart core, words that then touched and burned him and made him realize with some agony just what he had lost in his life. There had been that comezón of humanity in him, but he had blocked it out and then suffocated it, and soon it was nothing but a vapor. And that was when he had shed his last tear. He remembered seeing that woman in that time and in that place and in that country and in that other world where he had once felt emotions and had suffered and loved. The memory came rising up now and caught him unaware, a bad stench and a premonition to remind him that he would soon come to no good end, and that sometime, at a time he least expected it, in what he knew was now a too-short life-span, he would dine and be swatting flies in Hell.

The water was at first a shock to Emilia and then became a startling passage back from the cloud world. Isá had jolted her and brought her sputtering back to life. No, she hadn't wanted to come back. She wanted to go back, please let me go back, she said aloud, but no words came out of her mouth. Her eyes were enormous black holes, and through them she saw what was escaping her. Oh, that sweetness. Now it was gone. She was back from that cloud world. She missed it and would continue to miss it the rest of her life. Whatever was left of it, only God knew. She expected nothing anymore from anyone, not even the God she once thought she knew and loved. The Creator was once like her brother, Capundo, and her sister, Doro, the one she mourned with all her heart, the one she was closest to, the one she had so loved, and the one she never saw anymore. She had seen them both in the clouds alongside her mother, Anunciata, and her father, Persignato. Suddenly she broke into tears. Doro was with them! Doro! Ay, Doro. No one had called her, no one had told her. But now she knew, oh, now she knew that Doro was gone from this earth.

Emilia was back, but no one could hear her when she spoke. Her voice was a wisp of air, and her left side felt cold. And on the right there was no feeling at all. She still had a terrible head-ache, and her vision was blurred. She could see Isá, but instead of one there were two of her. Ay, she tried to laugh. Two Isás! Dear Mother of God, no! No one could hear her laugh, and what sounded like a strangled cry was really a fit of giddiness. A sudden chill ran through her, and she realized that her good dress was dripping wet. What had happened? Had she urinated on herself? She couldn't recall anything except the clouds. Hundreds of cloud families. Cloud couples, lovers holding hands. Now a solitary cloud. Now the cloud elders, looking at her, nodding. All of them so peaceful and serene floating in their ethereal world without concern for the complexities of human life, not having to pick up after anyone, not having to turn the sheets over to make sure that sleep would be unhampered, free. In her cloud world all was quiet, peaceful, timeless. In the other world there were the worries, the dread, the always wondering, the always losing, the always lost. In her cloud world there was no flesh to be confounded by, no aches or pains, no sore knees, no bad backs, her leg like a sail hanging free, the other dragged down like an anchor. There was no clutching of furniture as she made her way in a house that had become a maze, a house full of boxes, chores, work that would never be completed, no buttressing oneself against what seemed to be permanent, solid, but wasn't. In her cloud world there were no lies and also no hope. Thankfully, there was no hope. Hope she was tired of. The always wishing. The always clutching. The always longing. The always always always wanting. In her cloud world there was just the floating free in the eternal sky of blue. The sky that held her and sustained her, the Mother Sky of All Being.

It was so hard to come back.

When her eyes cleared some, she saw Mata standing behind Isá. And there was Ruley alongside him, and then she saw the Girl. When the Girl looked her way, she knew that Emilia had seen her, and she shrank back. Both of them knew that they had never loved each other. Why carry on with lies?

She lay in the water for what seemed a long time. It was cold at first and then very warm. She could hear Isá talking to her, but she couldn't make out the words. Words didn't exist anymore. All she knew were shadows where the words once hung. Syllables were intakes of breath, and her breathing came hard, then softer, and after a while she relaxed and fell asleep. In that sleep there were no dreams. The clouds were gone. Oh, sleep!

CHAPTER TWENTY-EIGHT

The Encounter

Arnulfo opened the door and went into La Tumbita. He felt as if somehow his space was being invaded, and this discomfort propelled him forward, an aggrieved lover, someone who is owed.

Isá was in her tub, not his, at the back of La Tumbita, taking her Sunday bath. He'd forgotten that this was her special time. It startled him when he saw her splayed out, eyes closed in her tinita, without a care in the world, little bubbles coming up from around where her panocha would be, open and wet.

Arnulfo hadn't realized how youthful and supple Isá's body would be. But of course it had to be—she was a hardworking woman. Hers was not the artificial exercise of the well-off, who stood in front of all sorts of modern machines to be pummeled and formed or let themselves be led into large rooms with other women whose faces glistened with the exertion of their dreams, women in black and red and light blue tights and soft leggings, their vacant faces flushed with the exertion of their imagined, made-over bodies.

He stood a ways from Isá, who sat in her tub soaping herself, a white washrag moving over her dark brown body, so soft it looked, so vulnerable. Her eyes were still closed. She hadn't heard him come in.

For a moment he said nothing but merely looked at her. Suddenly she felt a presence, his presence, and she opened her eyes. She said nothing but sat there, eyeing him with malice. Her look froze him.

He moved toward her, a little, maybe not at all, but she took it to mean that he desired her. And he, well, he wasn't sure if he did or not, he was just so startled to see her there like that. Without shame and completely so completely herself. If he did move toward her, which he didn't think he did, but he wasn't sure, he did have the thought, maybe he did back then for one moment, that yes, he could he could yes maybe he could . . .

Of course, Isá rebuffed him. She had to defend her honor, how dare you and all that. Nothing was ever said. Doña Emilia was in the hospital, how dare he think. And yet, if there ever was a time. Why should there be a time? Ay, why should there be a time?

She stood up in the old tub reserved for cleaning her chile, in such an overheated state that the water that had previously beaded on her face and softened flesh dried up immediately and left her without any trace of moisture. She had the cold, piercing eyes of a raptor, and if she could have, she would have seized him and torn his flesh. And frankly, he wished she had or could. He was tired, and that was surely one way to leave this earth—in a state of accepted abandon, the way a deer resigns itself to a bear, or an antelope to a lion. Eaten up, eaten away, eaten down, and then gone.

Arnulfo backed away, mumbling something under his breath, a faraway body-inverted sound of surrender and unease. It sounded like a moan, except he was so terrified after seeing her standing there, in her too solid flesh, all five seemingly enormous feet of her, looking so fierce and remote and decidedly female with the most enormous mound of female fur on her woman hill, that he moved backward in sheer fear and respect. He wanted to touch that dark pelt. It was like a drenched animal, hairs tilted down and resting on her thighs, but no, he knew that his touch would defile her, and thank God she was stronger than he would ever be as she rebuffed him with a dark and heavy look.

He looked at her one last time, and his look was one of child-like wanting. He wanted to suck on her large dark brown breasts, he could taste their salt and sandy grit, and then bury his face in her woman space, smelling that fecund earthen mud smell of a mature woman. He would then fall asleep like a baby, the baby boy he was, with her rough knowing hands petting his thinning brownish-yellow hair and then his sad little boy parts, cooing to him as she began to hum and then quietly sing the song one sang to troubled children late at night when most of the world was asleep. Coocoocoorucucu mi angelito . . .

But of course she wouldn't accept him, he knew that, but because he was Arnulfo P. Olivárez, tenía que darle El Try. Ay, ese pinche Try. That Try and This Try had been the up and down falls of his life.

And she, because she was who she was, sat down again, without any hint of awkwardness or shame or embarrassment, and farted loudly in the tub. The woman knew how to let a pedo fly! The air bubbled up and spread out to the far ends of La Tumbita, fanning the air with the known fragrance of the familiar: red chile and beans, and what was it, liver? They had had liver and onions the day before, and it was a good meal, now revisited. The smell, ay, it permeated the room with its aroma of the dark tubings and indentations of a woman's body. It was a profoundly meaty smell, that giant and protracted pedo of Isá's. He was impressed and at the same time aroused—if it could be said that a woman's prodigious fart could arouse a man. Likely it was her ability to feel no shame. It was both a relief to him and also terrified him. She was certainly more man than he would ever be, and both of them knew it. Why had he not ever noticed her before, really noticed her? Time wasted, alas, and now it was too late. Or was it?

He could hear and then see the little bubbles rising as she slithered her body down in the tub, where she farted again, this time a long whiney braying followed by a quick honk of a fart that rippled waterward and beaded the air with its little trail of gas. She lay back, her head on the backboard, and closed her eyes. She took the little white washrag, previously placed at the back of her neck, that place of power, the spinal cord and entrance of both light and dark intention, and swabbed her head. Then she submerged the toallita and placed it between her legs like a bandage of cloth. She didn't want him, need him, or care about him, not really. And this is what she showed him as she moaned with that cloth between her thighs, her pubic hair pooling up and waving in the warm water and then floating back and forth like soft reeds against the shore where she luxuriated, a woman in her flesh.

And when he was at the door, still peering at her because he could not believe how strong she was, she winked at him, as if to say not now, maybe later. Is this what that spirit eye, that strange cockeyed left eye of hers, said? He wanted to believe so. Her guiño, that little hint of a wink, gave him hope. Or maybe he was deluding himself with that imagined look. He couldn't tell what the truth was at that moment. He just knew that she, at this moment, wasn't telling him no or yes. That was the story of his life.

All his life he'd been trying out this and that, savoring this and that, probing and poking this and that, wanting always to get deeper, to get to the root and core of this thing, that thing, anything. Everything always slipped away from him, if truth be told. He couldn't hold on to anything or anyone. His hands always came up empty and longing for touch. He was a man jodido from his first breath to probably his last, and he and everyone else knew it. He had thought of killing himself several times in his life, he had the gun to do it, but those times came and went quickly as he felt his hot gancho and felt that terrible small hope. Too many men's penises have kept them going for too long, yes, over-extending their stay, and his fate was the same.

But when he was in México with his brother Caballeros, there was a respect from those strangers who knew he was a leader, a respected dignitary, the one chosen to represent. The same respect was accorded him when he stood on the Plaza stage, however briefly, and announced the Fiesta. What Fiesta can begin without a master of ceremonies, what marcha can begin without los padrinos, and what woman can be led from childhood to womanhood at her Quinceañera without the father to whom all grace and blessing should be given? The Fiesta could not begin without him, Arnulfo P. Olivárez, Master of Ceremonies. El Encargado. The one in charge. He moved away and remembered who he was once more. Yo mando aquí. I am the one who is in charge here. Me and no one else. I am the one in charge. Yo mando aquí. And don't you forget it. Please don't forget it.

He would show Isá who he was someday, and she would never look at him again the way she'd looked at him today, with pity and rage. Oh, he would show her, old Indian with that yowling darkness of the lost races of humankind churning up and laying waste his will. He would show her who he was, and she would beg him for his touch, and he would leave her wanting for more. Ay, who was he kidding? She was just an old acne-scarred woman with a dark nest. And who was he? Once a stately predatory bird of old, now a raving magpie!

Damn her flesh! And damn her living haughtiness that seeped through his skin and made him back out of La Tumbita in shame and in disgrace. He smelled bad now, like a small dark animal that had shit on himself. He hated her! And someday he would show her how much. But for now, just for now, she had won.

CHAPTER TWENTY-NINE

The Reason

Because he was the man he was, Don Clo thought he could do anything he wanted, get anything he wanted, and control anyone he wanted. And for the most part, this was true.

"I am not present, nor am I absent," he often thought to himself.

One of the few people who had ever gotten in his way was Rey Suárez. In his mind, Suárez was a lowly Immigration officer in a backwater town. He was an insignificant and sad man, and yet there was something that Don Clo admired in him. He didn't know Rey well but he liked him, and that was a problem. It was also a problem that Rey was a decent, honorable man. This is what made him so dangerous. He knew too much about everything without anyone having to tell him anything. He also felt deeply without letting on how thoughtful his ruminations were. There was something almost holy about him, if a layman could be called holy. Funny that he would think of him in these terms when his current best friend was the Spanish priest, Padre Manolo Rodríguez.

Manolito wasn't a holy man, he never would be, despite the fact that he worked his faith the way a mare works an open field. He railed against sin and corruption, but he was a great sinner and he knew it well, and this is what made him such a good friend. He knew sin inside and out, and like Clo, he was able to live as fully as he could given his lot in life. In addition, he appreciated Clo's poetry, his intelligence, and his breeding. They had the life of the mind in common. They both knew that inspired thought was lost on the swine who paraded around pretending to be living, breathing, intelligent flesh. Few men had the insight of a

Manolo Rodríguez or a Clodimoro Balderas. Among the rabble, they were singled out to be superior. It wasn't even that they had chosen their path, but rather that the world had decided their calling for them.

And yet few men were as astute and as decent as Rey Suárez. Don Clo longed to find that combination in a man, someone he could call brother. It was useless, perhaps, to seek the perfect friendship, knowing how little these things mattered in the scheme of his life. It wasn't necessary for him to have friends. In fact, it was better if he didn't. He disdained fawning attachment, anyone who got too close. He didn't like people to touch him affectionately, and aside from his wife, Lita, whose embraces he held and returned, no one was allowed near him. From time to time, from year to year, he may have had a friend or two. But a long-time, long-term friend was not possible. Clo did have Lita, but truly no woman could ever be his best friend, not even the mother of his two precious daughters. And as far as his children were concerned, they were just that, children.

It was a time of change for him. A charged time. He felt it with the oncoming fall wind. It was a now dry, now cold wind that brought the late summer rains and washed things clean for a little while, leaving and then returning with a humidity and torpor that reminded him of his early life back there, way back there in the forgotten place.

The summer was nearly over, and he felt a disquiet and a strange longing. His life felt out of balance, and this was rare. What was his life? A series of decisions toward the advancement of oneself. Steps always closer to his greatness of being. His singular life and spirit the most precious of all.

Men like Rey Suárez were the ones Don Clo feared the most— the utterly guileless, utterly selfless, those without ulterior motives or any sense of shame. There was nothing shame-filled about Suárez. The dishonorable, the ego-driven, the insecure, and the prideful he knew how to deal with and subdue; it was those lacking the giant mantle and golden crown of selfhood he struggled with the most. And he was a man whose sole job was to control.

That was his talent and his gift. He hadn't spent so many years going back and forth between the two countries, the United States and México, without knowing his place in the world. And that place was on top of the heap of offal that called itself the patriot. He had no use for patriotism. His work was aligned with power, those truly in a circle of control, and that world and that work had not much to do with the name country. He had allegiance to no one but himself and the others who were like him. He knew who they were, and they knew him. They were one and the same. They were kin and family, the only family each of them would ever really know. Brothers of the Darkness. Go ahead and laugh, that is how they subdued and controlled. No one believed they existed, and this was their great strength.

Once a decade or so, he would encounter a man like Rey. Rey was an unusual man. Americans weren't known for their lack of self, and their egos were so inflated that they were perfect subjects for subjugation, what they termed freedom. How small and self-absorbed their minds were, thinking only of immediate gratification and the instantaneous willfulness of their own ego.

Clo knew what it was to wait and what to wait for. He had it all planned out, all of it. He knew how men would act, what they needed, how they would attempt to fulfill their dreams. It was all so transparent, so vacuous, so petty, so small. Was he one of the few who could read the lower forms of mind and body that called itself human? Well, yes. Since he was a child he had known he was different, brighter, with a keener intellect and the will to achieve what others could not. He was able to leave his personal history behind—it was a shabby one at best, and wasn't worth holding on to—and become a citizen of this new world order. His talents had manifested themselves early, and he was singled out for his skills. He had gone to school in England, he was a Rhodes Scholar, that dark training ground of the power elite, and when he returned from his sojourn he was transformed, truly a man of the world, cultured, erudite, debonair, totally corrupt. And he was all this and more—he was impeccable in all things human, and he knew how to play the game masterfully.

He would never lack for money or power or the great amenities of this world; his charge was larger and more broad than the petty concerns of regular men. But he wasn't truly human, was he? Something was missing in him.

When he met someone like Rey Suárez, Don Clo wished he could exchange places with him for a day or longer. He longed to be inside Rey's skin and to know, however briefly, what it was to be a good man. Ha! If he met a good man, surely there was something aberrant or insane about him. And if there was, he would find it out. All men are insane at some point in their lives, and it was Clo's great gift to move that notch over to the point of madness without the person even knowing they were being manipulated. Insane men will do anything, and when they have lost all reason, they are the perfect tools.

Women, too, have their breaking point and can be controlled. But unlike men, they are stronger. To truly break them, one must know them intimately and love them, at least at first. Or if not love them, control them sexually. Oh, yes, Clo was a master of men and of women!

And this is where all the troubles began. Don Clo wanted the woman. And because Rey felt pity for her and intervened in her life, he lost what could have been his future. A future alongside Don Clo, and those like him. It was as simple as that. Rey paid with his life for hers. And he knew it. And yet he was still unafraid. And this was the unforgivable thing between them. The loan of the money was the least of it.

Evil always longs for its completion in the good. Goodness looks shyly and longingly at the Darkness. The Sun appreciates the dimness of the Night, and the Moon hungers for the light of Day. Men wonder what it is to be a Woman, and sometimes Women wish they were Men, to know their Power, what they perceive as Power, only to learn one day that the greatest Strength on this Earth and in all the Heavens is to know who you are, to truly know who you are.

Rey Suárez knew who he was. He was a man without illusions and with the force of spirit to understand that he was not the good, not the bad, not the best, not the worst. This understanding had cost him much, and he would never be able to rest in what he knew to be the suffering of the world. And yet . . . he had done his best in his time, in those terrible times and in those terrible places, to relieve what he knew to be anguish, misery, distress. What more could a man do in the face of mortality and on the precipice of extinction? All who walked and crawled and bled their way through this transitory world know what suffering is, none more than Rey Suárez, who held the stories of the world in his heart. And yet, if only he had been able to save himself and those he loved!

Don Clo longed to be friends with Rey, and yet he spurned him. And because he was a better man than Clo would ever be, Rey had to be removed. This is why he had come back to Comezón. To kill this man. It had nothing to do with the money he had lent him at one point to open the Mil Recuerdos Lounge; nor did it really have anything to do with the Young Woman whom he had bartered with Suárez to save. He ultimately cared nothing for her. She was yet another young woman, another pound of flesh and blood found in the blazing desert, only to be thrown back there like one would pitch out the carcass of a dog. This is how he would break Suárez, by letting him know that after he had helped her to cross into the United States, and after she was caught, he had helped to free her, only to have her blindfolded, kidnapped, held hostage, and raped. Yes, he was guilty. Only then had he used that disgusting insect, Mata, to take her back to that blazing desert where she'd first been found to die a terrible death. Only she hadn't died. Mata came back to tell him she had escaped, had not been found, and was believed to be alive. But that was not the story he would tell Suárez. He would break Suárez with the imagined story of what had happened to the woman about whom he had cared so much. He knew that between Suárez and the woman, nothing had passed except a loving humanity. They were not partners, lovers, or even friends. Suárez knew nothing about her except that he felt a pity and a tenderness for her bloody essence. Leave it to a fool like him to feel pity for a fellow man or woman. He was in the wrong line of work and he knew it. They both knew it. Suárez would believe the story of her destruction. And when Suárez was at his weakest, he would have Mata take care of him. Yes, why sully his own hands? Mata was in his pay, and Don Clo paid him well. Let him take care of things. He was the one to get his hands dirty, it had always been that way. And when Mata had outlived his usefulness, he too would be swatted and squashed like a fly. It wouldn't be too long, as the man continued to offend Clo, and in so many ways.

It was all so simple. Mata was in his way. Very soon he had to be eliminated.

But first there was Suárez to deal with. He knew too much, and that knowing was the all-knowing of the man who didn't care for what Clo represented. He looked down on him, yes, he did. And that would not be tolerated. For Don Clo was the man equally in charge on this side and the other. And in that regard, no era de aquí o de allá. He was from neither here nor there.

Clo would be meeting Mata shortly. They had a lot to discuss. But first he had to find Suárez. He looked around the bar and couldn't see him. He saw Manolo in a corner. Surprising to see him here. Things were not going as they were supposed to. Imagine seeing El Padrecito here. Truly, he was surprised. What was going on? But he settled himself, became a blank. A face without a face. He sat down and ordered another Rob Roy when the waitress came up. He would wait for Suárez. They would talk in the back or maybe go outside.

At that moment El Padrecito came up. It was clear he was very drunk. Very surprising. Oh, Clo knew he could drink. Yes, he drank hard. But never like this. Something was wrong. And from that moment on, when El Padre Manolito blessed him and held him tight, Don Clo knew all hell had broken loose.

CHAPTER THIRTY

The First and Last Meeting of the Society of Enlightened Naked Men

"¡Coño! ¡Qué estas haciendo, hombre? Put your clothes back on!" Padre Manolo yelled to Don Tomás Revueltas, who was standing in his living room. Don Tomás had taken off his shirt and was starting to remove his pants.

Previously El Padre had drawn all the curtains, peering out suspiciously even though it was very early in the morning and nothing at all was happening in Comezón. Or was it? Don Tomás wasn't sure. He had been summoned by El Padre, as a member of La Sociedad de Hombres Cultos Desnudos, the club they had formed not that long ago in this very room, both of them naked and bleeding from cuts on their thumbs as they professed undying loyalty to each other and their dreams in a ritual of sacred bloodletting. He was obligated to be here. There were spoken and unspoken rules that were not to be dismissed lightly no matter the time of the day or night. And although it was very early in the morning, around 4:00 A.M., the "Duende" hour, he knew he had to be here.

They had both been at El Mil earlier in the evening, and while the night started well, it took an ugly turn. Around midnight the owner, Rey, had gotten into a spat with El Padre, which led to a larger altercation with Don Clo, who, defending his close friend the priest, had insulted both Rey and his close friend Joe Kiratz, the town mayor, who in turn had been discourteous to Arnulfo Olivárez, who in turn had berated his close friend, but not really, Luisito Covarrubias. Things really got ugly around 1:00 A.M. when a nasty, sullen customer, a smart aleck in a black trench coat who called himself Bim but was none other than Edwardo Amor with his girlfriend, Vela, insulted La Pata. Rey reared up and hit the sonabitch, and he struck back. This was when everything started to go bad. Mata showed up to settle the crowd with an unpleasant and surly companion who he said was a cousin from Cuchillo. Cuchillo? No way. Everyone knew it was his lover, Mongroño "Mon" Mongrovia, from down in the valley by way of somewhere to the south of Hell. Okay, it's an exaggeration, but nothing good could come from all this pleito.

There were puta madres flying this way and that, coños resonating off the dingy walls, and more than one wátchale cabrón órale pinche puto flung to no one in particular with a sudden haunting grito that so startled everyone that for a moment things came to a halt. It came from none other than Arnulfo Olivárez, who, in a state of distress, began first to sing and then to weep uncontrollably. At one point, in a fit of sobbing, he spat up a glob of blood that fell to the floor. La Pata mercifully took him into her care and walked him to the restroom, where he remained with her a good twenty minutes while everyone settled down. Don Tomás had watched it all with a sense of worry.

There was a lot of sadness here, and hatred as well. The ugly men—those being Mata, Mon, and the young hippie, Bim, huddled in a corner in his all-season never-to-be-removed trench coat and all left at once. They were followed by Don Clo. Bim's beautiful girlfriend, with her dyed mercurochrome red hair, stayed behind and was befriended by Joe Kiratz. She had recently started to work next door at the Bead Shop, and now she and Bim were regulars at El Mil.

Don Tomás knew he had to walk the Padre home, and he did. He wanted to get him out of El Mil as soon as possible. Híjole, what was going on? Someone somewhere was going to get hurt. Don Tomás had gotten El Padre to bed, but he hadn't expected to be awakened several hours later by his frantic call insisting he come over right away.

When he got to the rectory, Don Tomás noticed that El Padre was in bad shape. He looked worse than when he had seen him earlier in the evening. And he looked so much worse than when last the society met. That was only several days ago, or was it longer? Since then Don Tomás had had trouble with dates and times. He, who had always measured his drinking to coincide with his meager retirement check, had blown that latter part of his monthly savings on a giant binge at El Mil the night before. The night before was only several hours ago when he thought about it. No wonder he was so tired!

He remembered Don Clo buying drinks for everyone in the bar. Why, he couldn't remember. He had seen the man before but had never really spent any time in his presence. It was only through El Padrecito that he'd been invited to sit at their table. In a show of generosity, Don Tomás ordered drinks for them and then later for the house. Was that it? He or someone was celebrating something. What, he couldn't remember.

Don Tomás looked over to El Padre. Where once a Lacrosse alligator had rested on the priest's white polo shirt, there was now a large hole and what looked like a cigarette burn. One hairy nipple was peeking out and tufted around the ragged circle where once the alligator has made his home.

El Padre's once white clerical collar, which he usually wore even with sport shirts, lay on the floor nearby. His pants were stained as well, and he was barefooted, his large hairy toes splayed on the old gray rug. He nervously dug them in and out of the tired pile. Don Tomás could tell he was agitated. Oh, more than anxious. He could tell that El Padre was overwrought, yes, and very sad. What was going on? In solidarity with whatever was happening, Don Tomás removed a worn-out shoe and his left sock, which, like the Padre's shirt, had a very visible hole.

El Padre then attempted to put on his collar, but couldn't get it on straight. He finally threw it across the room in a fit of childish frustration. Don Tomás picked it up, only to have it jerked out of his hands and then thrown back down and stomped on. Something was definitely up.

Don Tomás tried to help El Padrecito sit down on the couch when he noticed he was weaving, but still he was rebuffed. Suddenly El Padre plopped down on the battered and lumpy couch and started crying. Ay, Dios! It was a horrible night of crying men!

This blubbering reminded him of Arnulfo Olivárez. Tomás had had no idea Arnulfo was so sick, but now that he had seen him floundering about last night, he knew his time was near. Last night, last night! When was last night? Ay!

As far as the Padre went, something was definitely wrong.

After several minutes of consoling El Padre, Don Tomás was handed a letter.

Señorita Juliana Olivárez
Rancho Olivárez

After blowing his nose on the edge of Hermana Dometilia Domínguez's lacy tablecloth, Padre Manolito spoke.

"You are to take this letter to Juliana Olivárez."

"Juliana Olivárez?" Don Tomás said with a tremor in his voice.

"¡Coño! Didn't you hear me? Juliana Olivárez . . . "And at the mention of that never-again-to-be-mentioned name, El Padre started crying again. "I'm going away."

"Away?"

"Cabrón, what are you, a parrot? Are you going to repeat everything I say?"

"No, Padre."

"I told you I'm going away. Leaving Comezón."

"You're leaving Comezón? But you can't leave. Not before saying goodbye. To . . . to . . . "

"Never mention that name again to me."

"To . . . To . . . Ju . . . Ju . . . "

"What did I say? ¡Coño! I told you, never mention that name to me. That name has been my undoing!"

"It has?"

"Never mention that woman to me again . . . She is a curse to me, a curse!"

"Well, you deserve to say goodbye to her, to her, at least . . . "

"What do you know about anything?"

"Just what you've told me, Padre."

"¡Coño! What the hell have I told you?"

"I can't say, Padre, you told me never to speak of those things."

"What things?"

"Those things."

"Ay, Dios mío. YOU are the reason I'm leaving."

"I am? Pero, Padrecito, we are members of La Sociedad!"

"Qué la Sociedad ni que la Sociedad! Qué la Sociedad y este maldito pueblito se vaya al infierno! You and everyone else in this miserable town can all go to Hell! It's because of you and others like you that I have to leave. I can't breathe anymore. Your ignorance and lack of culture and horrible food are killing me. I'm dying here, do you hear me, I'm dying. I may be dead already!"

"What about hhhh . . . her?"

"What about her?"

"You can't just leave, not like this . . . She deserves you to be a gentleman."

"What do you know about anything. Nothing. You know nothing."

"I'll deliver the letter, Padrecito, if that's what you want. But think about it. You are a good and decent man."

"You're right, you're right. I need to say goodbye."

"Maybe it's not necessary, I mean, if you are going Away Away. I mean Forever Away. Are you? Maybe it's better that way if you just leave. I mean, if you are leaving for good and plan never to return. Although I wouldn't want that on my conscience. No, she deserves better. She's a tender girl. You might damage her for life."

"You have a point."

Manolo handed the letter to Don Tomás.

"You must give this to her when she is alone."

"Ay! When will that be? There's Isá Lugo."

"Yes, there's that harpy. What are you, weak?"

"No, just prudent. Ju . . . Ju . . . she's never alone. That bulldog of a woman is always there."

"She isn't now. She just moved out."

"Ah yes, the mother is in the hospital, and the old woman . . . yes, clever . . . "

"No, not clever, practical. I trust you. Implicitly. Are we not Brothers of La Sociedad?"

"But you just said that there was no Sociedad, Padre."

"Oh, stop it! ¡Coño! We're Brothers."

"I will never tell anyone what has transpired. I swear."

"You must be circumspect. A gentleman. Do not look her directly in the eye. She is a delicate rose."

Ha, Tomás thought, not so delicate, but yes, a flower.

"Now go . . . you have your mission."

"Padre, it's four in the morning. She'll be asleep. Can't I wait a few hours? I understand she has a temporary helper, someone sent from the nursing home, Comezón Gardens, to help her get by until Doña Emilia gets out of the hospital and Isá Lugo comes back. *If* Isá Lugo comes back. I heard Juliana was moving there, I mean to Comezón Gardens."

"She's moving there? Ay, Dios mío! What can be done? This is all too much for me. This is why I have to leave. Surely you know that. I suppose you could wait here for a while. Do you want some wine?"

"Not at the moment, Padrecito. Well, now that you mention it, a copita wouldn't be so bad. It would help us relax . . . "

"There in the kitchen . . . get two glasses. The Rioja is on the shelf above the counter."

"A very good idea."

"A goodbye toast for two Brothers."

"Are you sure about this, Padre?"

"I have to go away."

"You do? Why?"

"You wouldn't understand. Soy Español."

"Oh. Well. Maybe that says it all. Yes, that says it all. But where will you go?"

"Wherever I go, it will always be toward the one true thing, the one true vision, the one true place . . . "

"And where would that be?"

"¡España!"

And with that, El Padre stood up and saluted his mother country.

"Now bring the wine, Tomásito, bring the wine. I'm thirsty and very sad. Shall we sing a little as well? Did you bring your guitar?"

It was quite a leave-taking. It lasted a number of hours, and before it was over, both had fallen asleep, El Padre on the couch and Don Tomás on a nearby armchair. Both were snorers. Amazingly, they were both so tired and both so inebriated, they didn't wake each other up.

When Don Tomás woke up around eight in the morning, El Padre was still asleep on the couch. Don Tomás noticed that the letter wasn't on the table anymore. When he looked over to El Padrecito, the remnants of what had once been a letter were scattered around the floor near him, and part of the letter seemed to have been chewed up and spat out. El Padre had one word of the letter pasted to the side of his mouth, and as Don Tomás looked over at him, a lone smeared and moist word leapt out at him: ¡Coño! Surely there had been more to the letter than that. He peered down at the floor and saw a masticated phrase: Te odio y te quiero . . . I love you and I hate you . . .

Don Tomás decided not to wake El Padre. He figured he would set about his mission after they had both slept a little longer. The Padre would have to rewrite the letter, of course. After that, Don Tomás would deliver it to HER, and then return here to check on El Padrecito. Hopefully by then he could return home to sleep. Enough of the Brotherhood!

El Padre looked exhausted, as if he'd wrestled with angels. Or maybe Satan himself. He wasn't sure. Don Tomás did know he had a manda, a mission, and a promise. Maybe just not now. He would leave for Arnulfo Olivárez's house, hoping to God the man and then that woman weren't there. He would then have to find Juliana and hand her the new letter. Don Tomás only knew he had been given a charge. He would set off, but not before putting his clothes back on and going back to sleep for a little while. It was still too early for all this silliness, and besides, he was cold.

CHAPTER THIRTY-ONE

And Yet . . .

The tinita would never be the same. It's not what you think.

And yet . . . maybe it was.

Arnulfo was to learn about the damage to his beloved tinita only much later, after the dust had settled or at least reoriented itself in his beloved Tumbita, the hideaway that meant so much to him. Although there was something lonely about the space now. Isá had gone to live with Lucinda, who was still living with Ruley and his mother, Terri Ann. Of Mata, well, that story was still unfolding or folding in or was finished. It wasn't clear which. It was true that Mata had been seen with Mon and that they had left El Mil about the same time as Don Clo and the kid in the trench coat. Some say Mata worked for Don Clo, but that was never corroborated. And yet it was clear to Rey that they all knew each other, and in ways he didn't want to know about. If any one of them knew Don Clo, then they were living a double life on the wild side of darkness. Although from outward appearances he looked to be a fine, intelligent, and cultured person, Rey personally knew that he was a killer.

Rey had expected Don Clo to take him aside and lay him out, but it hadn't happened, not yet. He was waiting for someone or something, but he wasn't sure who or what. Don Clo had gotten very angry with Mata, and they had stepped outside El Mil with el chorreado, the young hippie, and then Mata took off. It was a mass exodus. No good, no good, no good things could come of this.

In this instance, S.S., the Sanctimonious Sacerdote, seemed almost an innocent, a lost babyito en el desierto. He left with Don

Tomás Revueltas, and then Arnulfo left with Luisito. Everyone seemed to be paired up with someone else.

Dying and then Death will do that to you, thought Rey. Someone dying in your life or you dying, and all hell breaks loose. ¡Dios mío!—had everyone gone mad in Comezón? Rey wondered, shaking his head.

Something was up, and Rey was concerned. Afraid, really. He decided to stay put at El Mil and clean up. He didn't want to be out and about when the mierda shifted out there in the world, which likely was imminent. Everyone was drunk except him and La Pata. And this was very, very bad and truly sad when you thought about it.

"You want some company, Rey?" Pata said in a neutral voice, expecting nothing. She was a realist.

"Sure, m'ija. You stay on and have a drink me with me tonight?"

"You got it."

They sat down at the bar to have a drink, he a carbonated water and she a Diet Coke. It was a good thing to sit down with someone who didn't need to drink, didn't like to drink, and didn't ever want to drink.

There in the hazy morning light of the blinking Budweiser sign, he noticed what nice root beer–colored eyes La Pata had. She had nice lips, too. She looked good with and without makeup. She was, when you had time to notice her, very nice-looking. And she was always kind to him. And she always looked at him as if he were special, someone to be respected and cared for. It had been a really bad night, and now it was a little better.

Little by little Rey had lost the taste for liquor. He wasn't a teetotaler, but almost. He had an occasional beer, not because he liked the taste anymore, but more out of solidarity to something. That something being his profession. He was a beer-monger, a purveyor of liquor, and that was how he made his money, from other people's grasping, delusions, sorrows, and supposed joy. It was a hard realization, but it was true. He would someday have to give up his work, and he knew it. Of course his mother had told him so all along, and she was right. When Florigunda said that she knew Rey better than he knew himself, she wasn't kidding. Florigunda never believed in jokes, not any at any time. She hated to hear them and never told any of her own. Her son's livelihood now and in the past had been her life's disappointment.

And yet she still had hope for him . . .

And yet . . . Rey thought his mother's life dream, her comezón, if you will, was based on a joke. That being her Amorcito Corazón, the dream of lost love. Ay, that was the biggest comezón of all. Love.

Rey knew in his heart he would never see his ex-wife, Dulce, again. Oh, he might see her and she might even come back into town, but he could never love her again the way he had loved her before. And it pained him. Would he find new love? Did he want to find new love?

Doubtful, and yet . . . he saw the way La Pata often looked at him. And once he looked back and then hurriedly away. She was an old drunk, no getting away from that, and she was someone who took care of old drunks.

And yet . . . she wasn't like most of the people at El Mil. She was more solid. She had suffered, and as a result she was transformed. Sometimes when Rey saw her taking someone's order or helping Arnulfo to the bathroom, he felt something tender rise up in him for her. It was good to see goodness. And she was a good woman, there was no getting around that.

In the midst of all the carnage and misery and intermittent happiness and exultation—that being the magical pulse of life—she was there to help her customers experience their fleeting joy and to take care of them when their dreams came crashing down around two o'clock in the morning. La Pata deserved something good and someone good in her life. She was attractive. She had a small, compact, no-nonsense body, a chiseled fine-featured face, and small hardworking hands. She was industrious and loyal, tough and sweet, but never cloying. She could spin you on your heels if you spoke out of turn, and she never held back from injustice. And she was fair.

As far as Rey could see, she had few faults. Maybe the only one he could see was that occasional overwhelming sadness. But then again, it was something only he saw deeply, for he held that same sorrow in his heart. It would never be fully alleviated, but when one saw that unnamed grief in another, there was a resurgence of hope in life somehow, and in the kinship and favor of blessing that this awareness and brotherhood brought on.

Of course he'd never mentioned this to La Pata, nor would he ever; and she, in turn, would never speak to Rey about their mutual affliction, that being what it was, their life in their flesh. But each knew the other, and they held their joint recognition in their understanding, and frankly, it was enough. If ever Rey were to sleep with La Pata, which he had never done and wasn't sure he ever would, sex being something so sacred to them at this time in their lives that if and when and maybe ever they were to come together, they would lie in sacred darkness and in the early morning light look at each other and acknowledge with complete understanding and great tenderness the wars that had gone on in their lives. As much as Rey had loved his wife, she never knew his darkness but only saw his light. And it wasn't enough to bind them the way a married couple should cleave to each other. The passion spent, the dream realized, the expectation assuaged, and the mystery explored, what remained was the quiet time in contemplation and acceptance. This Rey had never achieved with Dulce.

This is what he longed for and what La Pata wanted as well. He looked at her across the bar as she picked up a stray glass on table number 7. She was a professional.

But just what Rey was going to do in his next-to-last life, he wasn't sure. There were untold yearnings in him, more than one comezón, but for what, he wasn't clear about quite yet. He saw a woman in the picture. He did want that—a home, someone to come home to. He wanted to love and to be loved back. Isn't that what everyone wanted?

Well, maybe not.

And yet . . . maybe there was something more.

Rey had stopped looking at women when Dulce left him. Sitting there in the empty lounge with La Pata, sighing with relief that another boozy jodido crowd had left, he felt almost happy. Don Clo had come and gone. He had been afraid the man was coming after him to collect what was due. Yes, he owed him money, but even more, he owed him the life of that young woman. Don Clo had helped her get away from La Migra. Ay, La Migra! He was Migra once, an Immigration officer who tried to forget what was going on. He deluded himself into thinking that he was helping people. And maybe he had in his small way. He hadn't really started drinking until he took that job. And all the time he worked for Immigration, he was an ugly drunk. That was why Dulce stopped loving him and eventually left. Ay, that was back then!

And yet . . . was he doing the same thing here at El Mil . . . trying to help people who didn't want to be helped? Yes, he saw that it was the same dilemma.

La Pata put on C2 and asked Rey to dance. Surprisingly, he said yes. The door was locked, and no one else would be coming in.

La Pata felt warm and soft and strong in his arms.

CHAPTER THIRTY-TWO

Burning

Arnulfo leaned on Luisito, and it was a heavy leaning. He was feeling very, very tired, weary and melancholic. He had been at the hospital with La Gorda for part of the afternoon, and while she was doing better, he wasn't. There was just too much stress. Isá was gone, maybe never to return, and the woman who was helping Juliana was a skinny over-powdered mummy with high-arched painted-on eyebrows. The white cotton sleeveless blouses she wore revealed too much: he could see her wavy black sobaco hair that funneled down in humid rivulets toward her bullet-cone breasts, which were pooched up near her chin. So much random hair, and altogether too much unrestrained, uncalled-for, and unappreciated chichi was too much for him.

What was happening in society? There was a breakdown in morals, and this woman was an example of what had gone wrong. And she wasn't the only one, caray! The way young girls were dressing—in slips and with their dirty brassiere straps showing—was very unpleasant. Lucinda dressed like this now, in camisetas, ugly ripped-up t-shirts, and loose-fitting jeans that skimmed her backside and slipped downward, showing too much in that back region without a name, the scooped-out filleted soft-haired rump.

And now this temporary caretaker sent out to help from what should have been a professional organization had a breezy, lazy manner that he didn't like. She wasn't polite like Isá. She talked loudly and made unusual body noises for a woman. She was likely to hacer mal aire or honk a cough in your direction or blow her noise like a trumpet or snort like a man when you least expected it. Pertulia Provencio was her name, and she was on the ugly side of sixty. She wasn't ugly like Isá, with that inscrutable implacability of those who aren't afraid of their ugliness. She was a snively scrawny runty hangdog of a woman, all skin, bones, hair, and elongated chichis. That was it; her chichis were too large and overbearing for a woman of her stature. They were elasticized and probably hairy as well, he imagined, if he had to imagine them, and he didn't want to. She had to snaggle them upward to keep them under control in one of those push-'em-ups that women wore nowadays. It was awful to see an older woman like her without a shred of decency. Lucinda had no excuse, either, even though she was young. She, too, had no decency. What had happened to her?

How a woman like "Call me Perty" Provencio could go sleeveless was beyond him. If you cared to peer inside that humid nest sideways into her deep and twisted cleavage, he was sure you'd find some form of animal or insect life. Remember the story of the woman who had a black widow living in her beehive in the 1960s? Well, that might be Perty. Except in this instance you would find a live mouse or a host of cucarachas suckling on a large brown teat the size of a spark plug. He hadn't, didn't want to, and never would look inside or down her blouse. No matter how much he was aching. Funny, maybe the throbbing had stopped. Had it? He couldn't tell anymore as he touched himself just to see if he still had feeling down there.

To get away from Perty, he found himself retreating more and more to La Tumbita. He had the only key now. Well, as far as he knew he had the only key. Isá once had a key, but she was gone. He had forgotten to get the other key back from her. He'd have to change the lock. Although everyone in the house knew where he kept his key. By his bush. His shit bush near the back door. It was a sickly oleander that had never grown tall, but it was big enough to shield his privates in the moonlight when he didn't care to make wee-wee inside, waking up the whole damn house, which usually meant La Gorda, who was awake, dammit, waiting for him.

After what had been a mostly pleasant night at El Mil, he would head straight for his little bush and talk to it. He had many a conversation out there in the shadow of the big house, deciding this and settling that. Afterward he would drag himself along the resolana and then against the zaguán, trying not to make noise, but always tripping up against a piece of furniture or a box on the floor—one of La Gorda's many projects that lay scattered, in full view and in dangerous and precarious intersection with his body—usually stubbing his callo in the sore place. Now it was bleeding all the time. He wrapped it in gauze and would have to cauterize it again soon, it was such a flaming pustule of pure pain. La Gorda would have helped with his callo if she were home. He had to admit he really missed her.

Once that woman came to help Juliana out, he started going to La Tumbita more and more to get away from her. By the light of a very large moon, that's when Arnulfo noticed that the tinita was scraped. Scraped! As if something had bumped up against the metal and scratched the surface. What what what and when when when?

Manolo held Juliana in his arms. He had kissed her eyes first and then her forehead and then her cheeks, pulling in the smell of her hair, clean and slippery and freshly washed, for that was how he found her so early that morning, bathed and pure, ready for another day. The woman who took care of her was gone on some errand. Arnulfo was gone or asleep, he couldn't tell which. He was out of the way and so was the old witch, and there was no one but the two of them alone in that big house.

Juliana, la princesa, was alone. Solita. She coaxed him out of the house and into the little shack out back. She said it was safer and more private and that they could talk there, just the two of them. He would give her Absolution, no?

Few words were spoken. He didn't remember speaking, and he didn't remember her speaking much. She directed him to the little hut. He hadn't known of its existence, and he was surprised to find it so cozy, or part of it, anyway. It was he who had to push her in, bumping up against that copper tin, pulling this way and that to get her wheelchair inside. She asked him to take her out of her chair and set her on the couch and he did, noticing how heavy she was, all of her mostly dead weight. He struggled, and then she pulled herself out of the chair with a sudden and surprising show of strength. She was unafraid as she unbuttoned her white blouse and laid it open for him. She was not wearing a brassiere. Her lovely breasts heaved, and he felt her tremble with excitement. He could look at her forever, he thought, for she was beautiful there in the early morning sunlight of that little hut. In that dark place she shone brightly. She, Juliana Olivárez, was the sun. She was also the moon lighting the way out of his darkness. He stood there, looking at her, and she reached out her arms to pull him in.

"Let me look at you," he said thickly.

Juliana was still covered by a light blanket. He had never seen how short her legs were or where they ended. He was slightly afraid to look at her like that, and yet he knew he must. She was fearless and took off her blouse and then pulled the blanket off and settled herself on the couch as she pulled off her underwear, a soft pair of flannel shorts, like men's boxers, only with lace, something a woman would wear, a young woman without legs and the need to be covered. She struggled at them unsuccessfully, maybe out of nervousness, for she was nervous but not afraid.

"Help me," she said, and he did. Very gently he removed her underwear, and she sat or rather lay on the couch, for she was unable to sit upright fully by herself. She still had on her little soft white boots or shoes, and he said, "Let me." And it was he who took them off. It was he who stood or rather kneeled in front of her and took off one little soft sock, her misshapen foot like a little child's, a twisted fish foot with waxy pale toes, an archless quivering of bland useless flesh. He lifted it slightly, and then brought his mouth to it and kissed it. A foot like a tiny mollusk, humid and strange. A small snail a little dove a tiny flower a rose she was a rose she was a little girl she was a rose.

"Let me look at you," he said, a drowning man coming up for air.

He stood her up, her strong arms grasping for something to hold. Juliana held on to a beam of wood behind the couch and pulled herself up to some height to be equal with him. Manolo sat on the couch, ragged, nearly spent. He could endure little more.

He had looked at her long and hard and kissed her again and again. But she wanted more. She was rushing him. He just wanted to look at her, to take in her beauty, yes, her beautiful face, yes, her face her face. He looked away from her feet. She saw that look and covered them with her blanket.

Her breasts, one and then the other, were lovely and large and soft and sweet. He wanted just to look at her look at her, and she, she wanted him to make love to her the way any man would. Hard, with dark passion brewing and spilling over—she wanted the dark love that any man would give a woman at a time like this, a desperate time, a never-to-be-repeated time. But he, he wanted time slowed, not fast, even, measured, not furious. She wanted him the way she had imagined him in her dreams, impatient, demanding, ruthless. What was wrong with him?

What was wrong with Juliana? Manolo thought to himself. He wasn't just any man. He was Manolo Rodríguez, her lover, her spirit confessor, and maybe her savior. To save her he would need time. His time.

Juliana lay on the couch, and he lifted her up and rested her down so that she was lying fully on the couch and he settled in next to her and she pulled him to her and he said, wait, wait, there's no hurry, wait, why are you hurrying?

She wanted him then and fast, she wanted him to kiss her hard and then soft and then hard again and to come inside of her oh please soon please soon

But he wanted to look and see and understand

When all she wanted was him

She wanted him inside of her

But he was already inside of her

He was inside her mind her heart he was swimming in her
heart didn't she know that?
　But for her it wasn't enough
　She wanted to hold him there inside inside her precious inside
　Hold him there forever
　Knowing for them there wasn't enough time
　Maybe there was no time but now
　Not even now
　Let me look at you
　But at this she grew frightened and pulled up her blanket
　She grew cold
　She grew fearful with his fear
　He covered her up
　Held her for a while
　They needed more time
　Another lifetime
　When would be their time?
　Algún día, mi amor, algún día . . .
　Someday
　Someday will be our time

Slowly he placed her small feet back inside their little socks
　Pulled up her underwear
　She was wet and waiting
　But it wasn't possible now
　No, not like this
　She deserved more than this paltry Absolution for her sin of
loving him
　And his greater sin, of loving her
　She covered herself again, buttoning the blouse
　The sun was rising
　The day would begin for them both
　Oh, what a day it was!
　She knew he would go away
　He had to, she knew that
　He gave her the letter
　He had rewritten it

When I am gone a month, you can open it
So long?
Yes
And she agreed
She placed it there, next to her heart
In that place of mulberries
Bruised bloody fruit
The letter would stay there when she was moved to that home
When she met that other man, the young doctor
Who professed his love for her
She would open the letter, then
Read it to herself
Memorize it
And then decide what she would do
What was it to be?

Manolo Rodríguez was going away with Don Clo
To see the world
He had to
Sí, mi amor
It's not because of you, it's because of me
And she, Juliana Olivárez, did understand
What it meant to him
That coming together and that leave-taking
For if he returned he would be
Whole
Complete
Himself
The way she was
Whole
Complete
Herself
There could be no other way
And they both knew it

The tinita was never the same
It had been bruised by love

Arnulfo always suspected
    But he was never really sure
    Ay, m'ijta, my wish for you was only that
    That you would never know the loss . . .
    That loss . . . that love . . . that comezón
    And yet, how else would it be for you?
    You, who are an Olivárez
    We were once tenders of the olive groves
    Later we came from the nopales
    From that lonely road to this one
    We came bruised
    Knowing the taste of the bitter, forbidden fruit
    The ineffable joy, the sweetness
    And yet . . .
    What is life but this burning?

CHAPTER THIRTY-THREE

The Long Moco

"What is marriage but a long moco? Sticky, messy, sometimes seemingly never-ending. And difficult to dispose of."

"Oh, don't get all agüitado about it. Those of us who are married know what we're talking about," Arnulfo Olivárez said to Joe Kiratz. "You of all people, Joe Kiratz, should know what the hell I'm talking about."

Joe nodded in recognition. They sat at the back of the Mil Recuerdos, each with a beer nodding to the other.

"Olivárez," Joe said, "you should be a poet. Hell, you are a poet. A poet of your time and place. Comezón's Poet Laureate. The Poet of the Small Town. Poet of the Forgotten Fools and the Crazy Dreamers. You are a genius and a madman. And you speak the truth only when you are drunk. Which is good. For to speak the truth otherwise will get you exiled, reviled, ignored, or killed. People will always be slightly afraid of you, envidiosos, jealous as hell, or dismissive, which is another form of respect. People won't know what to do with you, how to deal with you, and as a result they will leave you alone. Which, when you think about it, is a great compliment. Some people will respect you from afar, which is the best way to respect someone, and when they greet you it will be from across the street. Best not to let any of those fools get too close. They will only get in the way and become, sooner or later, impediments. You are a man who walks the streets of Comezón without attachment and in your own way. Unfettered and free of love. For to love, well, let's just admit it, it's just best to be alone. After all these years, I've learned that aloneness is my greatest gift. You and I are alike in that regard, Olivárez. And this is what probably makes people hate you, stay away from you, dismiss you, or be envious of you. Your ability to see through them is your greatest gift. For you are a smart man and they know it. Damn you, hermano, you are blessed and cursed! And cabrón, you know it! Which makes people fear you, love you, and hate you even more. Although I don't think too many people love you. And that's good. That's a good thing. Am I talking too much? Sometimes I talk too much. But you understand, you get me. No? To be reviled is to be honored, and to be honored is to be a pendejo cabrón, a vendido. And that you aren't and never have been. You are a unique and singular man, an anomaly, forget I used that word, what does it mean? It means you are you. El único. Yes. One of a kind. It's probably a good thing, too. More than one of you would be too much. One of you is already more than most people can handle. Even I can't tolerate you for too long. Yes, I admit it. But we're here now, and for a little time we can speak truth. Marriage. Let me tell you about marriage . . . And while we're at it, let's include love . . . "

And with that Arnulfo dug a dried moco out of his rather large nose. He inspected it for color and size and then flung it across the room without thinking.

CHAPTER THIRTY-FOUR

El Comezón

I remember holding you hard against the night. Do you remember when we used to hold each other, Milia?

What happened to that love? After a while, so many people got in the way. Your mother, your father, your sisters, brothers, friends, even strangers. You can barely account for them. How did they end up in your life? Connected to you? Dependent on you? And you on them. How did it happen? And you ask yourself, what does all this suffering have to do with me? And what does my suffering have to do with the world?

Arnulfo sat in a high-backed hospital chair at Comezón Memorial. He was holding La Gorda's hand and stroking it from time to time, not lovingly, but absentmindedly. He could have been stroking his coat or smoothing down his hair. He was carrying on a conversation with himself, and to him it was all-important. Emilia was asleep and was awakened from time to time by an outburst from Arnulfo. He was very passionate about his subject, which seemed extreme for the time of day and setting. Emilia was in Intensive Care, and there he sat, talking about so many things, too many things, without thinking about her or her health. Frankly, he didn't want to think about her. She was sick, he knew that, very sick, and he didn't know what the outcome of all this would be.

With that thought, he looked around the room: gray, sterile, full of machines, an ugly room in which to die. Would she die? he wondered. She might, and then again she might not. It was unclear to him and to her doctors. She had a good chance of surviving, but how? Would she be able to walk again? Not that she was able to walk much before. Oh, now it would be worse. Would she be in a wheelchair, bedridden, incontinent, blind? Would he need to hire two caretakers, one for Juliana, the other for La Gorda?

He was resigned to whatever happened. La Gorda would now be his consentida, his little spoiled girl, now that Juliana was gone, maybe never to return. He couldn't take care of two cojas, two cripples, could he? Make that three, for he was sick as well. What to do? What to do? He squeezed La Gorda's hand, and surprisingly, she squeezed back.

CHAPTER THIRTY-FIVE

Hold That Chicken

It was very confusing standing there in the aisle in front of the soup section.

Arnulfo was reminded of his one joke, the only joke he had ever known by heart and allowed himself to share with others.

A man was sitting in a restaurant. When the waiter came up, he ordered pea soup. The waiter left to take his order to the kitchen. After he left, the man looked at the menu again and decided to change his order. He called out to the waiter, "Make that chicken soup." The waiter went back to the kitchen to change the order, but when he was gone, the man reconsidered his choice. He called out loudly to the waiter, "Hold that chicken and make it pea."

Arnulfo chuckled to himself. Hold that chicken and make it pea. Make it pea. Not pee, but pea. Get it?

People usually got the joke, but not everyone did. It was a simple joke, but funny, really funny. Or so he thought. Hold that chicken and make it pea . . . get it? It was a good English joke. Mexican jokes were always better, but you had to be a good storyteller to tell a joke in Spanish. And you had to be sharp to get the jokes. Very sharp. American jokes were like Americans. Medio tapados. Plugged up, not funny. He used to know good jokes in Spanish. But now he was forgetting things. Ever since Emilia had gone into the hospital. Ever since Lucinda had left home for good. Ever since Isá had left the house and moved in with the Terrazases to cook for Lucinda and her adopted family. Ever since his tripitas had gone missing along with his carne adobada and menudo on Sundays. Not to mention his güisos, red and green enchiladas, tortillas, sopes and sopas, postres, and his beloved ponche. Ever since he was alone at Rancho Olivárez, really alone without anyone, human or animal. Chamorro had gone missing right after Emilia's stroke, and despite Arnulfo's having driven the back streets of Comezón at all hours of the day and night, the dog was nowhere to be found. There was no trace of him. Maybe it was a good thing. Chamorro was getting old, and Arnulfo didn't think he could put him down. No, he knew he couldn't. The dog might have been worried about that and taken off, that was it. But who knows, maybe he'd come back. Ay. It was all a mess.

And it was all so sad. Emilia was in the hospital. Juliana was at that place. Isá was with those people. Lucinda was there as well.

As for that one—well, what happened to him was a blessing in disguise, if that was him. It had to be him, and not the one he thought it was. Because if it was the one some people thought it was, well, then there was no justice in this pinche world. And come to think of it . . . there was no justice!

Ay, the ever sinces that had happened were enough to break a healthy man's heart. As for him, his heart was already long broken. He barely had a heartbeat now, but that didn't stop him from moving through the store looking for powdered sugar doughnuts and his Sanka. He liked his coffee strong but was worried that he wouldn't be able to prepare it the way he liked it. Might as well just have instant coffee. Brace himself like a man for what was coming. Just what was coming he wasn't sure, but he was already bolstering himself for whatever the hell came his way, whatever sorrow, whatever pendejada was likely to come. Maybe there would be some joy. He didn't expect much, but then again. He would have to prepare himself the way Donacio had taught him, him and his grandmother. Doña María had given him some lessons in working things out, some hope in the absence of hope. He would have to re-remember what she had said, how it was out there in the pueblo with Donacio and Doña María. She had warned him that these days would come, and about what he needed to do to prepare himself to make the transition. He hadn't thought those days, which were now these days, would ever come. He'd been lazy and disobedient and had ignored her words and teachings.

Oh, those days, which she'd talked about then, were now here. So soon, so soon! It was too soon, and he still wasn't ready to let go of his life. Would he ever be? It was too soon!

He missed Emilia. Last night in the hospital she had reached her hand out to him, and he had held it for a long time. It was soft and weak. But she was still alive. She couldn't talk yet, but she knew he was there. He was grateful for that. No one was in the room with her. The old witch had gone home to that hellhole she was living in. He avoided her, knowing that sometime soon he would have to confront her again. He would ask her to come back home. And hopefully she would say yes. She would take care of Emilia, and Emilia would get better. Maybe the hospital could help her out with her health problems. There was that hope. And it was a good hope.

Juliana was safe. For the time being. Wasn't she? The last time he'd seen her, she couldn't stop crying. After all she'd been through. The going, the coming. And then the discovery. That had nearly killed her. But it didn't. Too many questions unanswered. They weren't sure about the dead man's identity. His face was burned beyond recognition. It was a horrible scene. Imagine finding someone hanging from the church balcony, a noose around his neck, wearing a bloodstained chasuble and with that poem on his chest . . . and the face, what was left of his face, burned off. It was enough to make a heart stop beating, the lungs stop breathing—the will and hope to live stripped from a man and thrown aside.

It was all so complicated.

And then things got better. The authorities—whoever they were now that they'd discovered the man hanging from the choir loft was Mata, the once and only real authority in Comezón, nasty as he was—the authorities, again, those vague abstractions from Santa Fe and Albuquerque, had determined that it was probably Mata swinging from that noose. And yet they weren't sure. There was the matter of the old poncho that had once belonged to Luisito that had been used to hang the man, whoever he was. It could have been Luisito up there hanging by that twisted neck. The two men were missing, and so it could have been either of them up there. Frankly, and it was sad to say, most people hoped it was Mata. A few not caring if it was Luisito. The bets were on.

And what of the other one—few could say his name without shaking their heads and muttering—what about him? Their once-exalted priest and confessor, Padre Manolo Rodríguez—where was he? What about the one to whom the bloody chasuble belonged? Should they wonder if it was him? More than a few people wondered about his disappearance. Just like that, he was gone. No money taken from the church coffers. Nothing missing except the heart of Santa Eulalia, the essence of God's representation in this little town. What El Padre took with him was people's belief in goodness. Arnulfo didn't want El Padre to burn in Hell; he already knew he was . . .

What El Padre had taken was his daughter Juliana's innocence. He had broken her heart and spirit. But then again, she wasn't so broken.

After La Gorda's stroke, Arnulfo had had to move Juliana to Comezón Gardens, the nursing home on the way to Albuquerque, near the foothills of the Lágrimas. All the better nursing homes were in that direction, the hopeful direction. It would have been harder for him to place her in a nursing home or any care center headed south—the direction of the Border, all change and struggle. Too much turmoil. Oh, it wasn't a matter of money, although he always worried about money, especially now that La Gorda was in the hospital. It was a matter of giving Juliana the best. And everyone knows that Mexicanos never get the best—in any direction. So Arnulfo took her to the best Gringo-based, Gringo-run, Gringo-staffed, and Gringo-peopled nursing home up in the heights, as close to the Lágrimas Mountains as he could get. And she was doing well there.

She'd started teaching a painting class and had informed him she was back in school, getting her GED. He didn't know what a GED was, but she seemed happy. Wiffie Urquide's mother, Provitora, one of the only Mexicans to have made the leap into Gringolandia, was a resident of Comezón Gardens, and she told El Wiffie, who told La Connie, her daughter-in-law, that a young doctor, a strong and good-looking Anglo, had taken Juliana under his wing. He didn't think she'd need the foot operation; as a matter of fact, she was in excellent condition, and not only that, every time she came into the room with her new motorized Roustabout, his eyes lit up. He was a single man, handsome, a güero from back east who had worked all over Central and South America with something called Doctors Without Borders, and his Spanish was very good.

Ay, so there was hope . . .

Hold that chicken . . . just hold it.

The soup section at the Save & Bag was huge, overwhelming. Should he get Classic Chicken or just plain Chicken? What about the Chunky Noodle? Should it be fortified or low-sodium? He had driven all the way to the west side to buy food. He didn't want anyone in Comezón to see him buying canned menudo or prepared chile. He couldn't live on a diet of tortillas de maíz and asadero with canned Old El Paso chopped green chile. He cooked up his chorizo but always ended up burning it. And his huevos a la Mexicana weren't Mexicano at all, they were an ugly mash that couldn't be eaten in any language. He wished he had learned how to cook, but now it was too late. Emilia had been a good cook when they first married, and later they both became used to Isá's cooking. Isá would come back when Emilia got out of the hospital, if she got out. Wouldn't she? Well, of course she was going to get out. She had to get out. He would have to have someone to help him with her, and who better than Isá? She was good with Juliana as well, maybe not great, but she was all right, and at a time like this, all right was just fine. And don't forget that the woman could cook. Except . . . what if Emilia . . . he didn't want to think about it.

He had never noticed how big the store was and how many things they had in there. He couldn't remember the last time he'd been shopping for food. Maybe just before he met Emilia and was living in that little apartment by himself. Even then he didn't cook, but ate practically every meal out.

He did go into a grocery store now and again to buy beer or an occasional pack of cigarettes or some powdered sugar dough-nuts. He liked his doughnuts in the morning with a cup of strong black coffee. Where was the Sanka? Where was the coffee section? He didn't know how to make strong coffee. He'd tried boiling the grounds, but that didn't work. How in hell did Isá use to make his favorite café de la olla? If only he remembered! He had asked her to come back, but she'd refused. Maybe it was because of that encounter in La Tumbita . . . no, that wasn't it. What was it, then? Women, he didn't know anything about them. He should by now. And he should know what kind of food he needed.

Let's see, he had a loaf of bread, white, two cans of Juanita's menudo, better to get the large can. $11?!! When did menudo become so expensive? Beans? What kind of beans? Onion? Ranch-style lean beef? Black beans? Black beans, no! No black beans. What section was he in? The Hispanic section. No wonder. He needed the Mexicano section. So that was why there was all the Peach Pineapple Chipotle and the Pickled Jalapeño Nacho sauce in front of him. Pinche Gabacho Wannabe Food. And the chile, ay, now it was either chili or chilli. And the beans, some-thing had happened to just plain old beans. Now they were barbe-cued, refried, or whole with all sorts of things added.

Let's see—what was in the cart? Four cans of Hatch green chile, extra hot, three boxes of MACS chicharrones with the skin on, asadero cheese, also Longhorn and chorizo, what brand? He needed beer, Kool-Aid, Cheez Whiz, what else? He couldn't deal with vegetables. Maybe he would buy a watermelon or some kind of fruit. No, no fruit. It gave him the runs, and he was afraid of diabetes. Fruit made him nervous and made him go to the bathroom. Watermelon was soothing, good on the stomach. He needed some Pepto-Bismol, Tums, and aspirin. Oh, and some callo pads. What section would the foot stuff be in? His corn was both-ering him again. He was wearing his Hush Puppies. He had to. He could no longer put on his boots. His feet had bloated up, and he could hardly walk even a few feet. It was hard to get his boots on, and even harder to get them off now that Emilia . . . damn!

The 16th of September Fiesta was coming up, and what was he going to wear? The callo had to heal. He needed to get his boots on. And what about the mariachi suit? It still smelled of pee.

Hold that chicken. It was a funny joke. He needed to laugh now. If ever he'd needed to laugh, it was now. Too many things gone wrong. Too many lives overturned. Too much suffering.

Just what kind of soup did he need?

He had spent a few minutes looking at the Adult Depends. It was awful to think that he might need them for the Fiesta. He didn't need to buy any. He could try out one of Juliana's . . . oh, the shame. But now no one would know. He often urinated when he least expected it. It just happened. A young woman stared at him as he was wondering if the extra-large pañal was his size. She wasn't really looking at him, but she somehow offended him. Out of spite and bravado, he leaned over and grabbed a box of Trojan lubricated ribbed condoms. Wait a minute! Chingao, the Pleasure Party Pack cost $24.99! What was the difference between Ultra Ribbed and Extra Sensitive? Should he go for the Natural Lamb? Por Dios, no, he didn't want anything to do with lamb intestines or whatever they made them out of. They might make fur grow on his peepo. He settled on the KYNG Extra Large Premium High Sensation Ultra Thins. Why not? You never know when you might need them. Damn, but it was expensive to screw these days. Oh hell, he didn't need them. It was likely he would never have sex again in this life. But then again, you never know. There might be a chance. No, hell, there wasn't a chance, not a pinche chance. And yet . . . he had seen the look Isá gave him. Cabrona, that look still burned him. She'd rebuffed him, hadn't she? And besides, she was a lesbian, wasn't she? Or was she? She had a mustache if you looked closely, and her voice was low. No, she was all woman. He'd seen that.

Life was very confusing.

He wanted to get a gift for Emilia. What do you get for someone who's just had a stroke but is doing better? She still wasn't able to move her right side, or was it her left? When her voice came back, she taunted him at the hospital, telling him he didn't really want to visit her. How did she know? He hated hospitals. Never wanted to die in one. He'd get her out of there as soon as he could. But he couldn't do it by himself. He would have to beg Isá to come back home. She needed to take care of Doña Emilia, her best friend. That's how he'd put it. He'd give her a raise, well, maybe. He wouldn't mention the raise unless it came up. It had to come up. Well, maybe not.

He thought of a line from a poem by the great Mexican poet Juan de Dios Peza: "Mujeres: Es el beso un paraíso por donde entramos muchas veces al infierno. Women: The kiss is a paradise where we enter many times into Hell."

Arnulfo's father, Bascual, had liked Peza's work and often quoted him. He could remember Papá declaiming lines from his favorite poems after dinner for anyone who would listen. After so long, it was hard to listen anymore. Papá was a bombastic old man, let it be said once and for all. Arnulfo wondered if that was how others saw him. Most likely. Unfortunately, he and Bascual looked alike. He, too, knew how to declaim and exhort and tell a good story like his father.

It was nearly time for the Fiesta. The rains were here. The chile harvest was ready. It was the uncertain time, between too cold and a little cold, between a sudden downpour and humidity. You never knew what to wear during the day, and at night you were stifling in your room naked only to wake up shivering. He kept his fan on, but then he got cold. He was cold, and then a sudden blast of heat unsettled him. There was no balance to nature. He remembered that he had to send his mariachi suit to the cleaners. Ay, maybe it was too far gone. It had been a rough four months. Yes, listen up, anyone who could hear him, it had been a living tomb of uncertainty and dread. He would have to have a look at his brown charro suit, the one he held in reserve and wore when he was in México with his fellow Conquistadores. It was a dark tan and hid spots well. It fit him a little tight in the chest, and the vest didn't cover his panza fully, but now that Isá was gone, he imagined he'd lost a little weight. He'd have to try it on for size. But first he'd have to ask La Gorda where she'd put it. See how it was? She just had to come home! The suit would go better with the Hush Puppies than with the mariachi outfit. They were about the same color. No one would notice. Well, maybe someone would notice. Luisito would have, cabrón that he was, always noticing things you didn't want him to notice! Maybe some other pinche joto out there on the Plaza would notice, someone who had nothing better to do than look at a man's shoes. The world was full of people with nothing to do and nothing to think about other than tonterías and stupid things like the style of a man's shoes. Ay, qué pasara en el mundo—what kind of world was it for the Julianas and the Lucindas?

Some good had come out of everything. Lucinda had thought she was pregnant but she wasn't, and she was still at Mata's. Thank God.

Juliana was in that place but happy there, and she might be coming home. Would she be coming home? Most likely. He had heard things about how well she was doing, etc. etc. At least someone was doing well.

Mata was dead, or if not him, someone else. Maybe it was Luisito. Pobre cabrón. It was hard to tell who the man was in the choir loft. Whoever it was, he was jodido. There were no words for the atrocities one man could commit against another. Así era. Life was too short.

Life was too short if you weren't careful . . . hell, it was always too short . . .

CHAPTER THIRTY-SIX

El Último Brindis

There is something to be loved about a town that respects its dead. How would that respect be gauged? What details would add up to the value placed on both life and its other face—passage to the portals of light?

Arnulfo hurried across the dirt and weeds. Hard to believe it was a cemetery, but it was. San Judas, Patron Saint of the Lost and Desperate. Patron Saint of Those at the End of Their Rope, Patron Saint of the Last Stands, Last Chances, and Never Agains. San Judas was the panteón where every Mexicano in Comezón had been buried since the time of the Mexican Revolution. No doubt all future Mexicanos would be buried here as well. The antepasados were piled up, heaped one atop another in the little overheated heat-starched plot of blessed earth that couldn't be mistaken for anything else but the Mexicano cemetery. Plastic flowers in all shapes and sizes and colors were on display, in varying states of decay and newness. The rows were also a haven for sun- and wind-battered silk flowers and gaudy wreaths, every other cross a handmade number with skewed Cholo, not to be mistaken for Gothic lettering, by minimally talented parientes, relatives who imagined themselves artists. Names were misspelled, and few cared. Jesús, who should have been nicknamed Chuy, became Chewey, and Güero became Huero. Rusty wrought-iron gates and cramped once-painted wooden enclosures bordered and defined scrabbly little plots of Astroturf and overgrown weeds. Here and there large dry tumbleweeds rested in desultory fashion. Now and again there was a halfhearted attempt at gardening, desert style.

The ground was full of espinas, and they were sticking to Arnulfo's Hush Puppies. He worried that they might not survive the onslaught of all the goat heads, and it was a shame, as he'd barely and finally broken in the damn little joto shoes. Yes, San Judas Cementerio was an awful little place, and there was nowhere else in the world he wanted to be buried. He felt a certain pride in his shabby too-bright day-glo Campo Santo and all its glory. It was puro Mexicano, and that's how he wanted it both in life and in death.

¡Caray! He was running late! Moving diagonally across the Dioses family and on to the Hermanos Cuellar, he saw near the northern end of the cemetery, very near the statue of San Judas, what appeared to be the funeral party. He tiptoed across Herminia Bocadas's neatly groomed plot and sidestepped a sad little grave that he knew belonged to his neighbor Timor Tuneltera. Timor's mound was full of hormigas, the stinging nasty kind, and they circled their little conical nests with fine sand for protection, creating spiraling pockets that dotted the harsh landscape, brown earth against brown sand. So this is what all flesh came to: food for these disrespectful hostile stinging red ants, insidious and arrogant, enemies who didn't give a damn whether Timor had played a beautiful guitar or not. He had been a good cook as well, and Arnulfo remembered how lovingly Timor cooked his cabrito until it was so soft it melted in your mouth. ¡Ay! It was too much to think about. He hoped the reception would have a lot of good homemade food, as he'd only had a can of Vienna sausage with some saltines for breakfast with a cup of Sanka.

The old and weary live too long, and the jodidos die miserably. He hated to think about how Luisito had ended his days. He hoped it had been fast. Hopefully he'd been shot first and then hanged and burned. If not, híjole, se chingó. It was true that Luisito had been a chingaquedito, but really and truly alguien lo chingó un chingo a la puta chingada madre, and there you had it. ¡Chingao!

Arnulfo might have avoided Luisito Covarrubias in real life, but hell if he was going to send him off into the vastness and wonder of it all without saying goodbye. Bueno, good riddance.

¡Vete a la chingada! No, no, Arnulfo, he said to himself. This is the final end of that puto, be respectful. The man had been a thorn in his side for years. Le odiaba. He detested him, and yet no one had been more faithful and concerned about Arnulfo's needs than the man who was about to be buried. He didn't know how he deserved to have the friendship of such a strange and mercurial little man, a cipher who adored him and drove him crazy at the same time. Tenía que chingarle or he wouldn't make the service on time! ¡A qué la chingada! ¡Chíngale, hombre, chíngale!

The body had finally been identified. Yes, that body. The one found hanging from the choir loft. The face was burned beyond recognition, and the body, or what was left of it, was hanging by stringy and crispy sinew. From all appearances it appeared to be, or rather, as the authorities said, it most likely was, the corpse of one Luis Adolfo Covarrubias, age uncertain, born in Comezón, son of Francisca "Pancha" Manteca Covarrubias. The plaid wool poncho fibers were the giveaway. They were embedded and burned into what once had been skin. Eeee, the corpse was a nasty thing, or so everyone said, sniffing the air and looking down. None of them had seen the corpse or what was left of it except for Lorenza Tampiraños, whose unfortunate duty had been to report the death. Why her? She was the one who had accidentally been locked in the church by a very drunken Padre Manolito. She'd gone, as was her custom, on that Friday night for the Adoration of the Blessed Sacrament to pray in front of the altar. El Padrecito never showed up, and after everyone left, she decided to stay on and pray and had fallen asleep in a back pew. She didn't hear anything until she was awakened by loud and unpleasant shouting. She heard various men's voices, including El Padre Manolito's. She thought she also heard the sheriff, Mata Terrazas, yelling, along with two other male voices she didn't know. One of them spoke beautiful Spanish, he sounded Mexican, and the other voice was of someone young but mean. She was so nervous, she crouched under the pew until they left. She knew she had to run to the bathroom immediately. She got up and sprinted to the front of the church. She didn't make it as far as the restrooms but locked herself in the sacristy, where out of necessity she had to take one of Padre Manolito's amices and use it as a towel to stanch her desperate flow. It was the lesser evil. She didn't want to urinate on it or into it, but what else could she do? It was either that or leave a smelly puddle on the floor. She was in the Altar Society and sometimes helped wash clothes or helped with the Mass, and she knew El Padre repeated the words "Lord, give me strength to conquer the temptations of the Devil" as he placed the oblong piece of white linen around his neck and shoulders. So she repeated the words and swore to wash the vestment several times and then return it to its rightful place in the sacristy as if nothing had ever happened. She wadded up the now smelly amice and put it in a plastic Walmart bag she found in her purse.

Suddenly she heard two men arguing, and after what seemed an eternity of abuse, she heard several shots. Terrified, she stayed in the sacristy for several hours, after which time she finally emerged, shaken and groggy. Everything was very still. She noticed there was a trail of blood leading from the altar and then all the way back to the choir loft. That's when she saw the body hanging there, a bloody banner for all to see. She was so frightened she fainted. She never told anyone that she urinated on herself again and that she also had defiled a priestly vestment. It couldn't be helped. It was nobody's business, anyway. By that time it was early morning and she was cold. She tried to get out of the church, but it was then she realized she was locked in. Ay, what to do? What to do? She returned to her pew in the back, which she wiped down with a few wadded Kleenex, and then lay down to pray the rosary. What else could she do? Later that morning she was awakened by Don Tomás Revueltas, the pseudo-sacristan, who was followed by Mayor Kiratz and a bunch of Anglo deputies she didn't know. No eran de estas partes. They were all strangers with fierce and ugly faces. Where was the sheriff, Mata Terrazas? No one had seen him, and of all the times for him to have gone missing, this was not the time! At least that fierce and ugly face was familiar. No one tried to interview her then. Well, maybe it was because she smelled of orín, who knows. In the melee she'd misplaced her teeth, which she later found in her purse. The desconocidos quickly led her out of the church, and that's all she knew until she read the paper the next day. In her haste to get home, she lost the plastic bag with the amice somewhere along the way. Santa María Madre de Dios, it had been too long a day. She called in sick to work at La Reina Mexicana and went straight to bed, a hot water bottle small comfort.

CHARRED BODY FOUND HANGING FROM CHOIR LOFT

That was the way the murder was reported. Oh, it was a murder all right. Someone with very evil intent had killed Luisito, let's assume it was Luisito, then set him on fire and then hanged him from the edge of the choir loft. But why, why? His arms were stretched out like Christ on the cross, and something had been written on his bloody torso. Someone said later it was a line from a poem. A poem? ¡Por Dios! Who would do such a thing? Only a demented poet, maybe?

Ay, how true it was that all poets were demented!

It was all a mystery, thought Arnulfo.

Who had killed Luisito and why? The who was more important than the why. Anyone who knew Luisito could imagine themselves wanting to kill him. He was obnoxious and a smelly drunk. The who could have been any number of people, both men and women he'd offended in his life. Hell, it could have been Pancha, his mother, who had no use for him. Women disliked him, and it could have been any number of women he'd insulted in some way or another during the course of his lifetime. As for men, he'd infuriated, exasperated, enraged, and hassled everyone in town. Anyone could have and might have wanted to kill him. But no one would have, despite any sense of mutual dislike. It was an outside job. Someone from outside of Comezón had killed Luisito, most likely by mistake. He'd probably gotten in the way in the way only he could get in the way, and someone had to shoot him to get him out of the way. What did they call it? Collateral damage. Someone in the way. An unfortunate puto caught up in the drama. A vato loco en el medio de una chingada. It was to be expected, and yes, it had finally come to fruition that el mero puto cabrón had gotten killed for being in the way.

And yet the cemetery was packed. Arnulfo ended up several rows down from the little tent that housed the deceased's family, which in this case might have been Pancha if she had shown up. She had forgotten the hour of the service and was sound asleep at home. Also, she was not a day person. Whatever goodbyes she had to say to her errant son, Luis, she'd said long ago. Really, no one expected her to show up, and she hadn't. So there you had it. The seats that should have been filled by family were filled by his drinking compadres from El Mil, Rey Suárez center front, and on either side of him La Pata and Emy. Emy was next to Joe Kiratz, with Don Tomás Revueltas next to La Pata. In the second row were Pep Turgino and a few other rowdies, including a vagrant named Pincho Puentes, who had known Luisito in his heyday, which wasn't much of a time of success, power, or popularity. Next to him was a recent drinking buddy, a thick-chested older biker from Galveston, Texas, named Jeeter Wenchley, who always had his pipe, Myrtle, in his mouth.

This disparate crew also served as the pallbearers, and each wore that same set of small soft white disposable cloth gloves, which would eventually be removed to form a crucifix atop the coffin, a simple wooden box. No muss, no fuss.

Jeeter was a last-minute call, but he was strong, and they needed him to lift the coffin. Although if you've ever lifted a coffin, it doesn't seem that heavy. This is what Arnulfo was thinking, feeling hurt that he hadn't been asked to be a pallbearer. Why, he wasn't sure. He couldn't stand the deceased in life and certainly not now in death. And he had come, and of all the people here, Luisito probably loved him the most. Well, maybe except for Chamorro, who was still missing. Where the dog had gone, he had no idea. It was hard to believe that Chamorro was nowhere to be found. Ay, it was probably a blessing he'd disappeared, as he knew he could never kill him. And yet, he would have had to save face as an hombre macho who lived by the Rules. That was the law of this desert land. The Code of the Pinche Machos. Kill the halt, the lame, the incapacitated, especially animals. A woman te jode. Return the favor. Never shed a tear. And never look back.

No one loved Arnulfo like his Chamorrito. And no one knew how much Arnulfo loved his little perrito cabroncito. Where the hell had he gone?

It was Arnulfo's great heaviness in life and his eternal come-zón to love those who didn't love him and to have those he didn't love so much love him too hard. Ay! If you call that fawning, overbearing attention love. He thought of La Gorda. She was getting better, it was true, and soon she would be coming home. But who would be taking care of her, he wasn't sure. He needed to talk to Isá. He needed to, but he didn't want to.

At any rate, he was here to pay his respects to someone he didn't respect, didn't love, and had never liked. God Rest His Pinche Soul. And yet he remembered getting roaring drunk with Luisito, the two of them honking into their cold beer like young boys, laughing their heads off at nothing at all and then pissing side by side in the alley behind the bar, one taunting the other to see which one's urine stream could reach the street. He remembered more than a few good times with the pinche difunto.

Joe Kiratz saw Arnulfo out there in the heat and motioned for him to come closer. He'd been hugging the shade of someone's umbrella and was grateful that Joe had called out to him. His feet were on fire and itchy as well. A few goat heads had penetrated the soft leather of his shoes. For sure he was going to have to get some new shoes before the Diez y Seis de Septiembre Fiesta, which was coming up soon. Hard to believe it was just around the corner. He hoped to God he would make it.

With a large lurching thump, Arnulfo sat down with the only real family Luisito had ever had: the denizens of the Mil Recuerdos Lounge. It was a somber occasion, and everyone felt it. They nodded to each other as Jeeter blew a circle of smoke rings in the direction of the coffin. To finish it off, he blew a large smoky cross that wafted off into the hot air. It lingered for a minute and then vanished with a swirl of dust. It was only 10:00 A.M., and already it was sweltering as only a late August day can be in a Mexicano cemetery without a stick of shade or shelter to be found because everything is so, well, Mexicano. And it would probably get hotter. The graves exuded a dry, dusty, eternal heat, and there were no clouds in the bright blue sky. All the goat heads were visible and ready to claw you down. There was a haze in the air that didn't bode well. Everyone longed for rain, but the monsoon season was erratic. There was an occasional too-brief breeze that everyone was grateful for, but it disappeared too quickly, leaving the overheated mourners disappointed and irritable. There was a petulant breeze coming from the west that would soon be moving to the southeast. The season was changing, the chile harvests were in, and the air smelled different. There was the strong, toasty, slightly burnt aroma of roasting green chile, the dry, meaty, earthy smell of vegetables, squash, and tomatoes, melons of all types, and cebollas, the onions so prized by the local farmers, as well as the itchy dryness of dust that wafted up and pricked Arnulfo's lungs. He coughed hard a few times and wished everything would be over with, and soon. A sudden breeze drifted over the small gathering and calmed them down momentarily, reminding them how very precious life was in comparison to the poor difunto who would rest forever in the turmoil of San Judas Cemetery, the final resting place of those soon to be forgotten in this world of rich and poor, white and brown, the have-nots not even having much at the very end of never having had anything.

Everyone was hungry and looking forward to the reception, which would follow the burial at El Mil. Rey had stepped up and offered to have the despedida at his lounge despite the fact that he had never appreciated Luisito in life. He was irresponsible and smelly, unpleasant and a buffoon, and worse: he was a pest. But alas, he was part of El Mil, and someone had to honor him this one last and maybe very first time. Rey had ordered trays of enchiladas, beans, and rice from La Única, and there would be a keg of beer and homemade lemonade that La Pata had made because she knew Luisito liked her limonadas. Oh, and there was pan dulce from La Reynita Panadería and a chocolate cake someone brought; it was a little caved in the middle, but it still looked pretty good. It was large and had a large white cross on it. People would take food at the last minute to El Mil, and they would acabalar, they would somehow have enough. That's the way it was in Comezón: everyone pitched in during a funeral, even if you didn't like the deceased, and most especially if they were related to you. This was often the case.

As the coffin was being lowered into the hard clay, the cemetery having been built on an old river bed, the little white gloves blowing in that intermittent breeze, suddenly from out of nowhere—and it was both a nowhere and a strange somewhere—came the voice of Luisito Covarrubias, which could be heard shouting shrilly, "He was stole-ed. He was stole-ed."

What Luisito was referring to, no one knew, and it was with great surprise that he was greeted.

No one knew what the hell he was talking about as he waved with one hand and held Chamorro, the missing dog, in the other. He looked the worse for wear, as if he hadn't slept for days. And he hadn't. But that story was to come later.

It was hard to tell whether the shock was greater at seeing Luisito in the flesh or seeing Luisito holding the small Xoloitzcuintle dog Chamorro in his arms. Both looked thin and tired and yet relieved. Arnulfo almost fainted when he saw Chamorro, but Jeeter caught him just in time as the dog ran up and licked Arnulfo's outstretched leg, which had been propped up on one of the coffin railings.

There were gasps and a few sobs, mostly from Lorenza Tampiraños, who was sure she'd seen Luisito's burned face hanging from the choir loft. This apparition brought back her trauma, and she had to be helped to the back row of chairs, where she sat panting like an overheated Chihuahua. She took her Sprite bottle from her purse, took a large swig, and then clicked her teeth in disbelief.

A visiting priest from the Congo, Father Gimy Juscard Malungu, stopped what he felt was a heartfelt and sonorous eulogy even though he didn't know the deceased. No one had understood his overstated and rambling monologue, but his presence was appreciated. Father Gimy was the itinerant traveling priest, doing duty in all the small farming towns of the lower valley, and had been called in to cover for the missing Padre Manolito, who had last been seen leaving El Mil in the presence of Don Clo the night of the murder.

Lorenza stood up and wailed loudly and pointed to Luisito, who pointed back, only with his middle finger. This caused Lorenza to crash down on the seat again and urinate softly into her already sweat-saturated chones, which had bunched up mercilessly in her crotch. Was there no end to her humiliation? Luisito looked at her as if he'd never seen her before, which he really hadn't, and decided then and there that she was an attractive woman and that he shouldn't have given her the dirty sign. Was she single? he wondered. He would have to find out.

At that moment Joe Kiratz came up with a tray of jello shots of tequila that he had prepared as a toast to Luisito, who had told him once in a quiet drunken moment how he wanted his funeral to be. Joe had dutifully written down his wishes and retrieved them from a dusty notebook he kept at the lounge, in which he wrote down the odd phrase or dicho as well as important phone numbers. He had brought it forth once it was announced that Luisito Covarrubias was the deceased.

The list of songs Luisito wanted played at the wake included "Volver, Volver" by Vicente Fernández, "Wooly Bully" by Sam the Sham and the Pharaohs, "Stairway to Heaven" by Led Zepplin, and "El Rey" by José Alfredo Jiménez.

A boom box suddenly appeared, and despite a slow drag at the beginning, each song found a grateful listener.

Luisito came up to Joe and took the first shot, and with a wink Joe began to pass around the little paper cups. Especially now, with the heat and the sudden turn of events, the drinks were greatly appreciated. Since the group was small, everyone got more than a few shots in different flavors: orange, lime, cherry, and a special ugly-looking mixture that no one could quite identify. Don Tomás Revueltas whispered to Father Gimy that the deceased was back from the dead and that the funeral was over, thanks be to God. The coffin stopped its jerky downward journey as the two confused mortuary directors, brothers Mingo and Mundo Mongrovia, twin brothers to Mata's cuchispete boyfriend, Mon Mongrovia, stopped the coffin midway. They would have to take the deceased, whoever he was, back to the mortuary and file a report. It was all a bother, dammit! La Pata hugged Luisito, and then everyone got up and mingled around the seats, patting Luisito and oohing and aahing as they enjoyed another shot while Vicente Fernández belted out the familiar, well-loved words and Chamorro jumped around and barked in syncopation and solidarity to "Volver, Volver" . . .

Este amor apasionado, anda todo alborotado, por volver.
voy camino a la locura y aunque todo me tortura, sé querer.

Nos dejamos hace tiempo pero me llegó el momento de perder
Tú tenías mucha razón, le hago caso al corazón y me muero por volver

Y volver volver, volver a tus brazos otra vez, llegaré hasta donde estés
yo sé perder, yo sé perder, quiero volver, volver, volver.

Nos dejamos hace tiempo pero me llegó el momento de perder
Tú tenías mucha razón, le hago caso al corazón y me muero por volver.

Y volver volver, volver a tus brazos otra vez, llegaré hasta donde estés
yo sé perder, yo sé perder, quiero volver, volver, volver.

Rey announced that the party was still on and invited everyone to join him at El Mil, give me ten minutes.

Father Gimy insisted that the group pause for a moment of silence in honor of the deceased, whoever he was, God bless his eternal soul. After that, the group convened back at El Mil for what turned out to be quite a memorable reunion.

All in all, it was a fine funeral, one Luisito would remember for the rest of his life. Joe later made copies of the tequila shots recipe at everyone's request and passed them around.

JELLO SHOT RECIPE

- 3 oz. package of Orange, Lime, or Lemon Jell-O (or all three, made one at a time)
- 1 cup of boiling water
- 1 cup of chilled tequila
- 1 tablespoon of grenadine syrup

Mix water and Jell-O until dissolved. Let it cool and then add tequila and grenadine. Stir.

CHAPTER THIRTY-SEVEN

The Letter

Juliana sat in her room at Comezón Gardens. It was a wonderful room, full of light and sun. Little rainbows danced on the walls, reminding her of the beautiful sunsets on the Lágrimas Mountains.

She had decorated it with her artwork, and everyone who came into the room liked it. She had even sold a little painting of Our Lady of Guadalupe to Mrs. Bonifacia Bixler, whose maiden name had been Gardúñez and who was a devout Guadalupana again. The "again" part was because she had only recently come back into the church since her husband, Norland, had died. Out of respect for him, she'd been going to the Church of Christ, but she admitted to Juliana in a moment of sharing that it hadn't been the same. All she said was "estaba muy seco—it was very dry."

Now that Norland had died, she was free to worship God the way she wanted, and "I'll tell you, m'ija, it's a relief." That little Guadalupe, done so artistically on a piece of fabric with a cro-cheted edge, was just the beginning of her newfound fervor, and such a hit in the nursing home that now Juliana had orders from various residents, mostly Catholic, and even one Mormon who had been a Catholic once a long time ago.

"Think of the Guadalupe as the female face of God, and you won't have any problems," Bonifacia said with pride, for after all, her Guadalupe was the first and would always be the best.

Juliana was so busy nowadays, between teaching an art class, taking a basket-weaving course, and learning to decorate gourds, that she wondered how she had ever spent her days at home taking a long nap each afternoon. She began each morning with her daily grooming session with her helper, Marisol, who was kind and very funny. On the weekend Herminia came in to help; she was a woman of the world and liked to talk dirty, which delighted Juliana. Already in a few weeks she'd learned so much: how to tell if a man wanted to have sex, when and when not to have sex, and how a woman used her hands on a man when she didn't want to have sex, full sex, that was—because you'd just changed the sheets or you had your Cross. And if you did have the Bandera Roja, there were other things to do that would ease things up a bit. Men were easy to please if you were a little creative.

It was a wide world that had opened up to Juliana, and she had taken it all in. It was hard to believe that at age twenty-eight she knew so little about the basics when it came to men and to women. Especially men! She was a total innocent, and Herminia let her have it.

"It's hard to believe that you, a beautiful young woman, are just learning about sex at your age, things you should have learned about when you got your first training bra and that first tampon."

"Tampon? What's a tampon?"

"Ay, ay, ay! Hija, you don't know about tampons? What in the world have you been using for your flow? Rags? Ay, no me digas. Well, it's about time you came into the twentieth century and learned to care for yourself. Are you on birth control?"

"Not yet."

"Not yet! A sensual young woman like you, with a figure like yours, and a face que 'sta rete chula con esos ojotes. We women have our sexual needs, and just because you're here and have little legs doesn't mean you can't have an active and healthy vida sexual. Even here. Now give me your palm. You don't know this, pero, h'ija, I read palms during the week. La Hermana Herminia. I see here in your palm . . . aha, mmm . . . I see a man coming and then going and then coming. And maybe going . . . it's hard to say yet what is in the future."

"You see that there in my palm, Herminia?"

"Right there. See that line? Pure sex. But more than that, real love. And more than that. A deep love. But more than that. I see a family."

"You see a family?"

"Children. A boy. A girl."

"A girl and a boy?"

"Yes, and a dog. A dog. But something is wrong here, it doesn't seem to have any hair!"

"No hair? Well, it must be a Xolo."

"What's that?"

"A Mexican dog without hair."

"Well, that explains that. I was getting bald energy. Híjole, I thought it might be the man I saw coming and going. I have to tell you I'm relieved. Now let's get moving. We need to go down to breakfast. Today we're having waffles. And you know how I love waffles! You don't know what a waffle is? Ay, Diosito!"

Breakfast. Lunch. Dinner. All the meals were good, hearty, nutritious, and healthy. Well, maybe there were a few that weren't that healthy, but they were so good. Juliana had never had a root beer float. She now loved root beer and floats. She'd never had biscuits and gravy. Okra. Artichoke hearts. Boston cream pie. Red velvet cake. Waffles. The list went on and on.

Life was not so bad at Comezón Gardens. If it weren't for her mother being ill and still in the hospital, things weren't so bad. Doña Emilia was out of Intensive Care and was now on the fourth floor of Comezón Memorial recovering. Another thing that was good was that Isá Lugo had gone away, hopefully never to return. Oh, she might return, but this time Juliana would demand respect and better care. She had her rights! Another good thing was that her father came to see her when she least expected it, and their relationship was almost tender. She knew he loved her. And here— or rather with her here and him changed the way he'd changed— he wasn't ashamed to love her the way a father should love a daughter, no matter what her body was like. Pobrecito, he looked very old and tired, and yes, thin! What was he eating? When he came to see her, he was always starving and would eat a hearty meal with her. It was good to see him. The two of them had their first Chinese food together, and that was very good.

The sad bad ugly thing about being here was of course La Situación. That being the absence of Manolo Rodríguez from her life. She was unable to talk to anyone about him, even Herminia. Although if she could talk to someone, it would be Herminia.

She held El Padrecito's letter in her hands. She would read it tonight after the basket-weaving class. It had been a month since she'd last seen Manolo Rodríguez. He had kissed her and she him, and then he was gone.

She thought that she should feel some kind of embarrassment after what had happened, but she couldn't feel any remorse. What had happened, after all? Nothing. A few kisses here and there, a little bit of touching, some talking, and that was it. After listening to Herminia, she realized not too much had happened. And yet it had. What exactly had happened, she wasn't sure. Was it foreplay? That was the word Herminia used when she described a woman's rights. A woman's rights? "Foreplay is right up there, m'ija. Don't forget I told you that."

The letter lay heavy in her hands. It was a bit scuffed. She had kept it close to her at all times and had practically worn off her name on the front:

Señorita Juliana Olivárez
Rancho Olivárez

After she'd gotten the letter, she'd smelled it. It smelled of what, was it liquor? Last week she'd licked the letter. It tasted bad. During the day and night, after she was cleaned up by either Marisol or Herminia, she put the letter in her blouse, near her heart. Yesterday for the very first time she forgot all about it and left it in a drawer on her nightstand. After all, it was smelly. Maybe that was a good thing. Manolo Rodríguez's face was receding. Thank God she had never given him his holy card. And too bad she had kept changing his eyebrows. She was beginning to forget what they looked like.

She fingered the letter. Today was the day she was going to read it. It was exactly a month since El Padrecito had left her in La

Tumbita with promises to return. It had taken her a time to get out of there, it was so crowded, but she had finally managed. She found herself in the garden near Chulita, her mother's favorite blood-red bougainvillea. It was there in the morning light that she sat in her silla de ruedas and wept.

Sitting in her new Roustabout in the garden of Comezón Gardens near the fountain, she had time to reflect on what had happened. She still loved Manolo Rodríguez. She would always love him. But he was not a good man. At least not yet. That's all there was to it. As to what was in the letter, ay, that was only for her to know.

A flock of blackbirds crossed overhead, filling the sky with a message from another world. The Ancestors were talking to her.

Maybe she would go to Spain to study art. Maybe she would go to the university and get a degree. Maybe she would befriend the blond doctor. She didn't love him. Not yet.

Anything was possible. Herminia had seen the future in her palm, and as Juliana held her right hand against her heart—in the place of mulberries, hope, and love—she knew just how miraculous life was—for Death had passed her by. She knew she was, entirely and completely, a child of this Blessed Earth.

CHAPTER THIRTY-EIGHT

La Fiesta

Ever since, they had been inseparable. Neither wanted to be separated from the other. After all they had been through and all they were going to go through, yes, there was that aspect of it as well. They knew that they were better off close to each other. And there was great comfort in that.

They both had been tried, tested, and tested again. That pinche jodido cosa called life had beaten, broken, and bent them both. And they were the worse for wear. And yet, in a strange and miraculous way, they had survived, surpassed, and yes, grown from the aberrant and chingao experiences of the last four months. That's when the chingazos began. ¡Cinco de Mayo! The Puta Madre Fiesta of All Fiestas!

Now Chamorro not only slept with Arnulfo but went everywhere with him. No cage or leash was necessary. No vocal command or movement of the hand restrained him or called him near. The Xolo never left Arnulfo's side. After what he'd been through—a kidnapping by a deranged man in a long black coat, sequestration in a strange and smelly house, no light for days, an ugly place to pee and defecate, terrible food, oh, the ignominy of having to eat Walmart cat food, seventy cents a can, and not his usual careful diet of ground beef with an egg for protein and his beloved red chile, why, there was no way to describe his exile from his beloved Rancho Olivárez! Thank God he had been rescued by, of all people, another crazy man, Luisito Covarrubias, el wine-ito. Ay, that was a story! And this is not to mention his terrible guilt and sadness at having to leave Arnulfo without saying goodbye. Oh, that had weighed more heavily than anything else, as he felt that his sacred duty had been taken from him. And then to find out that Doña Emilia was in the hospital and near death, it was too much! It was a period of his life he didn't want to remember! Chamorro knew that he would never leave Arnulfo's side until Arnulfo left his side. Both of them now realized that the final leave-taking would be peaceful as they lay snuggled one beside the other in the big bed in Arnulfo's room, both of them under the covers of that large wool Mexican blanket that was so heavy it buried you alive. Arnulfo was always cold now, no matter the outside temperature. His room was cold. The house was very cold. Even though it was September, there was a chill to the air. Both could tell it was going to be a hard winter.

But at least Chamorro knew he would not have to be subjected to an ugly death by a cold bullet behind La Tumbita, his still-warm carcass thrown into the basura, the ugly garbage bin behind the house, removed on Fridays and taken to the Comezón dump. When Arnulfo left this earth, he promised his beloved Xolito, either of them, whoever died first, would be buried with the ashes of the other, ever-faithful companions, the ever-loving Chamorro and the now almost reformed Arnulfo P. Olivárez. Arnulfo now only went to El Mil every other day and stayed for one drink, well, maybe two. He had to check in on Joe Kiratz and see how his book was going.

Every day Chamorro and Arnulfo said hello, good morning, how are you, I love you, and goodnight. The dialogue was open, constant, and very loving. Arnulfo had become a better and more loving man, less selfish. Both of them visited Doña Emilia, who had recently moved to Comezón Gardens, where she was recuperating. Chamorro was glad to see the couple growing closer. They also popped in on Juliana, who was still there and might even be staying on. Oh, things were uncertain still, but at least everyone was getting along . . . and getting stronger; they were, weren't they? Juliana was so alive, so full of energy now. Was she in love? Or was she coming into her selfhood, finding the strength she'd always had? She was so loved and appreciated at the nursing home. She was a friend to all, and no one imagined her going far away, most especially one young doctor who doted on her. Was she having a romance? they wondered. And if not, why not?

No one knew that Juliana was saving the money she made from selling her art, and that one day she was going to take a long trip by herself. No escort needed. No man to tie her down, not yet. For after all, she knew who she was and where she was going.

Doña Emilia was weak but hopeful, and Arnulfo was very weak but philosophical. Everyone had to die. Someday soon, Persi Izquierdo's La Sebastiana would stand in front of him in all her bony glory, opening up a ragged blouse and showing him her dried-up chichis, then tapping him on the shoulder and asking him to dance.

Arnulfo looked out at the 16th of September crowd. They were different from the Cinco de Mayo Gringo embriagado faces staring out at him, inebriated and full of piss and beer. This crowd was darker, humbler, more down-home. It was the plebe out there dancing to the Cumbia Cruisers, short little viejitas bobbing in a bowlegged beat, their in-control jefito dance partners holding them the way a woman should be held by a man who still knew how to hold a woman and steer her across the dance floor, which in this instance was the pitted cement in front of the kiosco, roughened edges carved out by years of shabby maintenance and outright descuido. Nothing was too well taken care of, but no one cared; it was late afternoon, and the darkness was coming on. Soon the night would be here, and then the fun would really begin.

The Plaza lights twinkled on and off and then stayed on. It was growing dark. Arnulfo had never seen the sky the color it was now—an incredible agave blue-green. He would, if he were alone, stare at it until it faded back into the darkness of the Lágrimas, which stood out like sentinels behind the horizon, but as Master of Ceremonies he had to stand guard over the crowd on the Plaza, an ever-watchful arbiter of the crowd's happiness. And why should he care what they felt or dreamed? This was his last year in this pinche get-up!

Arnulfo was wearing his brown charro suit, his second choice, of course, because his beloved mariachi outfit had suffered irreparable damage the last Fiesta and he hadn't sent it to the dry cleaners on time. Frankly, he was afraid to send it to the cleaners; the silver thread on the left arm was unraveling at the cuff, and the pants were stretched out in the como se llama, and the trap door was all húango, loose and stretched out from being pulled up and down.

It had been a bad year all around, and the suit's disrepair was testimony to the difficulties he'd endured in the last go-round as Master of Ceremonies. He was wearing his Hush Puppies, which weren't so hushed or puppied anymore. They looked old, and the soft camel color had shifted to a caca brown with some strange discoloration near his infected callo. He had dragged himself to El Paso recently, and Dr. Marías thought the callo needed to be operated on. Following the Fiesta, Arnulfo was ordered to wear sandals until the corn dried out and was able to be lanced and then sutured. An abscess or ulcer had developed, and now it was hard to stand, much less walk any great distance. It was possible that things would become serious if he didn't take better care. Like hell he was going to wear joto sandals and parade around town with his large hairy toes!

Arnulfo was using a bordón, a colorful cane that had once belonged to La Gorda, probably handmade by Persi Izquierdo, and come to think of it, he wondered why he hadn't used one before. It gave him a steadiness he liked, and a distinguished appearance that proclaimed he was an important man. The cane had also been useful when he tapped a rascal dog on the snout and moved him out of his path. Don Arnulfo P. Olivárez. Master of Ceremonies. Fiesta Director and Unofficial Mayor of Comezón, Nuevo México. Okay, okay. Córtalo.

Arnulfo looked out to the crowd. He knew many of the people out there dancing to a slow number. Wiffie Urquide and his wife, La Connie, came traipsing by, followed by Pep Turgino and his girlfriend, Wuanita, a big blond waitress with a little white mustache who worked at La Única, and caray, who would be waltzing by, Todo I love you, Baby, but Rey and La Pata, who now were an item. What was he doing here and not at El Mil? Oh yeah, now Emy was running the bar. The rumor was that Rey was going to sell.

Arnulfo had been sitting down in a chair near the kiosco that Luisito had brought him. Cabrón. The man was still out there bothering him and wanting to get close. He was like Chamorro, never leaving his side. Ay, maybe there was some blessing in that. Since the murder of whoever it was—no one was really sure who it was—Luisito had stayed close to Arnulfo as well. No matter how much interrogation had gone on about the events of his disappearance and then sudden return, Luisito was unable to reveal exactly what had happened the night of the killing. All he could talk about was that some clowns—he kept repeating that phrase—some clowns had beaten him up and then locked him in a house. He didn't remember where, "'member I was all cutted up and beated up and medio muerto." Everyone could tell he was terrified when he spoke about that night, and they soon realized he didn't want to remember any of the details of what happened. He had a bad cut on his face that became a scar that he was always rubbing, and after a while people stopped asking him about what had happened that night, the night they found the man hanging from the choir loft in Santa Eulalia Church. Luisito didn't remember much, and what he did remember he didn't want to remember.

Arnulfo stood up a minute to check out someone in the shadows.

Did he see out there . . . was it? It was a woman, yes, she seemed so familiar.

He knew her face . . . was it . . . no. Was it Dominga Maez Hornbarger?

Surely not . . . and yet . . . she looked young and then maybe not so young. No, it wasn't Minga. Minga wasn't really that attractive when he thought about it. Her face had a cold, hard look. The woman out there in the shadows was beautiful the way a woman in her maturity can be, but it was more than that.

The Lágrimas Mountains were now red, now purple, now dark blue. The woman stood out against the mountains in an aura of white. She seemed so familiar. The woman reminded him of Doña

María Quiroz . . . she had that kind of face, with high-set cheekbones and a straight, firm nose and full lips. She looked nativa, she was an indigenous woman, and she was smiling . . . smiling at him . . . Arnulfo P. Olivárez. The King of Comezón . . . Master of Ceremonies . . .

"Buenas noches, Damas y Caballeros . . . today is September 16th, Mexican Independence Day. In the early hours in 1810, Padre Hidalgo rang the bell of his little church calling for people to fight for liberty, for their freedom from Spain. And God knows we had to free ourselves from Los Ethpañoles!"

He spat out these words, thinking of S.S., the Sanctimonious Sacerdote, El Padre Manolito Rodríguez. Maybe he was the one who had hung from that choir loft not so long ago. He was the man who broke his daughter Juliana's heart, but then again, maybe not. She never spoke of him, and what little Arnulfo knew of their supposed romance, he had learned from, of all people, Luisito, who had all the chisme. Oh, let the dead man rest, whoever he was!

Arnulfo turned back to the Plaza crowd. Things were heating up, and soon the dance would begin.

"Estimado Público, on this beautiful and sacred day we are here together to celebrate what for Mexicanos is a great day of national pride and another year of freedom. Otro año, que Dios es servido. The 16th of September. Diez y Seis de Septiembre. Mexican Independence Day. This is México, don't you forget it. ¡Qué Viva México! ¡Ay, mi gente! ¡Qué Viva Comezón! Long live our little hometown! Long live our little world! Long live the story of our people fighting for their freedom! Let us remember our Ancestors, los Antepasados, all those who worked and loved this land, not just the you-know-whos who have money and big fancy cars and gave all the rest of us pedo and dragged us through the streets because we were inmigrantes. Let us call out for freedom from tyranny, oppression, and the pinche jodidos cabrones que todavía . . . "

The music was coming up . . . no one heard his last phrase, and it was probably a good thing. The song was one of La Gorda's favorites, the melody by Narciso Serradell Sevilla . . . "La Golondrina" . . . "The Swallow" . . .

LA GOLONDRINA
Por Narciso Serradell Sevilla

Adonde irá, veloz y fatigada
La golondrina que de aquí se va,
Más si en el viento se hallará extraviada
Buscando abrigo y no lo encontrará.

Junto a mi lecho le pondré su nido
En donde pueda la estación pasar;
También yo estoy en la region perdida
¡Oh cielo santo! y sin poder volar.

Dejé también
mi patria idolatrada
esa mansión
que me miró nacer.

Mi vida es hoy
errante y angustida
y ya no puedo
a mi mansión volver.

Ave querida,
amada peregrina,
mi corazón
al tuyo acercaré

voy recordando
tierna golondrina
recordaré
mi patria y llorare.

Arnulfo saw Rey slide by, todo huggy medio hunched over, his crotch close to La Pata, and caray, if she wasn't kneading his back like warm masa with her small hands. Mmmm!

He looked back toward the house . . . and then back toward El Mil.

Otra vez el burro al maíz . . .

Which way . . . which way . . .

Maybe he would go see La Gorda. Maybe not. It was already late. For sure tomorrow he would go see her and Juliana. He would spend all day with them. He was hungry. Monday was Roast Beef Day.

Rey wouldn't be at the lounge, not today, but Emy would be. It wouldn't be the same if Rey wasn't there. Times had changed. He'd changed. Who else would be there? Maybe no one, because toda la bola was out here in front of the kiosco dancing. Joe. Pep Turgino. Luisito. Pendejito, there he was on the dance floor with—who was that? Lorenza Tampiraños? Híjole, La Patada. The next thing he knew, they'd be getting married! Even Don Tomás Revueltas was sitting on a lawn chair in the cool night humming to himself and looking todo contento con su wine-ito in a little paper bag.

And who was that in the back there, under an ugly gray poncho—none other than La Gringa Seca, La Mercia Crawley, who would never put an end to the Fiestas as long as he lived. When she saw him looking at her, she looked the other way. Fregada had nothing better to do than sit in the darkness with a bunch of Mexicanos enjoying the cool night air and listening to the music of his people. He would forgive her this one time, pobrecita. He heard she'd been sick.

He promised himself that later he would go over to her and say hello and tell her how her friend Doña Emilia was doing.

A comezón exists in most everyone's heart and memory—which is really the same thing—a lost love, a never-found love, a love rejected or accepted, a love known but then strayed, a found love not known, a place, a thing, a goal, tangible or not, a lover, alive or not, dreamed or not, a phantom always loved. A God, perhaps, desired, rejected, never found, yes, a God, the many, the One.

Each of us has our little time on this earth, and who was he to give Mercia Crawley or anyone else pleito on this one sacred night?

Arnulfo hummed a line of the song: "Mi vida es hoy errante y angustida." Yes, wandering, anguished, he couldn't return home. Pero fíjate, it wasn't over yet. No, not yet. Chamorro nudged him as if in agreement. Híjole, but his Xolito was smart. Arnulfo reached down and patted his smooth, soft body.

Something caught Arnulfo's eye. Back there in the shadows was a woman. She was looking at him. He couldn't see her clearly. But he knew who she was. She was waiting for him. Let her wait a little bit longer. He was Arnulfo P. Olivárez. Master of Ceremonies of the Fiesta. Unofficial Mayor. The King of Comezón.

Yes, she was there. He could see her now. She was smiling at him with that radiant and knowing smile of hers.

Her name was Doña María Quiroz.

Alongside her stood La Destroyer.

And behind them stood Morning Light. And behind her, well, he couldn't see that far . . . and it was probably a good thing.

Arnulfo was a little sad the sun was going down. But oh, what a sunset it was going to be.

© (464866) Conaculta.INAH.Sinafo.FN.México.

María Zavala, "La Destroyer."
Ayuda a bien morir a los soldados.
She helps the soldiers to die a good death.

México, 1914.

Bendiciones

Thank you to those many people who have helped me to envision this world of Comezón. Many of them are Ancestors who have passed into the Cloud World, and to them I give my respect and deepest thanks.

This book is dedicated to my beautiful sister Faride Faver Chávez Diener Miller Conway, who was my biggest fan and who always supported me unconditionally. She believed in my words, and for this gift of faith I am so grateful. Your enduring truthful friendship has meant so much to me for so long. You were there when I came crashing into the world, and I know you will be there when I leave to join the stars. I love you, Febe.

Thank you to Juan Albert for giving me more than a few bon mots to spice up the book. ¡Qué Viva el Padre Manolito! Thanks also to Roberto Perezdíaz for helping out with the Spanish-Spanish slang.

I recommend the book *Too Late to Die Young* by Harriet McBryde Johnson. It helped me to understand the life of Juliana Olivárez, my protagonist. I am grateful to this wonderful writer and activist for her incredible testimony and education on disability awareness.

There are so many people to thank who have encouraged me over the years and have sent the elevator back. Renvoyez l'ascenseur: This term in French literally means to send the elevator back to those waiting for it. The concept comes from those small elevators that need several up-and-down visits and the assistance of the one going up or down and also the assistance of the one staying put. En otro sentido, the phrase means to return the favor. I want to thank special friends John Randall, Sandra Cisneros, Rowan

Evans and Joe Castner, Raúl Félix, Cristina García, Charles Lewis, Kari Sortland, Abraham Verghese, Alan Marks, and John Nichols, true friends of art and literature, for always sending the elevator back.

Dear friend and guide John Bilderbeck was always there to help and sustain me. He was there those Sundays when no one else showed up. We hooted and hollered to Santana and Cream and let out many a grito. We ate our ham sandwiches and drank our café de la olla, friendship always intact and sacred. Until he passed away, I didn't realize how deep our friendship was. Descanse en Paz, hermano.

This book began in the novel-writing class that Tony Hillerman taught at the University of New Mexico. He was my professor, my mentor, later my friend, and will always be an inspiration as a fearless advocate of creativity. He took our ragtag group of budding writers and made us believe that we could become novelists. Thank you, Tony, for your gift of faith. Thank you as well to Anne Hillerman, for continuing her father's tradition of generosity and love.

My thanks to my editor, Emily Jerman Schuster, for her care and always kind and professional guardianship.

A special thank you to friend and mentor Robert Con Davis-Undiano, a true lover of Chicano/Chicana Literature and a voice for Global Culture, Literature, and Art. I salute your vision!

Thank you to the University of Oklahoma Press, its editors and staff, for shining its far-reaching, powerful, faithful and steady light in the world of publishing. Few others support as you have and continue to do.

I'd like to celebrate the life and memory of Rawley Tandy, one of the 4B Buzzards, a kind, handsome, and lovely man with an exuberance for life who was a dear friend and who left us much too young ¡Alabanza!

My sister Margo Chávez-Charles, a talented teacher and writer, has been a strong supporter in times of bad knees, gimpy legs, and early and late phone calls. You know how it is, hermana! I thank you for the grace and beauty of your spirit and for other untold mercies.

My uncle Leonardo Rede was the inspiration for this novel. I never met him, as he died long before I was born, but he was legend to me. Gracias, Tío Nardo, por ese viaje tan importante. This book is inspired and informed and is dedicated in spirit Pa' mi Tío Nardo. Now you are Mountain.

My mother, Delfina Rede Faver Chávez, shines ever bright in my heart. She is and was my fortress of hope. In my book of life she is Legend.

My father, E. E. Chávez, was a man of great strength and will. He gave me the ability to face adversity and to call it opportunity. I attribute this gift to "lo Chávez." He also gave me his gift of humor and his powerful gift for making story. Thank you, Daddy!

My thanks to Daniel Zolinsky. Husband. You are Loved. No one has sustained me more these years than this wild, loving, generous "Fricano"—a French Chicano. You've taught me so much through your many unending gifts: fluidity, expansion, culture, spirit, love.

I want to thank my hometowns: Las Cruces, New Mexico; El Paso, Texas; and Ciudad Juárez, Chihuahua, México, as well as those beloved places in Far West Texas where my spirit was born and continues to roam: Marfa, Alpine, Presidio, and El Polvo. Beloved borderland!

¡Duende! ¡Qué siga la Fiesta!

Denise Chávez

Amorcito Corazón
by Pedro De Urdimalas and Manuel Esperon González
Copyright © 1949 by Promotora Hispano
Americana de Música, S.A.
Administered by Peer International Corporation
Copyright Renewed.
International Rights Secured.
Used by Permission.
All Rights Reserved.

Camino de Guanajuato
by José Alfredo Jiménez Sandoval
Copyright © 1954 by Editorial Mexicana de
Música Internacional, S.A.
Administered by Peer International Corporation
Copyright Renewed.
International Rights Secured.
Used by Permission.
All Rights Reserved.

Paloma Querida
by José Alfredo Jiménez Sandoval
Copyright © 1953 by Editorial Mexicana de
Música Internacional, S.A.
Administered by Peer International Corporation
Copyright Renewed.
International Rights Secured.
Used by Permission.
All Rights Reserved.

Volver, Volver
Words and Music by Fernando Z. Maldonado
Copyright © 1972 (Renewed 2000),
1978 EMI MUSICAL, S.A. DE C.V.
All Rights for the U.S.A. and Canada Controlled and
Administered by EMI BLACKWOOD MUSIC INC.
All Rights Reserved
International Copyright Secured
Used by Permission
Reprinted by Permission of Hal Leonard Corporation

Wasted Days and Wasted Nights
Words and Music by Huey P. Meaux
Copyright © 1960 (Renewed) EMI UNART CATALOG INC.
All Rights Controlled and Administered by
EMI FEIST CATALOG INC. (Publishing)
and ALFRED MUSIC (Print)
All Rights Reserved
Used by Permission